W9-AAW-229

"I HEARD YOUR VOICE INSIDE MY HEAD ALL NIGHT," RISA WHISPERED.

"How very gratifying." Blake covered her hand with his and curled her fingers over the clay. "I hope I said something worthwhile."

"Oh you did." Her throat clogged with the lack of air at his nearness.

"Did you hear me whisper to you all night as I lay awake and thought of you?"

"Yes." She wished she had heard more of the passion in his voice that was there now, instead of the danger.

"I said I want to remove your hair pins." His gaze defined her hair. "Spread your curls like a blanket of fire beneath you." He regarded one cape button. "I wish to undo all of these, and taste the peaks and valleys of your body." Her knees went to water. "And then, can you imagine what I will do last?"

"No." *Tell me.*

"Unhook your stockings." He pressed her to his torso. "Your corset. All your reserve."

The clay slid from her fingers.

Books by Jo-Ann Power

You and No Other
Angel of Midnight
Treasures
Gifts
The Nightingale's Song
Never Before
Never Again
Never Say Never
Allure

Published by POCKET BOOKS

JO-ANN POWER

Allure

SONNET BOOKS
New York London Toronto Sydney Tokyo Singapore

This book is a work of fiction. Names, characters, places and incidents are products of the author's imagination or are used fictitiously. Any resemblance to actual events or locales or persons, living or dead, is entirely coincidental.

An *Original* Publication of POCKET BOOKS

A Sonnet Book published by
POCKET BOOKS, a division of Simon & Schuster Inc.
1230 Avenue of the Americas, New York, NY 10020

ISBN: 0-671-03408-1

First Sonnet Books printing September 1999

10 9 8 7 6 5 4 3 2 1

SONNET BOOKS and colophon are trademarks of Simon & Schuster Inc.

Front cover illustration by Wendi Schneider

Printed in the U.S.A.

Allure

PROLOGUE

August 5, 1880

Dear Diary,

I am escaping! Tonight! I must pinch myself to believe it. My mistakes and my failures, I can at last put behind me. He has asked me to marry him, and I cannot refuse. His understanding is all I ever asked for, to turn my days to gold. Now I shall be happy.

I pray it will be so. Given the choice between bringing more shame to the title of countess of Rossborough, and doing what I must to save some shred of my self-respect, I know what I must do.

I hope to God that he and I may depart Sandown undetected and quickly. But after we are gone, I do wonder if we will be able to live in peace or if

"Maddie?"

She jumped in shock. "Aunt Elizabeth . . ." She jammed her pen in the inkwell. *Be calm. Calm. It is only your aunt.*

The elegant lady swept into Maddie's bedroom. "What are you doing?"

Maddie slapped shut her journal and shoved it into her desk drawer. Hands shaking, she grabbed the key and locked the drawer. She stood, smoothing her chemise over her ribs and stomach. *Where to put the key?* She leaned back against the desk and slid the key under the blotter.

"Are you writing in that diary again when we should be going down to the shore for Lord Hargrove's little supper? Why, you are not even dressed!"

"I will be. Soon. I promise."

"No more scribbling, Maddie. That pastime is for children, not countesses who have their social duties to fulfill." Aunt Elizabeth crossed her hands. "I will wait for you."

"No need to." Maddie's palms were going clammy. "A few minutes more, that's all." *Leave, please.* Her eyes drifted to her bed, under which she had hidden the satchel, packed hurriedly only minutes ago.

"I know how you dally, Maddie. Come along. Quickly now." Her aunt stoically took the only wing-back chair as Maddie went for the bellpull. "Do not ring for the maid. I will assist you."

Maddie understood by her aunt's tone she would brook no objection. "Yes, Aunt Elizabeth." *Best to be co-operative with her, go to the dinner party, then head for the boathouse to meet him.*

She made short work of the stylish sailing outfit, her aunt tying the sash and buttoning the tiny loops over her buttons. Her aunt praised her choice of the white and navy gown, then lifted her brow. "Lovely. Shall we go now?"

"Yes. Certainly." Maddie swept down the main stairs of Sandown Manor before her aunt. At the first landing, they both turned to see the American, Ben Woodward, galloping down to join the houseparty.

"Hello," he greeted them, stopping. "I see I am not the only one late for supper. May I?" he offered an arm to each lady. Maddie accepted, panic rising with each passing minute that she had to get away.

But as one of the footmen opened the drawing room door to the garden, Maddie caught sight of a few other weekend guests already assembled inside the pavilion created by the huge tent on the shore. A gust of wind blew her hair. "I think I will need a shawl. Do go ahead, Aunt Elizabeth. I will be along shortly."

Maddie gave them both a perfunctory smile. "Excuse me, please." She turned and took a few of the stairs up toward her suite, but paused when she heard the door close. Spinning to see if the footman watched her, she sighed in relief that he had retreated to his duties. But on the next floor, she spied a maid headed for the stairs and knew her route to her suite was cut off. She would have to do without her satchel.

She darted back into the shadows in the hall and took its length at a run. She'd take the back library stairs to the ground floor and out to the boathouse. No one must see her leave.

If they did, they would surely fetch her aunt and Maddie could not bear to be foiled now. Not *now* that her most heart-wrenching problem was about to be solved.

All of the guests must have gathered in the pavilion by now. A few lamps remained lit in the various rooms, and shed sparse light on the lawn that led toward the sea. But Maddie took it in a clip, reveling in the crisp air of freedom.

She had always adored sailing. Won so many races that her father had to praise her if only just a little for her skill. How very just it was that she should sail away into the night to make her life worth living again.

Breathless, her skirts above her knees, she scrambled down the grassy knoll to the dock and headed toward the boathouse.

"Maddie?"

She jumped at the gruff voice. "Oh, my God," she slapped her hand to her heart, then she recognized the man before her. "What are you doing here?"

"Taking a stroll before supper. Just like you are." He

stepped so close she could smell his bay cologne. "I am also informing you that John is not coming."

"What? Why?" She was too surprised to pretend she was not meeting his brother.

"I cannot let him run away with you, Maddie. You are not good for him. He needs an honest woman— and an honorable one."

Tears stung her eyes. "How dare you."

"I will dare anyone who hurts my family." Blake Hargrove stepped into a rare ray of moonlight and as if to make his huge figure more ominous, thunder rolled across the water toward them.

"I will not hurt him."

"Yes, you will. You do not love him."

"Go to hell."

"I have been there already." Blake thrust one hand into his trouser pocket, then took a puff on his cigar.

"He will come to me anyway."

"No. He has pride, Maddie. He will not take another man's *amour*. Nor will he marry you without my blessing—and therefore, without his share of the income from our father's trust."

"You will deny John his rightful due?"

"To protect him, yes."

"You are a bastard."

He threw his cigar into the water lapping at the dock. "Not a new term for me."

"To hell with you all. I don't need your money—or want it. I have my own. I am tired of all of you trying to control me. Get out of my way. I will make you sorry."

Blake paused. "Maddie, do not threaten me."

"I shall take up with Deville again. If I have to, I will . . . Oh, what am I saying?"

She ran for the end of the dock and one of Blake's sailboats. It was a small one, but—

"Maddie," Blake called to her, "a storm is coming."

"Why do you care?" She would go, meet John. He would be waiting for her in the cove south of here. He had promised her he would.

"Do not bother to sail out, Maddie. John is not in the cove. He left Sandown this afternoon, headed for the ferry and home." Blake's voice hit her like a wave.

"No, that isn't true." She was sobbing, cutting the air with her arm. "How can you do this to me? Go away and leave me in peace. Go, go."

And furious, he strode away.

Thunder boomed as she discarded her shoes and bent to jump into the little boat. She began to unloop the rope from the dock. *Damn Blake. Damn him. He doesn't know his brother. I do. John is waiting for me.*

"My, my. Where might you be off to on such a gloomy night?"

Maddie froze. "What are you doing here?"

"I could ask you the same thing. But I know where you're going."

"No," Maddie fell back. "You couldn't."

"I came to tell you what I think of you."

"I don't care."

"Actually, I came to show you how much I *care* for *you.*"

"Why would I be interested?" With this person, she could feign innocence. She had had so much practice.

"Because this little lesson is your last."

Fear choked Maddie. "Don't be silly."

"Odd. The word fits you exactly. Come, let's get into a boat."

"No." Maddie jumped away.

"Yes, Maddie. *Now.*"

1

The main thing is to be moved, to love, to hope, to tremble, to live!

Auguste Rodin

London, England
April 1881

*H*er palms lingered over him, smoothing across his chest, caressing the sleek muscles as if absorbing his strength through her skin. Her fingers traced the valley of his breastbone, down the ridges of his ribs to the flare of his hip, the cut of his thigh—and the fullness of his manhood. And then she defined his virility with a lazy fingertip, sweetly, thoroughly, examining each indentation of the huge fig leaf.

Fighting the urge to hoot in laughter, Blake Hargrove clenched his teeth as he stood by the door watching the young woman stroke the statue.

Still totally fascinated and suddenly frustrated, she yanked her tiny glasses down her nose to peer over the gold rims at the statue's bulging bicep. Her eyes narrowed on the flow of the marble, her finger following the blue vein that ran along the contour of the arm.

Who was she? This woman who savored the headless, legless marble man like his living lover? She was bold to stand here in a public place such as this tiny art gallery and explore the fellow as if he were flesh and blood.

Blake grinned at his errant wish that she were caressing *his* flesh. Lord knew, she certainly roused his blood. *Poor form, old man. Look at her walking suit, her carefully coiled chignon. The gleaming red hair. She's of a class which usually does not permit its women to go out alone, much less to a private gallery. Certainly not its back room either, filled solely by classical nudes.*

What's more, this lovely woman admired the naked male body with such abandon that she had not heard Blake enter the back room. Even now, she caught her tongue between her teeth in concentration and pushed her nose flush against the fellow's forearm. She appeared to be ready either to kiss him or lick him, head to toe.

Blake wanted to chuckle—or groan.

Time to break in on her reflections before he lost his own senses.

"Pardon me, madam," Blake injected, bowing slightly, though he hated to take his eyes off her for fear he'd miss another antic. Intrusion into the privacy of a patron visiting the back rooms of art galleries was a breach of etiquette of the highest water. Blake had spent most of his life among dealers and gallery owners, artists and their patrons, so he knew that one only compounded the crime of interrupting them if one embarrassed them for their appreciation of the finer aspects of a work of art. Yet, it was apparent from her gasp and her wild blush that he had committed both faux pas with this lady. "I did not mean to disturb you."

She dropped her hand from the Adonis as if Blake had shot her. "Oh! Forgive me—"

"I owe you the apology. I did not intend to frighten you. I had no idea someone was here in the private viewing room and I strolled in . . . evidently"—He gave her a rueful smile—"without a sound."

She faced him fully now, her opalescent eyes wide with her surprise and her attempt to hide her chagrin. She put down one hand to hold back the sway of her skirts, which nonetheless furled out to endanger a terra cotta Cupid and one jade geisha. As a result, her glasses teetered on the tip of her nose, and she grabbed them and jammed them into her left skirt pocket.

Blake felt like a dolt unable to put her at ease. "If *Monsieur* Bartholome had told me someone was here, I assure you, I would have remained in the main gallery and waited until you—"

"I was admiring him," she declared forthrightly, though her cheeks still flamed with her maidenly dismay. She began to furiously work something in her right skirt pocket. "He is superb."

But so are you. Blake strolled toward her, feeding a hunger to touch her as intimately as she had the work of art. Instead, he let his eyes caress her. "I rather enjoyed your perusal."

She blushed. A delicious cherry red spread across her high cheekbones. Her round face with winged brows, straight nose and jaw told him she herself could have modeled for any sculptor eager to create a new Helen of Troy. From what he could detect of her lush body beneath the gewgaws of the Wedgwood blue wool and endless petticoats, she had the full breasts and hips a sculptor would demand—and appreciate when he had finished molding for the day—and wished to spend the night refining his knowledge of her curves.

"The statue is well worth your attention," Blake changed his risqué tone, hating himself for his bluntness, hoping he might induce her to talk at length. "One of a kind." *Like you.*

Her pale eyes bore into him in curiosity. The color

of lightning, they shocked him. Pinned him in place as if he were one of the butterflies in his brother John's dioramas. John collected the most gorgeous array of creatures, but none matched this one for splendor.

Red hair, the French called Titian. Porcelain skin, the English termed rose. A mouth, so generous that most men would say it should best be busied in the bedroom. But her eyes were what held him. Long-lashed, cat-like and so bright, he could barely stand to look into them.

"Pardon me," he began, "but I must—"

She took a step toward him. "No, you needn't go."

"I never intended it. I was going to apologize further for my forwardness." *When clearly you are a woman of sensitivity.*

"It is I who have disturbed you. With my rather flagrant study of his . . ."

"Good points?" Blake suggested and could have kicked himself that he had spoken so brazenly to her again.

To his joy, she grinned. "Assets," she corrected him in a contralto rich as melting chocolate. "And if I haven't embarrassed you totally with my examination of this gentleman"—she tilted her head at the Greek god who stood between them—"I ask you to stay and admire him. He certainly is worth every penny of the asking price. I had hoped to speak with *Monsieur* Bartholome, but he is detained with another customer and I must," she said with regret, "go myself."

"But I could not bear to take you from your inspection of the Adonis. He is unique."

"Yes, indeed," she said with awe and a quick glance at the torso. "He is the only representation of the god of love who truly looks—" She colored outrageously. "—sensuous."

Her knowledge of sculpture made him blink. What

else did she know about this statue, sculpture in general, and how had she managed to learn it? Blake removed his gloves, putting them and his walking stick on the display table while he trained all his senses on her. "His sculptor is unknown," he offered leisurely, admiring the glow in her eyes at the topic.

"Yes, but we can tell from the type of marble and from his"—she cleared her throat—"fig leaf, that he was probably from an Athenian workshop of the first century."

"He was one of many works—"

"Bound for Rome on a ship owned by Agrippa of the house of Herod."

"But it sank," he added, "near Napoli."

"However, we do know he is the more modestly rendered of the entire cargo," she smiled at their shared enthusiasm and recited more details as if this were a contest. "In fact, the six dancing women and four satyrs—"

"Were so sensuous as to cause the fishermen who discovered them last year to cover them in blankets before transporting them to Rome." He was revealing that she knew as much as he about the provenance of the piece.

"So perhaps it was best they were shipwrecked because Herod's family would not have been happy to learn he had commissioned such interesting works."

"Nor"—Blake nodded, taking great pleasure in the way her lips parted in anticipation of what next he would relate about the torso—"would Agrippa's political supporters have been thrilled to discover that he was part owner of a Roman house of—" Damn, he had walked into this repartee to lure her into conversation—and now what did he dare to call this establishment?

"Prostitution," she supplied, but he could see it cost her a flush of her cheeks to mention it.

She was so young. Twenty, perhaps? Or a few years more. Women beneath the age of thirty rarely bothered to regard painting or sculpture. Those few educated enough to distinguish an oil from a watercolor, or a Praxiteles from a Michelangelo, were usually swept up at age nineteen by debuts and balls, swains and proposals, a suitable marriage, a country house and matching one in town, and then within nine months, motherhood. Few of them knew about prostitutes, in Victoria's London or Caligula's Rome, and nigh unto none would utter the word. This woman might be young, but she was educated in art—and needed to be schooled in the sophistication she would require to continue to appreciate it without demurring like a Madonna.

"Ah, yes," she admitted at his raised brow, "I do know about such things." Blake breathed a bit more easily that she had declared it with such aplomb. "But I realize that as a woman, I am not supposed to."

"That is only what society says. I believe that women should be educated in art, as in all other disciplines."

She tilted her head, her eyes shimmering like moonlight. "Whatever would become of the empire if all British women were so free?"

"I daresay the empire would benefit if we freed more women to admire art such as you have today." He sauntered closer and savored her. She was a delectable looking woman. Ripe as an apple. Her smile, wide and ready. Her skin, without powder, perfect. Her lips, unrouged, were pink and wet, too full to be the fashion. He wanted to chuckle at her because the way she squinted up at him, he could tell she was blind without her glasses. But when he got closer, she relaxed, her eyes huge pale pools that drowned his logic for a moment. "Until then," he said, summoning his thoughts, "most gallery owners will continue to cover their more intricately rendered art with sheets."

She tipped her chin toward the Adonis. "But he was not."

"*Monsieur* thinks it a crime to hide perfection." *If he has seen you, I wager he wants to unveil all your glories.*

"*Monsieur* should be more careful of his treasures."

"Especially for the ladies who venture to the back room."

"Of which I am certain there have been none."

"Until you."

"Precisely. And scandalously unescorted, too," she added with a wicked hint in that mouth-watering voice.

"But how can you appreciate a work of art with another chattering in your ear?" he mused.

She tisked. "Sacrilege. And to that end—" She sidestepped Blake. "—I will leave you to admire him in peace."

"But I could not bear to run you out." Blake felt a gnawing need to keep her talking. She was rare. A woman of breeding and intellect who understood and appreciated art. He met so few attractive women under the age of dotage who could discuss art with any twinkle in their eyes—and here was a connoisseur who discussed it with a charmer's blush.

"You don't. I need to go. I am late for an appointment." She dug her gloves from her skirt pocket—and sighed at the sight of the delicate crocheting clumped around a tiny ball of gray material.

"Clay." Blake recognized the substance immediately. After his four years of modeling classes in Paris—and his sister's obsession with sculpting, how could he not?

This woman mimed what Blake knew was a small curse under her breath. "I should have taken it out before I left home." She began to pick at her once white crocheted gloves, the holes of which were chock full of little dribs and drabs of clay.

He grinned. "Do you make a practice to walk around with clay in your skirts?"

"Well, of course," she replied with a merry dose of self-deprecation. "Doesn't everyone?"

"Everyone who wishes to sculpt." Blake put his hand out. "Permit me to help you. I am an expert at such activities."

"Really?" She paused in her picking to survey him with skepticism. "How is that?"

"My sister and I once carried balls of this stuff about in our own pockets. Stroking them, shaping them as we walked or talked or ate. Drove the laundress to tear her hair out when we left the clumps in our pockets."

"Alas," she sighed like a Drury Lane actress, "our butler was already bald."

"Pity."

"Mmmm, yes," she laughed, "but he resigned, nonetheless."

"Why?"

"I dunked clay in the family crystal and mucked the glasses so, he could not clean them."

"Ah, the trials of being an artist," he lamented.

"There are few of us. Fewer women, still. Your sister is a sculptor?" she asked, clearly eager to learn of another Englishwoman who had similar interests.

"Was." *Before she died.*

"I see," she said, chastised at his curt reply.

"What are you creating?" he quickly added. He did not wish to talk about Barbara, but her.

She looked away, then back at him. "I wish I knew. And you?" she asked after a glimpse of his hands. "Your skin is free of clay dust and charcoal. And your nails are unbroken. Not like mine." She raised her hands and turned them over once and again. She splayed her fingers. "They cramp and I—"

He caught both her hands in his. "Let me—" he

pleaded as she startled at his effrontery, then closed her eyes as he began to massage her fingers. "I remember the pain I'd get from sketching and afterward manipulating clay into their images. You have elegant hands," he murmured, "callused by your use of chisels and drills."

She relaxed at his ministrations. "But your skin is soft."

"I gave up my art."

"I wish I could," she said with anger, then snatched her hands away. "My apologies. I do not mean to be distasteful. You must think me ridiculous, fondling statues and then speaking so . . . bluntly."

"On the contrary, I find your knowledge of sculpting beguiling. Your honesty refreshing."

"You need not be polite, sir. Say you find me—"

"Different."

She snorted and tugged at the glove he held.

"Determined." He kept a tight grip on it. "And strong."

She blew a gust of air up to ruffle her bangs. "It is distressing to fight you for my gloves, you realize. Give over, will you?" she surrendered to the smile that teased her lips. "I am used to men and women who do not understand me."

"Oh, but I do. I, too, was once prone to insights and moods few others suffered."

That secret, shared so easily, quieted her. "Why did you abandon your art?"

"I was not superb."

She searched his eyes. Empathy blossomed in her own.

"And you?" he asked. "Why do you wish to give up yours?"

"I may not be superb, either."

"But you are not certain of that."

"No," she agreed. "Not yet."

"Well, then you must continue, must you not, until you confront all your doubts and have an answer."

"Meanwhile, I dabble."

He picked out one pellet of wet gray matter. "Dabbling is not working. It is play without purpose and can give you no peace. Am I right?" He watched her wrestle with his own bluntness, then determined to soften the blow. He withdrew his handkerchief from his pocket, rolled the specks of clay together and deposited the round mass in it. A glance at her left hand gave him a surprise—and a delight. *You have no husband*, he thought with a greed that stunned him because he had never cared to totally claim any woman. Not even a mistress.

"You wear no rings," he ventured, changing the tone of their intimacy so that she might not fly away from him. Handing over his handkerchief and her clay, he felt a glee he explained to himself as one artist exulting in another's freedom. The unvarnished truth was, he was delighted she was unattached.

"My aunt tells me I should."

He arched a brow, relieved he had gentled her. "Ah. The family heirlooms must be paraded, eh?" *When I would wager the most precious family jewel is you, dressed in nothing at all but your blushes. Or your chuckles.*

She chortled. "How did you know?"

I have an eye for treasures. "I too have an aunt who likes to remind me I must exhibit the family's bounty."

Her gaze drifted from his silk cravat and gold watch fob, to his ivory walking stick. "You do them proud. Down to your signet ring."

He relished the fact that she would take so much of him in and appreciate his attire. He grinned, wishing to appreciate her unattired.

"As for me, I hate the feel of that weight dragging

me down. My fingers can't move. Not to sketch or model. Even if I don't sculpt as often as I used to."

"And how often did you used to?" he asked, but he predicted her answer. There was in her every movement a vitality, an economy that spoke of a compulsion to move, to do, to try. He had once been possessed by his need to create and he knew how its demands could propel the body.

"Every day." She smiled, until in her eyes an apology gleamed. "Now if you will excuse me. I will leave you to enjoy the Adonis." She would have walked around Blake, headed for the front room of the little gallery.

"Why did you stop sculpting?" His question halted her.

She turned with a swirl of skirts that sent a bronze nymph somersaulting toward the floor. "Good heavens," she said as she caught it and hugged it to her chest.

He strode up to her. "Why?"

"A number of reasons."

"I see. And they are—?"

"Forward, aren't you?"

"Second only to persistent. I understand your challenges because my sister's were similar to yours—and so were my own." He felt such sorrow for her dilemma. "Why did you stop?"

"My tutor said I had ceased to develop. He claimed I could never excel unless I changed a great deal."

"Was he right?"

"Yes." She replaced the naked girl on the display table, patted her on the head and stepped away from any other objects.

"How?"

"He said I needed to grow older, experience tragedy or love before I could be—" She lowered her voice. "—a great artist."

"What was your response?"

"I was naïve enough to argue with him."

"If you believed in yourself enough to argue with him, why did you stop sculpting?" He waited as she summoned words which seemed too loathsome to utter.

"His criticism ate at my enjoyment of my work. I questioned every movement of the pick, each pressure applied to the drill."

"So you allowed another person's views to affect your view of your own work?"

"Yes," she acknowledged, "didn't you?"

"No. I stopped because I learned—I saw—" He put his thumb to his chest. "—in here that I was not unique. If you have certainty about your work, no one can make a judgment that affects your own view."

"My tutor is an artist with many patrons. Acclaimed. A maestro of the Guild of St. Jerome in Florence. He should recognize talent when he sees it."

"But he may not," Blake insisted. "He might lack the perspective."

"I thought of that. Once."

"And what happened?"

"Soon after we argued, I experienced tragedy. And now I find little to thrill me."

"So you lack inspiration," he announced with an insight that must have struck a chord because she turned her head to one side and stared off as if to find solace among the shelves.

"Yes, among other things. Conditions are not right. I have responsibilities now that I did not last year and I am constantly worried that I am making poor decisions."

"Self-doubt," he said, "kills the will to create."

Her exquisite face tipped up to his. Shock that he understood and gratitude that he did flowed over her expression. "Yes," she breathed, "but knowing what is wrong with me does not change things." She fiddled with her gloves. "I must go. I have an appointment at my dressmaker's and I must meet my aunt there." She tried to walk around him.

He hated the idea that they would part on this sad note. "Perhaps it is time you drew women as umbrellas."

She stopped in her tracks, spun and let laughter shake her shoulders. "Who does that?"

"A young French painter. A friend of mine. When he is too self-critical, he creates the ridiculous to inspire the divine."

"A wise man. Would I know his name?"

"Not now. But you will. Toulouse-Lautrec."

Humor dimmed as truth clouded her eyes. "Part of my problem is that I have not found the right inspiration."

He wished to give her one. "You could try a man . . . as a walking stick."

Her gaze examined the breadth of his shoulders. "Or a gladiator."

He resisted the urge to hug her. "I have a suggestion."

Her brows inched upward. "My aunt has trained me so well, sir, that I know I should not ask this next question. But my year in a studio in Florence among male and female students who were more worldly than I compels me to say my curiosity is aroused."

"I am indebted to your associates."

She chuckled. "What is your inspiration, sir?"

"A sunrise. A sunset."

"Available to me already."

"Not where I know it to be best."

"And where is that, sir?"

Be sensible, Hargrove. Don't tell her you'd like her to see the day begin and end in your bed. She is an English girl, gently reared, and winsome in spite of her artist's experiences.

"I give an annual weekend party at my home with more than twenty guests. It is on the Isle of Wight. The view of the sun and the moon on the sea is—"

Her face hardened to a mask. "At Sandown?"

He began to bow, take her hand. "Yes, I—"

She withdrew from his reach. "Not Blake Hargrove?"

For a second, Risa was struck by the irony of her situation. Here was a man she could laugh with, confide in. And yet, he was the man at whose home her sister Maddie had died. The man whom many thought had encouraged her sister's affections, induced her to come to his house party on the Isle of Wight, and then let her sail a treacherous sea alone. To die.

"Yes." He straightened, puzzled. "I am—"

"Blake Hargrove. My God. I have wanted to meet you for months. I hoped you would return from France soon so that we could talk—and now here you are, in a tiny gallery, of all places." *You must tell me more about the night Maddie died. What you thought, said, did, before and after she sailed away from your dock.*

He examined her so intricately this time, Risa felt as if he had photographed her. Memorized her. "I regret to say I do not know who—"

"I am Cerise Lindsay. You knew my sister. Well."

"Madelaine? She did tell me her younger sister was a sculptor, but you are ... so ..." He took in her hair and lips. "So very ... different from her."

Maddie had been five foot two, with chestnut hair and honey eyes. She possessed a nervous energy that reminded Risa of a high-strung tabby cat she'd kept as a childhood pet.

"I regret deeply how she died," he said softly, seemingly at a loss for more words.

But Risa was not. "So you said in your condolence letter to me last August," she lashed out at him with a civility that surprised her. "I have waited for you for six months to return from France so that I could ask you details about her death. Her drowning was no accident." *Maddie was an expert sailor. An excellent swimmer.* "It could not have been."

He looked as if she had slapped him. "The constable and the coroner were satisfied that Maddie lost control of her sailboat off the coast of Sandown."

"But I am not."

"So I see. If you would permit me to—"

"Apologize? What happened to my sister merits more than another of your apologies, my lord."

"I was not about to do that, my lady."

Risa had her mouth open ready to chastise him for the brief letter of condolence he had sent her last year after Maddie's funeral. "No?"

"I did that already. And evidently not to your satisfaction, either. So I was about to ask you to have tea with me."

She squinted up at him. He certainly looked sincere.

"I wish to talk with you at length about the circumstances surrounding your sister's death and—"

"I cannot do it now." *Why didn't you come to me last August after Maddie drowned in your little sailboat? Why not any day since then?*

"Ahhhh, hallo—" came the sing-song voice of the French ex-patriot who owned the shop.

"I can make an excuse and we can slip away," Blake urged her.

"I want to, but—"

"There you are, *Mademoiselle le Comtesse!*"

"I have a dressmaker's appointment in ten minutes,"

she told Hargrove. "I wish I could cancel or postpone it, but I cannot. Besides, my aunt is meeting me."

Maurice Bartholome sailed forward, hands extended.

"Bring her," Blake insisted.

"Her presence would complicate our discussion." *Make it into a shouting match.*

"Your aunt never liked me."

"Exactly." She feigned a smile at the shopkeeper who was now upon them. *"Bonjour, monsieur.* I regret to say I must leave. I will return day after tomorrow to talk with you. In the morning at ten. I hope you will take no other clients at that time," she told him, annoyed with the man who had kept her waiting so long that she must return to ask him why Maddie had come to see him last year before her death. "I must speak with you soon—and privately."

"Oh, but *mademoiselle,* I did not know you had arrived. And you, *Monsieur le Comte,* I did not hear you come in," he said to Blake Hargrove. *"Pardonnez-moi.* I was with another patron. Bah, it is my assistant who is the laggard. I try to train him to use his—how do you say?—his mutton head and tell me who enters, *n'est-ce pas?* I see you have met the lovely lady, *oui?"*

"Yes, Maurice, I have had the pleasure." Blake Hargrove glanced over at Risa once more. "I wish we had more time to continue our conversation."

"She is incomparable, *non?* And she shares a passion for art. Cerise Lindsay, the fourteenth countess of Rossborough. The oldest title in Britain, *oui, mademoiselle?"*

Lord Hargrove shot up a hand. "Please, Maurice, leave us, will you? I have to talk to the countess alone."

"No. Not here." She did not wish to speak in front of Bartholome.

The gallery owner's eyes drifted back and forth with delight. "Ah, if you will permit me, I suggest my office."

"Thank you, Maurice." Blake steered her toward the shop owner's private room off the gallery. "Forgive me for commandeering it, but we must have privacy."

She halted. "I cannot talk with you now. If I do not meet my aunt, there will be fireworks. Then the wretched gown will not be finished for tomorrow and surely the sky will fall." *Of course if it would, I need not appear at Court and make my debut bow to Her Majesty.*

"After all your vehemence—" Hargrove arched a brow. "—I am astonished that a gown takes precedence over talking with me about your sister."

She extracted her arm from his grip. "Our meeting here was accidental. And my appointment is one I cannot change." *Ironic as it is, I came here to London to meet you, and to disguise that, I agreed to my aunt Elizabeth's demand that I debut. Now, here you are—and the debut keeps me from talking with you.*

"Then I will call on you this evening."

"No. Never come near Park Lane."

Hargrove's ruddy complexion turned to ash. "I am not welcome."

"If it were only I in the house, yes, you would be, but my aunt is there and—"

"I understand," he said, "completely."

"I also do not wish anyone to think that you and I are the least bit involved. It would not do." *My Aunt Elizabeth and my cousin Georgianna would think me ready for Bedlam that I would even speak to the man who had spurned Maddie.*

Scandal mongers who had spread rumors last autumn that Maddie might have killed herself over Blake Hargrove's rejection of her advances would be surprised as well. The wags would hold a May Day fest if they learned that Risa met him at all, let alone privately.

"I agree," he said. "I must think of my reputation, too."

Risa tried not to gape. Her aunt had drilled into her head the fact that Blake Hargrove was one of the most renowned rakes in London. Over thirty years of age, he had never married, never even been betrothed, but many, many times he had taken a mistress. "By all means."

"*Mademoiselle!*" Bartholome was horrified at Risa's agreement.

"Please, Maurice," Hargrove waved a hand at the Frenchman, who took his cue and left them. "Very well, my lady. I need to talk to you too. At length." He frowned. "What are you doing after the dressmaker's?"

"The milliner's," she said with distaste for the fripperies of being dressed like a spring chicken. *Dressed for the kill*, she had always told Maddie that was really what Debutante Season amounted to. "Another day, I promise you, we will talk. And our conversation will not be very pleasant."

"I do not expect it, though I might wish for it."

She tried to ignore the sorrow in his voice. But she could not deny the sadness she felt at her realization that they might not ever be friendly as they had been here for a few brief minutes. "I will send round my card and communicate with you about a time and place we can meet." She yanked up her gloves.

"Make it soon."

"I assure you, Lord Hargrove, learning more about my sister's death is my sole objective in life. It is the reason I came to London. Why I cannot sculpt. Why I will not draw a happy breath until I discover all the facts about what really happened to Maddie that night at your estate."

"Name the day, the place, and time. I will meet you and tell you all I know." He doffed his hat. "I doubt it will do either of us any good, however."

Despair crept into her voice. "And why is that?"

"Because, my dear countess, I am as haunted as you by your sister's death. You see, I have just returned to London after spending six months in Paris trying to find clues to Maddie's demise—and I discovered absolutely nothing."

"Why would you find clues to Maddie's death in Paris?" He could not thwart her with such silliness. "Maddie spoke only a smattering of schoolgirl French and had visited Paris only once with her governess when she was fifteen. Maddie hated the city—and thought Frenchmen haughty. You must be mistaken."

"I see that you are, too, Lady Lindsay. About quite a few facts."

How dare you. "I hope you will enlighten me, then."

His hard green eyes suddenly swam with sympathy. "I pray you will let me."

2

One should either be a piece of art, or wear a piece of art.
Oscar Wilde

"You look so wonderful in that gown, Risa, I might even want to wear it." Ariel bounced down the grand staircase of Rossborough House in Park Lane.

"For which event, sweetheart?" Risa turned slowly in the barge that was her gown and glanced at Ariel's threadbare jodhpurs. At fifteen, her younger sister was willowy as a fairy, but earnest as a village brew master. "The hunt or the hunt ball?"

"When I get dressed for my debut with the queen"—Ariel lounged against the hall's centerpiece, the statue of Allure—"I'll wear my riding pants."

"And give Victoria the vapors." Risa pulled up on the low décolletage of her ivory satin Antoinette gown.

Ariel went back on her elbows and crossed one leg over the other. "If you stop twitching, you will even look better than *she* does," Ariel pointed up at the lady, upon whose rosy marble plinth she casually reclined.

"She, my dear, wears hardly any clothes." Only a diaphanous *robe de chambre*, typical attire for mistresses during the 1690s when she was carved. "Whereas I"—Risa put a finger to her nose to stop a sneeze—"have four layers. None of them where I need them to keep warm, either." She patted her chest, ruffling the fresh rose·buds at her bodice.

"What do you suppose that folderol weighs?"

"I'd estimate"—Risa grimaced at the famous statue of rare Carrara marble—"as much as she does."

Ariel chuckled, her cinnamon curls shaking. "I wish I could come see how you are going to bow, juggling that bouquet"—she nodded at the one dozen blush roses in the nosegay stand on the hall reception table—"and dragging that carcass behind you." She nodded at Risa's train.

"The very thought gives me a backache."

The item in question was at the moment being laid down the thirty-two foot foyer of Rossborough House and covering twenty feet of sea green Aegean tiles. Since six o'clock when Risa had risen to begin to dress for this day-long ordeal, the two downstairs maids and the two upstairs maids had squabbled over the honor to unfurl the massive accoutrement, embroidered as per her aunt's instructions in the de Ros family roses.

She rubbed her arms as a new set of goosebumps broke out. The bare décolletage and tiny cap sleeves both were required of every debutante by Her Majesty's Lord Chamberlain. No girl got past him or his gentlemen-in-waiting without them to enter into the presence of Her Britannic Majesty, the queen of England, Scotland, and Ireland, and empress of India. To make matters more complex—and eminently less manageable—the twenty-foot train was to be dragged a distance of one hundred and seventy-odd feet, the total of two Buckingham Palace drawing rooms, so that Risa might enter the monarch's presence, eyes demure to the floor, bouquet clutched to her bosom, hand out to balance herself as she dipped, her nose to go no less than two inches from the red carpet.

If entering Victoria's Debut Drawing Room was a challenge to a girl's grace, leaving was a threat to life and limb. Having struggled up from her Chinese kowtow, a debutante was to stand immobile before approximately one hundred other noble men and women as a gentleman-in-waiting collected her train like a sack of laundry, and bundled it over her arm, so that she could inch backward out the same door she had entered. Of course, each nerve-wracked lass did this without faltering—or glancing HRM in her noble eye.

"I had a nightmare last night that I wore my linen shirt and trousers that I sculpt in."

"Better than just your earbobs and shoes." Ariel recalled Risa's old threat to her father to sculpt in the all-together if he did not leave her in peace to work.

"A bit of comedy that would endear me to ever so many people, don't you think?" *Not precisely what I need to do to make friends—and get them to tell me about Maddie's last days. And the person who knows the most, Blake Hargrove, I have already antagonized with my sharp words.*

"Not if you wear your glasses."

Risa was pained. "A terrible vision, scamp."

"Aunt Elizabeth may think they're frumpy but they give you a regal air."

"Now there's a choice. I could be either naked and lewd, or frumpy and regal."

"Besides," Ariel went on, nonplussed, "if people don't know you're blind as a bat, they should. Then when they learn that you sculpt, they'll be impressed. You see the value?"

"Hardly."

"They will flock to buy your work."

"What work?" She had destroyed every piece she attempted since she returned to England.

"I tell you, your talent still exists."

"Ah, but *where* is a problem." Why it skulked about was the bigger one—and she found no way to call it out of hiding. *Unless you wish to sculpt a Roman gladiator come to life. Which you shouldn't.*

"Father said you had the best ingredient—persistence."

Which he called perversion. "Well, talent certainly has deserted me this past year."

Self-doubt kills the will to create.

Blake Hargrove's words echoed in her ears once more since yesterday. He was too intuitive. Too intrusive. Much too delightful for a man she must not become attracted to. Her older sister had died at his estate after an argument with him. And while the police reports and the judge's inquest records, which Risa had ordered sent to her through her solicitor, declared that Maddie's death was accidental, to Risa many questions about that night remained. So did others about the days and months before.

And from Blake Hargrove, Risa wanted answers. Lots of them. What was Maddie thinking and feeling before she sailed away? What had Blake and Maddie argued about? Could Maddie have cared for him so deeply that she would allow the sea to overtake her boat? Because he was the last person to see Maddie before she cast off, his description of Maddie was vital to Risa.

A clear picture popped into Risa's head of how Maddie must have struggled for air to survive, bobbing above the water line, gasping. . . . As before when the sight came to her, Risa cast it out.

If I can banish that horror, why can't I suppress that other image of a humorous man? A sensitive man who understood her artistic problem and tried to help her?

She could understand how Maddie would have been attracted to him. And Maddie had not been an artist whom he might try to inspire with the prospect of drawing umbrellas and walking sticks.

Or a gladiator. One with fluid grace, glittering green eyes and ebony curls across his brow.

"You see, you are smiling, Risa. Whatever your troubles, you certainly have not given up."

You are dabbling. Not working. Blake Hargrove again. Speaking inside her head so easily.

"You keep at it." Ariel's insistence echoed his.

Yes, I was caustic with him. Not a way to entice him to tell me all about Maddie's last days, surely. She would correct that when they met the day after tomorrow at the zoo. She had sent a footman to his house yesterday with a note to him and had no reply from him yet. But he would come. He had seemed eager to talk yesterday. And when they did, she would be congenial and—

"Risa? Are you here, Risa? If you bow to the queen with that scowl, she'll throw you out for imitating her."

"I hear she has a funny bone."

"Where?"

"Her steamer trunk?"

Ariel guffawed. "I'd believe that!"

"Maddie said it was so."

"Yes, well, Maddie said a lot of things." Ariel bit her lower lip. "Have you started your investigation yet? I mean, I know you said you would. That's why we are all here really, not for the queen. But with this debut business, have you any time?" She glanced up the stairs and toned down her voice. "I know you don't want to upset Aunt Elizabeth any more than she was about Maddie's death and all those rumors that she committed suicide. But I'd like to help. Anything, you want of me, just ask."

"Thank you, sweetheart." Risa was not going to tell

Ariel much. The girl talked with servants, Bobbies, delivery boys, then spread the news better than a broad-
sheet. "I appreciate it. I progress slowly."

"I'm surprised you even agreed to this debut."

"My dear, it was my idea. The best way to get to
London and explore this mystery further. Talk to people who knew her. Saw her." *Look what I've discovered
since September. Nothing new.*

Not a clue as to why Maddie paid all her bills before
she left London for Sandown. Not even a vague idea
where Maddie had gotten the money to do so. Correc-
tion: The *cash.* Because she had mysteriously paid in
cash. The family solicitor, Mr. McCordle, had told
Risa so. He had also learned, by tracing account
records from her bank in Florence that an M. Rossborough had sent monthly drafts to Risa in Italy from the
Chelsea Masonry Bank.

"But the Rossborough family bank account had always been in a bank in the City," Risa said to him.
"Why would Maddie open an account in Chelsea?"

"I have no idea, my lady. The other questions are
why did she use the name M. Rossborough and why
were the bank drafts paid for in cash and why did your
sister have a safety deposit box there?"

To none of those questions had Risa found any answers in the past months. And she had tried mightily
amid the task of acquainting herself with the challenges
of inheriting the large Rossborough estate which to her
astonishment was ten thousand pounds in debt.

She had not even found a key to the safety deposit
box. Not on the master key ring which each de Ros
earl or countess passed to the heir. Risa had personally
searched in Maddie's bedrooms here in London and in
Rossborough Manor for the thing. She had found
nothing.

Nor had she discovered Maddie's diary for 1880.

That in itself was very odd because Maddie had kept a diary for every year since she was eight years old. And she had hidden them either in their little treehouse at Rossborough Manor or in her favorite hidey-hole here in the attic of the London Park Lane house. Maddie had confided where she hid them. And though Risa had never taken advantage of her knowledge and read Maddie's private journals, she had hoped to read the 1880 diary to find clues to Maddie's behavior in the months before she died. But that route was closed to her.

No diary had been in her trunk with her clothes that came back from Sandown. Aunt Elizabeth had said so when Risa asked her last week.

"The maids at Sandown packed all of Maddie's possessions in her rooms there after the accident," her aunt informed her. "None of our maids up at Rossborough Manor spoke of one in her effects. I did not even know Maddie kept a diary."

"No one but I knew that, Aunt Elizabeth."

"Do you think she might have written things in there which would explain her actions?"

"Maddie poured her heart into her journals. I had hoped I could discover what she thought and did last spring by reading her entries." *But that is in vain.*

"Well, I hope you can enjoy some of the social whirl," Ariel chirped, and drew Risa's attention back to the present. "Maddie did. She liked being courted by all the men who came to call. Especially the Hargrove brothers."

"Why do you suppose they called together?"

"I'd say the earl of Sandown came because he was encouraged by Maddie. His brother John tagged along as a chaperone—but I think he was in love with Maddie, too."

This was something Risa had not known. "Did Maddie tell you this?"

"Oh, no. I plunked myself at the top of the stairs whenever they'd arrive. The earl's younger brother is very polite, but cannot hold a candle to the earl who is very, very beautiful. Like Heathcliff or Mister Rochester come to life, rigid and silent and . . . brooding."

Compelling. Like the Dark Angel by Donatello upstairs in the library.

Risa smoothed the family pearls at her throat. She had not told Ariel that she had accidentally met Blake Hargrove in Bartholome's gallery yesterday. No one knew where she had gone yesterday or why.

She did not intend to tell anyone, either. Not Ariel. Not Aunt Elizabeth, certainly, because that would start the lady's tendency toward tears and tirades against Blake Hargrove. She'd also demand all the particulars of the encounter and relay them to her daughter Georgie. Within a day, all London would know that Risa had met Blake Hargrove in a private art gallery owned by a dealer in Chelsea with whom her father had refused to do business.

Yet Maddie knew Bartholome. Had jotted a note in her diary of 1879 about meeting the man at his gallery. Risa had found that leather-bound journal in Maddie's special hideaway in an old trunk upstairs in the attic.

Risa had gone to see him yesterday because Maddie's interest in art had never been anything other than that of an owner. A disinterested one.

"Risa?"

"Hmm. Yes, what, pet?"

"I worry about you."

"You mustn't." *Did she sound too nonchalant?*

"You don't like being the countess of Rossborough."

"I find satisfactions." *A few.* She had rejoiced last January when she secured a loan from the bank in York for a new plough for her tenant farmers. She had negotiated with the manufacturer of the plough, saved one thousand pounds, and applied it to her late estate taxes. Then, she asked for lenience in paying the balance. Shire officials agreed, saying her word was good, and the bank soon followed by agreeing to a smaller interest rate. For the time being, her creditors were satisfied. She also had one hundred pounds she had failed to spend on one more debut dress, with which she would buy seed for her tenants for this spring's planting. But now she had to repay the bank and she did not like the solution to pay her debts.

She had to sell something valuable.

Land was the first commodity she owned in abundance. But to sell it was a solution which any de Ros would reject. Had rejected. Parting with de Ros land was considered a family sin. Her patrimony bade her not even to consider it.

The only other solution was to find some way to break the deeds on de Ros property and sell one or more of the famous pieces in the de Ros art collection. As it was, no art purchased by a de Ros had ever been sold, nor could it be, because all art conveyed with the property deeds to the houses and surrounding land in Northumbria and here in Park Lane. To dare think of parting with any of the priceless master sculptures or paintings brought a lump to Risa's throat. Yet, it was the best means to pay the remaining debts to the bank and the government quickly. The legal changes to the property deeds could take months or years, her solicitor Mr. McCordle had warned her. For that, Risa had to wait, but she had ordered McCordle to file the appeal to the courts.

Meanwhile, she imposed new standards of frugality on her Rossborough Manor in Northumbria. Cut the staff of footmen by two. Even sought to save money by bringing down two maids from Northumbria, rather than hire new staff for her London debut. But even if she had stayed home and rejected her aunt's insistence to debut, Risa had to meet next month's loan installment. She hoped McCordle hurried with his legal filings. She wanted to sell the small Rubens that hung to her right or the Canaletto to her left.

Her eyes drifted to Allure standing before her. This lady would bring a price so great Risa could not only pay off the loan in one lump sum, but have enough left over to invest it wisely and live, if she chose, like Midas for the rest of her life.

Allure was the white marble statue of a woman beckoning her lover to bed. The five-foot-tall piece dated from the early seventeenth century and was the only secular work by the master religious sculptor Gianlorenzo Bernini. Risa's great-grandfather had acquired it as payment for winnings in a card game and placed it in the front hall of his new townhouse in Park Lane. Allure had presided there in her half-lidded ecstasy, appealing to her unseen lover and arousing to all who entered there for over a century and a half.

If Risa sold this—if she sold *anything*—her father would roll in his grave. So, too, her great-grandfather would curse her to God. That gentleman had begun the renowned Rossborough collection over a century ago and his acquisitions not only graced the walls and halls, but filled the attic storeroom above the servant quarters.

But these burdens were hers alone. She would not share them with her younger sister, and so she tried to sound valiant for Ariel. "Being chatelaine of so much is a suitable occupation for a woman, Ariel."

"Worthy of your attention, do you think?"

"Perhaps more beneficial to more people than creating a work of art." *And perhaps selling a work of art to see*

*people thrive is also more worthwhile than hoarding a trea-
sure for the enjoyment of a few people.*

She put a hand to Allure's arm, and considered that
the polished marble sparkled less than she remembered
from her childhood. Was that a result of her disen-
chantment with sculpting or her acceptance that she
might part with the piece?

"What are Aunt Elizabeth and Georgianna doing
to that menu for tonight? Eating it? It's almost nine
o'clock and the queen begins to receive at eleven! If
they don't hurry, we'll be last in line." She flicked a
finger at the garland of roses across her bodice. "And
these will be brown." She sneezed.

Ariel winced. "Stop ruffling those flowers."

"Ariel, if I could just disappear into the potted
plants . . ."

"Our Disaster," Ariel recalled their father's pet name
for Risa. "This morning you do not have to waltz or
drink champagne or engage in any banter."

"Small consolation. Those are tonight's tribula-
tions!" *But I am determined to make a splash. Ingratiate
myself with Maddie's acquaintances and even Blake Hargrove, if he comes.*

She swirled toward the stairs and stopped, the train
tugging at her. Good Lord, how was she to maneuver
this leaden mass and curtsy eye-level to a mouse? "Go
rouse Aunt Elizabeth and Georgianna, will you, sweetheart? I want to be first in the carriage lineup to the
palace."

Ariel was two steps up when her aunt and her cousin
appeared on the first floor landing, both halting in
their tracks. "Oh, Cerise," her aunt's whisper floated
down the staircase. "You are a vision."

Georgianna oohed and ahhed. "I told you that
Madame Farnesse would do Cerise proud, Mama."

Georgie sailed down the stairs in a strawberry satin

that counterpointed her black hair dramatically. At her own debut four years ago, she had been named one of the Bright Ones of the Season. She'd done what was expected of her, too, when she accepted the best of the three marriage proposals which came to her.

She had, for her dusky beauty, her etiquette, and conversation, landed the second son of the Marquess Dungarvon. Lord Robert Dungarvon was a man of golden good looks, refinement, and a pension from his father of forty thousand pounds per year. This prize offered Georgie his name, a London townhouse in Kensington, ten servants to run the place and, most important, impeccable social connections and the right to be called "my lady." If he was given increasingly to imbibing too much liquor, he nonetheless adored his wife, bejeweled her and dressed her, though she had gone to him with merely five hundred pounds in dowry and the trousseau in her trunks, both given her by her uncle, Risa's father.

Georgie relished her good fortune. Aunt Elizabeth crowed over it. Maddie had applauded it, envied Georgie her husband, and lived for the day when she could emulate her childhood friend, debut and find a mate to take home to Rossborough Manor.

"The ivory is a superb shade," cooed her aunt as she faced Risa, hands folded before her.

"No other white would have done with that wild red in your hair," added Georgie as she circled her cousin, but asked Ariel, "Shall we dress you like this?"

"Riding pinks are my choice," Ariel folded her arms.

"An improvement over the faded chamois," Aunt Elizabeth rolled her eyes at her daughter and Risa. The subject of sending Ariel off to the York School for Young Girls was a sore one that came into their family discussions far too often for Risa's taste. She had withstood her aunt's and her cousin's urging that Ariel go to learn how to be a proper lady by proclaiming that her younger sister wished to be a Latin scholar, not a decoration on some man's arm.

"At least she did not ask to carry a book, Mama."

"She could also—" Risa took her formal length gloves and purse from a maid. "—speak to Victoria in Latin."

"Does she know Caesar?" Ariel beamed. *"Veni, vidi, vici?"*

"Yes, yes." Aunt Elizabeth sighed, acknowledging once again that Ariel was educated, if cheeky.

"Let us bury Caesar, please, and *go,*" Risa tried to divert any conflict among them this morning and motioned to the four maids to pick up her train. She was dying to be off before the tide shifted and her sister and aunt turned upon each other.

"Butterflies, darling?" Georgie trailed behind her.

"An army of ants." She teetered in the new slippers on the slick marble floor. "Fitzhugh has been cooling his heels in the box for an hour. He's probably nodded off."

"Poor old fellow. After this season, do pension him off, Cerise," Georgie waved her hand like an empress at a maid to fetch her stole. "We shall most likely sit in the carriage line up the Mall for at least an hour."

As Risa sailed out the door, she muttered, "Deliver me from evil."

No one did.

The minutes dragged by. It was ten. The court hairdresser rapped on their coach door and asked if Risa wished his touch on her coiffeur. She replied she did not.

It became eleven. Crowds grew along the Mall to call to the debutantes to come out and be seen. Risa considered it seriously as her muscles began to twitch with inactivity. Her aunt shooed them away.

"The doors will open now." Georgie licked her lips. "And we should see our carriage into the mews in, oh, half an hour perhaps."

It was twelve. Risa's stomach rumbled in hunger. The family carriage rolled through the Buckingham Gates, a patrol of the queen's Life Guard in their bearskin Busby hats marching past. One footman opened their coach door.

Risa alighted and arched her back. "Dragging cannon must be lighter than this train."

"Now, now, my dear," Aunt Elizabeth cajoled as two footmen opened the gilded doors, "smile. We are here."

"Just a minute, darling," Georgie fussed with Risa's train and directed her mother, "Let's furl this out on the red carpet. There. Must not drag it in the dirt."

If Risa ever thought that lifting blocks of granite and marble had benefited her, at this moment she knew its worth. She accepted the weight of the train with more ease than she predicted. So much in fact that Georgie whispered how stately she looked and how very pleased she was to be Risa's sponsor. Risa smiled and did not say she knew the reason that Georgie had volunteered for that role: She wished to insinuate herself into the presence of Her Majesty and take a bit of the day's glory home for herself.

They entered the main hall where at least a dozen young women stood in line before them. Their clucking mamas flitted about, arranging the fall of their daughters' gowns, primping their coiffures or fixing their pearls, patting their cheeks, assuring them, petting them, and stepping aside to allow them the chance to look over the young gentlemen-at-arms.

Risa stood like a statue, nerves eating her up. She chuckled at the irony. *Can't create one, so become one.*

She told herself that that perhaps, too, was for the best, as they waited another interminable half hour.

"Ooooo, we're moving." Georgie nudged her mother, who fell in behind Risa, next to her daughter. "Here we go, Cerise. Now remember, your card to the gentleman at the door. Then your eyes to the floor."

"Sounds like a poem," Risa reflected. "Look happy. Be snappy." She nodded at the formally attired man in a gray morning suit at the first door. "Bow deeply. Smile sweetly. Back outward. No coward endeavors this chore."

Her gown bound her, the flowers tickled her and made her want to sneeze again. Her hands flexed in the hot silk gloves. Itched for something to hold.

Then the man before her pivoted, hovered over her, and spoke softly in her ear. "Perhaps you need clay?"

His sandpaper voice buffed her jagged nerves. But the bewitching sight of Blake Hargrove gave her a jolt of pure pleasure she wished she could deny.

"Your card, my lady," he requested, white gloved hand reaching out to take her invitation.

"Why?" She held firm when he tried to take it.

Amusement sparkled in his emerald eyes. "Shall we play tug of war again?"

"Cerise?" her aunt sounded testy and Risa knew it was not due to the delay but to the fact that Blake Hargrove was here and talking to her as if he knew her—and cared about her.

"Please give me your card, my lady Rossborough. I am to present it to the Lord Chamberlain." He glanced toward the head of the line, offering her his profile, and taking her breath away with his starkly classic features. "Your turn will be very soon." He gave her a gleaming grin that spoke of the humor she treasured as much as his insights. "You have come early which is advisable. Good morning, Lady Dungarvon. How are you?"

Georgie reached around Risa to let Blake take her

hand. "Such a pleasure to see you, Lord Sandown. You remember my mother, Lady Elgin."

"I do. Good morning, my lady," he said to her aunt with a politeness that belied the bitterness of their last encounter.

Aunt Elizabeth had last seen Blake Hargrove at the inquest in Sandown days after the drowning. There she had broken into tears and criticized him on the stand for failing to dissuade Maddie from sailing away. She had told Risa it would be a cold day in hell when she wished to see his lordship again. Now she did her social duty and curtsied, *sans* expression. "Good morning, my lord."

Georgie jumped in, undeterred by her mother's dislike of him. "I had no idea you would attend this morning," she offered with a hint of coquetry.

Risa was appalled that her married cousin would flirt. Georgie had always been an opportunist, and a magpie. Risa knew she would also make it her business to learn if Blake Hargrove attended this to find a future wife.

Curiosity and possessiveness washed over Risa. What sort of woman would he desire as his bride? Had he desired Maddie? *Could he desire me?*

"I am substituting for a friend. Lord Tuttle."

"Ah yes," Georgie reflected, "I do know him."

"He was suddenly indisposed. I volunteered to take his place."

"Kind of you. You have not attended a Drawing Room since the year I debuted with . . ." Georgie clamped her mouth shut. "I forgot, forgive me."

"Do not fret," he absolved her, then focused on Risa. "I used to attend these quite often. One does when one is young and expected to observe the rituals. The last time I came was four years ago when my sister came out. Cold?" he took her gloved hands in his.

A frisson skipped up her spine. "A chill."

"Perhaps I might chase it away." He began to massage her fingers as he had yesterday, and his warmth permeated to her bones. Beside her, Georgie smiled, her aunt gaped.

He ignored them.

Then Risa's empty stomach growled.

"You're hungry, too," he turned so that her family could not overhear.

"I could eat an elephant," she confessed with a smile that he returned with one of his own.

"Wait a few minutes, I will find one."

His massage threatened to give her heat stroke. She chuckled. "Not enough time."

"Not the right place." He winked at her. "You will do well. You are not chattering." He nodded toward the talkative young woman behind them whose mother shushed her. "Or swooning." He inclined his head toward the girl just in front of them.

"I hope she doesn't faint."

"If she begins, the man before me will assist her out."

"And if I do?"

"I will rescue you."

She knew her expression held the gratitude she dare not speak before her aunt. "I must warn you that my past performances at such events are—shall we say—memorable."

"So Maddie told me."

Maddie shared family secrets with you? "Why, I wonder."

"Maddie adored your courage. She told me of your greatest disaster with love in her eyes."

"I hate to remember it myself. I was eight. I fell at the de Ros memorial day when I was to present the de Ros family roses and scepter to my father in commemoration of the king's grant to the first countess."

"Nothing like that will happen today. You are composed."

She laughed. *Near you* . . . "I am a jar of jelly."

"You look . . ." he whispered, scanning her hair, mouth, roses, eyes in one hawklike swoop, "like an angel. Your curtsy will be flawless."

Skin hot from his perusal, Risa grew wry. "I refused dance class and my father's interminable demands to practice this court curtsy. I never planned to debut. I wanted to use any funds for it to study art in Italy."

"You had plans to become a renowned sculptress."

"Yes. And I wouldn't be here now, if it weren't for my aunt pestering me about my family duty—and my greater need to have a ploy to come to London, research Maddie's death, and meet you."

"All the more reason to get this over with, so that we can talk."

"You will meet me then? At the zoo?"

"Day after tomorrow. The panther's cage." Blake nodded as a footman beckoned them closer. "But when I realized yesterday where you were coming today that you had to have a new gown finished, I came to see you," he revealed with such sincerity that she wished to have him tell her why. "I could not wait."

She licked her lips. Caught her breath. Concentrated on the fact that he wished to speak about Maddie. Not her.

He raised his chin, his eyes widening in recognition of some signal from the man before him. "But now it's time for you to make your bow."

She was reluctant to go just when he was revealing so many facts. "I want to go home," she whispered, gaze straight ahead, as he coiled her arm through his and pressed it to his warm side.

"Lean on me."

"Thank you." *Might I count on you for other things more important to me? Such as telling me the truth?*

"You're welcome." He led her forward one more step. "I wanted to see you again without rancor in your eyes."

She examined his. And found them deep and lovely. "That is difficult."

"Nonetheless, I have to try to return us to yesterday. Before the introductions—and the harshness."

"We can't."

"We must."

"I doubt it."

"What good will come of talking to me about Maddie if you will not give me the benefit of the doubt? Don't you see? I surprised you by coming here this morning to resurrect your initial impression of me. That man in the gallery was one you trusted enough to open your soul to him. Cerise, when we speak of your sister—" He lowered his voice more as they approached a footman. "—you must be prepared to believe me."

"I do not know you."

"Part of you does." He caressed her with his eyes. "Just as an inner part of me knows you. Understands you."

"That is the artist in me."

"And does that artist lie to herself?"

"Never."

"Then you lock her away from the rest of yourself."

Not surprised at his perception, she was rueful. "That artist is not often welcome out here in society."

"Perhaps she needs to rely more upon her instincts. Associate with those who nurture her. And with those who appreciate her."

"You do not have a reputation that allows a woman to trust you." *And against all logic, I want to.* "Rumors about you abound. That you charm many women."

"That I have had mistresses."

"Yes. That you enchanted Maddie. That she lost her head over you—"

"And perhaps took her life. I regret those rumors."

"You regret much."

"More than you know," he said with melancholy.

She felt a twinge of sorrow for him, but couldn't let compassion for him stop her. "I am sorry if I offend you when I say these things, but if we are to speak truth, then we must begin here and now."

"Then look at me. And hear me. I did not lead Maddie to believe I cared for her except as a friend. Whatever she thought, whatever she told your aunt about me, Maddie created the fantasy." His eyes narrowed as if he were in pain, as if he wished to say more, but thought better of it.

And near as Risa was, she recognized his statement was an honest one.

"Come now," he said, "we will talk again. Soon. Alone." He patted her hand. "The girl before you is almost finished her bow. Another step. Smile. Wonderful. Though I will say I like much better the way you grin."

That made Risa brighten.

He surveyed the hundred or so others who turned their heads toward them. "I take that back. Look like that and I see I shall have to beat off the other gentlemen who will come to call."

She was thrilled, she was dismayed, she was conflicted so that she whispered, "I don't want them to call on me."

"Neither do I."

She shot him a glance.

"I loathe a crowd, especially when I see a work of art I wish to admire at my leisure . . . alone." He flashed her a look of molten need. Then grinned like a dark angel. "Here we are. One more step."

She hung back, charmed by him, and hating herself that she was. But as she glanced about, her heart began to slam in her chest. "The Prince of Wales—"

"Smiles at you. He finds you lovely, but why not? A man would have to be blind not to see it. Good, Bertie nods. His wife Alex approves. You are now one of the Bright Ones. There, now, the previous girl is backing out. But she is a little woozy, and her train—"

"Is drooping."

"If she doesn't step on it—"

The material ripped. Her mother moaned. The witnesses slowly lowered their lashes against the offense, as the poor girl froze in place, and was assisted from the red carpet. Which left Risa standing at the door as the girl bowed herself past, tears already dribbling down her cheeks.

Blake's voice baptized Risa like fine brandy. "Think of umbrellas or walking sticks."

"A gladiator," was the only vision which saved her from the shakes.

"And to help you keep that thought," Blake took her hand and pressed something cool and squishy inside, "hold onto this."

She looked down.

He stepped back.

Blake passed her card to the Lord Chamberlain who pounded his standard and read, "Cerise Margaux de Ros-Lindsay, the Countess of Rossborough, the Baroness Lindsay!"

She opened her fist and chuckled. He had given her a wet gray ball of clay.

3

⤜⤏⤜⤏

The model must . . . impress you, awaken in you an emotion, which in turn you seek to express.

Henri Matisse

What a gladiator.

"Minus your sword," Blake muttered to himself over his failure to bring one to cut a swath through the throng greeting Cerise Lindsay in the Dungarvons' receiving line. *So now you are defenseless.* He grinned down at his empty glass. He'd never before contemplated dueling over a woman. But he was ready to take on any of the dandies who had so much as smiled at her in the past hour.

He took another flute of champagne from a passing footman and retreated to the garden. The breeze was crisp, cooling his desire to break in that line not one whit. He plunked his glass on the stone bench, pulled a cheroot from his wcskit and patted his pockets for a match. *Hell of a note, not to be able to smoke or even savor the champagne.*

"Shouldn't be surprised, old man, when you just want the woman."

"Good evening, Lord Hargrove," cooed one widow who had taken the air with another man. She arced a thin brow at Blake, making him wonder if she'd overheard him talking to himself.

He nodded. "I do hope so, Lady Dillingham."

"Perhaps it can be." This woman had once wooed Blake to her boudoir to display how dearly she wished to wed again. "Will you dance this evening?" She teased him now.

He never did. "Later."

"Surprising. Whatever the occasion," she cooed, "I hope you'll share your skills with many of us." And then she led her companion toward the ballroom.

Blake would waltz at this blasted affair Cerise's cousin Georgie hostessed to launch her into society, but he intended to do it only with her.

He fingered the cigar, turning away from the sight of the new countess of Rossborough at her duty.

But in his mind's eye, he still saw her.

Tonight, she had traded this morning's ivory debut gown for a candlelight affair that caressed her breasts like a kiss. Her dress was a froth of chiffon with a classical drape that reminded him more of a Grecian beauty's attire than a Victorian's. But it really mattered not what this lady donned, to him she wore nothing at all.

He picked up his glass and drained it.

Courtesy of his years of studying the human body, especially the female in art studios and out, he could visualize what lay beneath any fabric. Before yesterday, he had called it a blessing to be able to gauge any woman's physical attributes. It made him dispassionate. It kept him a bachelor.

But yesterday he had gazed into the fathomless eyes of Cerise Lindsay, shared her torments, and saw beyond the physical. More unusual, he had shared his most intimate thoughts about his own talent.

He had not done that with anyone except his sister Barbara. Until yesterday morning when Cerise Lindsay had voiced her doubts about her work, he had not realized that his decision not to sculpt had severed a part of him which brought him happiness. Yet, he was loathe to put his hands to clay again—and lose his heart to his work.

And as for losing his heart to a woman, the truth was that he had adored his mother, cherished his sister, and never found any their equal. But he was drawn to Cerise Lindsay and he told himself the reason was her artistic plight. They had that in common and so he had offered her the benefits of his own experience.

He had succeeded.

And with their introduction, failed. His urgency to see her again chiseled away at his nerves, until he had to discover what she had planned for herself that she could not meet him for days.

It took no genius to deduce that she debuted today. The queen received on Wednesdays at eleven. Young women needed new gowns to go. Mothers and aunts who accompanied them were atwitter with nerves over the gown, the event.

Blake decided to attend the Drawing Room as was his privilege, if he chose.

He chose. And having used his influence to insinuate himself in the way of her progress to the queen this morning, he congratulated himself that he had won another round of laughter and gratitude from Cerise Lindsay.

Like an opium addict, he had wanted it again.

So here he stood, chilled among the boxwoods, envisioning like some shy boy the voluptuous Cerise Lindsay and learning that his blessing had become a curse. He could measure Cerise's beguiling assets within a fraction of a groan.

Her legs were incredibly long, meant to twine with a man's. He squeezed his eyes shut that he could envision them around his. Her waist was small, ten or more inches smaller than those bounteous breasts. He rolled his tongue around his mouth, tasting no champagne but the cream her secret skin must be. More than all else, he wanted to hear that sultry voice whisper sweet things in his ear and watch those magnetic eyes focus on him once more in delight.

God, do let her dispense with the few people she had yet to greet and then he would snatch her dance card from her wrist and fill every damn line with his name.

He threw the cheroot in the bushes and strode inside. Arms crossed, he lounged against a wall to watch her.

She was greeting another man with a tight curve of her mouth. She was so nervous. So persevering. Public engagements like this were against her nature.

She would shine best in familiar surroundings. With intimate friends. Performing here was draining her. The taut lines around her eyes gave that away. If, as she had told him yesterday morning, she had come to London to see him, then he'd help her accomplish her goal with speed. He'd steal her away from these toffs who would try to charm her for her title or her land, and her lush body. They might even assume that she had money.

But Blake knew the truth.

Cerise's sister Maddie had run through what she had in her pockets, perhaps in her bank account, too. She had most likely passed on any debt because last winter Cerise had been compelled to go to a bank in York for a loan. His own curator, who was by coincidence also the Lindsays', had told him so a few months ago when Blake inquired if Maddie's successor gave the man any indications that she would sell Allure. Blake wished to acquire the statue for himself and since Maddie had passed away, he wondered if Maddie's successor would consider selling it.

Blake saw Cerise roll her shoulders as the last couple in the receiving line walked into the Dungarvons' ball-room.

Now was his chance.

Georgie and Robert Dungarvon, as host and hostess for Cerise's first coming-out ball were assuming their positions on each side of her. The first dance was by tradition reserved for the closest male relative in the family—and since Cerise's father was not alive, the honor devolved to Robert. Blake had no trouble with tradition, as long as he got what he wanted as well. So he walked up to the three, and began to take it.

"Permit me to ask—" He inclined his head at Robert and his wife but smiled down on Cerise. "—if I might claim your card, my lady."

Georgie struck her fan to her chest, shocked. "Lord Hargrove, how charming. You do not ever dance."

"Can you bear to be the one to change my past?" he asked a surprised Cerise.

"I'd be honored," said Cerise with dollop of humor, "to save you the second waltz."

He took her hand, kissed her fingertips in the skintight gloves. "Make me happier. Save me all of them."

Robert arched both blond brows. "Come, my lord," he said none too sober for so early in the evening, "give the others a chance."

"Bobbie, really," his wife reproved him and looked at Blake with encouragement.

"Forgive my breach of etiquette, Lady Dungarvon." *But I will do as I must when I want something priceless.* "Robert, I am sorry."

Cerise's full mouth quivered with laughter. "I promise to save two waltzes for you, Lord Hargrove."

"Oh, my dear." Georgie objected to giving him more than the traditional one. "You mustn't."

Cerise did not even look at them. "After that, my lord Hargrove, your toes will be mashed and you'll wish to sit out the rest."

"Ah, but you do not know my own skill."

"I welcome the test then, my lord."

He nodded, stepped backward and resigned himself to watching her take the center of the floor with her cousin-in-law. Meanwhile, Georgie recovered her shock and gazed upon them in approval. However, her mother Elizabeth Elgin whispered something to her, regarding Blake with distaste.

He did not care much for her, either. She was a stern woman, more congenial certainly than many a debutante's chaperone, but nonetheless one with whom he found conversation stilted. He had not understood her attitude toward him. He usually had few problems in that regard with anyone, man or woman. He accepted people as he found them and did not judge. Yet, Lady Elgin had never graced him with a smile. With her, he felt examined. Even . . . dissected. He knew not why, nor had he cared enough to question Maddie Lindsay about her aunt's motive.

Lady Elgin's younger niece, however, found him appealing. He felt it each time she put her eyes on him. He heard it in her voice. Cerise liked him because he knew her inner struggle with her need to sculpt. In spite of the rumors that Maddie had loved him and may have committed suicide over his rejection. So if art was the lure that drew Cerise and him together, bound them in laughter, he would use it to draw her again. Because he enjoyed her company and . . .

Well, why?

Because he needed to help her. Because he saw her challenges. If she took his advice, he knew he could save her some anguish. As he had not saved Barbara from hers.

But there was more Cerise could learn from him. He suppressed the mental image of what he could teach her about his own naked body—and hers. If he could, if he *dared* educate her in the fine art of passion, he knew he would cherish the moments he spent with her.

That, too, jolted him. His practice was to immerse himself in a woman and soon to tire of her.

But he doubted he would tire of Cerise Lindsay.

She intrigued him with her courage to work in a profession dominated by men.

"Bright One suits her, doesn't it?"

"Like few others." Blake greeted his friend, Benjamin Woodward. The lanky American was also appreciating Cerise Lindsay as she took the floor.

"It's the hair."

Like wine. "And the silver eyes."

"Uncanny, aren't they?"

They see inside your head. "Mesmerizing."

"Yep. Madelaine was a bonbon, whereas this woman is . . ." Woody licked his lower lip. ". . . a feast."

"Ah. Does the connoisseur announce his intention to dance with her?" Blake was certain his own possessiveness made his smile sardonic.

Woody drained his glass. "Soon as I can jot my name on that card of hers."

Blake hid his intention to keep Woody away. "You have taken too well to our customs."

This spring was the millionaire's second in England. Here to purchase old masters' works of art for his new home on Fifth Avenue, Ben Woodward had crossed the Atlantic last month to finish the job he'd begun last year. If in the process he took back to New York an English bride, Woody's mother would burst her buttons in glee. "My father," he had confided last summer, "made his first million dollars in Texas cattle, the second in silver. It's my job to do us proud and bring home a girl with gold in her veins."

Like Cerise Lindsay? Blake noted the gleam in his friend's eye and vowed Woody would have little chance to charm her. "One dance is all you are allowed per night."

"I can live with that if I learn where she'll be tomorrow night. How well do you know her? You looked chummy when you spoke with her in line."

"We have only just met." He did not add where or when. *Nor will I tell you she is a sculptor, lest you amuse her with your understanding of art.* "The most I know about her is that she has taken up the estate responsibilities which her sister's death placed on her." *And she is eaten alive by doubts she's doing well.*

"My bankers tell me this new countess needs money and borrowed it from a bank in York."

"Is that so?" Though Woody enjoyed gossip, Blake wondered if Woody had sought out the information—and why.

"Maddie mismanaged her estate." Woody took another glass from a footman. "Quite a few know. Did you?"

"I never asked." *Never had to. Maddie told me. Her debts were her motivation to discuss selling me Allure.*

Woody pursed his mouth, admiring Cerise. "Well, I have money." His square face went raw with lust. "I might find this countess of Rossborough even more charming than the last."

For Woody to speak so blatantly about Maddie and Cerise set Blake's teeth on edge.

Yet, Blake could say little without giving away the fact that he had met her and understood her quickly and more deeply than Ben Woodward could ever perceive. "She is not your average debutante, Woody."

"What do you mean?"

"She's not come down to London to seek a husband." *She wants to talk to me. And I plan to give her what she came for.* "You will have to excuse me now, Woody."

He left the American with a speed he'd apologize for later. Blake would not stand by and permit Woody to occupy her. Not until Blake had had his fill of her smile . . . and became as indifferent to her as he did to other women.

He calculated the spot where Robert would stop dancing with Cerise. Her cousin bowed to her and Blake took his place. "Hello, again."

She smiled up at him, her joy doused by politeness.

"Won't you look like you are pleased to see me, at the very least?" he asked with more disappointment than he planned to let her hear. "Did your aunt suspect that we had met before?" *Is that why you are wary now?*

He took her in his arms, felt the heat of her hand on his shoulder and the other in his palm. He had expected to be nonchalant with her, but he found his pride wounded when she tried the same tactic on him.

"Perhaps she said something to Georgie. But not me. I think she didn't speculate to me because you were very discreet this morning at Court." She was in such control of her expression, he wished he had brought a lump of clay with him to slap into her hand. He vowed he'd make her grin at him without it. "You are very good at waltzing."

"You are being kind again." Other gentlemen led ladies to the floor. "I am unpracticed, my lord."

"Blake," he encouraged her. "Then perhaps you need to practice with the right partner." He heard the orchestra rustle in their chairs, the conductor tap his baton.

The silence stretched until she met his gaze directly. "Your gift of clay this morning was a stroke of genius."

"It worked too, didn't it?"

"Pleased with yourself?" Her mouth twitched in a grin.

"Should I be?"

"Do you never answer a question directly, my lord?"

"After you do," he chuckled and drew her so close her body radiated a heat that set his skin on fire. "Did the clay help?"

"Oh, yes," she told him in that confection of a voice. "I created a good likeness with it afterward."

He cringed, playfully surveying the room lest he hug her. "Of the queen?"

"You."

The fires seeped into his bones. "Dare I ask to see it?"

"You may dare, but you may not see it."

"You destroyed it?"

"Oh, yes."

"I am crushed."

She laughed. "Literally."

"You must not be so critical." *I can help you learn how to accept yourself. And I do hope, me, as well.*

"Self criticism for an artist is a useful trait. Believe me, what I created was not worthy of you."

He did hug her briefly then, words inadequate to her compliment. But then she gave him more.

"I want to thank you."

I can think of a way. Let me explore those lips. "You are welcome."

"You helped me with a few words—and your lump of clay."

The violinists raised their instruments to their chin.

"Did you bring me some tonight?"

He firmed his mouth, enigmatic.

"In which pocket?"

"Suppose I let you search?"

"I accept."

"Here?" He feigned being scandalized.

She eyed his chest. "Which pocket might it be?" She nibbled her lower lip in thought.

"And I thought you innocent."

"Of what?"

"Devilry."

She narrowed her eyes. "You lie."

"On the contrary, I am being a gentleman."

"Of course you are. And I am glad of it. So, in a gentlemanly fashion, do tell me which pocket, my lord?"

"Inside my weskit."

She tried to halt.

He led her on, laughing. "You do not play fair."

"You do not play."

"I have forgotten how," he realized suddenly. Like an amputee who has become used to maneuvering without a limb, Blake had told himself he had accepted his decision never to sculpt again. But the artistic passion he had severed from his days had also cut off his ability to laugh. And like a throb of pain from a limb he thought severed, he felt a surge of joy that his desire remained. And the one who helped him recognize that was this woman, who had great problems of her own. With her art. And with him.

He tried to grin at her. "I should call your bluff."

"But you won't."

"Not tonight. Not in public. But I will continue to bring clay with me. And you must find it every time."

"For a price?" she asked, disturbed by the thought.

"For the fun of it." He cocked his head. "What did you think I'd say?"

"For answers to my questions about Maddie."

He drew back. "You do think ill of me."

"Less each time we meet."

"Thank heavens."

"Difficult for me when I have the unhappy goal of discovering more about Maddie's death."

He could play with her, toy with her affections, oh yes. He knew how—and instinct told him he had the advantage over her because she was a novice to the art of love. He was no novice to the art of love affairs. Between the two stood worlds of difference. He would not expose her to them. He wanted her friendship. Her respect.

"I wish to cultivate a more responsible image with you," he told her. "I want to help you learn about Maddie's last days. I also have a professional desire to help you return to your sculpting." That was what made their relationship useful to her and unique to him. It was so much more noble of him—and worthy of her.

Her gaze mellowed. "Whoever would have thought Lord Hargrove was so sweet?"

Sweet? No other woman had ever thought him so. Made him so. He had taken women to his bed since he'd been fifteen, and had never been told this. He liked women and sex. He had never needed more. He had his estates, his fortune and his brother and sister to care for. To say nothing of his art. Until he found he'd been no good at it. "Blake," he urged, inanity easier than any other way to navigate this conversation.

"Blake, I am Risa—and now that we are on closer terms, please just dance with me."

"Precisely what I came for." *To get closer to you.*

He vaguely noted that his hand wrapped her slim waist, and the indentation of her spine was deep, a luscious valley he wished to define with his fingers or better, his mouth. He turned away for objectivity and when he secured it, glanced down only to suffer a loss of air at the humor that turned up her mouth. "I like this mood better. What brought it on?"

She blushed to the roots of her red hair. "I can tell you are"—her fingertips pressed into his shoulder—"stronger than I perceived you."

"The gladiator image again, I presume."

"I should sculpt you that way."

"Do it then."

She was examining him, objectively as an artist.

As a joke, as a hope, he said, "I could pose for you."

Her mouth fell open with delight. "Never."

"Why not?" But he knew the answer. And the danger. If he removed every stitch of his clothes for her, his armor would be gone. A naked gladiator, his body would declare, as it did so uncomfortably now, that she fascinated him. That he desired her. Naked, with the social formalities discarded, he knew the day would dawn when they would kiss, touch, explore a passion the very thought of which had already altered his view of himself. From satyr to suitor. "Risa, why not?"

"You appeal to me."

He felt strong, invincible. She desired him, too. "When I shouldn't?"

"No."

Anger flared that she would deny the obvious attraction they had felt from the first minute they had spoken in Bartholome's shop. Of course, it was Maddie's accident, her death, and the rumors about her relationship with him that made Risa balk. He understood her point of view—and yet, he didn't.

He hadn't killed Maddie. Hadn't sunk her tiny boat. The god-awful storm had done that. A squall so quick, so fierce, no one on shore could have predicted its force. Yet, Maddie insisted on going out. He had tried to stop her, but she was so angry with him she went.

By all logic, Blake was not responsible. Though he felt he was because they had argued before she cast off. Because the sailboat was his. Because she was his guest.

The violins filled him with a haunting need to sweep the past away, a refrain he knew so well since Barbara's untimely death. He took Risa securely into his embrace, loving the strength of her young body, wishing he could talk with her privately.

But hell, he wanted to do more than talk. He wanted to touch her, illustrate to himself she was just another woman, a body perhaps more luscious than many another's, but just that. Not unusual. Not . . . irresistible.

"We are going to begin. Ready?" He stepped closer, melding her delectable curves to his own. Their proximity was more than etiquette permitted and she stiffened.

"Relax and enjoy this," he murmured and stepped out with her firmly in his grasp. And she followed. Trusting his lead, she waltzed better with him. Agility with her cousin was lacking because of the abundance of champagne Robert had already imbibed. Robert was no man to support her, lead her, help her.

But I am.

To illustrate it to her, Blake executed a turn which Robert had not done expertly. Risa did not follow him well, and Blake knew she did not wish to give herself up to the seduction of the music. Not with him. "Imagine I am someone else, if you must."

"Who would you suggest?" she was fetchingly gamine again. Her mood swings were faster than lightning.

"Do gladiators dance?"

"One does. Very well, I might add."

"Do not compliment him too much, however. He may throw you over his shoulder and run away with you."

"Do gladiators do that?"

"Barbarians do." He risked any impartiality with such frankness. She didn't want his admiration, even if she adored his humor. He moved his hand, held her more tightly as he led her along with him. If he kept on this way, he was going to learn secrets from her tonight. About her body and her mind. "I would do anything for a chance to talk with you. Now."

Her gaiety died. "I want to."

"That's why I didn't wait for the day after tomorrow. I persuaded Lord Tuttle to fall ill this morning." Blake relished the joy that lit her features. "That's why I came here tonight, too."

Her first reaction was to smile. She was a woman complimented. Her second was to frown. She was a sister, attracted to a man she thought had rejected her sibling. "Is that also why you are not a wallflower tonight?"

"To dance with you, yes. We are under such scrutiny. These people wonder why I am here. So does your cousin, her husband, and your aunt." He swirled her around the floor. "They cannot take their eyes off us."

She faltered a bit in self-consciousness.

"Meet me outside before the supper buffet."

"No. I need longer with you than a few minutes."

Blake took in her parted lips and her earnestness. He needed time too, to get close enough to her to become bored by her. "We need hours." *Afternoons naked in the sun . . .*

"I haven't had a chance to do anything today but act like a mannequin, dress and undress, dance and—"

"Then meet me tomorrow. First thing."

"By accident?"

"There is no other way."

"But I run the risk that someone will see us."

"I can arrange it."

"How? Where?"

"Go to your appointment with *Monsieur* Bartolome."

Her eyes widened. "Do you know why I want to see him?"

"No." Blake was puzzled at the question. "Should I?"

"I hope not."

He had no right to ask her for further information.

She thought a moment. "I wondered if after I left, Bartolome had told you why I wished to see him."

Why would he? And why would you think he would? "He didn't."

She was relieved at that. But only slightly.

"You can be a bundle of nerves," he declared.

"You noticed," she confessed.

"No wonder you have problems with your work." When she frowned, he knew he had struck a chord of truth.

"I have a lot of worries," she admitted.

"Not the least of which is the success of this debut." He allowed himself the torture of a long look at her mouth. "Am I right?"

"In this, as in so much else, I am sad to say."

"Why?" he asked in a gruff voice.

"What?" she blinked up at him.

"Why do you not like that I am right about so many things?"

"You are too perceptive. Intrusive."

"Intimate." Her breath lodged inside her. He felt it. He rejoiced in it. "It is the way we are, Countess."

"You read my mind," she regretted.

"Do you think the fact that we can see inside each other will change because you do not wish it to be so?"

"I could hope so."

"As could I."

She bit her lip. She would not ask for an explanation.

"Do you think a man likes the idea that a young lady—a scintillating young countess—can make mush of him?"

"Can I do that to you?"

"With one silver-eyed glance."

"No man has ever told me such a thing."

"They should. What's more, I fear many of the fellows here will try."

"I shan't listen to them."

He brought her closer to him, wishing she would listen only to him, resolving to become a better man, a nobler one. "I wish I had proof to give you that I did not hurt Maddie's feelings."

She swallowed back a reply.

"I wish we had met before this happened to her, then you and I might have enjoyed each other's company."

"I want to believe you."

"I must build on that."

She looked away. "When did you first meet my sister?"

"Spring, summer of seventy-nine. I'm not certain of the date. Why?"

"You met here in London?"

"Yes. I called on her when she first came to the city a few months after your father died." He waltzed with less vigor now, disturbed. "I went to see if she wished to sell Allure." As he spoke, Risa's features hardened. "I see that damns me."

She looked forlorn.

"In what way?" Did he sound as desperate as he felt?

"Maddie kept a diary every year since she learned to write. I knew where she hid them and their keys. I have not found hers for last year, but I did find the one for 1879 in the Park Lane house. In it, she writes of falling in love with a man."

"Surely not—"

"She refers to him as only 'B.' "

Blake faltered.

She grew somber. "Blake, did you seduce my sister?"

He halted—and had to lead her quickly from the floor before the next couple careened into her. "Come with me."

"No." She swayed. "Answer me."

He noticed others glaring at them, curious about their conversation and the abrupt ending of their waltz. He swept an arm around her. "Not here."

"I can't leave. You know what a scandal this would—"

"To hell with what anyone thinks." He scooped her up into his arms. "You have turned your ankle. Like a proper gentleman, I am coming to your aid." *And my own.*

She feigned a smile at concerned on-lookers. Through clenched teeth, she ordered, "Put me down."

"Not until I see to your foot," he pardoned his way past a few people. "She's twisted it," he explained to one old biddie who would have blocked his way. But he marched into the hall and made for the farthest door.

"Now," he said as he thrust it open, strode inside, then pushed it shut with his foot. He put her back against it, his hands to her shoulders. "Did I seduce Maddie?"

Anger flashed in her eyes. "I must know."

"I told you that is rumor."

"You have seduced other women."

"They cooperated. They were also women I want-ed."

"And—"

"I didn't want Maddie. She was pretty, she was shy."

"She was sweet."

"Naïve." *Conniving, too.*

"I suppose you require only sophisticated women."

I did. "Maddie was anxious to capture a husband. Not the kind of woman I normally am drawn to."

"Maddie was a woman worthy of your love."

He could not answer that without an hour to explain the things he knew, and those others he suspected about Maddie. "The fact remains I did not care for her that way. The heart does not love out of logic." *As if I am such an authority on that emotion. Better to discuss what I do understand.* "Desire does not bloom at will."

"Can you prove you did not seduce her?"

"An initial does not prove I did."

"Nonetheless . . ."

He dug his fingers into her shoulders. "Tell me. Am I the kind of man Maddie would be attracted to?"

"No. But then . . . she seemed to have changed a lot since I left for Italy."

"What kind of man would she like?"

"A sensitive man."

"I am that."

"But you also are aggressive, domineering."

"Cerise?" A woman's voice inquired through the door.

"What else?" he whispered.

"She would want a man who would compliment her."

"I would do that."

"Cerise?"

"What does Maddie say in her diary about B.? Did he dance with her?"

"Never."

"Give her gifts?"

"No."

"But I danced with you, only you. Gave you clay. So then. What else can I say to persuade you I am not this man Maddie denoted as B.?"

"Cerise!"

"Just a minute, Aunt Elizabeth! I must go," Risa said to him. "Meet me at the zoo—"

Blake grew hot with frustration. "What *did* he do?"

"Kissed her."

"When?"

"One day when he met her at the Flower Show."

"And on that she based her fantasies of him?"

"Yes, it was a short kiss, a delicate thing."

"A peck. What good is a kiss like that?" he scoffed.

"It shows he is gentle."

"When a man really wants a woman, he does not show her with some subtle sign of homage. What's the point?"

"He doesn't want to harm her sensibilities," Risa ventured.

"No," Blake countered, "he wants to arouse them. He wants to take her in his arms—" So he did. "And make her burn for him."

He edged his hands beneath her back, tender as he'd never been before, and soft as angels' wings touched his lips to hers. She shivered, but her mouth was lush and warm and opening to the brush of his. He groaned and ran a hand into her hair, taking her fully against him. And he kissed her, tasted her as if he had craved her a lifetime and not just since yesterday. He claimed her like the warrior she'd compared him to. Fierce and commanding, he led her from a homage of the lips to permit him the moist recesses of her mouth. The kiss drifted from languid to a wild exploration that made him question if he'd ever kissed a woman so thoroughly before.

Shocked, he raised his face. Wrapped her securely to him. Kissed her temple, her ear.

She yanked away. Licked her lips. Focused on his.

"Did I seduce your sister?" he repeated her question. "Maddie was not the kind of woman I find appealing."

Risa lifted her chin, valiant. "No?"

"I prefer a different type. Determined. Independent." *You.* He cupped her cheek.

A knock came at the door. The knob rattled. "Cerise, darling, you must open this now."

"It's Georgie." Risa closed her eyes.

"Come tomorrow to Bartolome's for your appointment. Come in a hired cab. Leave in the one that will be waiting at the curb."

"I will be there."

"Do. Or I might be so rash as to disregard all rules and come to you at Park Lane." He raised his hand to embrace her again, calm her fears, but instead pulled open the library door. "Come in, Lady Dungarvon. Your cousin is unharmed. I had to make sure she had not sprained her ankle. Forgive me my rashness to sweep her away." He left without a glance at Risa.

Tomorrow he would tell her exactly what he knew about her older sister. He cursed, doubting he could make the mix palatable so that Risa would ever want to see him again, much less talk to her.

But I want her to kiss me again.

So as he climbed into his carriage and dropped into the squabs, he knew he could ensure that.

All I have to do is lie about Maddie.

4

To create, to improvise, these are useless words. Genius only comes to a person who understands with his eyes—and his intelligence.

Auguste Rodin

"After yesterday, you are very tired, *mademoiselle?*" *Monsieur* Bartholome once again verged away from the topic of Maddie's visits to him.

Risa smiled, hoping to dazzle the art dealer more than she had in the last few minutes. "Presentation days are long, *monsieur;* but I adored every second of it." *More than I anticipated. Especially in Blake Hargrove's company.* She enjoyed her debut *because* he had been attentive to her. Because he had kissed her.

But he will not again. I won't let him. Not until I know more. Of the truth.

She skimmed a bronze cast of a fawn. As yet, her coquette's approach to the art shop owner was not opening him to her queries about why Maddie had come to see him two years ago. The man was a clam regarding his relationship with her sister and Risa predicted that she becoming a shrew would not pry him open, either.

She would show him a bit of her hand. "I know that

my sister came to see you a few times in the spring of 1879. She said the two of you got on famously."

His thin black brows darted high. "She told you she had come here?"

Was Bartholome afraid or simply curious? "She wrote about it." Risa did not tell him she had read it in Maddie's diary.

"I am astonished. Her visits were to be a secret."

"Really? Did she say why?"

He waved a hand. "It was the way she came—and then the reason for her visits. You see, Mademoiselle, your sister came alone. Heavily veiled. Alighting from a hired hansom. So much like you," the dealer's face pulled up in a doughy smile whose falsity did not compel her to share with him any of her own secrets. "I did not think it my place to investigate why she did these things."

Risa nodded, waiting for enlightenment herself on that score. "She always came like that?"

"*Oui, mademoiselle,*" he continued, vague about the first date Maddie had come, but not about the time of day. "It would be in the late morning. Just as you have now."

That would mean Maddie had escaped Park Lane while Aunt Elizabeth went to visit Georgie each morning.

Bartholome went on to say that after three such visits, Maddie had purchased an oil by a secondary artist named Edward Ritter. He was an apprentice to Hans Holbein, the Younger.

We own two original Holbeins. Both preliminary drawings for a portrait of Henry the Eighth. Both hang in the main gallery at Park Lane. Why would Maddie want an oil from the artist's understudy? And more perplexing, what had Maddie done with the painting? She had not hung it in Park Lane where most of the Rossborough prizes were displayed. No puzzle as to why she hadn't, either. She would not mount it on the wall for it to be shamed next to another work of superior talent. Nor had she hung it in Rossborough Manor house in Northumbria with the few treasures the family kept there for private appreciation. Risa took a mental inventory of the paintings on display in her home to the north and none of those works was one by an unknown artist named Ritter.

Yet, the central question remained and Risa turned to him with it on her lips. "*Monsieur*, did my sister tell you why she was purchasing this painting?"

"But of course. She liked the composition."

"I see." Before coming to England from Germany, Holbein had carved wood-block prints for illustrated books and painted oils whose subjects were religious themes. However, in his years in England, Holbein had painted primarily portraits of the pompous King Henry, most of his wives, and his three children. "I know little about this Edward Ritter, *monsieur*. What did he like to paint?"

"Portraits. This picture was special to your sister. The two young girls, she said, reminded her of you and her when you were both young."

"How so?"

"Ah." He looked serene. "She said it portrayed you both as happy."

Then the picture must have portrayed a scene of two children playing in their nursery with their mother, never their father. Even then, the children must have been no more than eight and ten years old, at which point Maddie developed a penchant for riding and attempting to charm their indifferent father, while Risa took to pencils, chalk, and clay to fill her empty hours after their mother became ill and passed away. That was equally as odd as what had happened to the painting after Maddie had taken it from the shop. "Did she perchance mention what she wished to do with the painting?"

"*Oui, mademoiselle.*" The Frenchman was pleased that he recalled this fact. "It was a present."

"A present." Risa was more confounded. "For whom?"

"You do not know then?"

"Obviously not, *monsieur.*"

"She said it was a surprise. For you."

That shook her. Stumped her. "Thank you, *monsieur.* You have been most obliging."

"You do not have it?"

"No." *Unless it is in the attic with the other items. Our Follies, her father had called those art works which he and his forebears had bought and learned later were second-rate works or worse, forgeries.* Risa smoothed her gloves. As she pressed the fabric to the base of her fingers, another thought disturbed her. "How much was the painting, *monsieur?*"

"*Mademoiselle*, that I do not remember."

"Surely, you keep records."

"*Oui*, but the transaction, it was last year."

Risa glanced toward his office where his assistant darted out of sight but, she was certain, not out of hearing. "Do you not have a ledger for your transactions?"

"*Certainement*, but at home."

Charisma, she told herself, was a commodity she needed to purchase by the ton if she wished to return to gain any more information from this man. "Well, in that case"—she waved a hand blithely—"perhaps you could recall the approximate price you quoted her."

"We did a . . ." He waggled his fingers. ". . . negotiation."

"Naturally." She held her ground. "And?"

"I think we agreed to a sum of"—he wrinkled his

forehead—"one hundred pounds, a little here, a little there."

Risa did not let her shock at the figure show, but asked, "Was that a fair price, *monsieur?*"

"For the market? *Absolument.*" Challenged, he set his jaw.

For Maddie, who was thousands of pounds in debt, to spend one hundred pounds for a painting by an un-acclaimed artist could be described only as frivolous.

Uncharacteristic, too. Maddie had never cared about the priceless Rossborough collection. Why should she suddenly take enough of an interest in a painting by an amateur to buy it?

"May I ask you a question, *mademoiselle?*"

"Please do." Risa gave the man a congenial look.

"Why do you come to me now? Has the person to whom your sister gave this taken a dislike to it? Do you not like it and you wish to sell it back to me?"

"Is that your policy, *monsieur?*" If it was, he operated his business in a unique way.

"I wish to make my clients happy."

"No. I will not try to sell it back to you." *Though if I had it, I would and put good use to that one hundred pounds. I could use it to repay some of my loan.*

He shook his head in that Gallic manner which suggested confusion. "I am at a loss, as you say."

"I am befuddled, too, *Monsieur* Bartolome. I had hoped to learn more from you. Thank you for your help. I hope I may return."

"By all means," he invited her but sounded unhappy with the prospect, "I am at your disposal, *mademoiselle.*"

"Good day." She hastened toward his front door, her confusion over this purchase of the painting driving her to a solitude in which she might make sense of it— and to her attic to hopefully find it.

"Good day, *mademoiselle,*" he bid as she turned

his brass handle, tinkled his little bell, and left his shop.

She stood on the walk and inhaled crisp springtime air. Questions danced in her head like evil fairies. Would they never stop accumulating? She needed an-swers.

Agitation mixed with relief, she noted a black cab stood at the corner. The horse, a tall red roan, shifted from one hoof to another as he pawed the cobbles.

She crossed the street. What if this were not the cab Blake had hired?

She smiled at the coachman who climbed down from his perch at the sight of her. Even if he were not the one Blake had hired, she did need a ride home. "Could you take me to Park Lane, please?" she told him as the door swung outward.

"The guv'nor wants me to drive out the Brompton Road," he muttered, and handed her up the iron foot-step and into the black interior.

"Guv'nor?" She searched the void for the one he re-ferred to—and the door slammed with such a jolt that she jumped. "Oh, my goodness! Oh, I'm sorry!" she tried to turn and could not finish because the hansom driver cracked a whip over the nag that sent the cab lurching forward, throwing Risa more off balance. Vise-like hands caught her and what was more, they were big, clasped to her hips. They were also as insis-tent as the brandied voice.

"Sit down here," a man commanded between chuck-les, and guided her to the cushions.

"Good heavens," she murmured as she adjusted her glasses and realized the man who held her firmly and plunked her by his hard thigh was Blake Hargrove.

"You are finished earlier than I predicted," he of-fered, while he flipped down the oilcloth window, thus sealing out the world and much of its light. Still in the dimness which seeped round the edges of the cloth, she could see his teeth gleam.

"You could have told me you were here." This man excelled at spontaneity.

"And let those on the street know you had an appointment?"

"I am pleased you didn't."

"Your business with Bartholome went well, I hope." He sat farther back, his handsome face now shrouded in the gloom. "You were quite adamant the day before yesterday about his being here to meet you today. You got satisfaction from him, did you?"

She pursed her lips. "You are being forward again."

"Yes, aren't I?"

"I need not tell you why I went to see him."

"And it is such bad manners of me to try to get you to tell me. I agree on that, too. So then, did he try to sell you one of his treasures?"

"No."

"Peculiar."

"Why?"

"He tries to make the most of every encounter." Blake wiggled a finger at her. "Why not take your hat off?"

The change in topic had her chuckling and her hand going to her hair. "Do you talk better when a lady is minus her accoutrements?"

His mouth twitched. "Always."

"And do you give her something equal to her efforts?"

His look told her he never failed at that. "What did you have in mind?"

"Your hat, your gloves." *Your knowledge about Maddie.*

He grinned. "Of course," he promptly discarded all items. "Now then." He helped her remove her hat, jabbed the huge pin into it as he placed it on the seat opposite them. "I think you talented enough to survive old Bartholome. He is a cunning animal. Whenever I deal with him, I feel as though I must come home and bathe afterward. I am never certain I have escaped his taint until I look myself over." In the close confines of the cab, Risa shivered as she felt the hot sweep of Blake's jewel-like eyes over her figure.

She removed her gloves, finger by finger. The horse clip-clopped at a faster pace. "If you feel that way about him, why deal with him at all?"

"He is well connected. Tells all for a fee."

"How else can he make a substantial living?" She had known about such leeches on the art world from her father's tales of dealers who often came to call on him. They picked his brain for bits of news about who had approached him to purchase any of the Rossborough collection. But her father had little to tell. Few buyers bothered. Most in the art world knew her family's penchant to sell nothing. Not even the lowliest of their prizes. And at that, the lowliest were always originals by masters. Never by their apprentices. *So why did Maddie taint the family's reputation by acquiring a work by a second-rate artist?*

Blake shrugged. "Bartholome also hears rumors that are useful to a sale of a work. Or a work similar to it."

She agreed. "For example, the selling price."

"Yes. And the name of the buyer. The purpose of the sale."

"Aren't most works of art bought so that the owner can appreciate them?"

"A few are purchased for other reasons." Blake crossed one leg over the other, nestling into the corner of the cab and drawing her eye to the length of his limbs. And to the way the charcoal wool clung to his corded thighs.

She felt flushed all of a sudden. "Which are?"

"Bartholome earns his commission on works he has sold—as well as information he can sell."

A pin-prick of amber light filtered in, casting a golden glow over his hands. Blake Hargrove's were huge, his fingers long. She knew their strength. From last night on the dance floor, and minutes ago here in this coach. She also knew their tenderness, from two days ago when they massaged her own fingers and yesterday at Buckingham Palace when they had slapped a glob of clay into her palm. But more than his hands, his profile fascinated her. He *truly* was a dark angel in this cab. She wished she could see him, place her own hands on his brow, his nose, his cheekbones. She needed to feel his full mouth.

On mine again.

She tipped up her chin, attempting to see into the murkiness. She really must get new glasses.

"You are squinting again," he said like an indulgent father. "Here," he slid closer, a ray of sunlight, thin but brilliant, gilding his black hair. "Better?" He grinned.

"Immensely." She forced herself to look away, his lips tempting her to touch, to trace, to learn the measure of his mirth. She sat straighter. She was unnerved. Needy of the clay that kept her steady.

He put his hand atop hers. "You fidget without clay. Why didn't you put some in your pockets today?"

"A habit."

"A bad one."

She tried to smile. "I was in a hurry to keep my appointment. My aunt stayed the night at Georgie's house and will return at one or two o'clock."

"So that is how you escaped her. I wondered, too," he said after Risa nodded, "if she asked about our conversation last night."

"Yes, she did."

Aunt Elizabeth took her to task for dancing so much and leaving the floor with the notorious Earl of Sandown. "He has kept models as mistresses and thrown them away like so many sacks of grain. He controls his estate with an iron fist—and many say his brother John hates him for it. His sister Barbara killed herself, probably over his meanness. How could you dance with him?"

Risa looked him over now. *How can I find him insanely attractive? Because, Aunt, I don't see the ferociousness you and the others do. I see a man who has lost his desire to pursue his art. A man without a purpose.*

"Are you going to tell me what she said to you?" he persisted.

"No. It would make you feel badly and put her in a poor light. I want this conversation to be constructive. So I will avoid such things and say I am thrilled you came." *I am glad to see you, even if I can't terribly well in this cavern of a cab.*

"And you look tired. You must be exhausted."

"Last night I was awake until four."

"I know," he told her in such a mellow tone she felt her blood flow quicken. "I heard."

"From whom?"

"A friend of mine."

She arched a brow in question.

"Ben Woodward," he supplied and drew her nearer by her hands.

"The American."

"Mmmm." He was taking each of her fingers individually and gently pulling each one out, then slowly releasing it back. She breathed deeply, easily. "I saw him at my club this morning. He is enchanted by the lovely countess of Rossborough who to his delight is also a sculptor."

"He told me as we danced . . ." She inhaled, shut her

eyes, and let her head loll back to the cushions. ". . . that he is a collector."

"Of art—" Blake unbuttoned the cuff of her suit sleeve to send his fingertips up to her wrist and stroke her there. "—and women."

She tried not to purr at his touch. "I thought him great company."

"Did you?" Blake said with pique. And from his sharp tone, could she also say he was jealous?

Her lashes drifted open. His face hovered above hers, his emerald eyes grim in the confines of the cab. "But not as much as you."

"Is that so?" his skepticism blossomed into a broad smile. "What evidence can you give me?"

"Oh . . ." She tilted her head. "If he had fascinated me in body or personality, I would have sculpted him."

Blake's fingers had reached the delicate skin at the inside of her elbow and the press of his flesh there sent a frisson up her arm and down her spine. The coach turned a corner and she slid against Blake and felt his body heat. "But instead you were moved to create my likeness?"

"Yes."

"Again?"

"This morning." She should move away, but couldn't.

"Am I now in clay?"

"Butter."

"Butter?"

"At breakfast, you wound up in the butter."

"I assume I am complimented."

"Do be, by all means." She wanted to give him some compensation for his kindnesses to her, even if it was an admission by her that he appealed to her.

"How do I look in yellow?"

Or nothing? She bit back a grin. "I like you better in ivory." She indicated the color of his stock.

"Thank you." He was suppressing laughter. "Dare I ask what became of me?"

"You were slathered on my toast."

"A noble occupation, to give you sustenance."

His joke was more fact than he meant it to be. "I thank you for that," she confessed. "Last night, yesterday, the day before."

"Still you do not carry clay."

"Do *you?*"

He raised one arm. "Search."

Her fingers flexed. She wanted to run her hands over him everywhere. How could she contain herself?

"Risa, waste any more time, sweetheart, and I will rush you into other things you may not want."

One look at his mischievous eyes and she knew he meant he'd kiss her. Hope made her smile. "What if I say I am tempted to wait?"

"How long?" His gaze devoured her mouth.

His husky voice ate up her patience. "No longer." She placed her hands over his heart, spread wide to feel each muscle of his chest. The power of him took her breath. Her touch seized his own. He trembled and her hands wended up over his shoulders to his nape, and she rose to put her lips on his.

Smooth as polished marble, but warm and giving, his mouth savored hers. His arms wrapped around her, pressed her so close, she yearned to touch his skin, there where his torso melted against hers. And all the while, he taught her fascinating ways two lovers' mouths might mingle and taste. Too soon he drew away. His fingers traced the outline of her mouth. "Like this, your lips ripe from kissing, you are a vision for a sculptor."

"Breathless," she admitted.

"Enchanting."

Enchanted. She let her passion live in her eyes. "And I still have no idea if you have my clay."

"Tormenter," he scolded, raised his arms and said, "Find it quickly, will you?"

She chuckled, and was glad she did when the feel of his fevered body urged her to bring him near and sample his kisses one more time. Her hands delved into his vest pockets, then his coat pockets.

"Ah-hah! It's in here. Rather flat and warm," she held it up.

He grimaced. "A pancake."

"Not for long," she said as she crushed it and worked furiously at it. "What do you think?"

"A walking stick?"

She pretended innocence. "You inspire me."

"I am not that thin."

She rolled her eyes in mirth. He was a stallion of a man. "Thank goodness. You would have been more pleased with my morning's effort in the butter," she said as she let the clay warm in her palms.

"I hate to ask. What did you make of me?"

She gazed at him. How very central that question was. What was her perception of this man at whose house Maddie had died so mysteriously, so inexplicably? She had spent the past eight months blaming him for negligence in her sister's death—and perhaps, giving Maddie motivation to let the sea drown her. Yet, within minutes of meeting him, Risa knew him to be comforting, consoling, instructive. Now she knew him to be irresistible.

"You are scowling. Is this a sign that you portrayed me as a fiend?"

"How uncharacteristic that would have been," she teased him to hide her baser thoughts from him and herself. "I am a better artist than to make you what you are not."

"What did you sculpt then?" He touched the tip of her nose. "No gladiator?"

"Alas," she sighed theatrically. "I had only enough for a medallion. I did your profile."

"I think you need another chance," he said as if he knew this was the very gift she should not presume to ask of him. "The full model."

Your entire body. "A bigger and better medium," she concluded with a daring that stimulated her to greater audacity.

"Plaster?"

"Bronze would be better." *Do justice to your skin tone, the hollows beneath your cheeks. The half-lidded passion of your eyes. And if I could have you to myself to pose in your naked glory, I would discover that . . .* "Marble would be best."

"I have an eight-foot block of Carrara marble which awaits an expert's touch." As if he meant to learn her own features to carve someday, he led her back into his arms. "You would inspire a man to try to do you justice . . . in stone or bronze or . . ."

Bed? He did not need to finish, his implication was so clear. So complimentary. So brazen that she blushed, but his index finger outlined the shell of her ear and the length of her throat down to the linen embroidery of her collar, and she could not withdraw from the mesmerizing power of his caress. "Has anyone?"

She swallowed, as the backs of his fingers skimmed up her neck and dove into her hair. "No."

"Someone must have tried." He circled his other arm around her waist. The coachman conspired to urge her nearer by rounding another corner.

With Blake's mouth a fond temptation, she could only speak the truth. "My teacher, yes."

"How did you refuse him?"

I escaped his greedy hands, gathered up the remnants of the blouse he had ripped in his attempt to put me in his bed.

"I told him that I chose to keep my clothes on until I felt comfortable to take them off."

"Wise woman."

She shook her head, rueful. "I am a product of my teachings."

"Remain modest until you are married."

Or desired for my soul, not just my body. "And even afterward." *When desire departs along with any love, and boredom replaces whimsy.*

"Afterward? Your husband will have no need for your modesty when you are in his arms. He'll want your trust. As you will have his."

"I think it must make for a good union." She felt swept along by the current of his gentleness and shivered.

He must have taken it as a sign she was cold, because he hugged her. "So I hear." He caressed her ribs, his hand beneath her breast. "I want you to trust me so badly, I ache with it."

Her blood heated. Truth would not be denied. "I am glad to hear it."

His eyes locked on hers as his hand weighed her breast and his thumb stroked higher and higher until it rubbed her nipple so tenderly, she gasped. As if he were a magnet, she arched into him, her body tingling with a strange need to have him kiss her there. "You want me," he groaned and hid his face in the wealth of her hair. Her breasts swelled and a fist of need clenched in her belly. And then he ripped himself away from her.

He sat up and helped her to do the same. He settled into the brightest light in the cab.

His eyes were bright as moonbeams. His lips were moist with kisses. But his words were thick. "I am going to tell you about my relationship with Maddie."

He put her hand to his chest. His heart beat a wild

tattoo. "I want you to look at me while I tell you this and ask yourself if I could be lying to you."

Logic came to her. "I do not think well when I am near you." She dropped her hand into her lap.

"Reason deserts us both then. Good cause to tell you this quickly so that you are back in my arms where I want you. More than your lips. And for much longer than a few kisses." He drifted farther away. "So hear me out. Because for none of my statements do I have any proof."

5

My picture was my stage and men and women my actors who were by means and certain actions and expressions to exhibit a dumb show.

William Hogarth

"Let me raise the shades," Blake offered.

"I'll sit closer. If I may."

"Please." She inched nearer and he schooled himself to refrain from touching her. "If after I finish, you still question my honesty—" He admired the red cloud of her hair and the delicacy of her face. "—there will be no reason for us to see each other again." At that possibility, regret trickled through his veins.

He drowned a fear he might not ever kiss her again after this discussion. "I met Maddie for the first time two years ago here in London." He'd begin with facts. His suspicions he'd save for later.

"After I left home for Italy soon after Father died," Risa told him, "Maddie wrote to me that she had come to London to settle a few business matters. She said she had seen only a few people. She was in mourning and did not attend any social activities. So then, how did you meet?"

"I sent a note over to Park Lane with one of my footmen."

"You requested the interview?"

He nodded. "Your sister agreed to receive me. I expressed my condolences on the death of your father and explained that I met him many years previously. I recounted to your sister a conversation I had with your father in which I told him that if he were ever willing to sell Allure, I would like to bid on her."

"But the de Ros-Lindsays do not sell any items from their collection."

"So your father told me. A tradition, is it?"

"At first it was, yes. Because we are a family whose inheritance is passed through heirs general, any first-born may inherit, male or female. In Queen Elizabeth's reign, the then countess of Rossborough asked for a royal writ that all goods within the bounds of de Ros residential properties be passed with the deeds to the next heir. No object owned by a de Ros house may be sold. Ever."

"Unusual stipulation," Blake commented, squeezing her fingers. At this physical level, she was willing to trust him. Would that he could keep it that way and build on it.

"What has this meeting with my father and you to do with Maddie?"

"I had heard that she wished to sell Allure."

Risa sat straighter. "Who told you?"

"My curator also happens to be your family's. I also understood that after your father died, your estate was in debt."

"So many people knew about our financial straits. But Maddie never told me." She straightened, more valiant. "How did you learn about my family's debts?"

"My banker told me."

She went rigid. "You have very informed associates."

"I did not ask for this information. Both bits of news came to me quite as a matter of course."

She wrestled with her belief in him. "Go on."

"I was surprised, having been told by your father in no uncertain terms that a sale was never possible. I went to ask her if the rumor about her wish to sell Allure was true. And if it were, I said I wanted to buy it."

"What did she say?"

"She had thought about selling it, but had decided against it. I let the matter drop and I left. I did not see Maddie again until last spring when she returned to your Park Lane house with your aunt to debut. I did not attend Victoria's Drawing Room last year. But I did go to the Dungarvons' opening ball in honor of Maddie. She was well received." *At one minute, demure, the next flirting with many men. Flamboyant, then petulant.* How could he tell Risa this without defaming the memory of her sister? "You and she do not act or look alike in any way."

Risa stroked his fingers absentmindedly. "Maddie resembled our mother. I resemble my mother's mother. A Scotswoman."

"Hence the fiery hair and the independence."

"That last I am still perfecting." She gazed at him. "With help from some interesting people."

"I hope you will call on me for more encouragement."

She pursed her mouth. "The probability increases."

"Wonderful." *Let me encourage you more. Take you down now to the spare comfort of this coach and encourage you to kiss me all afternoon.* He swallowed, feeling his temperature rise along with a feral desire. To hell with a gladiator. He felt like nothing so tame. Barbarian had been right, bent on running off with her.

But Risa's next words threw cold water on his primitive ambitions. "What about Maddie? Tell me how she acted."

He would not lie. "Damned odd."

"How?"

"As the Season wore on, I saw her more and I wondered if she were under some sort of strain." Glad to reveal this, he prayed to find the right words.

"Why?"

"She would be laughing one minute, then glance around a ballroom, and become morose, snappish."

"Ariel says that, too."

"Ariel . . ." The name was familiar. "Your younger sister."

"Who is smitten with you." Risa coiled a tendril of her hair back over her ear and he longed to do it for her.

"I have not met her, though."

"She would sneak a peek at you from the top of the stairs when you came to call on Maddie."

He smiled. "Resourceful of her."

"She likens you to a gothic hero." Risa toyed with a grin.

"Dark and menacing. My looks, but not what I am." *Though many have seen me that way. Especially my brother John.* Blake lowered his voice. "Not to you."

"I do not yet know what you are to me," Risa admitted with difficulty.

"We will continue as we are and discover that together," he promised, knowing he trod new ground in his friendship with this woman whose unique profession drew him as much as her dedication to her sister.

She traced his thumbnail with a fingertip. "What did Maddie think of you?"

"You mean, did she think of me romantically? Yes, early last April, she told me so, and I thoroughly discouraged her." Risa turned her face up to his. "I was never interested in Maddie. There was little in her personality I found to—" He focused on Risa's sparkling opal eyes. "—stimulate me. After I told her that in so many polite words, she looked elsewhere. The truth is that Maddie tried to charm a number of men. I was among them. She wanted to marry."

"I know she did. She wrote me often about wanting that," Risa nodded, and he now counted two facts on which Risa agreed with him. "Maddie was lonely. Ariel is good company, but after I left for Florence, Maddie had no one her own age. She pined for someone to share her life with." Risa paused, examining him. "She needed love."

"She did not find it with me." *Though she did with someone.*

The carriage slowed, but Blake did not take his eyes from Risa as he thought how he would reveal what he knew about this phantom lover whose face and name he did not know. Whose form he had glimpsed once.

"I believe you on that score. What I meant to ask was were you a threat to her?"

"No." *Only in one respect, with my brother John. Get to that quickly, man.*

"You look away," she said. "Why?"

"Permit me to go on in an orderly fashion. I promised I would tell you all. I will."

"Very well," she said, but remained on alert.

"When I saw Maddie last spring, we did not speak of Allure. Yet, by June, I once more heard from my curator that she wished to sell it. By then, my brother John had come down from Cambridge to stay with me in London for the Season. He studies as a biologist. Twenty-three and studious. Wishes to become an authority and teach. He came with me to a few social events. He is a congenial fellow, is a baron in his own right, has a monthly income from our holdings, a home, a parcel of land in Devonshire. Anyway, he went out with me, and met your sister at a dinner party. They got on well and he wished to call on her. I told him I had reason to—the possible sale of Allure—and so I sent round a note and we went."

The carriage lurched, then idled at full stop.

"Would you care to get out? Walk about?" he asked.

"Oh, no—"

"It's quite safe, I guarantee you. It is secluded here. Only four servants up at the house." He squeezed her hand again. "I need to stretch my legs." *Walk off the desire the confines this cab encourages.* He tugged at her hand. "Come along. Do you good."

He stepped out and helped her down to the drive.

"My heavens." She noted the brick Georgian manse in the distance, but soon devoted her appreciation to his mother's garden. "This is worthy of a painter."

"Yes." What he saw worth a portrait was Risa's hair ablaze in the midday sun. "An oil. In strong reds."

She colored, understanding his inference.

He took her arm, forcing himself to speak of his mother's roses and lilies. He led Risa along one manicured garden path into a maze of tall and sculpted boxwoods. "No one—not even my servants—may see us from the house here. Let's sit down on this bench. The sun is warm." *Making your cheeks pink. And your pale eyes glitter like noonday stars.* "Want to remove your jacket?"

She did so, and he found more delights for his soul—and temptations for his body. Her canezou beneath the jacket was a sheer ivory linen affair, nipped into the waist of her skirt. It conjured an image of the hourglass her figure had to be beneath the fine fabric.

He looked away, trying to focus on the terrain he could view. "This was the Hargroves' first home. Compared to the de Ros', we are upstarts named by Charles the Second to our earldom."

"For loyalty?"

"For honesty."

She admired him. "An inherited trait?"

"I work to have you think so."

She did not hide her smile. "I wish I could see the house," she said wistfully. "I have heard of your collection of Bernini there."

"Second only to that in Sandown. I think you should see both. To further your education as an artist. Two weekend parties. What do you say? Does your debutante's schedule permit a few days in the country?"

"Invite me and my aunt. I will make the time."

He grasped her fingers. He wished to hold all of her in his arms, especially because she would come visit him despite the talk that would ensue. So many rumors speculated that he had loved Maddie Lindsay. Though all of them were wrong, the stigma clung to him. That Risa would come to his homes, signified not only her courage and her curiosity, but also her interest in him. "I cannot wait."

She cupped his cheek. Drifted forward. Licked her lips and retreated. Then she stood and walked around him toward the rose arbor. "You are a sore temptation."

"My thoughts exactly."

She fingered the petals of a rose. "Tell me the rest. Quickly." She spun and faced him. "I need to be able to decide if I should leave you or get lost in one more kiss."

He admired her boldness and her honesty. "The rest is not pretty." *Not conducive to kisses or embraces. Only sadness and frustration.*

He unbuttoned his coat, removed it and his stock. The day was getting hotter, his subject no easier. He draped his clothes across the stone bench and went to pluck a pink rose from a bush. Removing its thorns, he wished he could do the same from the truth he was about to reveal.

"John fell in love with Maddie and wanted to call on her often. We did." He tucked the flower into her collar, and next to Risa's skin, the bloom was no match.

"It is unusual for two men, even brothers, to call together. Why did you?"

"Your aunt expressed her displeasure with John's suit. He asked if I would go with him and I said I would. John thought that your aunt would not dare to turn me away because of my position in society. And because your cousin's husband Robert Dungarvon relies on my knowledge and contacts to continue his agenting of art works."

"I had no idea Robert did that."

"Mmmm, yes. Supplements his monthly allowance from his father. Keeps Robert in buttons and bows for his wife."

"Georgie does spend lavishly."

"They both thrive in the social whirl. That requires more money than Robert earns in his trust, I am certain. I know from experience what it costs to keep one house, staff, and equipage. Meanwhile, income from farming declines as wheat from America is imported and drives down our prices."

"I have the same problem in Northumbria. My tenants' produce earns less money each year and the result is they cannot pay their rents. It is one of the reasons my estate is in debt. The reason I had to take a loan." She looked at him sharply. "Did your banker tell you I took a loan?"

"Yes."

"Do you know for how much?"

"No." He sighed, dismayed at other details he knew and had no right to know. "Risa, Maddie told me she needed money. That was why she wanted to sell Allure."

Risa's regret mixed with confusion. "Maddie needed extra money probably to send me to study in Florence." She walked away to the end of the boxwood semicircle. "Perhaps, she considered selling Allure to pay my tuition and allowance."

"That is a noble cause," he strode forward and took her hands in his.

"Yes, but the way she went about it was not."

"Her means do not justify her ends?"

"Maddie did a lot of things that surprise me, mystify me." Risa shook her head, not confiding what those were. "I am working in a void. Trying to answer a host of questions. Finding only more pieces to a puzzle, none of which connect."

He had no right to ask her to discuss them. "Let me help by telling you what I can." He took a deep breath. "My brother John fell head over heels in love with Maddie. He proposed to her in London and she told him she wished to think on it. . . . What's the matter? You're frowning."

"My aunt never told me John proposed. I wonder why." She pondered that a minute. "Well, then, what happened?"

"When Maddie arrived at Sandown for the weekend party, she accepted John. He was ecstatic and we were to announce their engagement when . . . something disastrous occurred." He jammed his hands in his trouser pockets and considered the sky, then Risa's patient expression. "I wish I could describe this next more delicately."

"Be blunt then."

"I had twenty-two people as houseguests that weekend. One of them I saw leaving the gazebo—and your sister—in the middle of the night. A man. It was not my brother."

Risa recoiled. "You are certain?"

"Maddie was unmistakable. Her height. Her voice."

"Maddie was raised to observe proprieties and . . . and . . . the man. Who was he?"

"I never learned."

"It could have been your brother."

"No. John has a limp. A childhood injury from a riding accident. The man who left the gazebo walked with an easy gait. Risa." Blake would now make matters worse. "I am about to tarnish my own character further by showing you how ruthless I can be for those I love. I told John what I saw."

He flinched at the recrimination in her eyes. Then she recanted. "I'm sorry," she whispered. "Were that sort of act to threaten Maddie's happiness, I would tell her."

Risa's compassion was cold comfort compared to the memory of John's violent reaction. "John refused to believe me. Said I must have been sleepwalking or drunk. I assure you I have never done either. Nor did I mistake Maddie for another woman. John heard me out, then told me to go to hell and take my suspicions with me. But I refused my support of their marriage. John went wild."

Blake hated to tell her this next, too, but he had to, didn't he? "You see, while John has his own title, and his own home, the majority of his income derives from the family trust. And I control that."

Risa drew near. "So that if he married Maddie . . . ?"

"I would withdraw his monthly income."

She clearly fought a battle between praising him and damning him. Finally she chose a middling ground. "Maddie had an income from her estate. Even if she did have debts, she could support a husband."

"John did not want to live off her income."

"Honorable of him. Many men do."

"Yes. Don't they?" Blake reflected on John's own high self-esteem. "I am proud to say that my younger brother has standards for himself. This is one of them."

"And when did this discussion occur between you two?"

"The day before Maddie died. John left Sandown soon afterward. He knows I do not ever lie. But still, he cared for Maddie. When he learned later how she died, he wrote me a scathing letter. To this day, he blames me for her death. John thought . . ." Blake gathered his nerve. "John thought Maddie had let the storm take her boat."

"Why?" Risa's disbelief changed to anger. "Why would he think that? Maddie would not kill herself over a man."

Are you convincing me or yourself? "Some do," he said with sorrow that made his guts clench. "My sister lost her husband's affections and she took an overdose of laudanum."

"Oh, Blake, I am so sorry." Sympathy washed over Risa's features. "To do away with oneself requires a . . . a certain courage, I think. I doubt Maddie had it."

He raised a hand, frustrated. "I wish I had another rationale. I don't."

"Forgive me," Risa murmured. "I must sit down." When she got to the bench, she stared at nothing. "I wish there were no more to learn about Maddie. I am in such a muddle."

He sat down next to her. "Risa." He put his arms around her, wanting to shield her from her torment that Maddie may have committed suicide. Such a fact was difficult to accept, he knew firsthand.

She curled against him, despair and the need for comfort overtaking all else. "Maddie could not have committed suicide. You'd have to prove it to me."

He gathered her closer, stroked her back. "If you say she couldn't hurt herself, then she couldn't."

Risa drew away. "You believe me?"

"You believe me. You didn't want to, but you do." He rubbed away concern from her brow and kissed her there. "You can find the truth. You are, more than all else, persistent."

"No help there. Frankly, I am stymied."

"What do you need? Who do you need to see? Tell me and I will take you there, bring them to you, whatever you want." He smiled, but there was so little to be gay about. Only that Risa trusted him enough to say she needed help. Would she consider getting it from him?

She reflected a moment. "If I tell you everything, I may hold no advantages."

Meaning you still question my honesty. "True. So tell me what you need."

"Not why."

"If that pleases you, yes."

"You will go to such lengths . . . for me?"

"Yes." He memorized her mouth. "I want to be the one who is close at hand when you investigate Maddie's last days or . . . sculpt or . . . kiss."

"And if I promise you'll be the only one I choose to sculpt or kiss, will that endear you to me when I ask you more questions you may not want to answer?"

"I don't think there are any of those, Risa."

"Good then. Let's go back to London. My aunt should be home from Georgie's by now, and I don't want her asking questions about where I've been."

"Why not?"

"Because going out alone with a man is scandalous. Merits a girl a bad reputation."

"There is more to it than that—and you're not saying. Tell me why you don't want your Aunt Elizabeth to know you've come to me." He knew Lady Elgin held a grudge against him. He could easily put it down to a matronly proclivity to dismiss him as a rogue.

"She does not like you."

"Evident from the first time she laid eyes on me years ago when I tried to buy Allure from your father. She takes a very strong dislike to me, I think, because she has heard I have had a checkered past. With women."

"Aunt Elizabeth disliked my father's philandering, almost as much as my mother did. My aunt's own husband had a scalding reputation in that regard, too. So it is natural that she applauds men who are faithful."

"Then there is hope I may be favored by her approval."

"How so?" Risa asked, searching his face.

"I have taken no woman into my protection—" At this polite phrase for supporting a mistress, Risa's eyes rounded. "—for over a year." *I was bored silly.*

"That is comforting."

The urge to kiss her slammed through him. "Is there some other reason to be wary of your aunt?" he asked, suspicion nagging at him at Risa's reticence to speak.

"She must have known that John asked for Maddie's hand. She brags about Maddie trusting her and yet . . . and yet she never told me about John. I wonder why."

Interesting that her aunt hadn't. Gratifying that Risa could confide this to him. "The omission worries you."

"Lately everything worries me." Risa waved a hand to dismiss that, but explained it partially when she said, "Oh, Aunt Elizabeth has a tendency to keep things to herself. She learned it, as we all did, from dealing with my father. He was, to put it politely, a tyrant. Yet, he was older than her only by five minutes."

"They are twins then," Blake concluded, as he saw

Elizabeth Elgin take on for him a new facet to her reserved character. She was a woman who might have become the premier noblewoman in all of England, save
for her brother's birth minutes before hers.

Blake wondered what a pre-emption of that magni-
tude did to a person. John had resented Blake's power
and influence. John was a boy, too, younger by a few
years, not minutes. John had learned to discard the resentment and devote himself to flowers and butterflies.

What had it done to Elizabeth? Did it make her en-
vious? Grasping? Something had made her controlling.
Inhibiting her niece even after she became the countess
of Rossborough in her own right. Maddie had told him
in bitter tones about her Aunt Elizabeth's iron-handed
nature. And did the woman do the same to Risa?

He looked her over. He doubted anyone could totally control her. Nor should they.

"My aunt has been good to us three girls. She was
widowed just before our mother died, and she raised
us, along with Georgie."

He took her hands in his. "You owe her a lot."

"Yes."

"But for some reason, you don't want to tell her
what you learn about Maddie's death. Am I correct?"

"You are."

"Well, then, I would urge you not to." He was silent
a minute. "What else may I tell you about Maddie's
death?"

"Did you argue with her before she sailed away?"

"Yes. When John told me they would marry even
though I had forbid it, I tried to see her all day. I could
not find her. When I saw her near the boathouse, I
caught up with her, told her I would not approve and
would not give him his trust money. She told me—and
these were her words—to go to hell. 'I don't need your
money or want it. I have my own. I am tired of all of

you trying to control me. Get out of my way,' she said and pushed past me. She shoved the sailboat into the water, got in and then . . . I never saw her again. Not until the constable called us to the shore the next morning and her body was there upon the sand."

"Was the boat safe?"

This change of topic wrenched him from grief. "I bought it new last season. It was in perfect condition."

"Could there have been a hole in the hull?"

"There could have been. I did not re-examine it just before she cast off, I am sorry to admit. I have never had any problems with my sailboats. One does not think of such things until a tragedy occurs."

Risa closed her eyes. "How true. What about the sale of Allure? Did Maddie say she would sell it to you?"

"No."

"You have never given her any money?"

"No, why would I?" He was perplexed at Risa's line of questioning.

"Not any cash as a down payment or . . . or a good-faith deposit on its purchase?"

"Never. I do not buy with cash or put deposits on my purchases. I write checks. Why do you need to know this, Risa?"

She licked her lower lip, agitated.

"Very well, don't tell me. What I will tell you is that Maddie denied me the purchase of Allure as retribution for my failure to bless her marriage to John. In fact, she yelled at me that she would chop Allure up for building stone before she'd ever sell it to the likes of me."

"The depth," Risa murmured, "of her hatred for you astonishes me. She was hardly ever enraged . . ."

"She was crying," he said with a lump in his throat, "when she cast off." He gazed into Risa's eyes. "I hated myself then. I hated myself more when I saw her body the next morning." The feeling resurrected another helpless memory of his sister's body the morning after she died.

Risa rose, her spine stiff as metal, her tone soft as down. "Tell me. When you saw Maddie cast off, in those last minutes, did you think she might kill herself?"

"I was so angry that I didn't think of anything," he admitted. "Later, I had another idea." This was the reason that led him to search out other clues about Maddie for the past six months in Paris.

"And that was what?"

"Maddie had another relationship that bothered me."

"With whom?" Risa whispered, aghast at the possibility and then at what she saw on his face. "No! Another man?"

"Yes. Though I doubt it was the same type of relationship."

"For pity's sake, tell me who."

"Maurice Bartholome."

"Bartholome. B. B. . . . No, he could not have been Maddie's lover."

"I agree. But I did see her arrive and leave his shop often last spring." *Then this year, I meet you there accidentally. Why?*

"What do you think she was doing?"

"Looking. Buying. Selling. . . ." He let the last word drift and the power of it forced Risa down to the bench again.

"My God," she shook her head.

"I realize you may not want to tell me why you went to see him, so let me help you think this out instead," Blake tried to sound soothing, though he wished he could embrace her—and did not think it wise. He feared she would fly from him in torment at what he was about to tell her anyway. Best to let her run if she wished. *Then pray, Hargrove, she'll come back to you. Wanting help and succor. And your jaded hide for companionship.*

"Risa." He lifted her chin. "Darling, don't look at me like your heart is breaking. You're breaking mine." *And I have not the right yet to promise to make everything all better for you. But I want to, more than anything I ever desired.* "Do you keep a list of all items in the de Ros art collection?"

"Yes. The master log is at home in Park Lane in the wall safe in Maddie's . . . in my office."

"I would recommend that you pull it out, examine it, and compare it to the items in the house. You have others on display up north in Rossborough Manor, do you not?"

"Not many. The Park Lane house is the showcase. But the family rule is that every work is listed in the log."

"Check the list."

She agreed, then her voice was choked. "Do you think Maddie sold something?"

Do you? What do you know? Suspect? Why did you go see one of the most disreputable art dealers in the city of London? He longed to ask Risa, but knew better now than to push her to reveal things. He'd bide his time. "That was my first reaction a year ago."

"I went to Bartholome," she said as she gauged his every move, "for another reason."

Blake waited.

"Have you ever heard of the painter Edward Ritter?"

The change of topic gave him pause. "Ritter. He . . . was an apprentice to Holbein. And he died young."

"Maddie went to see Bartholome about one of his paintings."

"Holbein's?"

"Ritter's. Maddie bought an oil by him. The problem is that I have not seen it in our house here or in Northumbria and I must go look for it. Search the de Ros log for it. Maddie paid Bartholome too much for it. Anyway—" She rubbed her temple again. "—Bartholome says she bought it as a present for me and I don't believe him."

Why not?

"Maddie did not care about art."

"Darling, she cared enough about it to visit Bartholome every Monday morning in May and June last year. I discovered her routine by accident one day when I went to see a friend of mine in the same street. The next Monday, I returned and there she was again. Veiled, but recognizable to me, emerging from a hired hack. I was intrigued. I feared she meant to sell something."

"Allure," Risa declared without hesitation.

"Yes. And I wanted her. Badly." *More than I ever wanted a real live woman. Until I discovered you.*

"Now I must find this painting by Ritter."

"Risa, I doubt you are going to find it."

Horror sprang to her eyes. "Why not?" She was nigh unto pleading, probably predicting that what he would say next would cancel out so many alternatives.

"Ask other experts about this. Verify what I say. Only four paintings by Ritter survive. All of them are owned by collectors of Tudor art."

"Perhaps this was another."

"And if it were, why have I not heard of it? I am one of the best art dealers in England, darling."

"A fluke that you haven't heard of it, perhaps."

"Possible, if it were not for other factors."

"Which are?"

"Ritter was lazy. He arrived to the studio late, drunk and surly. Holbein dismissed him. Ritter did not paint again. Sweetheart—" Blake wished he could soften this blow. "—He blinded himself in outrage and he died from hemorrhage soon afterward."

"I will check our log. The house. I'll cable my housekeeper at the Manor to look for this painting. And if I don't find it, I'll go back to Bartholome and ask him to show me proof Maddie bought this."

"If you return, I want to go with you. Bartholome is shrewd. He knows his business. He studied at the Beaux-arts in Paris, but failed as a painter. He became a dealer and an agent. He has worked for some artists who are wonderful, others who are second rate. Acquired art for patrons who are ruthless."

"I can go alone."

He clutched her arms. "He can be dangerous. Oh, you try my patience," he bemoaned when she raised her chin in defiance. "I will follow you. Wait outside."

"That is not necessary."

"I say it is."

Her pale eyes mellowed. "Thank you."

"You are very welcome." He wished she were more grateful and he more aggressive. He wanted to hold her at the very least, carry her off to protect her at the best. "It's getting late." He indicated his carriage.

"You'll come tomorrow? To meet me at the zoo and tell me what you've learned?"

"At the panther's cage. At one." He touched her nose. "Promise me, that if you need help, you will call on me."

"Yes," she accepted readily. "I promise."

Only after he had let Risa leave the coach an hour later, did he permit himself to brood over his failure to tell her the other secret he knew about Maddie. The one that plagued him. The one that would take more time and effort to explain.

Maddie had a relationship not only with Bartholome, but also with a less than illustrious painter who lived in Paris. And in six months of trying to befriend the man, Blake had learned nothing useful about how and why he knew Madelaine Lindsay.

6

Come, and in the fourth portrait I promise I will try to make you even more beautiful.

Pierre-Auguste Renoir to a female patron

"*I*t's not here." Risa ran her index finger down the ledger entries again. "It's just not here." She slapped the binder shut and fell back in her chair. "Why not, Maddie?"

Risa rubbed her eyes with the heels of her hands. Why would Maddie buy a painting by a secondary artist, pay a large sum for it, intend to give it to her, never do it, and on top of that, not enter her purchase in the family ledger?

This book was next to the family Bible in importance to the de Ros prestige. Begun by her great-grandfather in 1754, these well-worn pages numbered the works in chronological order of purchase. The entries listed the art work bought, its price, seller, history of previous owners and a brief description of the work. For a de Ros countess or earl to fail to enter an acquisition was the equivalent of failing to enter the birth, date, and time of a new heir to the eminent de Ros name.

Patience, she warned herself. *You're getting upset over a small matter.* Maddie was not often efficient or organized. Perhaps she bought the painting and forgot to make the entry.

Perhaps, she didn't want to, whispered logic. If—*if*—Maddie knew the painting did not meet the de Ros collection standards of excellence, she might not enter it at all. She would be ashamed.

Which brings me back to question why you bought it at all, Maddie.

Risa pushed back her chair and grasped the ledger to return it to the wall safe behind the desk. She hefted the bulky book and swung open the metal door to the vault. She shoved it inside—and something scraped across the bottom. The sound of metal rubbing metal made Risa pause, extract the ledger—and as she did, a key fell to the floor.

Risa picked it up, turned it over and over. She'd never seen it before. And to her knowledge, nothing else was ever kept in this vault but the precious de Ros ledger.

But this key was small, brass. She squinted at the engraving. Shoved her glasses on, but shut her eyes. Could she hope it was the key to the safety deposit box that Mr. McCordle had discovered was assigned to a M. Rossborough? Could this be the key she had searched for among Maddie's possessions in Northumbria and here in London? Risa brought it closer and read the engraving, *124.*

A key from the Chelsea Masonry Bank? *Please, let it be.* Chelsea.

Chelsea, where Bartholome had his shop. She hadn't thought of that connection before. Would Maddie go to see Bartholome, then use the occasion to go to a bank? Why?

No, Risa. You are getting ahead of yourself. Speculating.

*When you must stick to what you do know. What evidence
you do have.*

Could this key open M. Rossborough's safety deposit
box?

She would go tomorrow to the bank. Ask if they had
a box number 124. See if the key fit. After she met
Blake.

Risa dropped it in her robe pocket, shut the box, put
it on top of the ledger, swung closed the vault door and
locked it. As the de Ros heiress, Risa now possessed the
only key to this safe. Lose it and a de Ros would lose
access to the best proof of their hegemony in the art
world in Britain and on the Continent. The key to the
vault, along with the key to the attic storage room upstairs and another to the one in Rossborough Manor,
jangled against the others in the pocket of her dressing
gown as she closed her office door and floated past Allure.

The woman's half-lidded gaze stopped Risa in her
tracks. Never had Risa felt anything for this statue except an appreciation for it's creator's skill. But at this
late hour, and amid her anxiety over finding the key,
Risa touched the cool surface of her sultry eyes, her
open mouth, her breath—a hot surge against Risa's fingertips so real that she sprung back.

Risa stared at the lady. She lived passion.

Risa had felt it herself. In Blake's presence.

This lady pulsed with desire.

Risa had felt the same body heat. Often, just to think
of Blake. This lady understood whole-hearted lust and
fool-hearty commitment. And Risa wished she were
free of her distrust of Blake so that she might revel in a
devotion as deep and wild as Allure's.

Tomorrow, her senses whispered, *you may try again.*

Tomorrow, she promised herself, *you can test him once
more.*

Content to wait, Risa set back to her purpose, lifted her hems as she climbed the stairs, soundless in her slippers. She'd vowed to herself this afternoon in Blake Hargrove's garden that she would look for this Ritter painting. And she would.

She did not try this time to chill the warmth that swept her blood at the thought of meeting him again. In less than twelve hours, she would once more become tormented by his memories of Maddie . . . and tantalized by his humor, his affection for her—and his kisses.

Think of him later.

Best to think of him not at all, but she had lost that battle, hadn't she?

She raced up the steps, breaking her stride briefly to glance down the shadowed hall toward Ariel's and her aunt's bedroom doors. Satisfied both slept, Risa headed for the third floor where the servants' sleeping quarters were silent as death. Risa picked up her pace, rounding the narrower set of steps up to the fourth floor and the attic store room.

As she opened the door, Risa winced at the bong of the foyer clock. It chimed one in the morning. The storeroom was warmed well by the flow of heat upward in the old four story Palladian townhouse. It was also equipped by gas lamps at the insistence of her grandfather, who had often sat here for hours stroking his treasures, and had installed superb lighting by which to do it. She would have been better off looking for Ritter's oil in the daylight, Risa knew. But she did not wish to discuss her actions and her findings with her aunt. She kept her own counsel, saved her energy, and any further recriminations of her aunt for Blake's negligence concerning Maddie's death.

"And I'm going mad in the process, too," she muttered to herself as she gently closed the door and turned up the jet of one wall sconce.

The room, lined in heavy oak to keep moisture in lest the canvases crack from lack of it, equaled the circumference of the entire house, but sported shelves of varying sizes, reducing it to approximately the size of the morning room. One wall held paintings, stacked in racks according to size, face-to-back, framed, and tagged with chronologically arranged numbers which matched those in the ledger for ease in identification. Another wall held sculptures of plaster, wood, bronze, and marble. A third wall contained a mixture of works, paintings and sculpture, and these were the ones her de Ros predecessors hid up here to conceal the evidence that occasionally a de Ros lacked fine taste when spending the family wealth.

She scanned the room and found the ladder. She scooted it over to the third wall and climbed it, teetering on the top rung as she pushed aside each painting so that she might look at it.

The light was more than sufficient. Her patience was less. She went through the top shelf quickly. She did the same for the second. The third.

No. She sighed in renewed frustration, no oil of any of these resembled the Ritter which Bartholome had described.

Maddie, Maddie. Where do I look? What do I do?

Ask Aunt Elizabeth. That would be easy, quick. But prudent? If Risa asked such a question, she would have to tell her aunt why she looked for this painting, how she had found out about Maddie's purchase, Bartholome, and his name in the diary. Risa brightened, realizing she would not have to disclose to her aunt that one reason she searched for this painting was that Blake Hargrove told her he did not think Ritter could have painted it.

She need only tell her aunt that Bartholome said Maddie had bought it. Therefore, did her aunt know about the purchase and if so, did she have any idea why it was not listed in the ledger?

Tomorrow she would ask her aunt at breakfast.

And then, too, Risa could and should confirm the painting was not up at the Manor, either.

I'll send a cable to the housekeeper there. Ask her the question I know the answer to. No such painting by a man named Ritter is in the Manor storeroom—and by her own recollection, not on any wall.

So then. What do I do now?

Go back to Bartholome. Ask him more questions.

Risa drove her hands into her hair, lifting the heavy mass and massaging her scalp.

What other answer could there be to where the painting could be?

A servant stole it. Pinched it for extra money. Opportunity existed. Maddie had inhabited this house only for a few months off and on since she'd become countess. She had come here briefly in the spring of 1879 and to Risa's knowledge had not returned to take up residence until last spring when her sister prepared for her debut. In the interim, a servant could take advantage of her absence to filch a painting—or anything else in the house—and sell it.

Yet, instinct told Risa that had not occurred. The servants here were intensely scrutinized before they were hired by the housekeeper. Mrs. Alberts was an iron maiden, as vigilant in hiring staff of impeccable character as Aunt Elizabeth had been in hiring her. Her aunt followed de Ros tradition in hiring trustworthy staff, simply because all the priceless treasures in this house and up at the Manor demanded a secure household. Her father required from any applicant three references and an unblemished employment record. His sister enforced his rules, and after he passed away, continued the tradition when the elderly housekeeper had suddenly died one month after him. Those who came to work for a de Ros were not only grilled, but investigated for any hint of larceny in their souls. Furthermore, so that a de Ros could easily check into an applicant's past, all came from Northumbria. Except for the newest housekeeper, Mrs. Alberts.

So the likelihood that a servant has taken the Ritter is small.

A burglar, then? A steely boy could have cut a circle in the window glass and—*Risa, Risa. Bars on the ground floor prohibit that. If there had been a break-in, wouldn't Mrs. Alberts have told you when you arrived in London three weeks ago? Or cabled that there had been a break-in? Yes. Yes. So . . . was there another explanation?*

Yes. Bartholome lied.

She reached up to turn down the jet of the gaslamp and jumped at the silhouette in the doorway.

"Cerise." Her aunt was tying the sash on her robe. Behind her, Mrs. Alberts did not move a muscle of her stone face. "What are you doing? And at this hour of the night?"

"Checking to see what is here," was the first thought which popped into Risa's mind. Suppressing her anger at herself for failing to hear the two women approach, Risa dug in her heels. What she said was partially true and fairly obvious. It made Mrs. Alberts spin for the stairs, but it made her aunt startle.

"Why?" She walked inside the room. "There's been no theft. If there had been, Mrs. Alberts would have informed us." Elizabeth walked forward, the gaslight casting gray shadows on her once pink and pretty but now sagging face. "And where is the ledger? How can you take a tally without it?"

"I am using the numbers only. All of them are in order and none missing."

"Why are you looking?" Her aunt skimmed a finger

along one frame, rubbed off the dust and stared at Risa.

Risa sharpened her wits, careful of each word. "I went to see a man who buys and sells objets d'art. I had a conversation with him in which he told me he had sold a painting to Maddie—and I am searching for it."

Elizabeth brushed a loose tendril of hair back into her braid. "Who is the man?"

"Maurice Bartholome. A French émigré. His shop is in Chelsea."

Her aunt's jaw dropped, then snapped shut. "A dealer of less than stellar repute, I must say. Often tried to see your father. Who, naturally, would not let him past the foyer. Why, the idea that Bartholome would come to see Maddie—or that she would receive him—is preposterous. What is this painting he sold to Maddie?" She surveyed the shelves. "Is it entered in the ledger?"

"No."

"But every acquisition always is."

"Correct. So naturally, I must ask myself why Maddie would buy a painting and not list it? She would always do what was required of her . . . so why not this?" Risa was asking herself more than her aunt. "Why not this?"

Elizabeth tipped her head to one side. "I don't recall Maddie buying a painting. If she had, I feel sure she would have told me, but then . . . She had never purchased any work before. She didn't feel qualified. Charles intimidated her thoroughly from doing that."

Charles was Risa's father's name and her aunt always spoke the word as if it were a combination of venom and ambrosia. Both Risa understood from her own experience living with the man. The venom derived from the fact that her father had never treated his twin sister, younger by five minutes, as anything but a marionette. She was just another woman trailing in his wake, as she should be, like his wife and three daughters. She was put on earth to take what he gave, not ask for more, and marry whom he chose.

He chose a man whom he liked, but unfortunately was a profligate with money and his good name. Lord Reginald Elgin also took mistresses, which Elizabeth, for all her once-celebrated beauty, could never understand nor had she ever lived down. Or forgotten.

Risa knew primarily because Georgie told her so, tutored as she was by her mother's hatred of her wandering mate. Risa could also tell because her aunt never spoke of the man without utter disdain. Lord Elgin's gambling and carousing had shortened his lifespan. When he died four short years after they were married, Elizabeth did not mourn him for longer than the prescribed few weeks. She paid off his creditors, sold his townhouse and moved in with her brother at Park Lane and back to Rossborough Manor. She became her brother's chatelaine in lieu of his ailing wife and supervised the rearing of his daughters alongside her own. If Elizabeth had wished for another husband, or at the very least less dependence on her brother, she never voiced it. She seemed grateful for the roof over her head and the monthly allowance her brother gave her. Even Georgie claimed that her mother was content to act as her brother's surrogate in all matters pertaining to the running of the Rossborough estate.

"Risa! You dream too much. I asked you how you found out about this . . . this Bartholome."

"I remembered his name when I read it," she began and would have continued had not her aunt interrupted.

"Read it where?"

Risa strolled away, prickling at Elizabeth's persistence. Where was the kinder woman who had raised her sisters and Georgie? What had happened to that lady? Had she disappeared into the resentment that now was her aunt's most apparent quality?

Her aunt's prodding reminded her too much of her father. Risa preferred compassion and respect. Such as she got from Blake. "I have been reading a diary of Maddie's."

"Really." On the surface, the word voiced her aunt's displeasure with Risa's intrusion into such sacred domain as her sister's privacy, but beneath it lay a question.

Risa did not take umbrage, nor did she answer.

"You found the one for last year?" Elizabeth was finally forced to ask.

"No. For 1879."

That rocked her aunt back on her heels. "And?"

"There was this little notation of a time and address, plus the man's name. Because I remembered him as one whom Father disparaged, I decided to go ask him why Maddie came to see him. He told me she had come to him heavily veiled in a hired hack, and that she had bought a painting of two little girls by an Edward Ritter."

"My God." Elizabeth's hand fluttered to her throat. Oddly, tears formed on her lashes. "And . . . and it's not here?"

"I regret to say, no."

"Poor Maddie." Her aunt dug for a handkerchief and found none. Risa handed her her own. "She was so erratic."

Risa froze. "Even before she came for her debut?"

"Well, yes." Her aunt blew her nose and sniffed. "Yes. She was happy one day and just so irascible—"

"If you thought this, why have you not told me this before?"

Elizabeth lifted her shoulders. "Oh, you know how you think. Time brings perspective. Hindsight is so useful."

"I guess so," Risa conceded, but was irritated with her aunt that she had not said this earlier.

If Maddie was truly unstable, then she could have

gone into that sailboat and permitted the storm to take her away.

"But why?"

"Why what?" her aunt queried, so that Risa realized she had been thinking aloud.

Maddie was used to their father. A controlling man of the first water, Charles de Ros-Lindsay brooked no challenges. He was the man by whom Maddie measured other men. Maddie had learned how to survive such a man's control. By surrender. Had she learned so well, had she been discouraged so completely by another man that she would do away with herself?

Risa did not believe it.

"Perhaps it's best you go back to bed, Aunt. Don't upset yourself more."

"But the painting?"

"I will find it. Or not. Don't worry." She gave her a watery smile. "I will figure this out." *I hope.*

Her aunt dabbed at her eyes, nodded, and sailed for the door.

Risa fingered the key in her pocket. "Aunt Elizabeth?"

"Yes?" She looked over her shoulder.

"During the time when you and Maddie were here for her debut, did you ever see her go into the vault?"

"Not last spring. The spring before, she did. Right after your father died. Everything was accounted for then," she declared, eyeing the shelves again. "I remember the tally we did. Nothing was missing." Her gaze shot to Risa's. "There won't be now, either. Why do you want to know?"

Risa ignored that question for one of her own. "After Maddie died, you had the master de Ros key ring until I arrived in Northumbria and assumed ownership."

"I did." Elizabeth folded her hands over her stomach, her pose of intrepid control which she used on them all when they were children—and naughty. "I took it from Maddie's effects rather than let the maids at Sandown put it in with her clothes and toiletries. I did not think it fitting that the ring be out of a de Ros' hands for long. Why? Is there some problem?" she asked as if Risa were insulting her handling of the ring.

Risa was no longer an impressionable child, but a woman with a quest and a terrible riddle to solve. "Did you ever open the safe?"

"No. I had no need. Why do you ask?"

Was her aunt too defensive?

"As I was closing it tonight, I discovered this." Risa opened her fist to display it.

"What is that?"

"A strange key." Risa pocketed it. "I hope it is the one to M. Rossborough's safety deposit box."

"Good God, Cerise. You mean to say you will go to the Chelsea Masonry Bank?"

"Of course. How else will we learn if it is—"

"Cerise, stop this. Do not make a fool of yourself with the bank officials. Maddie could not have done this."

"How do I know? Maddie seems to have done a lot of things which were out of character for her."

"But she was too sweet, too . . . well, my dear, I shall say it out loud. Maddie was too dim-witted to do anything nefarious or underhanded. I am telling you that the reason that we cannot find any solutions to this puzzle she created is a sure sign that she was not well."

Risa ground her teeth. So as far as Elizabeth was concerned, they were back to Maddie being emotionally unstable. If Maddie were so overwrought as to commit suicide, then she might have been incompetent, and therefore, make numerous illogical decisions. And why was she so confused, so sad, so embroiled that she could take her own life?

What's more, I blame myself for part of Maddie's turmoil. She had to find the money to pay for my education, didn't she?

"Aunt Elizabeth, you know I do not believe Maddie would hurt herself."

"Because you do not want to, Cerise. You are overwrought yourself." Elizabeth mellowed, and put an arm around her. "I think you need to rest. You are not used to this social whirl, the late hours, and the champagne." She pressed a hand to Risa's cheek. "You look pale. Why not let me take the key and go to the bank and see if this opens a safety deposit box?"

"No. I want to do that myself, thank you." She would be immovable as marble when it served her purpose—and this did. "Go to bed, Aunt. Sleep tight. We will all sleep more soundly when we find exactly what Maddie was thinking before she died."

"I doubt you will find it consorting with the likes of Blake Hargrove," her aunt bit back. Then she recanted her acid tone. "Forgive me. I suspect you are meeting him when I go to visit Georgie. Are you?"

How could her aunt know? Did she have information? From whom? The footman who had delivered Risa's note to Blake could have told her. Elizabeth did, after all, run this house like the queen's army.

"You realize Hargrove will only lie to you as he did to Maddie? He will seduce you, persuade you that he had nothing to do with her death when we all know—"

"Thank you, Aunt Elizabeth." Risa stuck her hands in her pockets and did not move.

"You won't answer me. Have it your way then. You always do, don't you? I hate to see you ruin yourself. I do want you to know, however, that people are abuzz that he took you from the ball last night. Georgie and Robert told me today at breakfast. My dear, you do not want a blemished reputation."

"I do not seek any reputation, Aunt."

"Of course you do. Every young woman does. How else can you get a husband?"

"And what if I don't want one?" *What if a husband never was part of my plan for my future?*

"But—" her aunt sputtered. "But that is preposterous. You are the countess of Rossborough. The first noble in the land. You have estates to run and you need a man to—"

"I doubt it. I can add, subtract. I can decide, Aunt Elizabeth, as well as a man—and furthermore, why would I give my power away?"

Clearly her aunt had no answer to that—and the reason was she had lived by society's rules, taken a husband, been dishonored and discounted by him.

"I saw how my father controlled and did not consult nor ever ask advice of you, his wife, his daughters, his solicitor or his tenants. I think that got him into a stew which has robbed all the de Ros women of their rightful independence. So then, I ask you, why would I want a husband to rule me, *over*rule me, when the only man I have ever known well used us all as pawns to his power? No. I want no husband. Now, please, do not bring up the subject again."

Shocked at Risa's outburst, Elizabeth slowly turned and without goodbye, left Risa alone.

She waited until her aunt's footsteps had receded down the stairs. Then she lowered the jet in the sconce, shut the door on her frustration and made her way down toward her bedroom.

Each footstep she took, she heard another declaration.

Bartholome lied.

Bartholome lied.

The sound of the voice inside her head resembled Blake Hargrove's and his statement urged her toward her bedroom and solitude. Toward reflection and honesty.

No doubt about it, she concluded as she fell back against her door, the voice belonged to Blake.

She bit back a curse against her instinct to believe him in this—as in other things. She marched to her dais, flopped down on the mattress, arms out like one of Michaelangelo's angels. She never cursed.

Damn.

She was so attuned to him that he now resided in her mind. Helping her understand this maze that was the mystery of Maddie's last days. Telling her how he liked her, desired her. Calling her darling and sweetheart, terms no man—not even her father—had ever bestowed on her. Making her want to hear him again, making her want to kiss him again . . . and allowing her to do it whenever she wished.

She punched up a few pillows, tossed this way and that. She must try to sleep tonight. But how? When she posed the question over and over again why he, of all people, appealed to her—and why his voice became for her the still dark sound of reason.

And danger.

7

You will find the spirit of Caesar in this soul of a woman.

Artemisia Gentileschi

"*Y*ou're late." She complained to Blake when she finally saw him stroll up to the panther's cage the next afternoon. "It's twenty past one."

"I apologize. I was unexpectedly detained," he said in that smooth-as-marble voice that never failed to stroke her senses—and now pervaded her brain. To add to her thrill, she could feel his eyes sweep over her in frank but swift appraisal. "I like the hat. Forest green suits you well. But I loathe the veil. I prefer to see your face."

I could not wait to see yours. "Where were you?" she asked, sounding as if she had every right to badger him. And she bemoaned her possessiveness.

"Getting information for you. Greet me like a friend," he instructed like a tutor, but appeared more like a devil with a wicked tilt to his mouth. She surveyed the pedestrians milling about them, belying her need to capture his hand and skip toward any secluded bower she could find. "I've been asking a friend of mine who is a collector of Holbein if he knew of an oil by Edward Ritter which may have escaped my attention."

"Who is this friend?"

"Marcus Sudbury."

The foremost English expert on Tudor period art. An earl. Elderly. Eccentric. Receiving only those whom he deemed worthy of his time and inestimable knowledge. Which meant the likes of Blake Hargrove—and when he'd been alive, her father. "And what did he say?"

He took her arm and they began to stroll. "Sudbury has never heard of such a work."

"For the same reason, you cited? Ritter was unproductive."

"Yes. Undisciplined and after his dismissal, blind."

"Oh," she sighed, dejected. "I had hoped we'd learn more."

"I wish I could have discovered something new from Sudbury." He squinted at a flock of birds as they came to rest in a tree above. "Yesterday, when we spoke, Risa—"

Her thoughts spun. "I am so grateful for your help on this yesterday—and pleased you've come today, too."

He had a strained thinness to his lips as he tried for levity. "Dare I hope you have developed an appetite for my company?"

She glanced away from his delectable attire. He wore a creamy shirt, cinnamon weskit, covered by chocolate tweed walking jacket over well-cut trousers. Good grief, she was nibbling on him as if he were cookies for afternoon tea. And she had not come here feeling light and gay. Not after her failure to find the Ritter—and her success at finding the key. Yet, she was with Blake for less than five minutes and her mind, so filled with him already, took new turns down a sensuous path. Why did he lead her to passion and laughter? This man, of all others? She knew one reason. "Where have you hidden the clay today?"

He examined her.

"Shall I search you here?" she dared.

"My fervent wish. But," he said, none too happy, "I see you flexing your fingers. Something is wrong."

She did not camouflage her distress. "The Ritter painting is not listed in our ledger. Nor did I find it upstairs in the attic."

He took the news with calm.

They continued to walk.

She felt him mulling over the possible explanations. Finally, she halted, stepped closer, disregarded the surge of longing that wafted through her at the aroma of his cologne, and examined him as she had intended. How could she know him so well?

And did she now live in his mind, as he did hers?

She burned with the hope, though her mind said, *Become cool. Remain focused.*

So she eliminated the alternatives that he might consider and she had already dismissed. "No staff could have stolen it. De Ros earls and countesses have always hired young men and women, who might very well qualify for sainthood were they to apply for that post. No one has burgled the house, either. Locked up tighter than Newgate Prison ever since the place was built. Iron bars along the ground floor doors and windows. The housekeeper is a keen old hawk. No one would dare go in or out with anything in his or her hands that should not have been there. Mrs. Alberts would tear them to shreds."

Blake sunk more deeply in thought.

"What do you think?" she probed, eager to hear if his voice matched the one in her head.

"Bartholome lied."

"Precisely." She twisted away from him, quickened her pace. She hated to hear it, had to admit it.

He caught up to her, took her elbow. "Darling, don't go so fast. We're attracting attention."

His endearment seared her reason. "Phooey. Let them think whatever they will."

"Not a sound idea. They can recognize me, even if they cannot admire you through that hideous gauze." He gave a strangled sound. "They can speculate, darling, that we are having a lover's quarrel."

That stopped her. She faced him. "Are you accustomed to having arguments with women in public places?" No sooner did she ask, then she recalled his argument with Maddie. But her next impulse was to ask him why he continued to call her darling. Why she melted with joy whenever he did was becoming less of a problem, less of a mystery—and more of an addiction.

"Only with your sister—and in regrettable circumstances. But since I have only met you four days ago, I must ask for your indulgence of more time to build a sterling reputation for myself."

His apology took the wind out of her sails. "Why must you cloud what we're discussing with such declarations?"

"On the contrary, I think I am being quite clear. It is the least I can do . . ." He took her hand gently. ". . . when I want to do so much more."

He stared at her with a ferocity in his features that made her believe he could seduce any woman between the ages of eight and eighty. "I cannot touch you. We are in public. I cannot ask you questions about your investigation of Maddie. You will not answer me. But you do demand the truth of me. So let me tell you how I am attracted to you. Those words are the truth. And I must say them." He let go her hand. "Hourly if you'll let me."

"Hourly?" she teased, recovering some aplomb, but loving the prospect that she could receive so much attention and affection from a man. "Far from proper, my lord."

"Nothing proper and everything natural."

She blushed so badly her cheeks burned.

"I want to be with you. I want you at Sandown. I want you there soon. In fact, I'd like you there tonight. I will get you there to see the Bernini collection. To give you the marble to carve. To help you return to sculpting."

"To see the sunrise?"

"And the sunset," he promised in a tone as molten as liquid bronze. "I will invite people for another weekend. All to ensure that your stay will appear proper for public consumption."

Risa's imagination flew to a brilliant beach. She thought of afternoons sharing tea with him, and evenings dining alone. Sunrises strolling along sun-kissed sands. Or star-studded nights when she might remove his clothes down to his skin, learn his strength with her fingertips so that she might reproduce it for others who would then appreciate a virile man, sensitive and giving.

What importance was propriety or etiquette to that? What did she care for strangers who might criticize her for being friendly with the man whom her sister cared for? Those people meant nothing to Risa. They had not brought her encouragement, help, or hope. Not like he had.

Why refuse him when she could justify the visit for so many personal and artistic reasons?

"I yearn to view your collection by Bernini," she told him, her resistance to his charm cracking wider. She recognized it for what else it was, too. Her fear of sculpting was crumbling, falling away as if she had outgrown the cast of confinement. "I long to see how he duplicates religious ecstasy and compare it to the rapture I see on the face of Allure. But I also want to work. You have brought that out in me." She breathed freely for the first time in months, more than a year in fact, since Ambrusco had tried to seduce her and failed. "But August," she reflected on the month in which the Court and Society traipsed down to the Isle of Wight, "is a long time from now."

"I wish it could be sooner, but I fear if I make it tomorrow"—he laughed at his own impatience—"no one will come. And then what will happen?" he asked in a whisper.

"Why, that means we will have time to pursue our art."

He chuckled. "We?"

"Don't you have some small need to sculpt?"

"No," he said with finality. "I want to sce you do it. And the Carrara begs for the touch of an artist."

"I am honored you would give me such a rare and expensive piece of marble. After all, you have no idea if I have any talent." *Or how rabid I am at the prospect of using the most revered of marbles to let me try to do justice to you.* She dug from her pocket a lump of clay and raised it to his view.

He grinned. "I will take my chances. Especially now that I have persuaded you to carry clay. Dare I hope you have practiced sculpting me in that"—he was teasing her now, looking about to see no one overheard them—"or did I wind up in the butter again this morning?"

"No," she said and watched his features fall. "Neither. I did not have to."

He cocked his head. "And why is that?"

"I heard your voice inside my head all night."

"How very gratifying." He covered her hand with his and curled her fingers over the clay, then pressed it sweetly, all too briefly. Then with two fingers, he smoothed the edge of her veil. "I hope I said something worthwhile."

"Oh, you did." Her throat clogged with the lack of air at his proximity. "You told me Bartholome lied."

"Did I?" he said without a sound, turning them away from the path and the sight of passersby, beneath a shady tree. His fingers stole up under her veil and stroked in one long languid glide from her earlobe to her collar. "Did you hear me whisper to you all night as I lay awake and thought of you?"

"Yes." She wished she had heard more of the passion in his voice that was there now, instead of the danger.

He dropped his hand and she nearly moaned with the lack of his touch. "I said I want to remove your hair pins." His gaze defined her hair. "Spread your curls like a blanket of fire beneath you." He regarded one cape button. "I wish to undo all of these, and taste the peaks and valleys of your body." Her knees went to water. "And then, can you imagine what I will do last?"

"No." *Tell me.*

"Unhook your stockings." He pressed her oh so fleetingly to his torso. "Your corset. All your reserve. Teach you new and unforgettable delights . . . so that no other man could ever compare."

The clay slid from her fingers.

He picked it up and returned it to her with a narrow-lidded gaze.

"You undo me now."

"A reciprocal arrangement." He drew away and gave the appearance of a man out for a simple promenade. "For now I will stop. Wait for the right time. I want you more with every step we take, Risa." He took her elbow again. "I wish I could hurry the process, but I won't. Terrible trial, you realize, to learn such restraint after years of license."

She laughed. "You are too experienced for me."

"Yes, aren't I? But I will not injure your reputation."

"Too late," she objected. "When you took me away at the ball the other evening, you created speculation that we are nurturing a tendre—"

"I am." He smiled so broadly, he made her do it too. But his expression fell. "Tell me I am nurturing yours as well."

"Like no other man I've ever known."

"Thank God," he murmured. "My need to have you at Sandown has just doubled, darling. Soon. Soon you will be with me. And with that promise . . ." he led her toward a shady copse where a wooden bench faced a maze of trees and Dutch tulips bloomed in a rainbow of color. "Sit here. There now." He took her in, from hat to breast to toe, and set her afire everywhere his eyes went. "No one is watching. Tell me. How can I help you more?"

"You switch topics," she mused, charmed and irritated, "like lightning."

"Better I do that than act like that barbarian and carry you off. So. We march on. Together, I hope."

She was so bewitched by him, that she folded her hands over her clay and tried to become logical again. "I must speak with Bartholome. Call him on his lie to me."

"When do you wish to go?"

"I am so angry—" *and curious* "—that I would love to go now. But I can't." She planned to inquire this afternoon if the Chelsea Masonry Bank had a deposit box number 124 which could be opened with this key.

"Tomorrow?" he asked, hopeful.

"No. I am invited to a garden party." The reason she

was attending was because Diana Cliveden had been friendly with Maddie since they were in deportment class together, and Risa hoped the baroness would share a few minutes—and a few insights to Maddie's behavior last spring.

"Hosted by the Clivedens?"

She rolled her eyes that Blake knew everyone, everything. "Yes, and the rub is that flowers make me sneeze."

"Seek seclusion in the music room then." He winked. "I will meet you there."

To . . . talk? She'd had enough of talk with him. "You're going?"

"I am now."

"Good. Then I will go to see Bartholome Monday."

"The shop is closed."

"Tuesday then. At eleven while my aunt takes her brunch with Georgie and Robert."

His smile was rueful.

"What's the matter?" she asked him.

"After seeing you every day this week, I doubt I can wait until Tuesday for the pleasure."

Desire for him was suddenly tempered by a strong dose of reason. He was a handsome man, a determined one. "Have you pursued all your women with such dedication?"

"On the contrary, darling, I have no need to pursue them at all."

"I see."

"Let me make it even clearer for you." He drew near again, put a foot to the wooden bench so that he effectively blocked her exit and any others' view of them. "You are different for me."

She was enchanted all the more by his admission, and could not change that. Did not wish to now. "Is that because I do not pursue you?"

"That is last on my list. Your allure for me is something I see there in your eyes. A curiosity. A naïveté that I wish to help you preserve, protect. Any good artist needs that. But a woman of your class must be defended from the brutes who might court you, marry you, but never understand you. And I do." His voice caressed her like it had all through the night. "I find it hard to believe no man has swept you away with compliments and kisses."

"I once fell in love."

"And who was the fortunate man?"

"The vicar's son, all of age fourteen—who," she added with spice, "taught me how to kiss."

"What happened to him?"

She rolled a shoulder. "After he learned I sculpted he called me a heathen."

"He is gone and I will be delighted to let you compare him to me and show you what an ignorant creature he was."

"But his actions showed me—" *Just as my father warned me that my art would drive most men away.* "—that if I want to be an artist, I must be prepared to live alone."

"No lovers?"

"None . . . yet."

"Most artists take them," he offered.

"I have known no female sculptor who had a lover, and only one painter—and she preferred women."

Blake frowned. "Will you not consider a man worthy of your affections?"

"Until now," she blurted, "I met no man who brought out any affections. I know myself well, you realize, and I am too wedded to my social code to think of taking a man to my bed who is not my husband. But I am also stopped by the fear that a husband might forbid me to sculpt."

"Not all men are alike."

"But the ones who would smile upon my hours spent in a studio are few."

"Are you saying you will not love . . . or cannot?"

She picked at her clay. "I think I am capable." *I know it more clearly today than ever before.* "I need to meet the right sort of man first."

"You can do as you please. Because you wear skirts does not make you a less whole person than one who dons trousers. Do not let anyone intimidate you that way. Not anyone. Especially someone who says he loves you. Because if he limits you, he cannot truly love you."

His vehemence stunned her. His declaration overjoyed her.

Before she had a chance to say that, he loosed his grip and apologized, then strode toward the tulips.

She followed him, put a hand to his sleeve. "Only a few people have ever encouraged me. Maddie. *Signore* Ambrusco. And you."

"Not your father?"

"No, never. The first time he knew I sculpted was when I was nine and he found me chiseling an angel out of a fire log. He said women do not sculpt. 'They sketch or paint—and only in watercolors. You'll never snare a man if you act like you will only carve him up!'

"My father told me to use my looks and learn to please a man. In bed, out of it. 'Do that first,' he warned me, 'and then your husband may permit you free time to chisel.' "

"I am sorry," Blake said again. "But all men are not like your father."

"Most, I think."

"Yes. I agree." Sorrow engulfed his features. "My sister," he said, scanning the treetops, "wanted to paint. Oils. She was good. She could have been first rate.

With practice. Her husband criticized her unmerciful-
ly. She listened to him. She loved him, though as God
is my witness, I have no idea why. When her husband
threatened to divorce her for her devotion to her art,
she gave it up. I tried to convince her that a severance
of their ties would be the best thing that ever happened
to her. She did not believe me. She took her own life. I
blame myself for not saving her. I take that failure to
my grave."

Risa put her hand to Blake's. "You tried. What more
could you have done?"

"Insisted she move out. Leave him. He was not worthy of her. She was so sensitive and he abused her emotions."

"Blake, for all your good intentions, you may not
have been able to change things for her. And perhaps,
she loved her husband more than she loved her art."

Blake blinked at her. "It would have been a small
thing to permit her—"

"Would it? You were once devoted to your own art.
You know it can be a ogre, greedy of your time, your
mind. Gobbling up your days, sometimes your nights,
possessing you in tea parties and church and on your
way to the milliner's."

He got a crooked smile. "At debuts, too?"

She hugged his arm, pleased he was becoming more
chipper. "Whenever an insistent creature plunks clay
into your palm." She thought a moment. "Did you
ever consider that Barbara's husband may have loved
her so deeply that he was jealous of her work?"

Risa could see that might be a tremendous challenge
to a love affair—and a marriage. "Did you think that
your sister's husband may not have wished to take second place in her thoughts, ever?"

"No, I didn't."

"That's understandable. Because you are so used to

the demands of art, you did not consider it a challenge, that is all."

He smiled, painfully. "I wonder how you became so wise."

"Nothing to it. A year in Italy with *Signore* Ambrusco and I learned much." *And not all of it about art.* "I knew two sculptors whose wives left them. The women were afraid that their husbands would find too many charms in the arms of the studio models." Risa recalled how Ambrusco had tried to teach her about passion and instead, she had learned about lust—and disillusionment.

Amazingly, as if Blake not only resided in her mind but could also now see all within it, he asked her about Ambrusco. "He was not kind to you, was he?"

She lifted a shoulder. "Are tutors supposed to be kind?"

"It is the best way to teach."

"He did not like what I produced."

"But he liked you, didn't he? Too much. And in an inappropriate manner."

She considered one red tulip. Walked away from Blake and stooped to rub her thumb over the satin petal. "We started off well. He liked my work. I had shipped to him a number of small *modellos* I had sculpted before he would accept me for his class. At first when I arrived, he told me I was destined to be great, noted, a woman in a man's artistic endeavor. So rare. He told me that I understood the human heart, that I felt pathos deeply, accurately. I worked harder, longer."

Blake came to stand beside her. "Did your work please him?"

"Yes. I produced a few figures, a medieval knight on his destrier, and a tiny cat and dog. But Ambrusco began to tell me I was producing too quickly. My works were blithe. I needed passion. A grand love affair. He said he could teach me that—and he tried."

"Did he hurt you?" Blake asked in such a raw voice, Risa stared up at him.

"Not in any romantic way."

While relief swamped his eyes, Blake extended his hand to her. "Tell me what he did."

"One rainy morning, he looked at my modello for a fawn, a piece to accent his new commission outside the Florence city hall, and he told me to stop. The character displayed no depth of emotion, he said. I was recreating something I had seen rendered by another's hand. But I did not agree with him. He tried to console me by kissing me—and caressing me."

"And?" Blake held his breath.

"I did not like him in that way. I told him so. He said he took it well. But soon after, he began to criticize me in public—and I am sad to admit that his cruel words eroded my self confidence."

Blake cursed the tutor baldly. "Did you suspect he was punishing you for your failure to become his mistress?"

"No, not then. I—I'm still not certain he did that."

"Sit down again."

"What?"

He took her elbow to lead her toward the bench. "I wish to see you do my likeness in your clay. Now." He swept off his hat and gave her his profile.

She chuckled, but took her old seat. "All right. No peeking."

"No walking sticks, either."

"Mmmm." She began to press and pull at the clay. "I promise."

Within minutes, even though she had terrible glasses and had an obstructed view through her veil, she fashioned a representation she thought worthy of him. "There. What do you think?"

He took it in his palm. "You do me more than justice."

She tried terribly hard not to preen. "I think it could be better." *If it were your entire body, naked to my eye, I would render much more beauty.*

"All art improves with practice. You have captured me with realism and"—he grinned—"a bit more nobility than I may possess."

"Something to live up to, then, eh?"

He caught her chin and whispered, "You make me want to be more noble."

"You make me want to be more bold."

"We can both work for those goals." He returned the clay to her, then strode a few paces away, hands in his trouser pockets. "Risa, I want to tell you something more about Bartholome and Maddie. Something I did not tell you yesterday."

"What?"

"Bartholome has a few friends who live in Montmartre. He attended the Beaux-arts with them. Some are critics now. A few are painting, but only one makes a living at it. His name is Henri Deville. Another is a gallery owner who shows only the new art of the French."

"The impressionist painters?"

"And sculptors. Like Auguste Rodin."

Rodin's last few marbles were the rage of European art critics. His portrayal of men and women in the agonies and ecstasies of human emotion was a facet long neglected by artists. Most sculptors focused on the sacred emotions. "I'd like to meet Rodin. See his work," she murmured. "Some say no other sculptor rivals him for sensuality, except Bernini. And even then, Allure is the only representation of secular love ever created by an artist."

"I'll take you, introduce you to him."

"You know him?"

Blake nodded. "I worked in his studio for a year. He knows how to make marble breathe." He cocked his head. "He also employs a woman who is his apprentice. In many ways, she surpasses her maestro for excellence."

"I want to meet both of them."

"We will go then," Blake squeezed her hand.

"After we find out the answers to Maddie's strange behaviors," she acknowledged, and then realized she not only had promised to travel abroad with him, but, like him, she had used the pronoun *we*.

Blake nodded in self-satisfaction. "Slowly, you do see I am no threat to you. What else can I tell you?"

She smiled at him, thankful for his return to their order of business. "Has Bartholome lied before? To buyers? Sellers? Has he ever been associated with others who . . . who are less than honest?"

"Lied? I cannot say for certain. I will tell you that Bartholome takes a huge percentage when he sells a significant work. Ten percent as opposed to the regular five. Many collectors who wish to buy from Bartholome are not happy about his cut of the purchase price. But he does run a business with this man Deville. Bartholome collaborates with him on the production and sale of his paintings."

"That is not unusual. Many dealers act as agents for one painter."

"True. But Deville's works are different."

"How?" Was his style unique or, like Rodin, was his subject matter?

"Deville produces copies."

"Copies?"

"Of old masters' paintings."

"Which masters?"

"Mostly sixteenth century Dutch. Holbein included."

Risa rubbed her temple. More puzzle pieces. "This Deville . . ." She paused. Examined the tulips and then the green of Blake's eyes. "Does Deville sell his paintings declaring they are . . ." *Fakes?* ". . . copies?"

"Yes."

"All of them?"

"I wonder."

"Because you have no proof?"

"None." He scowled. "I spent six months in Paris trying to find out, and I could not."

"Why did you try to find out?" she asked, predicting an answer she would not like.

He stared at her, and this time she detected sorrow in his expression.

"What's the matter, Blake?" She got to her feet. "How did you try to find out?" Fear tingled her spine.

"I became friends with Deville's friends. They told me things I already knew about him. I became friendly with his favorite model. She was no help. I became better acquainted with his banker."

"His banker? Why?"

"One usually sees the sources of income when one looks at a bank account."

"I wish I could even look at an account," she complained, so undone by Blake's revelations that she forgot her own promise to reveal nothing to him about the complexity of her investigation of Maddie's source of cash.

"You let slip yesterday that Maddie paid all her bills in cash." He leaned down. "What's this now about an account?"

"You're changing the subject."

"Very well, save that for later . . . when you trust me more to confide that to me too. For now, I will tell you all of this. You won't like it. I don't. You won't understand it. To a great extent, I don't either."

The hair on her arms stood up.

"Maddie knew Deville. When we argued the night she died, she threw his name out. Perhaps she did not think I would know it, I can't say for certain. But she did say the word Deville and in a spiteful tone."

"You know him?"

"No. Know of him. I buy original works by acclaimed masters or contemporary artists. Deville is not an artist. He is an imitator. But in addition, Risa, he is a shark, gouging patrons for top price on works he paints which are, after all, only reproductions. Deville is also a roue. Goes to excess in all things. A gourmand. A spendthrift. A man who seduces many women to induce them to spend money with him. So because of his reputation, I wondered how Maddie knew him. It was a question that, after her death, plagued me, and sent me to Paris to investigate. From what I gathered in Paris for the past six months, Deville never met Maddie. But does know her name. When I mentioned it in his company, he was shocked I brought her name up so casually. Deville, I am sad to say, also knows Bartholome."

"Many people the world over know about the de Ros family collection," Risa said. "Deville could have heard of Maddie, how she was now the heiress to it all. My father was well-known, often consulted by other collectors, museum directors, and curators. Perhaps, so had Maddie, though others would quickly learn she knew much less than Father did about art."

"I agree. But is it not too coincidental that Deville knows Bartholome and both of them know Maddie? Sweet Maddie who knew little about art?"

"A good question," Risa replied, searching for an explanation which could absolve Maddie of any collusion, any nefarious scheme which . . . "Why didn't you tell me this yesterday?"

"I wanted to. If I had, would you have believed me? No, only today can you do that. Only after you revealed this bit to me about Bartholome and you investigated and learned I helped you with that."

"You're right. So then tell me what you think about Maddie and Deville and Bartholome's relationship."

"Maddie was involved with Deville and Bartholome. I do not know how or why. I did not like Maddie very much, it is true. I feared that she wanted to marry John for a reason less than love. More akin to desperation."

That made Risa angry, but this time, at Maddie. Maddie who created this puzzle for her. Maddie, whose behavior compelled Risa to find any and all pieces and put this patchwork together.

"Invite me to Sandown," she said, working on her goal to become more bold. "I want to come." *To be with you. To learn if it is wise that I care for you. To meet your servants. The maid who packed Maddie's trunk— who may know where her diary is. The coroner and constable who investigated her death.*

"So you will. Good afternoon, Cerise. I like the whole name, just as I like the entire woman." He tipped his hat. Leaned close to murmur, "Listen to me tonight. I will be whispering in your ear, in your bed."

She laughed. "I know you will."

"I will be repeating how I wish you could trust me totally. Because without that, there will be no reason for us to continue our relationship."

She sat there for many minutes more after he strolled away, absently pushing and pulling the clay into representations of him. Blake, aggressive. Blake, protective. Blake, seductive.

She dropped her clay into her pocket, eager to go to

Chelsea . . . but impulse had her digging out the clay again.

This time she fashioned him as truthful. Then vulnerable. To her.

Just as you are to him.

She accepted it. Put her clay away and stood.

She smiled at the flowers. Reveled in the spectrum of spring colors. Drank in the warmth of the sun.

She would be bold. Dare to learn if the emotion she felt for Blake was more than infatuation. More than physical desire. More than the allure of a passion she now needed to experience as completely as eating or breathing . . . or sculpting.

8

One does not achieve inner discipline until one reaches the extremes of art and life.

Michelangelo

"Robert will get me my punch, won't you?" Elizabeth glared at her son-in-law.

Risa doubted a walk to the punch bowl would sober him up. She had seen him tipsy on occasion, but ever since she had come to London, he was in his cups most of every day and night.

The young man bowed with a drunken flourish. "Course, Mother dear. To keep you happy, anything." He wove his way past a group of people who included Blake.

"Georgie," her mother bit off, "you must do something about his behavior. He makes a spectacle of himself. It is demeaning."

"What would you have me do? I emptied all the liquor in the house the night of Cerise's coming-out ball. I forbid the butler to order any more, but Bobbie bribes the man to buy it for him. Then he hides it. I spend my mornings looking for the next damn place he's stored it."

"Chastise him."

Risa sneezed. "Do forgive me," she patted her nose, pretending her stuffiness was getting worse. "The roses are not only—" She coughed, sneezed. "—giving me a red nose, but also a giant headache." She tried to ignore the bewitching sight of Blake across the lawn, earnestly discussing the azaleas like a horticulturist with one intent matron and her pretty daughter. "Forgive me, but I must go inside."

"Go, my dear," Elizabeth agreed readily. She hated to speak about men who had failed to keep their wits about them. But more than that, she hated to speak of relatives of hers who did that. "Georgie and I shan't lack for company. Do powder your nose." The lady smiled benevolently. She showed no signs of holding a grudge since their altercation last night. Unusual for her.

Eager to get away from her family, Risa passed Blake. He watched her openly. But the lady he spoke with had talons she put to his arm. Risa smothered a grin. Foiling Blake Hargrove was as easy as swimming through a tidal wave. Yet this mother succeeded admirably.

Risa took the opportunity to seek the morning room. When she had come through the receiving line, Diana Cliveden had discreetly invited Risa to meet her there for a few minutes to discuss Maddie.

Risa made her way beyond the rolling gardens leading to the house. She was eager to talk to Blake today alone and see what he would say when she asked him if Maddie had ever talked about her financial situation. If she'd ever mentioned money. Cash.

Risa wondered what he would say if she told him how she had discovered a hoard of it yesterday in a safety deposit box which had to have been Maddie's. It was certainly M. Rossborough's. The bank president confirmed that after Risa presented her key and he told her that number 124 belonged to M. Rossborough— and M. Rossborough had not appeared to open her box since last summer. July twenty-seventh was the last day according to the bank log of those entering their deposit boxes. Two days before Maddie paid off all her creditors in London. Who else could M. Rossborough be but Maddie? Maddie who had the means to hide the key in the Park Lane vault? The key numbered 124.

Yes, Maddie had kept cash in her safety deposit box. Lots of it. Five thousand six hundred pounds.

Risa doubted Diana would know how Maddie had gotten it. But she'd ask other questions of Maddie's friend. Such as was Maddie in love last summer and with whom?

Risa found a footman in attendance at the entrance to the ballroom, which today had been turned into a grand salon filled with buffet tables laden with every delicacy from watercress sandwiches to petit fours. The servant obliged her by instructing how she might gain the morning room and she was closing the doors as Diana came forward, hands out.

"My lady." Diana curtsied deeply to Risa who as the countess of Rossborough now outranked her. "I am delighted you came today."

"As I am to be here. Please call me Cerise."

Diana inclined her head. "It has been so many years since I've seen you. You were—what? ten or twelve?— when I visited at Rossborough Manor and you astounded Maddie and me with your little sculpture of us." Diana laughed gaily.

"I am glad you remember it fondly. It was not terribly complimentary."

Thin blond brows rose delicately. "Since then, I have often thought of myself as a vase."

"But it was an ugly vase. Unbalanced and—"

"The face you formed on it was mine. Thin. Pinched. Afraid of my own shadow."

"I was ten years old and did not mean to insult you."

"Ah, but you didn't. You awakened me."

Risa was awed. "How could I do that?"

"Growing up as a woman predisposes one to being— shall we say—fulfilled by other people. Your imagery of a vase, an object to be filled with other objects, does much to help me self-correct in times when I can become someone's wife or someone else's mother."

Diana Cliveden was no ordinary woman. In looks, she was as tall as Risa, but a white blonde of such fragile beauty that five years since her debut, she was still the Bright One by whom many women were measured, and found wanting. In personality, Diana was better known as a wife in love with her husband who was twice her age, and a mother devoted to her only child—a daughter. Beyond that, Diana was hailed for her role as a political essayist who agitated for women's rights to equal wages.

Risa was honored by Diana's admission. "I am overwhelmed that the vase helps you."

"And I am overwhelmed when I realize you were so young when you sculpted it. Such talent should be given to the world. I was so pleased when Maddie told me you were studying in Florence."

"Maddie insisted I go. She found the money to pay my tuition and living expenses." Risa watched Diana for any sign she knew about Maddie's financial woes.

"Maddie wrote to me that she had ordered you to go."

Risa recalled the scene with a sad smile. "She threatened to throw me on the street, bag and baggage, if I did not leave immediately."

"That was Maddie. Kind. Spontaneous."

"Thank you. I miss her."

"Shocking how she went."

"Yes. And puzzling to me. So much so that I want to know more about her last days. Whatever you know about Maddie last year, my lady, I hope you will share with me. I need your help to put my mind at rest."

"I will do whatever I can, Cerise. Please, do me the honor to call me Diana." She indicated a Louis the Fourteenth chair for Risa, then took the matching one for herself. "Forgive me for rushing you into this discussion, but your note indicated you were anxious to talk with me—and I must return to my guests. I want to help you, but I was not at Sandown. How can I, of all people, help you with what occurred there?"

"Maddie wrote to me often last spring that she had taken tea with you and then came to your annual garden party. So naturally, I hoped you might give me some insight into her behavior before she went to Sandown."

"Of course, we were good friends. Perhaps not as fond as we once were, but that was something time and space we hoped could cure, especially since we thought Maddie was to reside more in London—and marry." She smoothed the creases in her pale peach organdy skirts. "But that did not happen for poor Maddie."

"No. It didn't. I wonder if you can tell me how she acted last spring. If she was herself or . . . or different in any way."

"I think whenever a woman debuts, she changes."

"Really? Why is that?"

"She must choose a man, and soon, to marry. You must feel the pressure yourself."

"Indeed, I do." Risa gave her a smile that indicated her frustration.

Diana chuckled. "You have no problems. I notice our dashing American guest, Mr. Woodward, finds you captivating."

"Mr. Woodward is very persistent." At her debut reception, he had danced with her twice after Blake had so summarily left. Today the man was also too attentive, rushing to get her a glass of lemonade, inquiring after her health. "I am also afraid he is too terribly American for my taste."

"Oh?"

"He refuses to take no for an answer."

It was Diana's turn to laugh. "Where you are concerned, I understand other men do not, either."

"Ah. Yes. Dare I ask who?"

"The earl of Sandown."

"I presume you are referring to his gallant rescue of me from the disaster of falling from a turned ankle."

"Of course. And there is a buzzing of bees in my garden that the reason the man is here, taking up vantage points to watch you, is because you have charmed him senseless."

And I am struggling to ensure I do not become giddy with that power.

"What do you think about that, Diana?" She watched the baroness slowly mull that over. "What did the rest of society think of Maddie's relationship with Blake?" Diana's brows rose higher at Risa's use of his given name. "Did Maddie want to marry him?"

Diana hesitated.

"Oh, please. I am beside myself that Maddie was in terrible emotional straits last spring. That no one understood her or helped her or . . . or . . . God, I do not know what to ask, what to think."

"On that I would say you are right, Risa. Maddie was not herself at all last spring. Yes. She was under a strain because of her debut. But there was something else . . . an infinite sadness that would come over her, like a shroud. I often asked her if she felt well or if she were pining for a man and perhaps I might be able to help her."

"And? What did she say?"

"No. She felt well. No. She was not pining for a man. No. She would never make the mistake to fall in love with her husband. 'Not like my mother,' she would say. Yet, I often thought she was in love with someone. I did not detect the cause at first. But there was something that made her fidget. Something that made her fret. Something that destroyed her happiness all of a sudden at certain parties."

"Which parties?"

"Oh, I don't know if I can even categorize them. Balls, garden parties, riding on Rotten Row. She would turn, spy something, someone, and go to stone. All her joy draining. As if she'd seen a ghost. I would ask, and then learned not to because she would never explain."

"She never mentioned a man she wanted to marry?"

"One man?"

Risa nodded.

"Never one, my dear. I wish there were."

"What? Why?"

"There were so many."

That knocked Risa back in her chair. "Many?"

"One day it would be Sandown, and the next his brother John. Then it was Woody . . . Mister Woodward. Later it was John again. I never knew which way the wind would blow so I stopped asking her. Instead, I felt it my duty to warn her to stop acting like a firefly. I told her she had to become serious and take stock of one man, then let herself love him before she set her heart on marrying him."

"And what did Maddie say?"

Diana scoffed. "Told me to mind my own business. Said she would—*must* was her word—must be married before the Season was out. Preferably sooner."

Risa gripped the armrest. "Why would she do that?"

Diana gave Risa a flat look. "You will not like my opinion."

"Tell me anyway."

"I thought Maddie wished to do one of two things. Either become lost in a grand amour with a husband, or . . ."

"Or . . .?"

"Escape the watchful eyes and controlling hands of your aunt." As Risa tried to come to terms with both of those possibilities, Diana went on in a small sad voice. "Maddie never said those things, but in so many ways that was the message I picked up from her. I have no proof. No examples. Only my feelings about Maddie at the time."

"Yes, I see. And so," Risa said, saving these things to digest later when she was over the shock of them, "how did you feel when you learned she had drowned?"

"The truth again?"

"Please."

"I wondered if she had become such a ball of frustrations that she killed herself."

"I couldn't find you." Blake appeared in Risa's line of vision many minutes later. "I grew worried."

Risa gazed up at him, mute. She had sat here so long, while the sun warmed her body but could not penetrate the cold places where her heart ached for her sister.

"A footman told me he'd directed you here." Blake knelt in front of her. Took her hands in his. "You're freezing." He tipped up her chin. "You're so forlorn. Please tell me why."

"What do you suppose a person thinks of before she considers taking her own life?"

She saw her despair mirrored on his face.

He smoothed her brows with gentle fingertips. His eyes clouded with his own remembered misery. "All the things she should have done. Had no desire to do any longer. All the dreams that died. Or . . . maybe she thinks of nothing, except . . . release. I do not know. I have tried to imagine what hopelessness must feel like, and I cannot." He raised her hands to his lips, blessed them both with tender kisses, then gathered her into his arms.

She went to him willingly, her arms wrapping around him.

Sweet and strong, he held her tightly, his mouth moving against her temple as he asked her, "Why, darling? What's wrong?"

"Would a woman who intended to commit suicide, leave five thousand six hundred pounds in a safety deposit box she kept under a false name?"

He drew back to stare down at her.

"A woman whose estate was in debt, and yet who had not taken a loan to pay it off."

His green eyes grew sad.

"A woman who had paid all her private bills before she left London for a weekend house party on the Isle of Wight."

Surprise had him asking, "Maddie did that?"

"Yes."

"That alone sounds like someone who plans to go away, at least for awhile."

"I agree."

Risa pulled away, sitting on her legs, hands limp in her lap. "I wish I could understand what Maddie did. I have got to know. There must be answers to this that make some sense." She ran a restless hand up into her hair, undoing a few curls of her coif as she rubbed her scalp. "I will go see Bartholome Tuesday."

"I will be there," he vowed, and then she was in his

embrace once more. "You will come to Sandown in three weeks. It's as soon as convention will permit invitations to go out for a formal weekend."

"Oh, but a sailing event in May? It is not done."

"To hell with waiting. I will invite everyone who came last year. Your aunt, your cousin Georgie and her husband. Even my brother John."

"Will he come?"

"I doubt it. He does not speak to me, you see." Blake blinked away his sorrow over that. "But I will introduce you to the constable, the doctor who did the autopsy, the judge who presided at the inquest."

"Everything I would ask for—and more." She cupped his cheek. "You keep giving me reasons to thank you. I am running out of ways to do that," she murmured, marveling at his largesse.

"Do not despair," he said with raw authority. "I have a few new ones in mind I can teach you."

"I am a good pupil," she showed him how much she had learned from him already with a hard, quick kiss.

He caught his breath. "And I want this investigation over and done for you. This is the only way I am able to help. The best I can give you. And I will. Damn, the rules of the Season and the fact no one goes to Wight in the spring. We will. If I have to pay every person to attend, they will come."

"After the invitations go out, some of your guests might put their heads together and realize you mean to recreate the events surrounding Maddie's death. They will speculate about your motives."

"Unavoidable. Once they learn you are coming, too, they will have a larger bone to chew on."

"I am ready for the rumors," she resolved. "My aunt will not be happy to come to Sandown." She recalled how her aunt had criticized her for meeting Blake secretly.

"She might enlist Georgie and Robert to pick at you, too. Probably ask you to decline your invitation."

"Georgie has her hands full with sobering up Robert. I doubt she will have time to pester me."

"I saw that little encounter out in the garden. Robert's affinity for whiskey has increased the past year. It is ruining his business. He hardly goes to his shop and he miscalculated the price on a Delacroix last week, underbid on its purchase, and lost the patron as a client."

"Georgie might decide to refuse your invitation," Risa told him, remembering Georgie's inability to discuss the Sandown weekend at all. The loss of Maddie, Georgie claimed, was a tragedy she could not even speak about. "I doubt they want to relive those days over again."

Blake was glum. "Your aunt will not pretend for days on end to be civil to me, I fear."

"No, but I hope you will overlook that. She was shaken by Maddie's loss. She still cries over it."

Blake stroked her hair absently. "Often we don't realize how strongly we care until we have lost our loved ones forever." He hugged her and Risa knew he recalled his own sister and brother, both gone from him in different ways.

She turned his concerns away from them. "Others will ask you why you have scheduled this party. You will need a response. What will you say?"

"The truth. That I am eager to rush the Season. But my friends are not deaf or dumb. In the comfort of my own home where I will be near you day in and out, I think it will become obvious how dearly I care for you. I will not hide it or deny it. I will host this party, Cerise, no matter the rumors. I want you to see what Maddie saw, stay where she did, relive the party as closely as I can duplicate it. I want your troubles solved. I want your mind to be cleared. I want you to sculpt. I want you to smile."

He tried to do it himself, but failed. "I want you to laugh. That happens too rarely."

And for his generosity and his protectiveness, she thanked him in a way that was becoming the most thrilling part of their extraordinary relationship. She kissed him. Delicately the first time. A brush of lips that had him catch his breath. A winsome touch by which she meant to show him she was grateful.

But gratitude faded in the radiance of a passion that blinded her, and had her reaching for him a second time. And so she tasted him, still naïve in her ardor and timid in her power, the tip of her tongue tracing his lower lip.

He moaned and clutched her nearer. But ever so sweetly and deliberately, he opened himself to her. And her tongue flicked inside. And roamed. And played.

Until he turned her in his arms and rolled her beneath him. She welcomed his weight. Savored his warmth. Matched the wild way he possessed her mouth, and twisted up against him, twining her arms about his neck and urging him down. She learned the texture of his insistent tongue and the flavor of his tenderness. Both were rough and sultry and addictive. She kissed him till her breath was short and he dipped his head to spread kisses down her throat and across her chest. Through her layers of day dress, corset, and chemise, her body strained to merge with his. And he undid buttons with alacrity to give her what she needed. His lips against her heart.

"Cerise." His words were nothing more than moist wisps of air on her bare skin. "I'm going to make love to you at Sandown. Stronger than this. Better than this." He kissed her fiercely and drew far away, so far away that he stood and brought her to her feet. "Longer than this."

A tear slid down her cheek. Its presence surprised her completely.

But not him. He lifted it carefully from her cheek. "Come to Sandown prepared to seek all the clues you wish to solve your sister's death, darling. But also come prepared to open yourself to me totally. I want you— and I won't take any less than all of you. Your trust and your affections." He stepped against her, his desire for her so blatantly evident as he crushed her close and explored every little recess of her mouth. "I intend to show you that a man can please a woman physically and love her mind as well. Then when he's done, he can walk away and wait patiently for her to return to him until she finds her ambition and feeds her soul."

He shot his cuffs, straightened his coat, walked half way to the double doors before Risa had recovered enough of her reason to call his name.

He turned, and from the grim look on his face, he suspected she would debate his decisions.

"A woman should do that, too, I think."

"What?" he asked, confused.

"Please a man physically, love his intellect, then wait patiently while he feeds his ambition and his soul."

A slow smile parted his handsome lips. "I agree."

"You've never met one who can?" This connoisseur of women, had not found one to suit him?

"Not whole-heartedly."

She would test him. She loved doing it and learning new facts about him. "Because you haven't searched for her?"

"Because none of them was you."

9

The artist does not draw what he sees, but what he has to make others see.

Edgar Degas

None of them was you.

His discovery pleased him.

It also astonished him. Propelled him home to Upper Brook Street immediately after he left her in the Clivedens' morning room. Compelled him to work like a drone to recreate his Sandown event and drove him to summon his young secretary from his supper to pen invitations to the twenty-one people who had attended last year. This year, they would add Cerise, who would take the place of her deceased sister.

"It's almost two in the morning, Jameson, you should go to bed." Blake smiled at his young secretary and indicated the study door. "Please do. What plans we have not completed can wait until tomorrow. Thank you."

"You're welcome, my lord." The fellow said with a grin, tired though it was. "I don't mind, sir. You are not usually a hard task-master."

"Thank you for that," he bid him, and waved him off to his third story bedroom up in the servants' quarters.

I am not usually so driven. But that is because I have never been so charmed by a woman. So needed.

Nor so summarily rejected.

But he had turned that tide.

Cerise accepted him now. Finally. After days of revelations and discussions. She trusted him enough to confide facts about Maddie to him. The safety deposit box. The cash inside. What had been wrong with Maddie that she behaved so oddly? Would they ever know?

He would try his damnedest to find out.

He rose from his desk, picked up the vellum envelope with Cerise's name scrolled on it. Then ran a hand across the back of his neck.

Weary, he felt invigorated at the prospect that Cerise would come to Sandown and they would try to put an end to this mystery together. And then . . . then Cerise could sculpt again. Laugh more often. Make love with him.

No. You cannot do that.

Blake was stunned at the sound of a voice that had never before intruded on his thoughts about a woman. Not a woman he desired.

Two weeks, he argued with himself, is long enough to wait. In fact, too long.

Too quick.

He leaned back to stare up at the ceiling.

What the hell was he doing acquiring a conscience about a relationship with a woman at his ripe age of thirty-four?

His conscience, Blake noted with amusement, had no retort for that.

He caught a glimpse of himself in the wall mirror. He walked toward his reflection, placed his hands along the sideboard.

He had always understood what attracted him to
women. Their bodies, always. Their humor, if they
had it.

God knew, Cerise Lindsay possessed ample measures
of both.

But what did he possess that attracted her?

Over and above her need to hear the facts about last
year's weekend party, Cerise had found something in
him. A saving grace. What?

He smiled ruefully. *Your persistence.*

Your devotion to helping her.

Well, yes. He certainly agreed with his conscience
on that fact.

What else?

Your looks?

He scoffed. He had always thought himself in-
scrutable looking. Mixed with the sharp profile was the
square jaw, the deep-set eyes. Strong coloring, too.
The swarthy skin, the black as hell hair, the thick
brows, and the beard he needed to shave twice a day.
He was no dandy. But a rather big brute.

Ironic, that, since he had such sensibilities which led
him to draw and paint—and finally sculpt. He had always been athletic, too. A good horseman. A better
sailor.

A finer sculptor. Or so he believed.

An excellent portraitist. Or so he'd been told. But he
had never believed any of the praise because he could
not perform the penultimate task of a true artist: he
could not paint himself.

As he looked in the mirror now though, he grew curious. The intensity in his features had never interested
him. Those were attributes he accepted as God-given,
permanent. They also lured women. When he painted
himself, he had always used oils, black and gray, relieved by a few splashes of white. A chiaroscuro like a

Baroque portrait. He had never liked himself that way. Somehow, never thought the portrait complete—and had no inkling of what to add.

The vividness of his coloring struck him now. Why did he see himself suddenly in a palette that included the bronze of his skin, and the green of his eyes and the red hot need of his desire for Cerise Lindsay?

Had he viewed himself in only one portion of the spectrum? Had he not seen the total personality of the flesh and blood man before him? Was that why he could not find praise for his works? Had he lived that way, too? In only one portion of his soul?

Perhaps he had. Especially when it came to relationships with other people.

Certainly with women he had remained aloof.

Oh, he had had many affairs. Liaisons which lasted days or weeks. One went on for more than six months. All occurred on the Continent, most in France, either years ago when he studied there, or since when he visited to buy art.

One of his affairs had been with a Russian émigré, a widowed grand duchess of elegant tastes and a rapacious appetite for his attentions. That affair had been his most recent and his last when he ended it more than a year ago. When he had returned this past November to Paris, she had sent round her card with an invitation to dine, but he had declined. He had been celibate since he left her—and he liked it that way. He preferred solitude to the companionship of a woman who wished to dominate him.

All of his other affairs had been with women who could not play for power. Did not know how. Most were models, women for whom their body was the only ware they had to show and sell. Women who came from the working classes with little education, few prospects for a secure future. Women who had an

extreme physical beauty of face or a haunting volup-
tuousness of form. Women who possessed proportions
that aroused artists' inspiration or interpretation.
Women who learned how to stroll about chilly ateliers
naked for hours, pose for days in the most beguiling
and often erotic, sometimes even lewd, positions, that
artists might learn the contour and function of their
flesh. And at night, they learned the extent of their audience's appreciation of their efforts. Often such appreciation led to continuous work, a long-term
relationship with the artist, who if he were talented in
his rendering of her, could make his model famous,
too.

Blake had never had an affair with any woman of his
class or country. In that, he observed the gentleman's
code. English women of Victoria's court were brought
up to be modest, ignorant of sensuality, sometimes
downright repugnant of sexuality. Perhaps that ensured
their virtue. It certainly kept their husbands assured
that their heirs were legitimate.

Blake had only occasionally thought about getting an
heir. He was of marriageable age, established socially,
and set financially, a target for many a matron's efforts
to settle her chick with him. But he allowed himself a
few years yet before he needed to chose a mate with
whom he would do his duty and sire a child. He liked
women, but as he had told Cerise yesterday, he had not
actively searched for one whose characteristics suited
him. He had been too busy, keeping his estate prosper-
ous, dabbling in buying and selling art when his own
artistic ambitions proved to be no more than vanity.

Meanwhile, after the death of his father, he took on
the rearing of his younger brother and sister. He enjoyed the role, perhaps at first for its total power, but at
the age of eighteen, had not been inclined to be affec-
tionate, as their father had been.

John and Barbara had not enjoyed his rule. They saw him as cool, rational, "a soggy bit of old toast," Barbara had yelled at him once. Even though he had been sympathetic and supportive of John's academic bent and Barbara's artistic one, Barbara had married too young—perhaps to escape him—and John had been unable to marry the woman he wanted because Blake forbade him.

Had John's desertion of him—and Barbara's suicide—shown Blake that love was an emotion one proved with acts and words? Heaven knew with Cerise Lindsay he tried to show and declare often how dearly he wanted her.

Now he shocked himself with his willingness to show her just how badly he needed her.

By not taking her to bed.

He laughed at himself in the mirror.

"What a joke, Hargrove. You want her. Persuade her for days to trust in you, and when you finally achieve it, you cannot take your prize. Why?"

Because you told her you wanted to become more noble.

To be worthy of her, yes.

He had told her she was different from any woman he had known before. She asked for nothing from him but the truth. She did not try to manipulate him to her needs but stated what she required.

She had been his greatest challenge.

And she would become his treasure.

His finest one.

So he could not take her to bed on Sandown, could he?

He had to marry her first.

Because he loved her.

10

❧❧❧❧

Show me an angel and I will paint you one.

Gustave Courbet

Sunday trudged by slow as a turtle. After Blake finished signing the invitations Jameson had penned, he sent the man off to draft a cable to his housekeeper on Sandown to prepare for the event. He wanted her to review her notes about last year's weekend party and learn what she had served, when, to whom, and what entertainments they had each day and night.

He told her to notify the Sandown staff to refresh their memories of last August. Since then, he had promoted one footman to pantry butler, and lost the services of one maid. Temporarily, he had the butler return to his job, while he asked the housekeeper to search for the former maid and rehire her if she could. At any price. Blake wanted every one of his staff to man the same posts, serve the same guests as they had last year.

Then, he himself sat at his desk with pen and paper to refresh his own memory. He started with an outline of the days, filled in what major events he recalled, then began to jot notes of little things. Snatches of conversations. His guests' attitudes, remarks, glances. Their affections or the lack for any of the others in the party.

The exercise cleared his brain, lowered his anxiety.

Unfortunately, it unearthed nothing startling.

Most of his guests at the event were true sailors. Enthusiasts who lived for the regattas at Cowes in August when Bertie would come down, sail about on his own skiff, and take huge parties of his set out for bacchanals on his yacht, the *Serapis*. Blake invited his own guests because they had gone to Cambridge with him or enjoyed his art collection or his incomparable scenery.

Ben Woodward, the American, had lavished his attentions on Maddie and then later another lady in the group, a debutante with a lineage as old as Blake's and just as illustrious. As the weekend wore on, the girl turned her affections toward another bachelor, an older man with blue English blood in his veins. Matthew and Lily Pierce would attend Sandown this year as man as wife.

Most of the weekend, Blake's brother John had been petulant, following Maddie around like a wounded pup, until Saturday when John told him she had accepted his proposal.

Georgianna and Robert Dungarvon had enjoyed themselves tremendously that weekend—at least in the beginning. Georgie, for all her coquettish ways, doted on her husband, and the man wore the attention like a benevolent emperor wears his laurel wreath. Blake had invited the couple, not only because they were gregarious, but also because Robert was attempting to agent a sale of a Bernini bust from its Italian owner to an English collector. Robert wished to examine Blake's fine collection of Berninis at Sandown in order to deter-

mine the price his client should offer. Robert had done
so and been blissful, it seemed, until the day of the supper party on the shore. Robert and Georgie had had a
falling out while Robert was stinking drunk in the middle of the day. The two of them argued so loudly while
standing on the front lawn that the housekeeper grumbled to him about their lack of decorum. Georgie put
an end to the spectacle by stalking off to ride one of
Blake's mares for the afternoon. Where she went,
Blake did not know, but she did not reappear until well
into the dessert course that evening. Robert had disappeared for the afternoon, Blake thought, to his room to
sober up. Blake did not see Robert until dinner.

Yet, Elizabeth Elgin was the most vivid character
Blake recalled from that weekend. Polite as he had always been, she tolerated him. Barely. So clear was it to
his guests that Woody had been moved to comment, to
which Blake merely shook his head.

"No wonder poor Maddie is skittish as a mustang,"
Woody concluded on Friday morning over breakfast.
"Lady Elgin would frighten a Comanche."

"Has she driven you off, Woody?"

"The coy countess of Rossborough has done that
herself, my friend. Yesterday, she told me after leading
me about for months with the bit in my mouth, that
she's chosen a man. I'll look in other pastures for my
mare."

Blake had not known until the next afternoon that
Maddie had accepted John. Still, Blake had winced at
Woody's imagery.

"What? Does my anger show?"

"Woody, if you mean to take home an English girl,
you need to understand their sensibilities are different."

Perhaps his failure to take Blake's advice was the reason the American still lacked a bride.

Woody had shot out of his chair. "She led me on. No woman does that to me." He threw down his napkin and left the dining room. Blake recalled that that evening, Woody seemed back in good spirits again.

Blake tapped his pen against his list. He'd keep this out, continue to think about those days on Sandown, and to add any other tidbits which might come to mind.

He went to bed Sunday night and slept more soundly than he had the previous one.

Monday morning, he summoned his four footmen before him, handed over the invitations and charged them with their delivery. Each servant took a horse from the stable and had orders to deliver the large envelopes embossed with the Sandown crest of doves and coronet.

"I do not trust these to Her Majesty's post, but to the four of you to safely deliver into the hands of each house's butler. Thank you, you may go," he said and returned to his study. He closed the door and tried not to brood over the town's reaction. Especially Lady Elgin's.

By two o'clock, he could wait no longer to know. He called for his butler to have his gray brought round, ready to ride on the Row. Mondays were the premier day to appear. It was the opening of the week, and the Season's debutantes took to their mounts if they cut a fine figure on a horse, or if not, to their open landaus.

He hoped to catch a word with Cerise. If she came. And if she did, he prayed she would not be escorted by her harpy of an aunt.

"Outrageous!" Aunt Elizabeth threw the invitation across Cerise's study. She had just returned from brunch with Georgie, who had received a similar invitation at home. Georgie had come with her mother, dressed to accompany Cerise to the Row. "How *dare* he even think we would darken his doorstep."

Cerise had expected her aunt's reaction and stood, her riding crop tapping against her boot. "I am going, Aunt Elizabeth."

"You condone it," the lady said, her words venom. "You have met him, encouraged him. He has pursued you, made a laughing stock of you at your debut and . . . and what else? Tell me. What else?"

"Aunt Elizabeth, I ask you not to continue in this vein. I am going to Sandown. I must."

"To be seduced by that . . . that *viper.*"

"Why do you dislike him so?"

"Ahhhh!" She brandished an arm. "He has won. Don't you see what his plan is?"

"Yes. I do."

"To get you to his home. Wight is no place for Society until August. He is a cad taking you there—"

"Inviting me, us." She pulled on her gloves. "I think it very generous. Very wise."

"Wise?" Elizabeth's eyes narrowed. "Why?"

"The earl of Sandown duplicates the weekend that Maddie died."

Elizabeth's face fell. Her body might have been marble.

"He does this for me. That I might relive Maddie's last days."

"Oh, my God," Elizabeth breathed. "There is no limit to the man's audacity."

"Yes, he is bold. I admire that." *I will emulate it.*

"You disgrace yourself."

"To discover what happened to my sister?" She shook her head. "To see where she died? How?" *Why.*

"Maddie died because she was upset when she cast off and she could not handle the squall."

"I doubted that in September when I came home and read the police and coroner's reports, and I doubt it even more since I've come to London."

"Your inquiry only drags out the time when you should be recovering from Maddie's loss. You must come to terms with it, you know. You must cry. You have not shed one tear. You must—"

"In good time, yes." Risa thrust up a hand. "But I will learn why Maddie acted so strangely. Having a safety deposit box under an assumed name. Yes . . . shocking, isn't it?" Risa debated, even now, if she should reveal that there had been cash in the box.

"You did not tell me," her aunt whispered.

And you did not ask if I discovered anything new after I told you I was going to the Chelsea Masonry Bank to see if it could open the deposit box owned by M. Rossborough. Why? Don't you care? "No. I have kept these things to myself. I did not wish to deal with your reactions."

"Was there anything inside the box?"

"Cash. More than five thousand pounds."

Elizabeth put a hand to her chest. Swallowed. "What have you done with it?"

"Nothing."

"But—"

"Oh, I tell you my fingers itch to grab it and pay off most of my loan. But no. I will not spend it until I learn where and how Maddie got it. And that's that." Risa glanced at Georgie, who remained flush against the study doors, stiff as a corpse. "I am going riding. Will you come, Georgie, or will you stay with your mother?"

"You cannot go alone," her aunt objected.

"I will do . . ." Risa replied distinctly, "as I wish." *See Blake, draw him, sculpt him. Daily. To feed my own desire to work—and show others a strong and sensitive man.* "If you are not coming, Georgie, I can take my maid."

"No, I'll come. Let's . . . let's go. It will be all right, Mama." She went over to buss her on the cheek.

"The hell it will!" Her curse riveted Risa and Georgie for a second. "After this Sandown event, the de Ros' will never be able to hold their heads up in polite society again." She sailed forward, reached for Risa's hand. "I beg you, do not do this to us, Cerise."

"I must." Risa shrugged her off. "I owe it to Maddie."

Her aunt looked desolate. "You are going to sell Hargrove Allure, aren't you?"

"What?" This rocked Risa.

"Mr. McCordle told me you have begun legal proceedings to be able to sell our collection. Hargrove wants Allure and he will take it from us, won't he? The wretch. The—"

"You went to see Mr. McCordle? Why did you do that?"

"I had business of my own with him yesterday. An investment I wish to liquidate. The subject of the collection came up. He was surprised—" She folded her hands. "—that you had not told me what you'd done."

Risa had no desire to justify it to her. "It is not done yet, Aunt Elizabeth. And Allure still stands here, does she not?"

"Not for long if Hargrove has his way."

"I will not discuss this any longer." Risa put her hand to the doorknob.

"Don't do this, Cerise. Please. Do not go to Sandown."

She spun on her aunt. "I will go. Come if you like, or stay here. I will learn how and why Maddie died." Tears stung her eyes. "I fear she gained some of this money to spend on me. I fear she may have died because of it. I will continue whether you like it or not."

*   *   *

Blake took up a post at a crook in the road and waited more than an hour. He prepared to leave, so disappointed Cerise was not coming that he felt like an
addict denied his daily dose. He flicked his reins, but
drew up, cheered when he saw Georgie Dungarvon—
and then Cerise.

Both rode black geldings. Georgie wore red. But
Cerise captured him, shimmering like a mermaid from
the sea in an aquamarine riding outfit that made her
complexion white as snow, and beneath her tiny toque,
her hair flamed like sunfire.

"Good afternoon, my lord Sandown," Georgie inclined her head. "Lovely day, don't you think?"

"Stunning," he told her but gazed at Cerise. "You
look well." *Ravishing.*

"And you, my lord," she gave him a watery smile.

"We received your invitation," Georgie offered.
"Robert and I are pleased to accept."

"I am thrilled." He waited for Cerise to do it more.

"I will come, too," she told him in a voice that held a
rasp.

Alarmed, he examined her closely. Had she been crying? "I will endeavor to show you a wonderful holiday,
my lady."

Her mouth parted in a firmer smile. "I know you
will, my lord."

"And your aunt—" He could wait no longer to
know. "—does she come as well?"

"She has not yet decided," Cerise said simply. Yet
whatever Lady Elgin had said, Blake would set good
odds was not so simple.

"I will speak for my mother when I predict she will
be honored to come again this year," Georgie stepped
into the breach. But clearly, that was all she would provide in the way of information.

He rode with them both for a few minutes, but the

opportunity to talk intimately with Cerise never came. Rather than torment himself, he bid them goodbye, doffed his hat and trotted home.

He would have to wait until tomorrow at eleven to see her again—and the torture of not knowing what her problems might be, eroded his composure.

How could he possibly wait for three weeks to have her near to hand from dawn to dusk?

"Good morning, my lady," Blake bid Cerise, trying to remain merely polite the next day when he saw her in the back room among the naked statuary in Bartholome's shop. He had not slept well again last night, worried about her.

She responded with a nod, a welcome in her eyes, but not upon her lips.

"Are you well?" he asked, smitten by the sight of her. She was a confection in dark chocolate crushed satin, iced in swirling *passementerie* of thick vanilla. He mentally licked it from her skin.

"Perfectly," she said in a severe tone that told him he was in trouble with her.

God, hadn't he known that most of last night?

He smothered a chuckle. "What did I do, sweetheart?" Damn him, if she did not drain his brain of rational thought. Throughout last night, his rest was deep but short, brimming with dreams. In each one, he undressed her languidly, each tenderness a lure to heighten her desire for him—and sate his for her. In each one, she responded with an abandon that had him hard with wanting when he'd awakened.

Three weeks. What absurdity.

Patience was a virtue he had never cultivated for a woman.

Yet, he smiled. Now he cultivated it for himself as well. To become that nobler man.

From the guest list to the *blancmange* on the dessert menu, he would duplicate the five day event. If he could recall the conversations, he would make his guests recite them, too. Everything would be as it was last August first.

Except when it came time for supper, Cerise was not going to sail away. There was no need for her to take Maddie's part. Did she even know how to man a sail? No matter, he would not permit it. Heaven forbid something happened to her. The very possibility swept through him like a tidal wave. He could not lose her. Not for any reason. Not for a lifetime. Not for a day.

But he would wait to have her.

Knowing her had changed him.

"It's ten past eleven," she scolded him, failing to pretend indifference in front of the approaching clerk.

"No matter the time of day, you look good enough to eat, darling," Blake whispered, lifting a coral carving of an Indian goddess. "A truffle, I think, in that outfit."

That broke her and she tried not to laugh. "I thought you were scrumptious the other day at the zoo."

"Only then?"

She chastised him with a roll of opalescent eyes, then went for her target. "What delayed you today?"

"Lack of sleep."

"Bad dreams?"

"Delicious ones, counting my breaths until I could see you again. Until I could learn why you sounded so drained yesterday. If your aunt is haranguing you—Ah, good morning, young man." Blake hailed the clerk who scurried before them. "I am here to see *Monsieur* Bartholome."

"I'm sorry, milord, he hasn't arrived yet this morning. Is there something I can help you with?"

"When will he be in?"

"I don't know that, milord. When he's indisposed, he'll usually send round a note, but he hasn't today. I opened the gallery." The clerk straightened his cravat with flighty fingers and smiled apologetically.

Risa picked up a statuette of a nymph, feigning interest in it.

"I see. Perhaps then, you can help me." Blake set his walking stick against a display table and removed his gloves. "I wonder if *monsieur* has found the listing for the sale of a painting. Last year. An oil by Edward Ritter."

Risa looked at Blake as if he were a genius.

"Ritter. I don't think I know of any paintings by such an artist."

Blake recounted Ritter's affiliation with Hans Holbein.

"If *monsieur* did find it, he did not tell me."

"A pity," Blake responded. "If he had, I would have paid significantly to buy it. Ritter is becoming popular."

"He is?"

"You had not heard?" Blake queried, pretending disdain.

"No, sir. I . . . Wait . . . I remember . . . The two of you were here a few days ago, weren't you?" The clerk looked so pleased with himself. "Yes. You wanted to know about your sister, didn't you, milady?"

Cerise replaced the nymph. "Yes. Do you remember her? The countess of Rossborough?"

"Yes, milady, I do. Nice, she was. Always treated me well. Some don't, you know. Think I am, well . . . I am just the clerk."

"Did you ever notice anything unusual about her?" Cerise pressed, drawing near to Blake and inspiring that burst of hunger for her whenever she was close.

"How do you mean?" the clerk asked, his little eyes blinking like a bird's in his eagerness to please.

"I can't say," Cerise waved a hand. "I was hoping you could tell us something."

Blake noted that she used the plural *us*. He grew concerned that the clerk would note this confirmation of their companionship. But the clerk did not bat a lash—and Blake breathed more freely.

That Cerise accepted him as part of her was not just a triumph to Blake, but a comfort . . . and a lure. A triumph that she cared for him enough to automatically speak of herself with him as a unit. A comfort that she recognized his kindness for what it was—a desire to be with her and help her solve Maddie's mysteries. A desire so strong, he spent his many minutes jotting down every snatch of conversation he could recall with Maddie, so that he might solve this puzzle with Cerise and move on to the exciting prospect of enjoying himself with her and courting her.

Not seducing her.

And please God, marrying her soon. But even that prospect had him gritting his teeth. September was the accepted month for weddings. That seemed an eternity away.

Where was his patience?

Gone. Deserting him. Again.

His eyes betrayed him and fell over her profile. Aphrodite with an up-turned nose, and those full, pouting breasts. She was, quite simply, the most sensuous creature he had ever seen. This morning at breakfast, he found himself playing in his own butter—drawing her face. The first time he'd sketched in over five years.

And if his skills were rusty, his imagination was not. Desire to draw her again and again leaped into his conscious mind like an animal set free from a cage. He went to his study, took out pen and ink, drew, but threw his effort away. She deserved a skilled artist to

capture her beauty, just as she deserved a strong man to
encourage her in pursuit of her own art.

And I am that man.

He grinned.

She caught it, even though she had been deep in
conversation with the clerk. She frowned up at Blake,
and when he cocked a brow, she returned to her discussion.

Blake wished to hurry her along. He not only had to
know about her aunt's reaction, but he wanted to tell
her all he'd done. He also wanted to learn what her social schedule was for the next few weeks. He had no intention of waiting until she arrived at Sandown to see
her. Sunday had been too long without her, and yesterday's brief encounter only put him on a rack. He did
not intend to suffer any more than necessary.

She was smiling at the clerk, her generous mouth
curving up in a warm smile.

My God. This charming creature would be his wife.

If she'll have you.

Would she?

Only if she loves you, Hargrove.

"What do you think?" Cerise beamed up at him.

"I think we should leave," he reached for his walking
stick, hat, and gloves.

She didn't like that answer. "About coming back tomorrow to see *Monsieur* Bartholome. To ask him about
the Ritter," she prodded.

"Oh, yes, of course. We will. Tomorrow."

"Right you are, milord. *Monsieur* will have returned
by then. He's not hardly ever ill."

Blake bid him goodbye, then took Cerise's arm when
she finished lowering her veil.

"What was the matter with you in there?" she asked
when the shop door had closed behind them and they
were heading for their respective cabs. "You were so

mysterious and then suddenly you were . . . I don't know . . . wool gathering."

"Happens to me often these past few days."

"Hmmm," she muttered, unhappy with him still. She put on her gloves, smoothed the fingers. "I thought he knew more about Maddie than he said. Did you?"

He paused at a street light and gave her a wobbly smile. "Darling, I confess I was not listening."

"Not like you to be preoccupied. Was it," she speculated, "something he said?"

"Something I want."

"What?"

"I must not tell you on the street."

She glanced about. "Where?"

He chuckled. He took her elbow and led her around a corner. It led to a service alley and no one was about. So he said be damned to the daylight and the possibilities that someone might see them. He circled an arm around her waist and branded her lips with his. The net of her veil abraded him.

But she was more than soft. More than warm. She was so willing that she pressed herself against him, her tongue touching his through the veil.

"Oh," she sighed against his mouth when she was done, "I thought I was going to have to wait for three weeks for this." She licked her lower lip and made his blood hammer in his veins. "Thank you," she said as if she had tasted peppermint candy. "I needed that."

"So did I." He kissed her again, backed away, all business now he had his ration of her for the day. "What was your aunt's reaction to my invitation?"

"She was furious. We had a terrible row. She forbade me to come."

"And?"

"I told her I would. She fears it will cause a scandal."

"Only a choice bone to chew that I duplicate last August's event."

"Yes." Her gaze avoided his.

"Why is that a problem for her?" *Doesn't she want to clarify what happened to Maddie?*

"She says you wish to seduce me as you did Maddie."

"And why does she think," he asked, his blood boiling, "I would do that?"

"Because you want to buy Allure."

"I haven't asked."

"She thinks you have."

He scowled. "Why would she think that?"

"Because she went to see the family solicitor yesterday morning. She went to conduct business of her own. While she was there, she learned from him that I have asked him to look into changing the terms of how the de Ros art is owned. I want to sell Allure. I have a large loan to pay. I need money. Since you were the primary prospect to buy Allure, she thinks you are still interested."

"And she thinks I will use any means to buy it." He shook his head. "I'll be damned. I have never been so maligned by anyone." He stilled. "Do you believe her?"

"No," she whispered, "I believe in you." And then she pressed the most innocent kiss to his lips to prove it. "I'm coming to Sandown—and in the meantime, I am escaping society and my aunt by doing what I need. I am sculpting in the tack room. I had hopes you might come . . ." She walked her fingers up his coat buttons to his mouth, where she traced the outline. ". . . and model for me. Tonight after dinner. At nine?"

He did feel like that gladiator now. Savage and conquering. He pulled her into his arms again. "What would you like me to wear?"

She tilted her head, the visions that danced in her brain enticing him, making them both grin.

"Come in whatever you like. I'll give you what I think is appropriate."

He breathed fiercely. "Which is?"

She chuckled. "A sheet?"

"I'll blush."

"Will you? I rather thought you couldn't."

He thought that over. Had knowing her made him innocent again? No, no one could unlearn the bawdy sophistication he had acquired. But Cerise made him feel young and fresh and spirited. With her, he felt as if he should blush. And that stirred his desire for her to high pitch. No woman had ever offered such an erotic proposition to him and caught his imagination as strongly.

"I am capable," he told her, "of many things you do not know about." *Love. Marriage. Devotion.*

Her gaze danced across his features. "I hope I am, too," she breathed.

He was nigh unto dizzy with the need to hear her explanation. "Of what?"

Her hand wended down his chest, to his waist and rested on the hollow beside his hip bone. "To sculpt you . . ." She swallowed. ". . . nude." Her lovely eyes locked with his. "I told you I wanted to be bold."

He realized she was asking for his cooperation. "If I encourage you, I fail to reach my own goal." Indeed, any nobility he hoped to achieve would be gone the minute he touched her like a lover.

"But you already did."

"My past with women has not been—"

"I didn't mean that."

He stepped back, out of her reach. "What then?"

She was blushing now. "I meant you are honest. You have principles. Scruples."

"More of them where you are concerned."

She beamed. "Yes. I think that's true."

He smiled back at her. She had the high color and bearing of a woman who knew she was cherished. That look he had seen on many women's faces. Women he had favored with his attentions. But never with his adoration. "I think you'd better go home, darling. Make certain your studio is in order."

"Be on time. I hate waiting for you." She stood on tiptoe, kissed him deeply, all too briefly, and then she strode off, somewhat wobbly in her stride.

He watched her, silly as a boy in love for the first time, as she raised her hand, hailed her cab, and rode away.

The irony of her decision had him chuckling to himself. She had become bold. And he had to become even more noble to brave it and not make love to her in her studio.

As each second ticked by, September became a less and less reasonable month to marry.

Minutes afterward at home, he curtailed his moonstruck attitude with a determination equal to the task before him. To make the weekend party a useful recreation for Cerise, he had three long letters to write.

He sat down at his desk in his study and wrote personal notes to the constable, the coroner, and the judge on the Isle of Wight. In each, he informed them that Madelaine Lindsay's sister was coming to his home May fifth and would they mind receiving her so that she might ask a few questions of them regarding her sister's death?

The constable was a boyhood friend of Blake's. They had gone sailing and fishing together each school holiday that Blake came home to Sandown. Arnold Crowley usually caught more fish than Blake, who went to sea more for the danger of riding the waves than the pride of catching fish.

Blake had seen Maddie's body that next morning
after the supper on the shore. Arnie had found her,
south of Sandown spread out upon the beach.

Maddie was discovered, caught among the broken
planks of her boat, tangled in seaweed draped about
her battered body as it dashed against the rocks a mile
from where she'd cast off.

Blake could recall Arnie's words, quite vivid in his
language, about how he found her that morning.

"Laying on her back, peaceful as if someone'd laid
her down. Her one hand was to one side, her other
over her bosom. If it weren't for the gray look of her
skin and the poor bruising she took about the head and
chest, she could have been napping on the beach."

Napping. Would to God she had been.

Arnie had been thorough in his investigation of
Maddie's death, interrogating every one of Blake's
guests and staff. Arnie had gained much admiration for
his politeness. Upper class English society looked
down its stiff nose at officers of the peace. So admiration after such an ordeal was a triumph for Arnie.

"An amiable fellow," more than one of Blake's guests
had mumbled at the end of the day of questioning.

No such commendation came to their lips for the
judge who presided over the inquest two days following the discovery of Maddie's body. Sir Giles Evelyn
was seventy years of age and wrinkled but showing
every bit of his starch. On the stand in the village of
Sandown's tiny hall of justice, the elderly man presided
with a cantankerous discipline. Sir Evelyn had been
trained to his profession in London, and by his de-
meanor and with his stentorian voice, never let anyone
forget it. He had asked some very pointed questions of
Blake.

After Maddie's Aunt Elizabeth had broken into tears
and criticized him on the stand for failing to dissuade

Maddie from sailing away, Evelyn asked Blake about the condition of Maddie's sailboat.

"Had you noticed any defects in that sailboat?"

"No, sir. I checked all eight that I own, the week before, as I usually did before my annual weekend party."

"Did you have any trepidations about your guests using any of the boats?"

"No, sir. None at all."

"My lord, you knew a squall lay offshore, did you not?"

"Yes, sir. I heard the thunder as the countess of Rossborough and I were standing on the dock. I am sad to say that I warned the countess not to go out on the water, but I did not try to stop her. I take that failure to my grave."

Blake rose from his desk, reaffirming his vow then to make up for his sin of omission in a valid way. He would discover why Maddie was so irrational that night in her argument with him. Why she was so determined to marry his brother. He wondered even now.

And the old feeling that she hid something from them all resurfaced.

Dear God, man. You are like a dog with a bone.

Everything was so unrelated. So illogical. It tormented him then—and now. His guilt over not inspecting her boat, her revelations that night before she cast off, the mysteries Cerise had discovered of safety deposit box and the cash inside added up to . . . what?

Only this growing fear that he had missed something vital in his remembrance of last August.

Madelaine Lindsay had been outraged with him that he would not bless his brother John marrying her. He had been shocked to his soul when she drowned. Never thought there was any foul play to her death until afterward when he started to think about Deville and Bartholome.

Now, some thought she may have committed suicide. Diana Cliveden did. But he'd thought Maddie had gotten caught in a storm she could not navigate. At least, he had thought that at first.

Was that more a literal metaphor than an actual one?

Was Maddie involved in something else with Bartholome and Deville that she could not escape? Why else did she know such disreputable men? Men who made their living in art, but did it in a less than honest method. If Maddie were involved with them in any kind of venture that was dishonest, what did that have to do with her death at Sandown? Miles away from her home, from Bartholome, Deville, and Paris.

Whatever else there was, the fact remained that when he left Maddie casting off, he was angry and so was she.

The other fact was that a faulty hull or sail were the only causes Blake could have suspected for Maddie drowning. Maddie was too adept with a sail. She bragged about it as her only talent, while her sister had a more viable one. Other people confirmed that Maddie was a superb sailor. Otherwise, Blake would have forbade her to sail. He knew a squall was coming. He could see it on the horizon, an umber rolling mass.

But you were too angry that she had agreed to marry John. Manipulated him into proposing to her, running away with her.

He had worried about her when she did not return to come to the supper party on shore. But he had not worried enough to inquire of her maid if Maddie had come into the house and gone to bed.

On the contrary, he went to his suite and tried to sleep. He did, exhausted over his discussion with John and then his argument with Maddie.

But Blake's anger died quickly the next morning

when Arnie found her body washed up on the shore and called them down to identify her. His grief was soon accompanied by guilt at his failure to stop her from sailing. Then, he began to brood over Maddie's outbursts to him.

His shock over her violent death multiplied at the grizzly knowledge that her body had to be autopsied to determine cause of death.

Blake ran a hand over his eyes now. The last letter he must write was to the coroner.

Doctor William Viner was the most acid-tongued physician Blake had ever met. Fortunately, Blake nor his household were rarely ill. Viner, local rumors had it by way of Blake's housekeeper, had been a physician in London at St. Margaret's Lying In Hospital. He had sold his practice in Harley Street a year ago in the spring, in the interest of taking his wife from the capital city. Mrs. Viner had contracted a nervous disorder that drove up her blood pressure, and sought the serenity on Wight.

Doctor Viner purchased a cottage in Sandown, thereby becoming the only physician residing on the island, save for one in Cowes upon whom the royal family often called.

Sir Evelyn had insisted on an autopsy of Maddie's body in accordance with the law for all accidental or sudden deaths. Lady Elgin had become hysterical, insisting it was a sacrilege to cut up her niece when they all knew what had happened to her. She had drowned.

Viner had withstood the invectives of the grieving and irascible aunt, and quickly done his duty. He confirmed that Maddie had died with air in her lungs. Or rather just one lung. The other was crushed. Viner conjectured that this had been caused by the boat battering against her chest.

No one had ever questioned him. Why should they?

What she had probably been doing, said the coroner's report, was trying to swim with one broken leg and a collapsed lung, while clutching one of the planks. Perhaps for hours. He knew because he found splinters imbedded in her chest. And water in her left lung.

She had been angry. She had drowned.

The evidence pointed to it.

The circumstances pointed to other mysteries leading up to the time of her death.

Blake had known that. Felt that.

Cerise had proof her sister had acted strangely. But she did not believe Maddie had the ability or desire to kill herself.

As Blake recalled his last words with Maddie, he agreed that the woman who stepped into that boat that night was too angry to ever commit suicide. So if she had not drowned, how had she died? Why?

If he and Cerise could answer that, they might put this investigation to rest.

And God knew, he wished for the speedy end to it.

He had a woman to woo and wed.

11

Is my nose really a little crooked?

Louis XIV of France to his brother
upon viewing Bernini's bust of him

"You're early." Risa was chuckling as she opened the door of the tack room to Blake that night. "Take your coat off, and your cravat too. I will hang them here and build the fire higher, too, so you won't catch cold."

"And what is this?" Blake asked about her attire of tunic and trousers of linen.

"My working clothes. You've never seen them? In Ambrusco's, all the students wore them, men and women."

"I've never seen you in them. Charming."

"Useful."

For work—and play.

Forcing down his erotic thoughts, Blake glanced around her little room in the stable of her Park Lane townhouse. He had come to the back door as she told him. He did want to remain discreet about their meeting, but he feared her aunt might arrive and raise a ruckus. He was wary of the woman to the point that he wondered if she would use such knowledge to injure Cerise among Society.

"Cerise, I am concerned about the propriety of me coming here." *Not enough to stay away, but still.* . . . He let her lead him by both hands farther into the tiny room where she had covered the only window with a sheet and placed a desk, and a chair to one corner.

"Don't. I have told my aunt that if she does not approve of me—"

"She knows, then, that you invited me here?"

"Yes, I have nothing to hide, Blake. I want to draw you. You are going to give me the Carrara at Sandown, and I must be ready. Be worthy of it." Her complexion was paler than normal.

"Darling," he cupped her shoulders and stepped against her. Warm and soft but oh, so strong, her body fit his as if she'd been designed for him alone. Beneath her linen, she wore—the good Lord bolster his patience—nothing but another layer, a camisole, maybe knickers. But no corset. And his need to have her physically drove him on. "We can wait for this modeling. Wait for your visit to Sandown where I can trust my servants to a fault."

"But I can't wait. You know it. I must practice sketching and building a clay and then a plaster model before I ever touch the Carrara. That will take me days, weeks. Perhaps all these weeks between now and your party."

"I don't want your aunt arguing with you because of me."

"A lost cause, I'm afraid. Oh, yes, I care about her opinion of me, Blake, I won't deny it. But I want to sculpt. You encouraged me to. Now—" She was staunch and yet so vulnerable. "—will you deny me?"

"No," he brought her close, buried his lips in her sweet-smelling hair, which tonight flowed loose about

her shoulders like a fairy queen's. He caught up hand-
fuls of the gossamer and thrilled to the fantasy she
wove around him. "Not I." He looked down at her. "I
have longed for you since you left me this morning."

So he chained his passion for her and kissed her. An
artless meeting of mouths meant to enchant her, meant
to please him, never tempt him to greater intimacies.
But as was the case with her, he saw his control slip
with each moment he embraced her. His hands roam-
ing the gentle curve of her spine, he silently praised
her for her lack of corset and whale bones so that he
might be tortured by the lush pressure of her breasts to
his body. He felt the urge rise to strip her of the linen
and find what delights her naked skin might offer. Yet,
he knew nobility did not come with such abandon and
he tore himself away.

"Mmmm," she kept her eyes closed, a smile curving
her lips. "I'd ask you to do that again, but I doubt I'd
be in the mood to work."

He grunted. Pulled away from her to walk about.
"You've gotten rid of the tack."

"I had the stable boy store it in the main stable. I
told him to set up a few bales of hay for a modeling
platform, too. I covered it with a blanket and a soft
sheet. I wanted you to be comfortable while you do
this."

"Darling, I shall be anything but comfortable."

"Oh, but you must try." She looked stricken. "How
can you pose for me for hours if you are not relaxed
and, oh . . ." She dropped her jaw as he removed his
weskit and began to undo the studs of his shirt. As he
finished the last to let the shirt gape open, she swallowed. Loudly.

He draped his shirt and vest over her chair, walked
forward, so full of pride he could impress her so. "Do
all your models affect you this way?"

"No." She touched her tongue to her upper lip, mesmerized. Her gaze left his face, probably for good, he thought wryly as he watched her learn the contours of his chest and ribs and drift back up to define his shoulders. He recalled the first time he'd seen her and she had put her hands all over the Adonis, and he had wanted her then to do the same to him. She walked around and around him now, as if he were the finest piece of sculpture. Finally, she traced a fingertip down his bare chest to his trouser band. "None of them was you."

Her first touch took his breath. And as if an electrical charge ran through her, she snatched her hand away.

He recognized her words were the same declaration he had made to her at the Clivedens' days ago. He saw her shiver, then press her thighs together. If he could do this to her minus only his shirt, what could he do for her without a stitch? His mouth watered. "But you've seen naked male models before?"

"Mmm-hmm," was all she was able to say as her gaze drifted down his chest time and again.

"Well, then, we are safe."

She seemed pained. "We are? From what?"

"Shocking you."

"Oh . . . you . . . definitely . . . do not shock me."

He reached for her hand and put it to his chest. "You set me on fire." She blushed and tried to pull away, but he shook his head. "You may touch me. You will have to, you see, because I think you have just turned me to stone."

"You are the warmest stone," she whispered, spreading her fingers and caressing his torso.

The hardest stone.

"And rough," her fingers curled into the hair on his chest, "but smooth." She flowed closer and was trailing little kisses up his throat.

"And you," he warned, as he took her arms and stepped back, "are making me insane. Tell me where to stand, how to pose."

She crossed her arms. He had no idea if she had suddenly become objective or if she were restraining herself from touching him. "Move in any way that you normally do. I begin to understand you as a gentleman. Now I want to see you as a man."

"You won't render me as a gladiator?"

"No. Just you."

"You wish to carve a Carrara of the earl of Sandown?" He was skeptical. "No one will want one of me."

"And if I do?"

"Well, then." His breath lodged in his throat. *Could you want the flesh and blood man for all your life?* "You must have what you want."

"I do like you so when you indulge me."

He grinned, spread wide his arms. "Tell me what to do. How to stand. I am yours."

Her features radiated the purest joy he'd ever seen on any human face. "As I hoped," she said and led him to his makeshift dais where she placed him.

Where she kept him for another hour—and did not ask him to remove any more of his clothes. Nor could he for fear he'd ruin any of her sensibilities.

So he allowed her to twist him and turn him, this way and that, her fingers skimming his body, until his muscles ached and his loins throbbed.

Watching her examine him, feeling her touch him, position him, was akin to feeling a tidal wave build inside him, rise and roll him over and over. She drew him as she put him, then repositioned him for more. The delicious agony had him wild to end this—and dedicated to never leaving. She looked him in the eye, she surveyed him from head to waist, but no lower.

If she had, he wondered what her reaction would have been. He fantasized about it. Her open mouth, her heaving breasts. Her thighs, pressing together time and then again as she drew, as she stood, then stared at him, met his gaze—and saw and understood his torment. Then matched it with her own raw desire.

But she was disciplined. Perhaps, because she was a virgin in what was her first—and please God—only love affair, she could turn from the desire that sparked between them like lightning. Though he was grateful she did, lest he lose his own thin thread of control, he also rejoiced in her dedication. He saw it in her face as she rediscovered her love of her art. The way she bit her lip, donned her glasses, dashed lines across the paper, smudged, then redefined him as she wished. And he did not move, he did not complain, he did not register the strains or pains for all the satisfaction she brought him with her newfound devotion.

At the end of her spurt of work, an hour after they'd begun, she rolled her head on her shoulders, put down her red crayons and sketchbook and glasses, stood and walked toward him to help him from his stance to the floor.

"Come sit down," she led him to a stool and stood behind him to massage the muscles in his neck, his shoulders, arms, and back. He spun around and took her to his lap where he did the same for her.

"Will you want me again tomorrow night?"

"At nine." She sighed at his ministrations, her head falling back, her hair cascading over his arm like a red river, exposing her elegant throat. "You will come?"

"Any time you want me." He kissed the pulse throbbing at her throat. Skimmed her ribs up to her breast, and beneath the linen tunic he lifted one full breast, his urgings to undress her slicing through his discipline. She overflowed his hand and he groaned, imagining how beautiful she must be beneath the beige fabric. Soon, he'd know. Soon.

But not now.

He forced her to stand. Did so himself. Ran his hands into her hair. Like a hot curtain, her curls flowed around her. No work of art had ever been so lovely. "I must go," he turned away.

Her fingers circled his forearm. His name was on her lips. "Darling," she called him for the first time, "won't you kiss me before you go?"

"If I do—" He fought back the urge to do more than kiss her. "—I won't leave at all. Chin up," he said and lifted her face with two fingers. "Our abstinence won't be for long."

"How long?"

Until I am certain you love me. "Until we have enough time together to know clearly what we want from each other."

"It becomes clearer to me daily."

He hugged her. "With or without your glasses?"

She cuffed him.

"Dream of me," she said at the door when he had dressed.

"Always. What can I do to make certain you dream of me?"

Whimsical contentment gave her a languid look. "Promise to come back tomorrow night, prepared to remove your . . ." She arched her brows. ". . . shoes."

He chucked her chin. "You are becoming dangerous."

"I rather enjoy it, too. Tell me, do you like earbobs?"

"On you? Yes. Why?"

"I often said that to be perfectly happy, I could gladly wear nothing more than earbobs and . . . shoes."

"I await the day when I am treated to that sight. Goodnight," he pecked her on the cheek and got the hell out of her studio before he removed her clothes. "See you tomorrow morning at Bartholome's."

But Bartolome was not in.

Blake and she departed the man's shop, and this time Blake did not pull her to the alley to kiss her. And she missed the benediction of his lips.

She did not let it destroy her delight to have him come and model for her. So that night when he came again to remove his coat, weskit, cravat, and shirt—to pose, to do as she asked, to buss her sweetly on the cheek, and promise to meet her at Bartolome's at eleven the next day, she vowed to take matters into her own hands.

The next morning, Blake was already in the shop when she arrived. She sailed in, dressed in the aquamarine he had admired, prepared to launch her newest attack on his senses. She had sketched into the wee hours, unable to get Blake from her mind. She saw him as vulnerable, strong, the most human type of man to sculpt. The sweetest type to kiss. The best type to make a husband and a father. The kind of man a woman could admire, and influence to become nobler.

And she smiled that she had influenced Blake Hargrove to become that better man. She saw it in the tilt of his head, the authority of his stance, the command of his arm.

"Why, good morning, Lord Hargrove," she tried to appear merely congenial. "You look chipper today."

"Yes, thank you," he replied in a similar vein, as Bartholome's clerk paused in his chatter. "You look wonderful as well. I do like your earbobs."

"Thank you. A pair of my favorites."

"I say, they match your shoes, don't they?"

"Only in a certain light." She hid her grin when she

saw the clerk wrinkle a brow, puzzled at their exchange.

"I was talking to *monsieur*'s assistant and he is telling me that he is worried about Bartholome's continued illness." Blake was anxious, Risa could see. "I asked him if he went round to call on him."

"I did, sir. No one answered, sir."

"He might not be there at all," Risa replied.

The clerk shrugged.

"I would encourage you," Blake told him, "to go round again. He might need a cup of tea or a good scone to help him recover whatever his malady is. Good for your advancement, you know, to do that."

"Yes, sir, I will take your suggestion."

"Where does he live?"

"Bayswater Road, sir."

"The number?"

"One hundred and twenty."

"Not far away," Blake pulled on his gloves. "Why not take my suggestions? You won't be sorry."

"No, sir. You're right. I will."

Scant minutes later, Blake and she were in the street, frowning at each other.

"Let's go visit him ourselves." Risa told him, putting up her parasol.

"Not you."

"Why not?"

"It will look odd. A couple calling on a bachelor in the morning. Bayswater Road is not the best part of the city. And—"

"I don't care. I cannot let this go on. I must know about the Ritter," she insisted.

"I agree. I will go now. Alone. You go home."

She did not like it, but she did it. And fretted all day about what he would have learned from Bartholome.

* * *

That night after a silent Aunt Elizabeth had departed the dinner table, Ariel asked to be allowed to visit
the tack room, too. Cerise doubted the wisdom of it,
but agreed to let her sister come if she stayed for only a
few minutes. Risa needed to know about Bartholome.

"What's the matter, Risa?" Ariel took the stool.
"Don't want me to see his lordship posing? Is he—"
She leaned forward. "—going to be naked tonight?"

"Absolutely not." *Not yet*, came the thought that had
her wanting him that way so badly she had to turn
away to hide her blushes.

"If you are worried that I might be offended, I won't.
I've been looking at our collection of naked men and
women all my life."

"Short as it is—" Risa wiggled her brows evilly as
she picked up last night's sketches. "—I could always
make it shorter, scamp, if you persist in this line of
questioning."

"Boo. Such a dash of cold water you are." Ariel sauntered over to her and picked up a drawing that lay
upon the desk. "Or maybe not. . . ."

"What do you mean?" Risa's curiosity stirred.

Ariel chuckled. "I told you he was dark and beautiful, but now here he is rather like a dying Gaul, isn't
he, with all those heavy muscles, and that big body? I'd
like to see his hips and legs though, wouldn't you?.,"
she rattled on while Risa imagined all too well how his
thighs would be sculpted beneath her hands. And his
hipbones would jut out and his manhood would not lie
limp as most good statuettes did, but rise for her. "He
looks in pain, but of course . . . What's the matter? You
do, too."

"Nothing, nothing," Risa waved a hand.

"We know he's not in pain, is he? He is . . ." She
paused, checked Risa's eyes, then bounced forward.
". . . in love."

Risa froze. Secured her glasses and stuck her nose closer to the portrait.

His half-lidded eyes. The soft moue of his lips. The lax way his hand beckoned . . . like Allure did her lover. Never had she seen a man so enchanted. How had she not seen it as she worked?

Did you?

Had she drawn him that way from life? Or her desire?

She groped backward for her chair.

"What's the matter?" Ariel prodded, chipper as a bird.

"Nothing. Everything," she decided, "is very right."

Because I feel the same way about him.

She loved him.

She smiled, sat straighter, ran her fingertips over the sketch of him reclining on the dais. When had she fallen in love with him? At Court? At her ball?

In his carriage when he poured out all he knew and told her the truth about Maddie and his own sister. Then at the zoo, he had become more than her mentor. He had become her suitor.

Ariel chortled. "Wonderful." She spun for the hay bale, and stepped up on it. "I'd like to see you infatuated with a man."

"Less time to worry about you?" Risa managed.

"About all of us." Ariel began to imitate a few of the stances in which Risa had posed Blake. "Aunt Elizabeth doesn't want to go to Sandown."

"What an understatement." Risa stood with her sketches in her hands. "She does not have to. Although I would appreciate it if she could summon the courage for it."

"Hmmm, yes. And Georgie says she'll come. So I wonder, can I come too?"

"No."

"You are a cold kettle of fish."

Not cold. Not indifferent. In love. With Blake Hargrove. She looked at another sketch of him. Sensuous, virile man. *And he wants me.* Pride swept through her. Desire for him followed.

"I need to go to Cowes." Ariel stomped her foot, then lifted her chin. "For my education. I need to see Osborne. And *Serapis.* They say Bertie's boat is a floating palace. Did you know that POSH means port out, starboard home because he refuses to face the sun when he sails, and he had his yacht outfitted with two new suites so that he could change them as he wished?"

"If you know that, why do you need to go to Wight to see it?"

"I wish you would reclaim your sense of humor, Risa."

Another reason perhaps why I struggle to sculpt.

"Don't you see how broadening it would be for me? Bertie has his yeoman prepare ten-course dinners, just like at Marlborough House and up at Sandringham, and afterward, they strip the deck for dancing." She waltzed a bit around the hay bale. "I should like to dance on water with Bertie. Wouldn't you?"

"Yes." *Like I do now on air.* "Think you will meet him if I bring you along?"

"I'll do my damnedest—ur—my best to do you proud."

Risa was laughing now. She shook her head, ended the day dream, and drifted back to the image of Blake waltzing with her at Sandown for days . . . and nights.

"Good, then. I can come!" Ariel applauded.

"Aunt Elizabeth would have a seizure."

"Oh, pooh. When does she not?"

"Ariel, please, don't pester me on this, my dear. If you come, so much will be thrown out of kilter." The plans to duplicate the weekend in each detail. *My hopes to investigate thoroughly each fact.* "You and she do not get on. She'll be picking at you and you will pick back. I will be the mediator and I don't have time to—"

A knock came at the door.

Ariel rushed to open it, only to have a huge bouquet of white roses thrust in her face.

"Hello!" Blake glanced down, surprised. "Ariel, I presume."

"Yes, my lord," Ariel curtsied, recovering her surprise with the joy of cuddling the roses. She thrust out her hand. "I am delighted to meet you at long last."

"And I you, my lady." He bowed himself. "Here for the unveiling, are you?"

"Oh, no, my lord. I have already seen the sketches. You are," she said with reverence, "quite lovely."

"Not precisely the word I would choose."

"But you'll take it, I presume."

"A man always takes a lady's compliment." His gaze rose to Risa, searing her with the heat of his greeting. "I am glad you saw the sketches, Ariel. I may hope the artist will share them with me."

"Risa didn't show you?"

He shook his head, his eyes upon her still.

"Why not, Risa?"

She grinned so knowingly that Ariel laughed and Blake arched both dark brows. "My secret. Artist's prerogative."

Ariel tisked. Took Blake's hand and led him toward the dais. "I tried out your pedestal."

"Platform," he corrected.

"Pedestal is the right word." Ariel winked at him. "You have not seen the drawings and I have, remember that."

"Ah," he grinned. "You whet my appetite." He caught Risa's little chuckle. "May I see them tonight?"

"Just what I need. Two of you to pester me. Time for you to leave, Ariel." Risa tipped her head to the door.

"Risa won't let me come to Sandown with all of you."

Risa halted in her tracks. "Ariel."

"May I come, sir? I am a very good person. More mature than other girls my age."

"Woe," said Risa, "unto us."

"I have no objections, Ariel." Blake asked Risa with a look. "If your sister approves." He strode forward and took Risa's hands. "What can it hurt to bring her?"

The possibility dawned on Risa that with Ariel there, she might be able to take up Ariel on her offer to help her. After all, few could get a servant talking the way Ariel could. Risa surrendered with a smile. "Better than worrying about what mischief you will get into here."

"Oh, you are such a brick, Risa!" The girl hugged the stuffing out of her. "I shall be of help to you too. Ever so quiet."

"Oh, please don't do that," Risa feigned horror. "I would think you needed a strong cup of licorice tea."

Ariel stuck out her tongue. "You would dare it. I will be quiet, I promise."

"Off with you." Risa opened the door, even though she could not suppress a grin. "I have work to do."

"Some work," Ariel muttered, but flounced past her. Then she spun and curtsied. "Good evening, my lord. I shall be the best guest you've ever had the occasion to invite. Despite what my sister says."

"Go!"

Ariel waggled her fingers at him. "Do you play gin?"

"Of course," he said. "Are you good?"

"Terrible. But Risa will win your socks off your feet. Do not bet her."

"Oh?" Blake said, a conspirator now. "Why not?"

"She cheats."

"Out!" Risa pointed toward the alley.

"I'm going. I'm going."

Risa swung it shut behind her.

"Colorful child," Blake offered.

"Imagine the excitement during her debut." Risa rolled her eyes at him as she went to stand before him.

"I can hardly wait. The men will queue up for a dance in a line a mile long as if they are going to the opening of a new Gilbert and Sullivan."

"Never tell her that," Risa warned. "She once had aspirations for the theatre. Sarah Bernhardt or Ellen Terry could not hold a candle to her." Risa imitated Ariel, one hand to her heart, one to her forehead, a dying diva.

"That bad, eh?"

"Aunt Elizabeth had to take away all the feather boas in the house."

"How many were there?"

"A dozen or so," she said with a snicker.

"Why does one have a dozen feather boas in the house?"

Risa pursed her lips. "They were mine. For various characters. Red for Cleopatra. Blue when I did Juliet. I also owned a few purples and a green."

"And how did Ariel get them?" His shoulders were shaking in laughter.

"Because I was the one who got her to play actress with me. But when I decided to dedicate myself to art, Ariel said she had to give the world one of us."

"Smart girl."

"Do not encourage her. If anyone condones it, she will run off to a music hall."

"She might be a success too."

"She will have a good life, I will see to it. She'll have money of her own. A dowry. A debut. A husband."

"You will be good for her. But . . ."

"What?"

"I wonder how I can put this."

"Don't be delicate. Say it."

"Could you choose for Ariel—and thereby restrict her growth?"

"Inhibit her?"

He nodded. "Wound her spontaneity?"

"Her creativity, you mean." The thought had merit, and irony. "You have a point I had not considered."

"But you will now?"

"Oh, yes. I worry about Ariel without a mother and father. She is aggressive, more so than I was, and my boldness caused problems for me that . . . only now I am recuperating some of my strength and perspective."

"Ariel benefits from the model you are for her. From what I see, she is not like Maddie in any way."

"You are right. Maddie was . . . well, the average girl. She wanted normal things. A husband. A man who loved her. Children. Happiness. She did not get any of those." *Perhaps that is my fault, too.* "And I want Ariel to have them. She deserves to be happy. Happier than Maddie."

He lifted her chin and whispered, "Happier than you?"

"I am very happy lately," she said, meeting his frankness with her own. "Becoming more so daily."

"Despite your worries and the mysteries about Maddie?"

"Despite those."

He hugged her. "There are a lot of things I do not know about you. Cheating at cards, doing a great imitation of Cleopatra. The fact I can make you happy. What else should I know?"

That I love you. "That I prefer to sing the songs from HMS Pinafore. But I'd never win rave reviews."

"No?"

She fought a chuckle. "I sing the tenor parts best."

"Sing for an audience of one then. Me."

She circled her arms around his waist. "When?"

"Soon at Sandown."

"Some evening at sunset?" *Or sunrise.*

"Whenever you wish."

"I wish for often," she said and stood on her toes to kiss him. Once more, he broke away to glare at the ceiling.

"You don't like," she asked with a catch she could not get out of her voice, "the way I kiss, do you?"

He stared at her.

She knew she sounded spoiled, and didn't care. "You could teach me if I'm so awful. I had only that vicar's son to practice on, so I'm willing to learn. I'm a very good pupil and I—"

He made a strangled noise. Then swept her up as he had from the dance floor the night of her ball. She caught his lapel to keep her head from spinning. This time he laid her to the hay and spread out beside her. His hands were on her cheeks, tangled in her hair, his mouth on hers before she had her senses righted in his topsy-turvy world.

"Your problem is—" He kissed her hotly, seizing her in a melting sensation that made her arch against him. "—you kiss too well."

"Then let's perfect yours." She twined her arms about his neck and forced him down to her.

"This is not wise," he said between one torrid kiss and the next.

"Nothing about our relationship has been," she replied when she could, her hands pulling down his suspenders and sliding his shirt out from his trousers. When she met skin, she pressed herself to him and ran her hands up the rigid muscles which yesterday she had only touched with her artist's skill and her woman's imagination. "Did I tell you—" She thought she might be cooing like a morning dove he felt so divine. "—that you feel as strong as you look?" She soothed him when his flesh quivered at her touch.

"Sweetheart—" He thrust a leg between hers and spread her wide to nestle there. "—in your hands I am clay."

But her palms were on his heart, and his mouth was on hers once more. And then she realized that one part of him was not soft at all.

He reared up and back, lifting her to a sitting position and raising the linen tunic in one urgent stroke that left her bare to his gaze. His eyes. His hands.

His mouth. His mouth went everywhere. To the shell of her ear. And her throat. To the point of her raging pulse and down between her breasts. And when he kissed her there, blessing her nipples with the most tender kisses, she shifted, eager to be free of her trousers.

"No," he protested, stilled. He began to roll away.

She slid up and back, and in the process, the trousers skimmed down her legs.

He caught his breath. He did not look away.

She reached out her hand.

And he closed his eyes. "This would not be good for my nobility."

"I think you have perfected that. I am trying to perfect my boldness." He did not move. "Oh, Blake, why not come back to me and learn if we can be perfect together?" Because wasn't that what love accomplished?

12

To give body and perfect form to your thought, this alone
is what it is to be an artist.

Jacques-Louis David

"*I* know it already, Cerise." He tried to focus on the
desk, her chair. Anything but the lovely sight of her
naked body, set out like a gift for the taking. "You said
before, you doubted you could take a man to your bed
who was not your husband."

Her lashes fluttered closed. Her skin was a porcelain,
blushing rapidly with his rejection. But she snapped
her head up. "I've changed my mind."

His gaze swept along the length of her. Her slim feet,
her elegant legs. The arc of her hip and the sweet curve
of her waist. And her breasts were the most luscious
charm of all. Full and firm with pale rose nipples. How
he wished that he could put his lips to those again and
feel what gossamer they were. *Think, man!* "Why?"

She colored to the roots of her hair. "I want to learn
passion." She swallowed. "With you."

"And I yearn to be your teacher, but I am not—"

"Don't you dare say you are not worthy of me or I

will scream like a banshee." She rolled a shoulder, and retrieved her tunic. "I thought you would want me, too, but I suppose I was wrong."

"No." He bent down to her, knowing that to touch her even briefly could mean his undoing. He took her mouth in a ravenous kiss that dove into the inner recesses of her mouth. "I have wanted you since I first saw you with your hands on that Adonis."

Her pain riveted him. "Then what is your objection to—?"

"Because I love you."

The look on her face was a portrait he would remember to his dying day. Her lips parted, her eyes stared into his and then glistened with tears. Her cheeks bloomed with a rich joy and her voice sounded like a sigh. "Blake, darling."

He did not turn away, but wrapped his arms around her. "I can't make love to you."

"Mmmm, of course you can."

"I won't."

"Oh, please." Her fingers skimmed his chest, and as she pressed her hips to his, she arched back, a woman in rapture, and said, "What will become of you if you don't?"

I'll go home and call myself ten times a fool. He chuckled, shocked he could laugh at a time like this. "I will get a special license from the archbishop tomorrow morning."

That got her attention.

It certainly gave him pause.

"What are you saying?"

"I'm not." He cupped her face. "I'm asking you to marry me." *Asking if you want me for tonight or forever.* If she refused him, then he had to leave, didn't he? Lest he lose any integrity he had gained in the days since he'd met her.

"Have you ever asked anyone else?" She sounded so serene.

"No."

"Wanted to ask anyone else?" And now she was logical.

"No." How could he live with her refusal? "If you are declining my offer, I must know now, because—"

"I love you."

It was his turn to stare into her eyes.

"I love you," she repeated as she curled her arms around his neck and drew him down with her. "I love you. How many times would you like me to say it before you take off the rest of your clothes?"

He grinned and stood, discarding them with an efficiency that was a record. But when he was completely naked, he wondered if the sight of his need for her would frighten her.

Her mouth dropped open.

"Speechless," he said, unsure if he should take her in his arms just yet.

She widened her eyes on him, grinning. "Honored is the better word."

Relieved and oh so eager, he pressed his body down against her silken length. "You make me humble."

She licked her lips, shut her eyes, rubbed her mouth on his. "You make me ache."

"I'll make you feel better. Trust me."

"I do, I do." Her nails bit into his shoulders as she undulated against him. "And oh, you feel wonderful." She grabbed fistfuls of his hair and kissed him madly.

He felt like hot satin. How had she never known a man could feel this divine? She had run her hands over so many male models to learn their contours, their dimensions, their physical might, the flow of their movement. But whenever her fingertips touched Blake, she understood his ambitions and his triumphs, his regrets and his defeats. Was it that the two of them were so similar? Perhaps so. What other explanation could she give for knowing that much about him—and wanting to know so much more?

And why waste time pondering a knowledge that was meant to be felt, and not explained?

Her hands ran down his back to his hips. Against her thigh, she felt the evidence of his desire for her. She moaned, a hunger to have him inside her gnawing at her.

But he kissed her until her lips throbbed and her head spun. Against her back, she felt the softness of the sheet and the give of the hay. But the sound of his voice permeated her senses.

"I love you," he said against her ear. "I need you," he told her on a sigh. His hands caressed her, stroking her throat and breast and thigh. He rose to his knees, her legs around him. Open to him, vulnerable to the point of blushing again, she basked in his appreciation for her.

For eternity, she would be able to sculpt him as he appeared now. The sight of him a few minutes ago declaring his love for her had thrilled her. But the sight of him adoring her body would live in her heart and find expression in a lifetime of days with him.

"Cerise, my dear love," he said in awe, "you are a work of art."

Suddenly burning with embarrassment, she tried to cover herself, but he stopped her. "Let me look at you. Please. I have wanted you. Imagined you like this, wanting me." He trailed a warm hand down her throat, over the peaks of her breasts, making them tingle, making her writhe. "You'll never want another man, I will make certain of it now."

"And if you don't hurry, I shall have to find one quickly, sir."

He laughed lightly, his fingers moving up her thighs to part her wider and trace one fingertip inside her. "Now?"

She lolled her head on the hay.

"Or now?" he bent and swirled his tongue around her, laved her to a high and needy peak, making her groan.

"Yes." She was pleading with him.

"But I must do this." And he hovered over her. "And this." He poised at her entrance. "And . . . this." He slowly filled her until she was without any thought except that he was big and hard and sweetly heavy. He was looking at her as if he had never seen her before.

"What's the matter?" she smoothed a lock of hair from his brow.

"Nothing. Everything is . . . better than I thought it could be."

She wiggled into a more comfortable position. "Me, too." She wondered though . . .

"What?" he prodded.

"Are we finished? Or is there . . . more?"

He eased himself farther inside her. "That much more."

She bowed upward. "Oh," she panted, wild with the sensation of clamping around him. "How impressive."

He put his lips to her shoulder. "Darling, we will be even more impressive together in a minute."

"Why?" She clutched his shoulders. "Are you leaving?"

"Going this far." His arms rigid, he inched upward a bit more to make her wince in pain. "And waiting for you." Then he spread little kisses across her cheeks and crooned, "Tell me when you are ready to go on." He took a nipple in his mouth and rolled his tongue around it.

She could drift along with him exciting her like this

until the stars fell down. "Don't stop," she urged him when he cocked his head at her.

"Like that, do you?" He dropped a kiss to the breast he abandoned and another to the other which he had not yet thoroughly tasted. "Don't worry. I'll come back for the other," he vowed and began to move in and out of her with such a strong, even rhythm that she began to move with him too. But soon, she knew only how lush they felt together. How erotic. How right. So that when he increased his pace and she followed him, she reached the summit with him and hung on to him for dear life as tremors shook her to her heart. His reaction was to clamp his eyes shut and freeze, his head dipping forward. In a minute, he breathed again and sank over her.

And then, there was between them, nothing but peace.

She curled against him, snug on the hay. He cast an arm around her waist, binding them together as their breathing slowed.

She wanted some reaction from him. She put the cause to her newness to the act of love, or her need to be praised as he had so many other aspects of her nature. Another part of her was curious what their union meant to him. If he enjoyed it. How he had enjoyed it.

He tipped up her chin. "Why the frown? Are you hurt?"

"No. That is . . . No."

He chastised her with a sideways glance. "What?"

"Did you like that?"

"Far too much, I'd say."

"Could you explain that to me. I mean was it . . . um . . . ?"

"Unique." He rubbed his thumb over her mouth. "For you too, I do pray."

"Definitely. I should know these things about you, if

I am to be your wife." A horrible thought struck her. "Unless now that we have done this you don't wish—"

He pressed his thumb across her lips. "Do be quiet, darling. I am going to marry you. And now that we have done this—"

"Not *because* we've done this—"

"Good God, no. But because we agreed to it *before* we made love—"

"So then you . . . did like what we did?"

He took her hand and led it down to cup around him.

Her eyes widened at his girth.

"I would say that explains my delight."

She cleared her throat. "I think it does."

"Good." He tapped her nose, rolled away, and caught up his shirt. "I am going home now."

"But I haven't drawn you. You can't leave."

"If I don't, we will do this again and again."

She lounged back on her elbows. "What a grand idea."

He shook out his trousers. He shot a glance at her and his hands went lax. He dropped his trousers and leaned over her to bring her lips to meet his. "My love, we have just performed the most wonderful act in life. I want to do it again. I could, too. But I won't. This was rash on my part. I did not protect you from conceiving a child. I should have. You and I will marry soon, but we will do it in such good time that no one ever suspects I took you before we were man and wife. And I will not rush our marriage because you carry my child. I care about you, your reputation."

And Risa cared about his. Certainly, his had suffered after Maddie died last summer. So many thought Blake could have stopped Maddie from leaving the shore. Even she had criticized him for that before she met him. Other people, her aunt included, chastised him for seeing Maddie too often, above and beyond the etiquette of a bachelor calling upon an unmarried young woman. "I see your point. And I would like no blemish to mar your reputation, either."

He reached for her hand to help her up. "I must go, but when I come back tomorrow night please wear more clothes."

"Planning to elude my charms?"

He thrust his arms into his shirt and then his vest. "I will come prepared to protect you just in case I can't."

"Ah. Perhaps, I will wear just earbobs and shoes."

He narrowed his gaze. "Why not a corset?"

Why not just a corset? She grinned. "I'll be all bound up and won't be able to work easily."

"Such are the trials of an artist." He kissed her hair. "Goodnight. Dream of me."

"I won't have problems doing that."

"As for me, I will walk a bit. I should go try to rouse Bartholome."

"You went this morning," she complained.

"But he didn't answer his door." Blake smoothed a curl behind her ear. "I want to talk to him."

Risa eyed him. "You mean you are going to demand it."

"Something like that, yes."

She was not happy about this. Blake would be bold. He might be too much so. She was about to say it, too, when he said, "I hear you objecting. But I fear he is avoiding us. I cannot let him do that. Come now, give me a long good-bye."

"Bah! If I do that you may never leave!"

He pretended to twirl a villain's mustache. "We will place that on our Sandown agenda."

"Becoming longer every day." She kissed him deeply, then watched him gather his coat and leave.

* * *

As Blake approached Bartholome's townhouse, he tore his mind from fears that he may have made Cerise pregnant with that delicious act of making love to her. Whether she was with child now or later, he was going to marry her before September. To hell with the custom to meet a debutante in April, court her in May, propose to her June, and woo her in the heat of July and August.

Blake pushed aside his thoughts of taking Cerise into his mahogany tester bed and climbed out of the hansom he'd hired to take him to Bartholome's flat.

The front door was locked, as this morning, but it was made of wood thin enough and old enough to push open. But when he forced it open with a push of his shoulder—an odor hit him.

He stopped for a second. Curiosity drove him inside the first floor flat, fear rising with his gorge.

He fished his handkerchief from his pocket, put it to his nose, and silently closed the door.

He called out once more.

But the gas lamps burned at low level. The shadows in the sitting room glowed bronze and black. The drapes were drawn, the quarters quiet.

"Monsieur?" Blake called.

But no one answered.

Blake halted in the middle of the Turkish carpet. Assessed the shop owner's penchant for medieval wall tapestries and Napoleonic furnishings. Lavish did not describe the décor so much as sumptuous.

His nose twitched. *You know this odor.*

His heart picked up a new tattoo. He knew it from Sandown when he'd been ten and his dog had died of old age on the patio of the loggia and no one found him for days.

Oh, my God. He shot forward.

The small kitchen was orderly.

The bedroom a shambles. The four-poster was un-
made. Clothes strewn over the bed and chairs. The ar-
moire open. And before it, on the floor was Maurice
Bartholome.

Dead.

For days now.

Blake clamped his handkerchief more tightly to his
mouth. Images of Barbara and Maddie swam before his
eyes. It took all his energy not to wretch. He strode
forward, went down on his haunches. Felt Bartholome's soft, dark flesh. His eyes were open, his
blood a black pool in a dry halo round his head as he
lay upon his pale Aubusson. Someone had shot him. In
the head. From behind.

Blake straightened, panicking. He noted what light
he saw came from a street lamp that filtered through
the sheer curtains at the only window in the room.

Quickly, man. He urged himself on. Unnerved at
finding a dead man, he was afraid someone might come
to misinterpret and accuse him of the murder.

What to look for?

The gun that had shot him.

No. Not here. The murderer would take it with him.

Was there evidence of who the murderer was? What
he wanted?

Blake scoured the room. *Concentrate.*

Bartholome was still dressed in his day clothes. Blake
leaned forward, rolled him over a bit to look for his
watch. The gold of it and its fob twinkled in the
gloom. His wallet was still in his trouser pocket, too.
Robbery seemed less likely a motive.

Blake rose. Walked into Bartholome's dressing
room. All seemed in order.

You don't have much time. The police could come. . . .

He ran a shaking hand through his hair. Took to the
hall. And noted another room existed.

Its door stood ajar. Inside, the gas burned more brightly.

He edged around the jam, careful though it was silent as a tomb inside. It was Bartholome's office. Blake walked in, stood by the desk, noted no window in this room, and spied file drawers—and a money box.

Open and empty.

A ledger. Open, filled with names and dates and amounts. Alphabetically listed.

Blake's heart pounded like a mallet.

Lindsay. Lindsay. No Lindsay.

He should leave. Took one step . . . and turned back to the ledger.

R. Rossborough. Was there an M. Rossborough here?

Hurry.

13

❧❧❧

Be sure not to say that it's by me.

*Francisco de Goya to his friend upon
viewing the artist's early work*

*R*isa rushed from her studio to the main house behind her butler. Why was Blake here so early?

"My lord Sandown," she tried to smile as if this were perfectly normal for a man to call upon an unmarried lady at nine o'clock. She offered her hand.

Blake took it to his lips. "I know it's very early, but I must speak with you." He locked his eyes on hers.

Fear lurked there. *What's wrong? Did Bartholome do something awful to you?* "Yes, of course." *That must be it.* "Thank you, Morris, that will be all."

"Would his lordship like coffee served, ma'am?"

Blake refused it politely. "Just let us talk."

"Come to the morning room. A fire's lit." She pivoted, but noted Blake's footsteps did not follow her. She looked over her shoulder.

He was examining Allure as if he had never seen her before. Walking around and around her.

"What is the meaning of this call?" Aunt Elizabeth

appeared from the dining room, sailing forward. "My lord, this is most irregular. To call at nine in the morning is the highest outrage." She stood foursquare before him.

He looked sad, but staunch. "I apologize, Lady Elgin, but I have no choice. I must see Cerise."

"Cerise you call her now." Elizabeth stepped forward, her color high, her fluffy pink dressing gown detracting from her high dudgeon. "You, sir, must think it your special provenance to disgrace my family. First Madelaine and now Cerise. Will it never end?"

He set his jaw. "I am dismayed you think so poorly of me, my lady. I could stand here and object. One day I will argue with you point by point, but not today. I do not have time."

Elizabeth gasped to be so summarily dismissed.

Risa took Blake's arm. "Excuse us, Aunt—"

"You encourage him! How *can* you?"

"Aunt Elizabeth, you and I will talk later."

"You ungrateful child."

"I am no child, Madam." Risa stared her down, and Elizabeth was quelled for the moment.

Blake was full of his purpose. "Forgive me, Lady Elgin."

Elizabeth was only slightly reproved. "How can you expect to improve yourself in my eyes, my lord, if you continue to ruin the reputation of my nieces?"

"I never did that, Madam. You may take my word or not."

"You expect me to accept your hospitality after you insult me this way?"

"Expect you? No, Lady Elgin. I do not. I would hope if you are so loving of your nieces as you say, that you would come to Sandown again this year for Cerise's sake."

"To be her chaperone."

"And hopefully her friend." He bowed slightly.

"Aunt Elizabeth, do give over." Risa hooked her arm through his and had her aunt narrowing her gaze at them. "Blake is here to see me and it is urgent. You and I will meet later to continue our debate." Risa led him down the hall.

"You look terrible," Risa told him when she had shut and locked the doors behind her. "Have you had breakfast?"

"I didn't feel like eating." He paced before the fire, rubbing his hands, his eyes, rolling his shoulders.

She had gone to bed reliving their minutes together making love and awakened with smiles and anticipation of more evenings spent in precisely the same way. Expecting to see him at Bartholome's shop at eleven, Risa had wondered how and where she might gain a few minutes alone with him, to kiss him at the very least. But her emotional need to show him her love was now channeled into another sign of affection. She went to him, halting him in his tracks as she ran a hand down his cheek. "Darling, tell me what has you so disturbed."

He took her in his arms. "Why do you wear your linen? Were you sculpting?" His voice was ragged. His eyes were weary, haunted.

"Yes. Thanks to you I am up before the birds and at my worktable sketching. Sit down, over here." She led him to the settee. Held his hands. And waited.

"Bartholome," he said at last, "is dead."

She sat blinking.

"I know it is incredible. So was the sight."

Risa's mouth dropped open. "You went to see him last night after you left here?"

Blake nodded.

"But when did he die?"

"It must have happened days ago."

She still did not understand.

"Cerise, I saw his body when I got to his flat. He was shot."

"He committed suicide?" was her first thought. Her second was that it must have been hideous for Blake to view such a tragedy.

"Sweetheart, he was murdered. The bullet entered the back of his head."

"My God. You were there." She ran her hand down his cheek. He was cold, so very cold. "Oh, Blake. You were alone and . . . What do the police say?"

"I do not know."

She began to tremble, a quake that built along with fear for his peace of mind. And his safety. "You were there alone and found him? Did any one see you? Did you talk to anyone?"

"I was careful. I left no traces. But I had to tell you."

She felt her blood pounding in her head. "Poor man. I did not like him, but—who could have done this? To murder him. Why, it is abominable to even think—"

"Cerise, my love, listen to me. There is more you must know. There are many people who could dislike Bartholome enough to kill him."

"How could you know that?"

"I searched his flat. I am not proud of myself. I do not like myself for intruding, but I thought I had cause and . . . Oh, hell, I am not an objective observer of death, either. Barbara's death did me in. Your sister's made matters worse. But I mean to tell you something else."

She did not want to hear it—and predicted she would nonetheless value it.

"He told us the truth when he said he kept his ledgers at home. I found last year's and the one for 1879. I skimmed them."

"And? Did you find the listing for Maddie's purchase of the Ritter?"

"No. I found numerous payments to many people. Some of the names are pseudonyms for well-known collectors in England. It is obvious to me what the names stand for because I know this world, live in it, work in it, talk with these collectors regularly. Most of the people Bartholome listed have had a long-standing relationship with him. When the police find his body—and his ledgers—they will have to make sense of the names before they are able to make sense of Bartholome's activities."

"Was Maddie listed?"

"No."

She was relieved, but at his next words, she was not.

"M. Rossborough was. Numerous times. I did not have a chance to count them. But the name was entered beside differing amounts of money. Hundreds of pounds usually. Different initials in another column beside each sum. And then I found one very large amount on July twentieth of last year."

She had wanted to be bold. Here was another opportunity. "How much?"

"Five thousand pounds."

Risa could not catch her breath. "Five thousand pounds? Why? Why would she take money from him?" *Was this five thousand pounds part of the money in the safety deposit box?*

Blake stroked her hands. "I have a theory."

"Tell me."

"The initials beside each listing represent an artist. JR. Joshua Reynolds. HH. Hans Holbein. Those are two listings beside pseudonyms which I think translate into the names of the foremost owners of those artists' works."

"And what were the initials beside this listing for M. Rossborough?"

"GB."

"GB. GB. What could—" She shot to her feet. "Gianlorenzo Bernini. We own only one piece by Bernini. Allure." She could not believe it. "*Allure?* But that makes no sense. None at all. What about Allure? A purchase? No, no, it can't be because she stands here and . . . Oh, you don't think . . ." But from Blake's expression he did think the same as she. "Could it be he paid Maddie to let someone make a . . ." The word was poison to her tongue. ". . . *copy?*"

Horror that Maddie might permit such a thing to happen to their family's prize possession drove Risa toward the front hall. "Wait here a minute," she told Blake, shut the door firmly behind her and walked along the corridor toward Allure. She glanced inside the dining room as she passed it and saw that it was empty. Aunt Elizabeth had not returned there. Where had she gone?

Quickly, Risa surveyed the other rooms along the hall. The library door was closed. The drawing room door was open and Risa hurried in, but it too was empty.

Risa retraced her steps to the morning room and stuck her head in to call to Blake. "Come with me."

The two of them went to stand before Allure.

Risa knew from her studies with Signore Ambrusco how often copies were made of great paintings or sculptures. Tutors in many European art schools required novice art students to copy the great masters' works. In this way students learned the basic techniques of design and rendering. Instructors graded students on how precisely they duplicated the original artists' works. Only after excelling at such copying were the best imitators encouraged by their tutors to attempt to paint or sculpt in unique ways. Some of these proficient students were able to innovate and achieve fame, if not also fortune. Many of them did not.

Among those who were good copyists, a few continued to imitate great artists—and earned a very good income doing it. With the help of dealers who paid them large sums of money to imitate originals and sell them as such, copyists had duped many collectors into purchasing forgeries. And the traffic in forged art treasures increased each year. Most of the bogus works came from Italy and Greece. In fact, the Italian government had recently enacted new laws which prohibited the creation of forgeries and their shipping across its borders. But the Italian condottieri were often unskilled in identifying the forgeries, and many perpetrators were arrested but never prosecuted.

"What do you think of Allure?" Risa asked Blake barely above a whisper. "You know Bernini's work better than I."

"Darling, I can only speak from the collector's point of view. As a student, I was never required to copy a work by him. So I can speak only on the quality of the marble." He walked around it, touching Allure's extended hand and then peering into her dreamy eyes.

"And?"

"Aside from the fact, my love, that the expression on her face compares poorly to the one I saw on yours last night, I would say that this is definitely Carrara marble."

Warmed by his reference to last night, she smiled at him, but returned to her examination of Allure. "The sparkle is definitely that of Carrara. I've never seen any other Italian marble as bright."

"And Bernini insisted on only Carrara for all his works. But Carrara is still mined in Italy."

"Yes, but could someone make a new block of marble appear as if it were mined and carved almost two centuries ago?" she asked.

"Marble does not deteriorate over time, unless it is

outside in the elements. It is the most stable of mediums. That is one reason it is so very popular among sculptors and so expensive. There is no way to tell when the block was mined."

"Well, then, what do you think of her craftsmanship?"

Blake ran a fingertip over Allure's mouth. "The artist must have kissed his model before he sculpted Allure's lips." Blake smiled at Risa. "Yours are more lush. But the artist did the best he could. I would say that he was very skilled. His use of the chisel is deft. His last polishing of the surface is certainly as fine as Bernini always insisted for his works."

He straightened, tipped his head toward Allure. "What of her composition? You have been able to look at her all your life. Does she seem the same as she always has to you?"

"Yes—and no." Risa recalled how she had felt only days ago when she had looked at Allure with less admiration than previously. "Recently, I looked at her and did not think her as beautiful as before. But her pose is correct."

"Are you certain, Cerise? This is the only work by Bernini of which no one has ever made a plaster or bronze copy. We have no means by which to judge its authenticity but your eye."

Risa took her time examining the marble lady. "Her arm is as elegant in its reach and her body is as replete as before when I have admired her. Her desire for her lover seems as strong as ever it was." Risa admired Blake. "I know now how she feels. What she wants from him again."

Footsteps approached from the main staircase. A maid cast her eyes to the carpet as she scurried down the steps and then disappeared at the end of the first floor hall.

Blake was thinking. "So, this statue is made of Carrara, but if it is new or old, we cannot determine. The
skill of the artist is so superb as to render both of us in-
capable of judging if its creator were Bernini or another person. The composition seems to you to be the
same as it always was, but you did have occasion to
wonder if the statue thrilled you as much as it did when
you were a child. Why was that?"

"I thought my failure to appreciate it might stem
from my discouragement with my own artistic endeavors. A sad state to have been in, but—"

"Lucinda? Come back here!"

Risa shot a glance up the stairs. "Aunt Elizabeth is
about to chastise her maid. We really do not want to
listen—or her to come out and overhear us. Let's return to the morning room."

But once there with the doors closed against inter-
ruptions, Risa was beset by one more question.

Why would Maddie become involved with Bartholome?

But Risa knew the answer.

*Money. To buy me an education. Money. To buy herself a
debut. Money. To get herself a husband.*

Blake asked her where her thoughts led and when
she told him, he said, "You know that I wondered why
Maddie visited Bartholome. Then, too, why she would
fling it in my face before she cast off in her boat that
she was going to work with Deville again."

"Didn't you once say that Deville makes copies of
paintings?"

Blake sat back in the settee. "Perhaps he has expand-
ed to sculpture. Or he has an associate who is a sculptor."

"Have you ever suspected Deville of copying a piece
of work to acquire the original and sell it?" she pressed.

"That is a good point," Blake nodded. "It takes a few
men with lifts to raise and move a block of Carrara the

size of Allure. If that had happened here, at least one of your servants would know about it."

"So I should try to find a way to ask if any of them have seen Allure moved," she said. "I can do that. Meanwhile, I am afraid for you. Once the police find Bartholome's body and his ledger, they will start to look for suspects. If the shop clerk tells him that we were there, they might want to question us." She went to sit beside him. "And if they ask you about last night . . ."

"The police have no reason to call on us. None to suspect me."

"Are you positive you left no evidence that you had been in his flat?"

"Yes, I am. We do not know if the police will be able to figure the ledgers out. They will probably talk to his clerk, and perhaps he will tell them we were there, but what of our visits? We could not have been the only ones in the shop in the past few weeks."

"No."

"Still, the police might come to you to ask questions about interpreting the ledger because you are the foremost dealer for art in England."

"You flatter me, darling."

She thought of her own self-perception and how it had changed in the last year, sharpened in the last ten days since she had met this man. "Do not doubt that you are hailed as an expert. Tell me, who else would the police consult?"

"Marcus Sudbury, certainly. Robert Dungarvon, too."

"What is Robert's expertise?" Risa asked, not knowing anything about this aspect of the man who had lived in her family circle for the past three years.

"Reformation and rococo art."

"The same periods as you?"

"Yes."

"So Robert knows Bernini's works?" When Blake nodded, she sat back. "How is that?"

"His father, the marquess, once owned a few pieces by Bernini which he sold to me a few years back. Robert learned about Bernini at his father's knee."

"Could Robert know Deville?"

"As much as anyone in the art world, I suppose, yes. But I doubt he would admit it. Reputable dealers don't."

"I see," Risa said, her mind whirling. "I wonder if Aunt Elizabeth ever heard Maddie mention Deville."

Blake frowned. "You've never asked her?"

"I wished to avoid the challenge of explaining where I learned about him. But that was in vain because she suspected from the first that I was meeting you anyway. And then there is the fact that I didn't feel—" She pondered a minute. *Feel* was certainly the right word, though she could not explain it in rational terms. And she must put reason to it. Her aunt deserved that kind of consideration. "I didn't feel she should be worried or included in my investigation."

"Do not ask her now, either, unless you feel it is the best thing to do."

Her look was sharp. Her thoughts were not as protective of Maddie as they had once been. "I must focus on finding the cause of Maddie's odd behavior." *And her death.*

He met her with his own truth. "My feelings, too. Your aunt is so opposed to me. Always has been. Though I may have been known as a nobleman with bohemian tastes, darling, I was never so disreputable that people, even respectable women, cannot come to think of me as suitable at some point. Even you have come round, and you thought I had not only seduced your sister, but perhaps contributed to her motivation to act irrationally."

"I will ask my aunt."

He gave her a half smile. "You *are* brave."

"So good of you to think so," she told him more gaily than she felt. *To ask my aunt such a thing should not create such a reluctance in my soul.* She stood and lead him to the door.

He embraced her. "Promise me you will be careful."

"Of Aunt Elizabeth?"

He shook his head. "Wherever you go, be prudent about who you talk to about Maddie or Allure."

"No one knows. I have kept most of the information I've learned to myself. And as for attending social events, I have rejected most invitations since I have become enamoured with my work again." She ran a hand over his dark satin hair.

He was chuckling. "The maestro is very complimentary."

"See to it she continues to be."

"How may I comply?"

"Come promptly tonight at nine."

Risa found her aunt in the conservatory, tending her hot-house lilies. The lady had changed her clothes from dressing gown to a faded frock. And she looked up at Risa, but huffed and returned to her pastime.

Risa strolled forward, yearning to discover reasons why she did not trust her aunt enough to tell her everything she had learned about Maddie. Yet too, Risa wished to make amends and enlist her aunt's cooperation, even if she knew she could not gain her approval. "I just asked Lucinda where you were because I want to talk to you. She told me you are not going to see Georgie this morning. Unusual for you."

The woman pierced her with a knifelike glance. "Are you asking me why?"

"No. I do not need to know," Risa considered the

bud of a hibiscus. "I was being polite. More than you have been to me lately. Or Blake Hargrove."

"Why should I be?"

"To me?" Risa scoffed. "Because I am good to you. Because you love me, perhaps?"

"No need to be sarcastic."

"No need to be obtuse, Aunt Elizabeth. I want you to know that I like Blake and I will see him, when I want, for as long as I want."

"And Society—"

"I do not care about. Society has not done a thing for me. Will not wave a wand and grant me happiness. That I must do for myself. I will do *what* I must to make that a reality. And I *must* continue my investigation of what happened to Maddie. I hope you will co-operate with me."

Elizabeth dug into a pot of earth with a vicious stroke of her trowel. "What would you like me to do?"

"Be polite to Blake Hargrove. Now and in the future. He has helped me tremendously with learning about Maddie's last months alive. That deserves some kindness in return, don't you think?"

Elizabeth wiped her brow with her forearm. "That depends on what else he is doing."

Her implication, her search, was to learn how Blake acted with her in the tack room. "He is generous with his expertise and his time to help me with my work."

Elizabeth snorted. "Work."

Risa wanted to leave in disgust, but she tried once more with this woman who had brought her up. "You taught me to be polite. Now you tell me not to be. You have changed, Aunt Elizabeth, changed mightily from the woman I remember in my nursery. I can only guess what made you bitter. Whatever the cause, it is your challenge not mine. In the meantime, I ask you to please let go of your prejudice of Blake. Especially if you wish to accompany me and Ariel to Sandown—"

"Yes, Ariel told me she is coming. Imagine, taking a girl along on a Society weekend. Whoever heard of such a thing? Hargrove must have coal for brains. Ariel will be into everything. Gossiping with the servants and pestering the stable boys to saddle up a horse every hour of the day and night."

"Blake invited her. And she needs some fun." Risa did not add that Ariel led him to it. "You need some yourself."

Elizabeth's trowel clattered to the floor. She stared at Risa. "What fun can I have returning to the place where Maddie died?" Her lower lip quivered and she dug in her pocket for a handkerchief to wipe her sudden tears. She blew her nose. "You cannot tell me that you are going just for fun. Don't try."

"I wouldn't." She said with difficulty.

"You are going because you want to be with *him*."

Risa nodded, though she blushed. "I do."

"Maddie is turning in her grave."

"Stop this!" Risa demanded, and waited until her aunt and she had more composure. "I will not argue this with you. There is nothing to debate. I have fond feelings for him. I will not hide them from you or anyone. I want to prepare you for whatever becomes of that."

Her aunt ground her teeth. Picked up her trowel.

"I do have to ask you something. A new fact I learned."

"From Hargrove?" Elizabeth asked with derision.

Risa did not answer.

Her aunt grew exasperated, saw Risa had the upper hand and said, "Ask. Ask. Get it over and done."

"Did you ever hear Maddie speak about a man named Deville?"

Her eyes blinked. She seemed to become smaller, weaker. But she blinked her eyes again and said, "No."

"Thank you," Risa managed to smile and walked away.

With each step she took, she felt a vise grip her tighter and tighter so that she closed the door behind her and fell back against it.

Risa held no doubts about what she felt now.

Aunt Elizabeth had lied.

14

⚜

Exactitude is not the truth.

Henri Matisse

*T*he carriage bumped along the coast road from Ryde Pier down to Sandown, but Risa refused to dwell on the inconvenience. The sun was so white, the sky so pure blue, the water of the Channel so crystalline today that she inhaled the salt air and felt a momentary relief from the tension of the past two weeks.

"I could live here. Could you?" Ariel chirped. Crafty girl, to ask it for herself, but probe Risa's thoughts, too.

"Definitely." Risa removed her toque, smoothing the peacock feathers absently, while Aunt Elizabeth remained fixed on something outside her coach window. She regretted the fact that her aunt could not rejoice with her that they came here to answer all questions about Maddie's last few days.

Why is that?

And why did you lie about Deville?

Risa knew her aunt had changed slowly, surely through the years. She did not know the cause, but she could speculate that it was her father's suppression of his sister's individuality. Then, too, the fact that Elizabeth's husband had been unfaithful left her with a dislike for men who took lovers. The woman who had acted like a second mother to Risa, Maddie, and Ariel had soured over the years into a bitter person.

Risa could not change that, but she had become more aware of her aunt's behavior. And she was tense, snappish most of the time. Especially after she learned from the housekeeper that Risa had asked a few servants about anyone moving Allure.

"Why are you pestering the staff about such a topic?"

"I wanted to know if she had been moved. She seems off center."

"She does?"

"I thought so, yes."

Elizabeth stood unmoving.

"Why do you have a problem that I asked, Aunt Elizabeth?"

"I have none, I suppose."

After all, Risa thought, *this is my house, my statue, and my staff*. But her aunt had trod away before Risa said it.

She knew her aunt hid much more from her than merely an acquaintance with the name of Deville.

There was nothing she could do about it now, but concentrate on seeing Blake again, and ferreting out more information about last year as the other guests arrived at Sandown.

She inhaled the spring air. It was warmer here on Wight than in London. It was greener, sunnier. She might even prefer this brighter climate to the tall towers of Rossborough Manor. The twin black needles had always put her in mind of gargoyles hovering over the cliffs of the North Sea.

"I think you will like Sandown," Blake had told her

three nights ago as he bussed her on the cheek and said goodnight.

She sighed at the remembrance of his brief embrace.

His restraint was laudable, she supposed, but since he was to leave for his estate the next morning to prepare for the party, it also made her want much more from him. Since he discovered Bartholome's body, Blake had come to her studio to talk and to model for her, but he did not make love to her again. When she asked him if he had failed to bring the protection he spoke of that first night they'd made love, he had gathered her close and declared, "Oh, I have something just in case we find ourselves in a spot. But I have thought this over, Cerise, and I do not feel proper about making love to you in your tack room. Not on a bed of hay, darling. I think you deserve better."

Perhaps they both did. "I am disappointed," she told him, but she was still a creature of decorum, even if she had become a woman of pleasure when it came to loving him.

"Wait until you come to Sandown," he urged. "There, enjoying a few minutes to ourselves can be so much easier, more comfortable, and secure from intruders."

Risa let him go reluctantly, but understood his need to go down to Sandown a full ten days earlier than his guests. It was a small comfort that she was to follow him in three days with her aunt and Ariel. She justified this departure to her aunt by saying she must begin to carve the Carrara before Blake's other guests arrived.

But that was not the whole truth.

Before they came, she wished to become acquainted with Sandown, the building, grounds, its servants. Blake had told her that the constable who had investigated Maddie's death agreed to see her tomorrow. The day after, she would meet with the judge who had presided at the inquest and the coroner. After that, she would have a week to sculpt, to enjoy Blake's company and this invigorating sea air before the guests arrived for the party.

Her fingers folded together with the tension those interviews aroused. She drove the anxiety away by concentrating on the prospect of shaping her ideas into realities in stone.

She fairly burned with the need to work. To stroke the marble, massive and crude beneath her palms. To measure its dimensions and all its possibilities. Its potential. To be certain before she took up her hammer or gouged one nick, that this mass could render her subject in the best way, the only way the subject should be shown. That this stone was cut and ripped from its gorge, its rightful resting place, to become the medium in which a subject might dwell. From which it might burst as she chipped and chiseled and drilled and sanded.

She fingered the clasp of her reticule. Inside she had tucked her sketches next to two of her *modellos* and a few of her tools, a gouge, and a claw tooth. Wrapped in a thin leather case was her most specialized tool—a flat chisel which she had specially made in Florence to fit her hand.

She crossed her arms, closed her eyes. Drifted to the dim but indelible memories of moments when she could feel marble pulse with the life trapped inside it.

Was she not doing the same thing now?

Struggling to emerge from her past, her fears about Maddie, her old and out-moded ways of thinking about how to pursue her work, and take care of her family, her estate, her tenants. Straining to cut the ties imposed by her father's rejection and her aunt's indifference and her tutor's manipulation. She was yearning to find a new way to live that might let her work for their good, yet leave her energy and heart to work for her own fulfillment.

To sculpt.

To be enveloped by each project's special unspoken promise that from this she might learn. About herself. Others. To find aspects to the human which pleased her, repelled her, compelled her to refine their images, and then illuminated other characteristics she had not seen. Those discoveries, unplanned and unnamed as she began a work, were the seconds of ecstasy she lived for.

And now, as an artist in love with her model, she wished to work for more. She longed to demonstrate to Blake in this tangible way that he embodied that nobility to which he had so dearly dedicated himself. And as a woman of her station and rearing, she was prepared to discard any restrictions those mores imposed on her. To enjoy the fruits of her love for him, by permitting herself the rapture which she'd tasted once with him and vowed she would again. He had asked her to marry him and she would as soon as she laid to rest the mystery of her sister's death.

For the first time in her life, she felt honored by a man. As his equal. Not his progeny, property, or pupil.

Still, the question dogged her: as a woman, would her passion for him lead her to lose herself in him?

Emerge from her own medium only to walk into his.

How bold was she? How independent?

She had never been in love before and the prospect of exploring her desire for Blake for the rest of her life left her light-headed. Giddy as that could make her, she pondered the distasteful prospect that she might be seduced by the fantasy of being loved, taken care of— and controlled by the man's needs and schedule. Would marriage to Blake mean she would be obligated to his needs, and perhaps too, in time the arrival of babies, the necessities of running a household? And in her case, she had the responsibility of running Ross-borough's estate as well.

Her head would begin to ache with the endless round of responsibilities which love and marriage could bring her.

If she had never thought marriage would be appropriate for her before these last few weeks, she wondered how it would suit her now that she had rediscovered her compulsion to sculpt.

Yet she need only take one look at Blake, experience a few minutes of shared laughter or silence in his company and the possibility that he would control her diminished.

She told herself that he was not made that way. Yes, he had had mistresses, but that spoke of other facts, didn't it? His virility. His lack of desire to look for a wife. Even the event for which he tortured himself most—his failure to save his sister from taking her own life—showed his inability to control events.

He was no ogre. But was he the type of man who would change into one with marriage?

She told herself to discuss it with him. He was open to conversations about delicate matters. Had he not volunteered to divulge all he knew about Maddie?

More convinced she should not worry that Blake would ever try to dominate her, she assured herself that she was right to have chosen Blake as the subject for the Carrara. The snowy marble, quarried from mines near Florence, was the type which artists coveted for busts and demanded for nudes. Men like Michaelange-lo and Bernini required it for their studies of biblical heroes and saints of the church.

But Risa hoped to take Blake's gift of the white stone and with it make a more secular statement. Over the past few weeks, she had molded him in clay, carved him in wood, and created four plaster casts. From those, she had drawn three-dimensionals and found the one *concètto*, the theme, she would employ. She would portray him as a man in love.

"You are going to ruin that hat, Cerise, if you don't stop stroking it," her aunt warned.

"Of course." She put it to the squabs. "It is one of my favorites."

The lady once more did not smile. *But at least you are civil. Compliant. No longer peevish or argumentative.* Risa wondered often if her aunt thought she believed her statement that she had not heard of Deville. Risa did not bring up the subject, but she probed the woman by mentioning other facts.

When she had received a cable yesterday from the housekeeper at Rossborough Manor that the woman had found no painting by Edward Ritter among the de Ros collection, Risa had declared she was not surprised.

Her aunt had agreed. "After all, who was Edward Ritter that the de Ros family should care to add his work? I have never heard of him. Bartholome led you astray. Why, only he knows."

When Risa had read the newspaper story in the *Times* two days ago at breakfast about how the owner of Bartholome's building had summoned the police to the gallery owner's flat and discovered his body, Risa had expressed surprise that Bartholome had been murdered.

Her aunt had muttered something about how regrettable violence was.

When Risa rhetorically asked who might have killed him, her aunt shuddered, said, "Indelicate to even think of it," and then became quiet.

Risa was curious to know the reason her aunt had been so curt. Yet she did not ask. Her aunt could easily deny any interest in Bartholome.

"Ooooo," Ariel crooned, "if that is Sandown, I will stay forever."

Risa craned her neck to see the Palladian simplicity of Blake's home. Atop a bluff, the pristine stone façade was bathed in brilliance of the midday sun. The house was the very antithesis of Rossborough Manor. Newer, invigorating, it stood like a maiden casting her slim arms toward the sea as if waiting for her lover to come home.

"He has enormous stables!" Ariel enthused.

"I wonder how quickly Lord Sandown's grooms can saddle a horse?" Risa said.

"I'm faster," Ariel grinned.

"I'm certain. Did you bring any books if it rains?"

"Cicero."

"Refining your rhetoric?"

"Of course. For when I meet the queen."

Aunt Elizabeth scanned them as if they were clowns.

Risa turned away, determined not to let her aunt's indifference or even her bad manners mar her visit with Blake—or stop her from her investigation.

The coach swayed as the driver turned them into the long cobbled drive up to the main block.

Emerging from the house and onto the lawn were two men and a woman. One man and the lady were dressed in service gray and white. These were the butler and the head maid. But Risa smiled at the sight of the taller dark-haired man whose broad shoulders and long legs, even at this distance, illustrated that this was Blake.

Risa could not take her eyes off him. He wore a soft white shirt which flowed over his shoulders and chest, billowing in the wind like a swashbuckler's. His jodphurs of chamois fit the planes of his hips and thighs with a snug beauty which had Risa mentally sketching those dimensions.

And her mouth watered.

"Good afternoon." Blake swung open the coach door himself, his butler attending to the luggage with the driver.

Blake extended his hand to Aunt Elizabeth first because she sat nearest the door. "Welcome to Sandown, Lady Elgin. I hope your ferry ride from Portsmouth was comfortable."

"Bracing. Thank you, my lord." She sounded affable.

"I am delighted you have chosen to come," he told her, meeting her gaze frankly.

"And I am grateful for the invitation. I wish my nieces to have an enjoyable holiday."

"And I shall do my best to provide it, I assure you."

"I hope so."

Risa breathed more easily that at least Elizabeth would not go at Blake tooth and nail every minute they were here.

"Hello, Ariel." She bobbed him a curtsy. "Ready to enjoy the sun and sea?"

"Absolutely, sir." She cast a glance toward his stables. "I am also ready to ride."

"My grooms have been notified they are to be at your beck and call." Blake had learned of Ariel's passion for riding and reading from Risa these past few weeks they spent together in her studio. But he turned his keen green gaze on her finally. "And what may I offer you first, Cerise? Tea? A few minutes to rest?"

A kiss? "Tea would be very nice."

Blake did not take his eyes from hers and yet, said to the maid. "Ida, please see to it the cook lays out a full tea for us in the drawing room, will you? Gerald, here—" He indicated the butler. "—will see to your trunks." Blake looped his arm with Risa's and led her toward the house. "I have assigned each of you a separate suite. Ariel will be in the nursery wing. I hope you do not object," he said as much to Ariel as the others, "but I wanted to give everyone who is returning this year the same rooms they had last."

Elizabeth swiveled her head around.

"I wanted everything precisely as it was last year, Lady Elgin. Best, I thought, to recreate the atmosphere and encourage everyone to remember details."

Elizabeth nodded, but focused on the doorstep. "My lord, I must tell you now I see no reason to go through this. London is abuzz with your intentions. The de Ros family is, once more to my dismay, on everyone's lips. This re-creation of your weekend will only dredge up sorrows none of us can wash away."

"Your objection is noted, Lady Elgin, but we go forward in any case. Cerise wants this, needs this. And she shall have whatever is in my power to give her." He squeezed Risa's hand. "And as for those invited, they may have spread the word at what's intended here, but they have all accepted my invitation. I shall make the experience a useful one so that we may all put this tragedy behind us and move on to a happier future."

"Excuse me, won't you?" Elizabeth avoided commenting on his intentions. "I should like to retire to my room. May I ring for tea there later?"

"Anything you wish," Blake bowed.

Elizabeth strode ahead of them to disappear inside with the maid.

Ariel scampered to keep up with Blake and Risa. "Not to worry about Aunt Elizabeth. She will shape up nicely before the other guests arrive. I overhead her telling Georgie that she would rise to the occasion. She does not wish to bring any more shame on the family—and Georgie was pleased. You know how Aunt Elizabeth likes to please Georgie."

"I do, indeed." *The only person who can influence her is her daughter.* Risa sighed. "Not to worry about her alienating people makes my task easier. They will be more relaxed and cooperative when I ask them questions."

Ariel came to a halt. "May I go to the stables, sir?"

"And the library. I have a complete collection of Pliny."

Ariel put a hand to her chest as if struck with love. "A true hero!"

He chuckled. "Go!"

When she had walked out of hearing range, he moved a fraction closer to Risa, and his voice stroked her senses. "Tell me you missed me."

Her eyes locked on his. "Minute by minute."

His gaze narrowed on her as he inhaled her scent. "You look scrumptious. Smell divine. What is that perfume? I have never noticed it before."

"Truly you've forgotten me"—she was rolling her eyes at him—"because it is the same as ever."

"That just shows you then, I must not let you out of reach for too long."

"But what do I get for the continuing pleasure of your company?"

"What would you like?"

She smiled wickedly. "One hearty token of your affection"—she touched a gloved fingertip to her lips— "for each day you've been gone."

"Three kisses." He snorted. "A pauper's sum."

"Enrich us both." She teased as they climbed the steps. "Don't limit the number."

"You become more bold as we go on." He looked impressed. "You test me sorely."

"Expect more of it, too," she said as the butler opened the front door for them and Blake's fingers tightened on her elbow.

Blake led Risa inside, had a footman take her reticule, hat, and gloves, then proceeded down the hall.

But Risa refused to budge. In the center stood a marble of such drama and beauty that her blood had surely ceased to flow for the awe that struck her.

"Oh, Blake," she whispered and drifted forward to the Bernini statue she had heard described countless times. She put her hand out to touch the dazzling power of Daphne in flight from Apollo, the man who would possess her.

Blake stood to one side, silent.

"In Allure, Bernini captured a woman in love. But here he creates a woman afraid of it." She skimmed the folds of Daphne's sheer gown, the arc of her arm as she reached up beseeching Zeus to transform her into a tree to escape the affections of her persistent lover. Her fingertips changed so gradually to leaves, and her toes became the roots so subtly, that Risa could detect the transformations of flesh to tree in finite increments. This lady was desperate to be free, her fear of her lover as palpable as the starry Carrara. "Her mouth is open in a scream. She thinks he will hurt her. She is so young, naïve."

"That is one reason he wants her." A note of brooding was in his speech. "He wishes to be her first lover."

"Many men's desire."

"A natural one, I think."

"Primal," she added.

Blake considered Apollo. "It is true that he wishes to initiate her. But he also wants to keep her and ensure no other will possess her." He studied Risa's pulse beat at her throat. "That too is a man's normal instinct."

"She wonders how much of his desire is lust and how much pure regard." Risa strode around Daphne to put the statue between them. *What is yours?*

"I can understand how she might fear Apollo's attraction is temporary."

"She has good cause. He had enjoyed so many lovers."

Blake stepped toward her. "Before he met her, he looked for excitement. Never intimacy. But look at his face," Blake instructed, and Risa did, but then examined his own. "He wants that now. Can you doubt his devotion?"

"There is determination there, too, and it seems daunting. She wonders if it can also be ruthless."

"Some men's can." Blake considered the lovers before him. "So she runs because she fears his love may control her."

"And so it seems better to become a tree—" *Live alone.*

"Than a tyrant's lover."

"Yes."

Blake frowned. "When a man falls in love, he wants to change."

You have, haven't you, for me?

A muscle ticked in his cheek as Blake said, "And clearly, Daphne can learn from this, too. She never knew a man who would accept her as his equal."

"Her father wished to dominate her." *As mine did me.*

"Perhaps, if Daphne had given Apollo a longer time to prove his devotion, they might have each changed for the better together."

"Time is a great healer," she offered. "And a requirement for change."

"Yet . . ." Blake paused. "It is the nature of his desire for her that he wishes to consume her, be consumed by her, surrender himself. It is a very frightening prospect to lose one's self."

"It is the same for a woman," she confessed.

Blake came forward to thread his fingers in her hair. "He wishes to nurture her."

"As she does him."

"Protect her."

Her hands rested on his chest. Beneath her palms, his heart beat double time.

"He wants to save her from other men," Blake declared, "tragedy, illness, sadness, everything, anything."

Risa pressed a kiss to his heart. "She does not want to be protected."

"I wonder . . ." He grew wistful.

"What?"

His thought became conviction. "If he would not wish to be protected by her."

"From the same things," she saw where he lead. "A mutual dependence then?"

"Is that not love?" he asked on a whisper.

"Oh, yes," she breathed and kissed him with triumph that they had found it together.

Satisfied, he held her for long minutes afterward. "Would you like to see the rest of the house?"

She looped her arm through his. "First, the rest of your collection."

"By all means."

He led her past expanses of red silk-lined walls crammed with scores of works by Rubens, Titian, and Raphael. Through the oyster and pink ballroom hung with grand court portraits of Hargroves done by Reynolds. The dining room adorned in hunting scenes; the yellow morning room awash in the new impressionistic works by French artists Degas and Matisse, a few old and scenic Delacroixs and two studies by a young American painter, a woman named Cassatt.

"She likes to do children," Risa noted an oil of two toddlers. "A unique study. She has an understanding of them, doesn't she?"

"She found her forte."

"An artist's first challenge," Risa confirmed as the task she needed to finish.

"Then, having found it, to stick to it to perfect it. Let me show you the greatest wonder of Sandown." He took both her hands and walked backward into his drawing room where he quickly shut the doors upon the household and let her gape.

Far from the stark spare lines of the Palladian house, this room spoke of the Baroque. The lavish, the gilded, the gaudiness of gold leaf, *trompe l'oeil* walls which duplicated a French garden maze of roses and boxwoods, and such a profusion of lilies Risa could smell their thick perfume. Dotted about the study, which resembled a thinking man's retreat, stood the innumerable creations of the Italian sculptor Gianlorenzo Bernini.

A bust of a cardinal, another of a German elector. A brace of deer, their eyes startled, bodies stunned into stillness, the essence of innocence disturbed. In one niche stood a pedestal which served as base for a few *modellos*. One life size relief caught Risa's attention.

And she walked forward.

She had traveled to Rome one holiday when Signore Ambrusco had permitted his students a holiday. She had gone with a friend, a boy of fifteen who also studied with Ambrusco, and they had rented an inexpensive *pensione completa* near the Vatican. Every day for five days they had gone to St. Peter's to study masters' paintings, frescoes, statuary, and architecture. Before she had seen St. Peter's, she had favored the few works by Bernini which resided in Florence. After she saw the wealth of his productivity in Rome, no other sculptor's works elicited such empathy from her.

The sensuous qualities he could call forth from the stone melted it to flesh. Facial expressions seemed so real, she saw them reflected in her own mirror. Eyes stared or snapped or smiled, soft with love, hard with hate, warped in fear. Mouths spoke. Hands appealed, defended, or caressed. Feet strode or stood firm.

Like Daphne in flight or Louis the Fourteenth in his smugness or David with his sling-shot conquering Goliath, Bernini captured the moment of fiercest emotion. Set it in stone. Cast it free.

The *modello* she viewed now was one of those final works she had seen in St. Peter's. It was no taller than twenty or so inches, but it arrested her more than Daphne and Apollo. This was another couple, a *concètto* or theme which was so intimate, Risa felt her cheeks flame in embarrassment that she had intruded. And yet the subject was a sacred one.

It portrayed an angel's visitation to a woman. She was Saint Teresa, a medieval supplicant. The woman, young yet ageless, reclined, her head flung backward, her cape falling about her hair and torso, as she experienced the sight of God. From the drape of her clothes, to the fall of her hand, she swooned, a woman in rapture.

In that moment, Risa knew her own, because her instinct to sculpt a human man in love was so very right. Bernini who had found his forte in the depiction of pagan or Christian religious themes, had perfected his art by depicting the glory of one woman's view of infinite love. Only once had he ventured into the secular— and another woman's view of her lover. Only once when he had created Allure.

Risa would create the modern rendition of love in the form of the man who was her own lover.

Her eyes sought him. He had stood silently to one side, his attention, she instinctively knew, had never swerved from her. His gaze caressed her and he smiled, a small but telling joy. "What do you see that makes your face light so?"

"You. The love I did not see on Apollo's face, I can see on yours."

At once, she loved him more, feared his love less.

She also trusted herself more to grow, to remain herself, and yet also become his wife. Amid that she could accommodate the demands of her life to her work.

She cupped his face, reached up on tiptoe and placed her lips on his. His arms circled round her, his mouth claiming hers. This was the kiss she had lacked for so many days, wild but sweet, sure and strong. He pulled away, laughing, "With that kind of reaction to viewing the collection, I wonder what you will do when you see the block of Carrara."

"Why wait to learn?"

The butler knocked and came in to announce her tea was served in the drawing room. Her hunger for food could not match the one she had to see his studio and the marble.

"Shall I say we will take tea later?"

"Please."

He waved his man away, then strode to the garden doors and held out his hand to her.

"I cannot see your studio." He had told her it was along the shore, the easier to have marble blocks delivered from ships. "Where is it?"

"Beneath the horizon," he pointed toward the sea. "The lawn runs down to the shore. You cannot see any of it from here, but I assure you it is there."

"Wonderful."

"Don't you want to change out of your traveling clothes?"

"I can't wait."

"Put on your walking shoes?"

She wrinkled her nose.

"You can even go barefoot if you want," he chuckled. "The grass is thick, the sand is soft."

She found a chair and sat to unlace her shoes. As she reached up to unsnap her garters, she heard him clear his throat as his gaze zeroed in on her ankles, then rose to her knees and her thighs. But she grinned, rolled down her stockings and stuck them into her skirt pockets. "Can't have the servants finding my hose strewn about, can we?"

He ground his teeth and grabbed her arm. "Let's go."

"How fast do you run?"

"Faster than Apollo." Then reached out to bring her to him. His body was deliciously hard and his words were urgent. "You change before my eyes and I am thrilled to watch you."

"I don't run from you, though."

"No, thank God." He kissed her hand. "Go on, darling. I'm right behind you."

She got a lump to her throat, but darted away, nimble as she had not even thought of being for ages. He walked in a measured pace right behind her. She exulted in the velvet grass carpet beneath her feet, the sun overhead, the dunes, the grains of sand, fine and warm and wet with surf between her toes.

The studio was a little house with no windows toward the Manor or the north, but glass along the east and south. The house stood high upon a thick foundation, necessary to support any heavy mediums he would bring here to carve.

She stopped at the top of the steps.

"The door's open," Blake told her. "Go in."

She thrust it open. The marble sparkled at her like a block torn from a white star and set to earth.

She moved forward, awed as she had been by Daphne and Apollo. But here, she felt not the results of another artist's vision but all the possibilities of her own.

Here was the rough marble which she would carve

with all the knowledge and insight of her past to cut and mold her future.

The block was at least eight feet tall and over four feet wide. Enough to cut a standing figure of a muscular man, a naked man, feet spread, hand out to the woman he gazed at through the eyes of love.

Risa would name the piece *Devotion*.

15

One must be bold to extremity: without daring and even extreme daring, there is no beauty.

Eugène Delacroix

"Good afternoon, my lady," the maid in gray and white bobbed a curtsy as Risa rushed through the door to her suite. "I am assigned to you during your stay."

"Thank you." Risa smiled, catching her breath from her run up to the house. "What is your name?"

"Mary, ma'am."

The girl was not a day older than sixteen. With a fresh scrubbed face that age would sharpen to a sultry beauty, she moved briskly. She had been unpacking Risa's trunks, hanging her gowns, placing her corsets and camisoles and petticoats in bureau drawers.

"You are efficient, Mary." This was the personal maid who had been assigned to Maddie here last August. Blake had told Risa that this girl had left his employ last winter. She had gotten an offer to work for a couple in Cowes, north along the coast road.

"Mary is a very lively girl," Blake added. "She had been in service with me for over two years when she left. She reads, writes, and wishes to better herself. So when she had this opportunity to earn more and travel to London occasionally, I thought the idea a good one. I wrote to her and her employer, and asked if she would return here for this weekend. She agreed, but I gather from her employer, not readily."

"I don't blame her," Risa said. "I'm rather jumpy myself." Then she went silent. "Do you have any idea why, other than she hates to relive the weekend?"

"Well, darling, I thought that if anyone should ask her that, it is you. I also think that if Mary does know something that could help us in our endeavor, she would be more likely to tell you than anyone else."

Time to find out what Mary remembered.

"Have you been in service a long time, Mary?" Risa began to dig out her sketchpad, pencils, and chalk from her reticule and put them into the top desk drawer.

Mary continued to fold lingerie and tuck it into the chest. "Yes, ma'am. Since I was five when I helped my mother in the scullery where she worked in the village."

Risa detected a hesitant note to her voice. "Lord Hargrove tells me that you were a great asset to him."

"Did he, ma'am?" Her round face split with joy. "I'm happy to hear that. I liked it here. He is a good man."

"Yes, he is." Risa opened the desk drawer and dropped her things inside. Then she walked about, appreciating the cheerful yellow damasks of the upholstery and the Aegean green of the silk-lined walls. *Maddie had lived here, left here to go to her death.* "Lord Hargrove told me you served my sister last year."

"Yes, ma'am. All of us at Sandown Manor have been assigned our same jobs as last August. 'Cept for me, o' course. I am to do for you."

"I am happy to have you, too." *Should I tell you now why?*

Mary lifted a stack of linen from a trunk drawer.

"I will take a set of those, Mary."

The girl's forehead wrinkled.

Risa shook out one set. "These are my work clothes."

"Pants?" Mary's eyes went round.

"And a matching tunic."

"You can wear those?"

"It is easier—" Risa shook out a set of them. "—to sculpt when you are free of all restrictions." *Physical and mental.*

"His lordship told us you are a sculptor. But doesn't your aunt harp on you to put more clothes on?"

"She knows it would be useless, as well as very impractical. Once I start to hammer at the marble, I will be covered in dust. A corset and skirts would only hinder me. And I would ruin them with my reaching and climbing all over the marble."

"That is a huge piece, ma'am."

"You've seen it?"

"Yes, ma'am. You cannot help but see it from the shore. Through the windows. The staff always thought his lordship would come back from London and begin to chip away at it someday."

"Why do they think his lordship stopped sculpting?"

"He didn't have the heart for it after his sister died. She would always tell him how good he was. I'd say he misses that."

"Yes, encouragement can do a world of good. Help me get out of these clothes, will you, please? I am eager to get to work."

Mary placed the clothes on the bed and began to unhook the back of Risa's gown.

"You do not look much like your sister, ma'am. Beggin' your pardon, ma'am, that was forward of me to say. I am sorry. I won't—"

"Oh, but I want you to be frank with me, Mary." *Tell me what you saw. If you saw Maddie's diary. Packed it and—*

"I hope I am not too forward, ma'am, when I say I liked your sister. I thought she was so pretty. . . ."

"And?"

"Beg pardon, ma'am, but—"

Risa turned to look at her solemnly.

"She was so unhappy."

At Mary's honesty, Risa swallowed the lump in her throat. "I think so, yes. Do you—did she ever give you an idea why?"

"No, ma'am." Mary cast her eyes to the floor and Risa wished she hadn't.

"Please look at me, Mary. I would hope that if there is any recollection you have of my sister that you think is . . . indicative of why she was unhappy, you would tell me. I loved my sister dearly."

"That's good to hear, ma'am. I had one, too, and I lost her to the sea, too."

"You did?"

"Yes, ma'am. She was a baby, younger'n me and she was taken in the tide."

"The undertow?"

Mary nodded. "She and me went swimming. It was this time last year on my day off."

"Not that long ago. Your memory and your sorrow is still fresh." *As new as mine.*

"Yes, ma'am."

"I am so sorry. Can you"—Risa wondered if this could ever be true for herself—"talk about it easily?"

"Maybe. I dunno. She was four and my ma gave her to me to mind. Sara walked into the water and next I saw, she weren't there. We found her body the next day. Most times, we don't here unless they drowned real close to the shore."

Risa froze. *No one ever told me that.*

"They get washed out to the ocean."

"They do?"

"Yes, ma'am, but, that's no matter." She sniffed and rolled both shoulders back.

"It is important." *To me.* "Why do the bodies not wash up on shore?"

"After about a mile or more, the undertow takes them far out until they get caught up in another current. The constable says they drift off toward France, but it's too far, you see, before the fish begin to eat them. I tried to save my sister, I did. I jumped into the water and swam to look for her, but I couldn't find her. My ma does not look me in the eye yet." Her lower lip quivered and she bit it white.

"She will, Mary. You tried to find your sister and that is the most important thing." *I wish I could have had the opportunity to save my own.* Risa thought it too early in their relationship to put a hand to the girl's arm and try to comfort her. So she smiled with sympathy. "Thank you for telling me about her. And the currents."

Risa turned back so that Mary could continue to unhook her dress.

"Would you care for a bath, ma'am? Or can I get you anything before I finish unpacking your clothes, ma'am? Maybe some tea?"

"A bath would be soothing, thank you, before I go to work. Tell me . . . did you ever see any of Lord Hargrove's sculptures?" It struck Risa suddenly that, amid all the rare and glorious art here, she had seen none of his.

"Before Lady Barbara died, he used to sculpt and paint and such. But I never saw him at it. The housekeeper tells me when his lordship was a boy, he was at his carving and whittling every day. He told us yesterday when he called us up before him that he was going to give you that big marble block in his studio, and that you were to have free reign of it and the grounds."

"He has been very kind to me."

"And all of us here. He is a good employer—and we do like him, if you don't mind my saying so, ma'am."

"I don't at all." *But you liked working here so well, why did you leave?* "Why do you ask?" Risa drew closer to her.

"I know your aunt does not care for my master. She didn't last year. She seems to have a few prunes struck in her craw, pardon my bluntness, ma'am."

"It's fine. Go on."

"Your lady aunt did not like my master. I would say she disliked him from the start. She was always complaining to her maid here about him and how he pestered your sister for a statue that she didn't want to part with."

"Allure?"

"A what?"

"Nothing." Why would that bother Aunt Elizabeth so much that she would complain to a Sandown maid about it? *Because Aunt Elizabeth was afraid that Maddie would sell Allure . . . and the statue would no longer be available to copy.*

The probability that her aunt was involved in such a scheme had Risa sitting down.

Was Aunt Elizabeth the one who controlled the forgery of Allure?

She was in charge of the house. Had been for years when her brother, Risa's father, was alive. Aunt Elizabeth had personally hired the new housekeeper. She could have given anyone access to it. *She had the keys until Maddie inherited . . . and then after Maddie died, I did.*

"Do you have a headache, ma'am?"

"What? No, Mary."

"But you look ill."

"I'm not. Truly. Please, help me with my corset."

But Aunt Elizabeth had the keys for a short five days or so, between the time Maddie died and I arrived to take over the estate. Certainly, if she were involved in the forgeries, wouldn't she have looked for the key to the safety deposit box?

And if she did, she did not find it because it was in London in the vault. And she traveled from here to Northumbria, never stopping in Park Lane.

But had Maddie ever told her she had a bank box?

Oh, Maddie, did you hide the money you earned from Bartholome?

Did you hide it from Aunt Elizabeth? And she killed you for it?

Repulsed, Risa put a hand to her mouth.

Diana Cliveden had told Risa the day of her garden party that she thought Maddie wished to escape Aunt Elizabeth's rule. Perhaps Maddie did.

But that did not mean that Aunt Elizabeth was involved in art forgery.

What else could it mean?

Could Risa ask her aunt and expect an honest answer?

"Mary, I wonder . . . if you ever saw my sister writing in her diary?"

The girl was startled. "Oh, yes, ma'am, every night. Before I would brush her hair out, she would write in it."

"Do you know where she kept it?"

"Kept it?" The girl thought Risa was challenging her. "I never read it. Not that I wanted to, mind."

"No, forgive me, I wasn't questioning your ethics, Mary. I do want to know what happened to it."

"Happened to it? How do you mean?"

An inkling struck Risa that Mary was hedging. "Did

you pack my sister's possessions from this room after she died?"

"Yes, ma'am. In her trunk."

"Did you pack the diary in there, too?"

The girl said nothing.

"Mary?"

"If you think I pinched it . . . Well, I didn't, it wasn't like that at all, I tell you. I wanted to save her embarrassment."

"Really? How?" *Why?*

"I knew she wrote about her . . . um . . . meetings with men."

Men. Plural. Had Blake been right that Maddie had been involved with another man here besides his brother?

"She was a sweet lady and your aunt did not treat her kindly. And the night of the supper party on the shore—the night your sister died—I saw your aunt come in here and try to jimmy that desk drawer open. I was hanging up her day gown in there."

Risa followed Mary's gaze. She had a clear view from here to the dressing room door.

"I thought your aunt was trying to read your sister's diary. I didn't know, but that was what I thought and so then, I said to myself, why is she doing that? She has no right to see that and I knew where your sister would always put the key to the drawer. Over there in the blue vase on the mantel. But then the next morning when I heard from the housekeeper that your sister was dead, I came up here to pack her clothes and I went to look in the vase. Because her diary were hers, too. But the key was not there. So I—I started to look in all the jars on the mantel and it weren't in any of them. So then, your aunt comes in and says to me as I'm packing her clothes, 'Have you seen Lady Lindsay's diary?' and . . . ."

"You said no."

The girl folded her hands. "I said no."

"Did my aunt know you had been in the dressing room watching her try to get the drawer open?"

"No, ma'am. I never told her that."

"So what did you do?"

Mary gulped. "I had all your sister's belongings packed and I was tidying up when I pushed the blotter back and there was the key. I opened the drawer and took it out and hid it in the dressing room, then I locked the drawer back up again, and put the key on top of the blotter."

"Didn't my aunt return?"

"For the diary? Yes, ma'am, I think that is the reason she came back upstairs the following day. Before the inquest."

"How do you know she came up here?"

"I saw her. But she didn't find the diary. Ever."

"Mary, where is the diary now?" *Could I dare hope it is in the dressing room still?*

"I took it with me when I left, ma'am. It is in my room in Cowes. I never read it. You need not fear that."

"I don't, Mary. I am very grateful to you for what you have done." *Preserving the only link to Maddie is an act I will praise you for forever.* "But could you please get it and bring it to me?"

"Lord Hargrove may not want me to leave, ma'am. He asked me to come here for this weekend."

"I know, Mary. Please do not distress yourself about this. I am certain that Lord Hargrove will let you go to Cowes to bring her diary back. I will ask him myself. I must read it, Mary, and learn why Maddie was so unhappy here."

"It was because she wanted to get married, quick like. And no one wanted to marry her."

"She told you this?"

"No, ma'am. I have ears, though I am told not to listen, and I can put things together. And your sister, she was in a hurry to get married. If it weren't going to be Lord John, then it had to be someone."

"Why?" When Mary did not answer, Risa persisted. "Why?"

"I don't know that, but I thought that she was running away."

"Running away?" Maddie was a countess with responsibilities, how could she think to desert them? *But it was a reason for her to pay her bills in cash.*

"I never heard her say that, but the afternoon before the supper party on the shore, she came in, wild like, and packed a few things in her reticule."

"What happened to it?

"I emptied it and put all her clothes in her trunk to be sent home."

"What else do you think of her actions, Mary?"

"Oh, ma'am, I have been trained to be discreet."

"I am certain you have, Mary. But tell me anyway what you think of this."

She winced. "I have been taught by the housekeeper to look the other way. I do. Your sister never said anything to me about having gentlemen, but I know she did."

"Here?"

"Yes, ma'am."

"But how could you know?"

The girls' eyes shifted to the bed. "I change the sheets. And last year, for your sister, I changed them often. I know the days she was here, she had a man to share her bed."

"Do you have any idea who it was?"

"Yes, ma'am."

Mary was reluctant to go on, but Risa asked, "Who?"

"Lord John. Lord Hargrove's brother. I saw him leaving here one morning before the fires were lit."

Risa felt ill. Maddie had slept with John Hargrove.

"Many women take . . . lovers, 'specially at weekend parties. I was told so by Mrs. Porter and my new housekeeper, too. It is not my place to discuss what the guests do."

"Did you ever tell anyone else?"

"Oh, no. Never."

But Blake knew. Blake disapproved.

"Your sister, ma'am, may have had more than one. From this window here one afternoon"—she indicated the oriel facing the maze—"I saw her kissing a man in the gardens."

"Did you recognize him?"

"No, ma'am. The trees cut off my view. Besides, it is not my place to meddle, is it?"

"But—was it John Hargrove?" *Or another man? The same man Blake had seen.*

"Lord John Hargrove has a limp and this man didn't."

Oh, God. Blake had been right about Maddie's behavior. She was flighty. She had taken lovers. She wanted to marry. To perhaps run away.

Why? Why leave everything she had ever wanted? Her title? Her estate? What compelled her to run?

"Mary, draw that bath for me. I will be back as soon as possible." *Right now, I must talk to Blake. About Maddie. And John. And this mysterious other man.*

"Your cook is excellent, my lord," Ariel had tucked in a second serving of the roast beef.

"I'm delighted you think so, Ariel," Blake smiled at her, then took stock of Elizabeth's and Risa's plates. "I know she will be glad to hear that a majority of our guests like the fare." He lifted a brow at Risa's untouched plate.

"I assure you my appetite," Risa informed him, "is more for work." *And your company.*

Risa had come downstairs after her discussion with Mary to learn that Blake had gone into the village on business. His butler said he was not to return until just before dinner. And Risa was left to bathe, go to the studio, bathe and dress again.

Blake's mouth twitched with humor. "Humor me then. Eat a little. Attacking that rock in my studio without sustenance means you will surely faint away."

Ariel scoffed. "Risa's never fainted at anything."

"Strong, is she?"

"Very. She hasn't even cried over Maddie's death."

Risa stilled.

Elizabeth sucked in her breath, and reproved her niece with a keen cut of her eyes.

"Real grief is very difficult to display, Ariel." Blake informed her. "One reason why we are here recreating last year's event is to see if we can't give your sister the opportunity to properly mourn Maddie."

Risa stared at him. Once more, she marveled at how well he understood her.

"Really!" Elizabeth stood. "How indelicate to talk of this. Cerise, I am astonished that you sit there."

"Oh, Aunt, what would you have me do? Deny the truth?" She turned to Blake. "I won't."

Her aunt threw down her napkin. "Forgive me, I am suddenly ill."

"Your aunt simply cannot abide any discussion of last year," Blake murmured after the lady had gone from the dining room.

"Don't we all wonder how she will act when the other guests begin to arrive?" sighed Ariel.

"It won't matter," Risa assured them both. "She will endure it. After all, she chose to come here. I gave her the chance to refuse. She did not take it." *Thank God.*

Risa put down her own napkin. "Could I ask you to walk with me along the shore?"

"Perhaps, Ariel—" Blake began.

"No, please, Ariel, don't. I wish to speak with Blake alone."

"I can read a book until bedtime. Go." Ariel smiled.

Blake came from his place at the head of the table to pull out Risa's chair for her.

"I want to see the marble before Risa begins to hammer at it!" she called after them. "I will have another dessert first."

"Do that," Blake invited as he and Risa headed for the hall. "Does she have aspirations to sculpt?"

"None." Risa breathed in the salt-sea air when he opened the garden doors. "If she does, she has the spunk. But having another artist in the family should give her a few advantages."

"Mmmm," he reflected on that. "Perhaps."

"Did Barbara benefit from your pursuit of art?"

His chin came up, and Risa could feel from the tension in his body that he disliked the subject of his sister's artistic bent. "She was seduced by the aura of the lifestyle. It seems to offer great freedom. From schedules. From responsibilities. From norms. That appeals to the heart. The mind can be seduced by the glamour, drawn by lures of self-expression, acclaim, fame, fortune. The mind can therefore be deluded by them."

He looked at Risa, but she knew he saw her through the lens of his own disillusionment with his artistic career—and his torment over his sister's death. "Not everyone can reach their goals. The heartbreak of failure can gut you." He considered the moon. "It can kill you."

Risa strolled alongside him across the lawn toward the water's edge. "The disillusion can be temporary. You taught me that."

"Ah," he said more rationally, "it is easier for me to say it, easier for me to accept it, now that I no longer create anything myself."

"I would like to see your work."

"Not worth your time," he proclaimed, retreat in his words.

"I should like to be the judge of that."

"I saved a few."

"Here?"

"Yes. My old studio in the south wing."

He was not offering so she asked to be taken there.

"I do not go there myself."

"Why not?"

"I do not look at my failure."

"What discouraged you so?" she asked, but knew.

"My failure to acquire any large commissions. Any great reviews. And then about the same time, Barbara began to have problems with her own pursuit of art. Her failure combined with mine was more than I could bear."

"So." Risa screwed up her courage, treading into forbidden ground. "How long will you blame yourself for what happened to Barbara?"

His surprise that she knew mixed with a savage anger—and remorse. "Because I encouraged her, and I should not have. She was fragile. Even more than I was."

"You are not fragile."

"Ah, Cerise. Look closely, darling. I can be broken. Wanting and working for things I cannot have."

"That is why you do not sculpt?"

"My own disillusionment coupled with Barbara's death destroyed my will to create."

"How?"

His features were silvered by the moonlight and she could see despair there. "In this business, you never know just how weak you are until you look one day to see you are broken by its demands. Until your belief in yourself is trampled. Your dreams smashed." He squinted at the moon. "It is a tragedy, my darling, when your own desires turn against you.

"The greater tragedy for Barbara was I never saw it. I saw only her ambition and her hope. When she fell in love and wanted to marry, I warned her that her fiancé might not encourage her. I knew him. He was kind, he did love her, but he was a man of his class and expectations, and she . . . she thought anything was possible. She was adventurous, believed that life was fair. But she was naïve, too coddled by me to brave the inequities of the art world. She would crumble at the criticism of teachers and dealers and agents. She would quake at the criticism her husband began to give her about her long hours of work, her failures as a hostess and his wife. He wanted her to have children, and she asked that he use a means of contraception—" Blake glanced at Risa to see if she knew of such devices.

Female models Risa had met in Florence insisted their lovers use them. "Condoms?"

"Yes. He refused her. She came to me, frantic for advice. Heaven help me, I told her she could get a device herself. I told where she might buy a cap. I criticized myself, called myself hideous that I had helped her deceive her husband, but my God, my God, what was I to do? I wanted her to be happy. I wanted her to have what she wanted from life."

"Because you had not."

"Yes," he breathed, in awe that she perceived it, and in agony that he had to admit it.

"What happened to Barbara?"

Blake's nostrils flared. "Her husband found out that she was using it. He made a terrible row. He hit her. He left her. Told her he would not come back unless she gave up her painting and sculpting and agreed to have children. He needed an heir. And she could either give him one—or he would divorce her."

"Oh, Blake."

"She gave in. He returned. She tried to live his way. She couldn't. She would sneak into her old studio to draw. She came to me, asked me to let her visit me each day in London so that she could paint and sculpt. It was in her blood, like liquor or opium, she had to have the ecstasy. Everyday. Or she would die."

He jammed his hands in his pockets and walked away from Risa. "I let her come. But what good did it do? Her husband found out about it. He took her home and threatened her again. She gave in to his demands and abandoned her work. She took to laudanum. A way to drown the pain of loss. But it did not help. She saw no future for herself. Her dreams of an artistic life were gone. Her marriage to the man she loved in tatters. What was there left for her—" He swallowed, all sound gone from his voice. "—but to die?"

Risa wrapped her arms around him. He shook with grief and when he turned in her embrace, he took her by the shoulders. "I don't want that to happen to you."

"It won't." She smoothed his hair back from his temple. "You have given me such support that I am stronger now. Beyond that."

"I am happy that I've helped you. I worry about you. I want you to have what you want, need. I love you, Cerise." He brushed his thumb over her lips while her mind sang his declaration over and over. "I love you with a quiet madness that astounds me. I have never felt this way about any woman before—and God knows, I have had so many, I should be jaded. You make me feel like Apollo, darling. Fresh and young and absolutely wild to have you." He proved it with a dark deep kiss.

"But you bear some similarities to Daphne. You cannot be controlled, and I fear if I show you how needy I am of you, you will misinterpret my love and perhaps . . . disappear."

"I have never known anyone to love me that strongly."

"I do." He ran his big hands over her face. "And I want to be everything you need in a lover."

"Blake, you are."

"I still fear others may hurt you." He kissed her until her lips parted and his tongue took possession of her, until her body wept for want of him—and his heartache. "You don't know how cruel this profession can be, my love. Ambrusco was an amateur. There are far worse ghouls than he. Reviewers who have no training, no knowledge of your art, and yet they hold themselves up as authorities over your style, your intent. Other artists who will befriend you to learn your secrets, then betray you, defame you, undercut you, to advance their own careers. Agents who can dupe you into believing they like your work, but then desert you for other artists because they want them as clients. And patrons who will torment you with blithe promises of commissions they never intend to pay you. You can work for nothing. For years. To earn only despair."

Just as he had buoyed her up, so would she do for him. "And yet you encourage me. Give me the Carrara. Why?"

"A horrible dilemma. I want you to have what you want, I told you."

"But you would shut me away from the slings and arrows of failure?"

"I would to God I could."

"You can't."

"But I want to. I want to."

He grabbed her hand and ran down the lawn. In the

haze of her desire for him, she understood he took them both from the view of any in the house who might see them in the moonlight. He led her inside the studio and pressed her to the wall, his mouth upon hers as he trailed his lips down her throat to her shoulders. In the cool air of the evening, Risa felt the heat in Blake's hands as he lifted her breasts and stroked her.

"I'd like to touch you, too," she worked at his shirt studs. "Let's take this off and then my clothes."

"I wanted you in a bed." He was rueful as he turned her around.

"Mmmm." She plucked pins from her hair as he undid her gown. "You will have that opportunity for years to come. Tonight we are here—and you must be creative about what we shall use as our mattress."

He had her dress unhooked, but was fumbling with her corset. "First thing I do as your husband is burn all of these damn things."

She shimmied from her gown as he unlaced her and she felt her breasts become more free by the inch. When he had the contraption gaping, she flung it away, and spun around to caress him with her breasts. The effect had her eyes fluttering closed.

He set her world on end when he swept her into his arms and carried her to a pile of drapes which were soft as sheets when he laid her down. But instead of resting beside her, he surveyed her. "I told you once I would delight in posing you as I wanted." He leaned down to spread her hair upon the material. Then positioned her hands, palms up. Finally, he traced a finger down her chemise, around her nipples, to her belly and one of her garters. "You are a vision, Countess."

She examined him from this angle. He looked like a colossus of Rhodes. "I need a vision, too, my lord."

He quickly obliged her, removing every bit of cloth. And the sight of him aroused, was, from her vantage point, truly magnificent. She licked her lower lip. "Interesting pose. I could sell a statue of you like this and make my fortune."

He narrowed his eyes at her. "And what would become of your reputation?"

"Mine would be scarlet. Yours," she chuckled, "would be appropriately . . . cast in stone."

"You are," he said with a growl, "becoming a very audacious woman."

She grinned. "What a compliment."

He stretched out alongside her. "Let me see if I can give you something else you'll like."

"Oh," she soothed, as he unhooked her garters from her stockings and began to roll them down her legs. "Do try. I will tell you when to stop."

The next morning when she awoke in her bedroom, she noted that every move she made pulled a muscle she hadn't known she possessed. He had made love to her, at last count, three times. And true to his decision not to get her with child before they married, he had used sheaths to protect her. While she praised his care, she applauded his skill at lovemaking more.

So much more that she put her head into her pillow to stifle her laughter. She could recall many delights of their night together, but for none had she told him to stop.

16

*Men incline to believe that they fill all of one's life, but
as for me, I think that no matter how much affection a
woman has for her husband it is not easy to break with a
life of work.*

Berthe Morisot

"*I* am astonished that Mary never came to tell me any
of this," Blake said to Risa the next morning in his
study.

"So am I." Risa had found him there after she had
taken a late breakfast. She had surprised him as he reviewed a set of handwritten papers before him on his
desk. He had kissed her once and would have again if
she had not become serious and said she must recount
for him a conversation she had had with her maid yesterday afternoon.

"Mary seems to be honest and well-meaning. You
will let her go to Cowes, won't you, to fetch Maddie's
diary?"

"Of course, she can be up and back before supper. I
will send her in my coach." Blake reached for the
bellpull. "I'll have my butler order it brought round
while she gets ready to go. I will have him bring her to
me to tell her she's to set off immediately."

"Good. Thank you." Risa walked to his window which faced the lawn down to the shore. "Have you heard from John if he will come here for the recreation of the weekend?"

"Not a word. I am not surprised."

"I really would like to talk to him. Do you suppose he would come if I wrote and asked him to?"

"Come near me? I doubt it. He told me he never wanted to see me again. That was the day he left here."

"The afternoon before Maddie died," Risa said. "I will send him a letter and ask him to come. If he refuses me, so be it. At least I tried."

"The more immediate question is what to do about your aunt."

"Yes." Risa took the leather chair which faced his desk. "I was so stunned yesterday afternoon by Mary's revelations that I asked myself more questions than I could find answers. I cannot bear to think that Aunt Elizabeth knew about or condoned the forgery of Allure—and perhaps other art as well . . . and yet, what else can I conclude?"

Risa sighed. "She knew Maddie kept a diary and she must have seen her put it in the desk drawer. But why would she go down to supper and then return to Maddie's room and search for it?"

Blake scowled.

"What are you thinking?" she asked him.

"Wondering precisely when that was." He began to shuffle through the papers on his desk, then ran his finger down one.

"What have you got there?" Risa sat forward.

"My notes on the weekend. Ever since we began to plan this I have tried to refresh my memory of the event by jotting everything down that I remembered." He skimmed the next page and the next. "Well, I have nothing here to tell me when your aunt came down to the shore. Much of my memory of the evening is blurred by my anger at Maddie."

He sat back in his chair, rubbing his jaw.

"Lacking any new insights, I will go write your brother my letter."

"Yes. Best to do that as soon as possible. Tomorrow I have arranged an appointment with the constable who found Maddie's body. He is very kind. A friend of mine. You may ask him anything."

"Good. And so today, I shall go to work in the studio," she told him. "My hope is that while I measure the marble and begin my final sketches, I will have some inkling of what I must do about Aunt Elizabeth."

"Do? You mean confront her with what you have learned?" His voice deepened with alarm.

She nodded. "What else can I do? I cannot find the answers to my questions in any other way."

"I do not think it wise to prod a lion in a cage, darling. And your aunt is one, certainly. She chafes at being here because she must live through this again. And if she is guilty of anything, we will learn it. She is transparent in her anxiety now." He rose and took Risa's hands. "Please, I beg you, say nothing to her about what you know or suspect. The truth will come out, I tell you. That is why we go through this re-creation of the weekend."

"You are right. I must be patient." She pecked him on the cheek. "Will you come down to the studio later?"

"You want my company?"

She hugged him. "I adore it."

"So I do recall." He touched her cheek. "Are you sure I won't disturb you?"

"Pleasantly so, I would say."

"If you say I can," he hesitated.

"I have worked in a classroom studio with eight others. Why would I not want you in the same room with me when I work?"

"When I was at my best work, I could not bear company," he admitted.

"You are not me," she insisted. "Say you will come."

"Yes, of course." He walked her to the door. "Will you work long? You look tired."

"I am . . . but more in the vein of delirious with exhaustion."

"How appealing." He smiled.

"Can I expect you to continue the practice?" she teased.

"And keep you awake all night?"

She grinned. "And speechless, too."

"Your silence was eloquent."

She backed away from him. "Come to the studio whenever you like."

"I promise."

She had opened the door when another question disturbed her, and she closed it. "Blake? The man whom Maddie saw in your garden was one of your guests."

"Yes."

"Was there any man among them whose name begins with B?"

"Ben. Ben Woodward."

"The American? I wonder if Maddie would have found him attractive."

"She did," Blake said. "She encouraged him, so he told me, but later here she refused him, two days before she died."

"My God. She really did want to get married badly, didn't she?"

"Yes, it seemed that way to me."

"Blake, you know Ben better than I do. Could he have hurt Maddie for rejecting him?"

"I have asked myself that question about each one of

my guests last year. Of them, I would say that Ben resented her decision. Could he have drowned her? I cannot see him doing that, but then, I have recently learned that love can change a man. I am certain hate can do it too."

Disturbed by her conversation with Blake, Risa told herself to concentrate on the marble. She would show him that she could work with him near. She always had been able to do that. In fact, she liked variety in her days. She liked people, travel, books. She loved him. She would always want him near.

As for the mystery of Maddie's demise, she was working on that too. With Blake's help.

So she sat before the block of marble on the floor, crossing her legs in the comfortable linen trousers. From this vantage, she could view the stone from the same angle as she had seen Blake last night. The image brought a smile to her lips and summoned a fresh urgency to sketch. She had brought her pens and chalk and sketchpads with her from her desk and had them spread around her. She opened her pad and reviewed her preliminary drawings of Blake's face. His expression was the one he had worn the first night he told her he loved her—and last night here.

Risa sat, hand on her chin, appraising the sketch and the form of the marble. The size and shape of it did conform to the figure she wished to carve from it. One problem was to decide which side of the stone would look best for the front of the figure. And the marble had subtle veins, detectable only in brightest sunlight. If she chose well, she could be assured that the translucent veining would run the appropriate way. Up Blake's thighs, up along the planes and arcs of his arms to give her the essence of the living breathing man.

Excited about her project, she began to take measurements with the set of tools Blake had put out for her. Afterward, she took a long roll of paper from his supply on a drum by the wall, set it out along the floor and began to sketch in the dimensions which the finished sculpture would take. She reassured herself that the marble could duplicate the size and power of the man. It would be her artist's role to ensure that the marble represented the theme of a man in love.

The sun had set when she was finished with her dimensional plans. She tidied the studio, and made her way up to the house.

Tomorrow, she would have a few of Blake's footmen build a wooden vise at its base to ensure it did not budge when she began to hammer out the first major chunks. As they built the vise, she would calibrate the size of the sections of the figure and then, perhaps the next day, she would be ready to make the first cut.

With such a profitable day behind her, Risa hated to end it, but looked forward to supper and Blake's company. However, the meal was an even more tense affair than last night's. This time, Elizabeth retired quickly after the cheese and fruit were served.

Ariel had detected the underlying currents. "My lord, I wonder if you would mind if I asked the maid you assigned me to accompany me to the ruins of the Roman villa outside the village tomorrow?"

"I have no objection at all." Blake deferred to Risa. "If your sister thinks it acceptable."

Given Ariel's interest in Latin and all things from ancient Rome, Risa had suggested this to her back in London. "I understand the mosaics are beautifully intact. I wish I could go with you. But I do want to get as much as possible done on the Carrara before the party."

Blake studied Risa. "If you are to finish that piece, you will need more than ten days."

"Yes. After the guests are gone, I had hoped you would invite me and Ariel and Aunt Elizabeth to stay on, at least until I finish it." The projected time to finish such a large marble would be at minimum four months.

"You may stay as long as you wish, Cerise. I must return to London."

"Oh, but why?" Ariel asked with sorrow.

Risa felt as if he had already deserted her.

"I have business to conduct. My estates in Surrey need attention, and I have a client who wishes to buy a Rembrandt from a Bourbon prince. Poor fellow needs the cash to pay his tailor's bills."

Ariel was disappointed.

Risa was stunned. "I think I will take a walk along the beach. Excuse me."

She ran upstairs to her suite, fetched a shawl, and hastened from the house. The wind was brusque, the shawl of little help.

She had made her way to the studio without thinking about her destination. Inside, the chill of evening pervaded, but at least the wind did not cut her as it had on the shore.

She walked round and round the marble, trying to fathom why Blake was leaving her here after the party. Then she heard his footsteps on the stairs and soft across the floor.

"You are angry with me," Blake said without greeting. "I'm sorry. I broke that bit of news badly. I should have discussed it with you alone first."

"Yes. You should have."

"You must not think that I go away because I do not wish to be with you."

"Define for me what you would hope I think." Her mind, she thought with rueful amusement, turned to the practical.

He came to stand behind her. "You have done your sketches. And you must concentrate on your sculpting. You know that is the only way you will summon from the marble what you want."

"I will get the best from the stone. I know it now. It is," she asserted, "a glorious feeling. But I need you, too. Stay with me."

"You know what will happen if I do."

We will spend our days and our nights together. "Is that a terrible possibility?"

"I want to marry you more than anything else in this world, but—"

But? "If love is not nurtured," she said with conviction about her mother's love and her aunt's of their cheating husbands, "it dies."

"I have always thought that love endures all. Even lack of physical expression."

Risa shook her head. "Can it? This is the first time I have been in love, I do not know." Another thought occurred to her. Cruel, in some ways, it was necessary for her to ask of him. "Don't you wonder if in your absence, I would be driven to discover it with someone else?"

"No," he whispered while his arms wrapped around her, pressed her back against him. "Not someone else, Risa. Some *thing.*"

"What could that be?" She wanted to rest her head back against his shoulder, but she would not surrender while he tried to justify leaving her.

He kissed her ear, her throat. One of his hands held a breast. She sighed as he pressed her closer. She arched against him, straining to feel his strength. Through her layers of gown and petticoats he did no more than hold her while she imagined he caressed her as he had last night.

"Why?" He spun her about. "Because I must leave while you finish this."

"I do not understand."

"I want you to work here without interference. Without influence. I want you to have nothing else occupying your mind."

"Why?"

"Cerise, it has been a long time since you sculpted every day. I think it best you discover one love at a time."

"You think my love of art can exclude my love for you?" She was incredulous.

"Art is a demanding lover." His expression drained. "I want you to be certain that you want both of us."

"How can you question that?"

"You are young, darling. And very talented. I can see it in your sketches and *modellos*. I also see the fire in your eyes before and after you work. Finish this statue and then you will know if you want me, too."

"And what if I take longer to decide than a few months?" she shot back, fearful he would eventually turn to another woman to fill his need for companionship and sex.

"I will wait for you," he whispered. "Forever, if need be." And then he left her alone.

The next morning, she had a different perspective on their debate. She had slept fitfully. Memories of how he had made love to her stirred dreams of his mouth on her, but then he would say, "Goodbye, Cerise." And she would jolt up in her bed, searching for a way to make him stay.

But she would not ask again.

She would use other means.

So she donned armor. A spring green gown, better meant for the afternoon because of the depth of its décolleté. She wore her newest corset, and had Mary's substitute tighten the bodice to the point of bursting.

dALLURE271

Blake liked her breasts and he would have full sight of them this morning. Temptation, Risa thought, could be used by both partners in a match.

The maid who tied her corset was a friend of Mary's, so she said. Risa asked the girl if Mary had returned from Cowes.

"Yes, ma'am. Late last night she came in, and she is still sleeping."

Risa would see Mary later. She marched downstairs to the dining room.

Luckily, Blake was alone, frowning at his uneaten breakfast.

Good. "Lovely morning, isn't it?" she asked him as she surveyed the sideboard and took her own chair.

"Is it?" he grumbled.

"Are you reading the newspapers?" she asked and saw the untouched pile by his plate.

He handed them down to her.

"Thank you." She nodded politely at him and then the footman who came to ask her preference for tea or coffee. She took tea and proceeded to drink it in silence.

When she looked up, Blake met her gaze. She smiled back serenely.

Searching for her mood, he found her satisfaction, and nothing had made him scowl worse since she had met him. By the time the footman appeared to take away Blake's plate, he was rising from his chair.

Risa did not contain her chuckle. "It does not seem as if you had a good night's sleep, my love," she called as he was about to open the doors.

"On a bed of nails."

"My bed was very comfortable."

"Yes," he snorted, "I imagined it was."

She stood. "Have an appointment, do you, before we leave to see the constable?"

"No."

"May I help you with some problem until then? I am good at arithmetic. If you have books to balance or—?"

"You damn well know my problem is the lack of you."

She passed him by with a chuck under his chin. "Of your own making, darling. If you wish to see me before ten, you know where to find me."

He ground his teeth.

She departed for the studio. Pleased with her performance.

But, curse the man, he did not come to join her.

Clearly, luring him to her with her physical charms was not going to persuade him to change his mind about leaving her.

Why not?

He loved her. She believed that.

What could she do to make him accept her position? Simple conversation was obviously not going to work. She had to illustrate to him that to live without her would be a meaningless existence for him. How could she do that?

The constable was a jolly fellow. Not the usual sort of dry chap she thought would take up the post of protector of the peace. He was also efficient. He reviewed his own notes with her and Blake. She remembered them from the set he had sent through her solicitor last October. Nothing had changed. Except she now knew more, suspected more.

"I understand," she said when he was done, "that when people drown here off Wight, the bodies of the deceased are not often recovered."

"Yes, ma'am. That is true," Arnold Crowley told her without apparent thought to hiding the truth—or dismissing it. While this fact seemed crucial to Risa, to these two natives of Wight, the fact seemed so ordinary that both of them had discounted it as useful.

"I learned this yesterday from my maid at Sandown Manor. She was telling me about her sister's death."

"Mary Billings. Yes, that was sad," Crowley offered. "Always is to lose someone accidentally like that. The undertow, you see."

"I do. You see nothing odd in this, do you?" Risa asked of Crowley and Blake.

Blake rubbed his cheek with a finger, pondering.

Crowley shrugged. "When we have a body, it helps us answer our questions. We had one here, my lady."

"If the only bodies found are those that drown close to shore, then my sister must have suffered some foul play. Why?" she asked the question she saw in the policeman's face and Blake's. "Because Maddie was an excellent swimmer. She could have survived a boating accident in shallow water. Unless she was injured—or dead—before she left shore."

"But," Blake said, "I saw her get into the boat."

"And cast off. But how far did she sail out? You do not know," Risa insisted.

"I had left the dock, it's true," he said.

"Lady Lindsay," said the constable, "we have no indication of what your sister did. Only your conjecture."

Risa sighed, reconciling herself for now. "Thank you very much for your time. I hope I was not too much of an imposition on you, Constable."

"Not at all, Lady Lindsay. I am pleased to be of service." Risa began to rise.

"Arnie?"

"Yes, my lord?"

Blake sat opposite Risa in Crowley's office. "I wonder. Could you do me a favor?"

"Yes, of course. What?"

"Read that portion again about when you found her body. What you wrote about how she looked."

"Oh, Blake, ahem . . . my lord, you know she was not pretty." He glanced at Risa. "I don't want to offend you, ma'am."

"If you have anything to add," Risa said, "I am not squeamish. What is it that bothers you, Blake?"

"About the bodies not washing up on shore. Pardon me, darling, for the bluntness—" He squeezed her hand. "—but Arnie, please, read the portion of your report about how Maddie looked."

Crowley read it aloud. The constable had found Maddie's body, near broken planks of her boat, seaweed and debris around her body as it lay atop the rocks.

"Yes, yes." Blake was urgent. "But when you described to me that morning how she looked, you said she was lying on her back, and your words were 'peaceful as if someone had laid her down.' "

"Aye, Blake. She looked serene as an angel."

A chill walked up Risa's spine. "Are you asking if she could have been laid down there?"

Arnie's eyes popped. "Oh, Blake, I don't know—"

"Why not?" Blake persisted.

Arnie's brows knit. "I don't recall footprints along the beach. Even if there had been, the tide could have swept them away. Besides, Blake, you said she cast off. If she got into that boat and sailed away, are you saying someone captured her in their own boat, had some altercation with her, then placed her on the beach?"

Blake shook his head, forlorn. "Christ, Arnie, I don't know. I suppose that is possible."

"Possible, yes. But who would do that? Assuming it had to be one of your staff or your guests, Blake, who was missing from your supper party?"

Risa felt the vise of fear. Aunt Elizabeth returned to

Maddie's room. Had she been gone long enough to also hurt Maddie? No. No. Her aunt hated boats.

Arnie sat erect. "Are you suggesting someone may have killed her?"

Blake stared at him.

"We are not certain."

"No," Risa told Crowley. "We have only unanswered questions. The same as we have always had."

"I tell you this," Arnie asserted. "I interrogated every one of your guests and staff, Blake. It was my duty and you know I left no stone unturned. Have to, in these cases. So if you suspect that Madelaine Lindsay's death was not accidental, you had better tell me."

Neither Blake nor she had a cogent answer for him.

"He is a kind man," she told Blake when they were once more settled in his brougham. Already she was discarding her hat and gloves, unbuttoning the high collar of her dress in the growing heat of midday.

"Would a man who is unscrupulous enough to meet an unmarried woman at a house party, be ruthless enough to . . ." She could barely manage the words. ". . . hurt her?"

"If she threatened to reveal their affair. Yes. He might not wish the scandal. My love—" He tipped up her chin and when he brushed her cheek with his thumb, she could not back away. "Only four bachelors came to the party last August. Ben Woodward. Then there was Lord Matthew Pierce, who met Lily Nesbitt here and married her last autumn, and stays, I am told, fast in love with her."

"And the other two were John and you," she added.

"Yes."

"So assuming the man Mary saw in the maze—and the one you saw in the gazebo—are the same man, we must conclude that he was a married man. Oh, Maddie—" She mourned for the rashness of her sister. "—what happened to you?"

She wrinkled a brow. "Did you ever wonder last August if some man here may have hurt Maddie?"

"Not until lately. After Bartholome's death, I wondered if it were possible. Yet we have no reason to connect the two deaths. We know that Maddie knew Deville and that there was the fifty-six-hundred pounds in the safety deposit box. We also know Maddie received five thousand pounds for the sale of what we think was a copy of Allure."

"Which came to Maddie through Batholome."

"Yet," Blake added, "Bartholome was not here the night Maddie died. He could not have hurt her."

"Neither was Deville."

Risa grew numb from frustration. "If Maddie was murdered by someone here, we have no means to connect the forgery to her death."

"But was it a coincidence then that Maddie died accidentally, after paying all her personal debts with money she'd earned from forging pieces from the family art collection?"

"I don't think so, Blake. I never have."

But how did the facts connect?
Did Aunt Elizabeth know?

17

The big artist does not sit down monkey-like and copy.

Thomas Eakins

As their coach drew up the drive to Sandown Manor, Risa told Blake she wished to change into her linen to work this afternoon. But more than that, she wanted to ring for Mary and ask her if she had brought back Maddie's diary.

Blake let Risa go without objection. But he stood in the drive, watching her closely. Risa could feel his eyes on her as she departed. *Good for him to miss me,* she thought.

Upstairs in her suite, Risa pulled the bell for Mary. It took only five minutes or so for the girl to appear. But the look on the girl's face gave Risa a start.

"Where is the diary? Did you bring it with you?" she asked the girl.

"I'm sorry, ma'am, but I was not able to do a very good job of saving it."

Saving it? "From what?"

"Well, ma'am, my room at my new position is in the loft."

Most house servants slept in tiny rooms well above stairs. Most often, they slept in large dormitories with many others.

"Yes, and?"

"I left my belongings in the drawer of my settle and while I was here they had a rain and a big leak in the cistern on top of the roof. The dormitory flooded and my drawer got washed out. All my small clothes and two of my uniforms, they were ruined."

"What happened to Maddie's diary?"

"I have it."

"Where? What condition is it in?"

"Here." The girl took a shriveled drab leather book from her apron pocket and handed it to Risa.

Risa's heart fell. "The pages are stuck together."

"Not all of 'em. Some you can open."

Risa did. But the ink was smeared, most of it illegibly so.

She groped for her chair. She had set hope on this book helping her find the answers to some, if not all, of her questions about Maddie. And now, there would be precious little of that. A few turns of the warped and mildewed pages told her that.

"I am so very sorry, ma'am. I never thought anything like this would happen."

"No, of course you didn't, Mary. It is not your fault. These kinds of things are acts of God. We cannot control them." Risa sounded more accepting than she felt.

"There are some pages you can read, ma'am. I saw some. Oh, I didn't read too much, I didn't, but when I saw what had happened to the book, I was so upset that I had to look, you see."

"Yes, I do, Mary." Risa squeezed the maid's hand. "You have done so very well and I thank you."

"If you don't need me any more, I can go."

"Thank you, yes."

"Would you like a pot of tea while you read, ma'am? I could get it for you."

"No, Mary, I only wish to sit and try to read my sister's entries. Thank you."

The girl bobbed. "Welcome, ma'am, I'm sure."

Risa opened the book before Mary closed the door. The inks were blue or black, all run together now like small dark rivers frozen on the page. *Dear Diary*, Risa could make out on many of the pages because she knew Maddie's handwriting and the words were repeated over and over. She could decipher a few words, but fewer complete sentences.

The diary began in January and Maddie had put in a few large words about how she hoped the new year was happy.

Risa paged through until she found a few pages from the spring. They were clumped together and Risa had to peel them apart. On one in April, Maddie scrawled that she had enjoyed her presentation to the queen. *Rapture*, she had written afterward. *I am one of the Bright Ones. This means someone will love me, ask for my hand— Thank God. B. surely won't.*

Tears formed on Risa's lashes.

A few weeks later in May, Maddie had boldly printed, *I AM RUINED*. But the rest of the day's entry was too washed out to make any sense of the squiggles of ink.

Ruined. How? The usual meaning of ruined for a young woman was that she had succumbed to a man's seduction or she carried an illegitimate child.

It was possible, but oh, Risa's heart ached to think that Maddie had become pregnant.

Doctor, Risa found on one of the next pages, and brushed away a tear from her own cheek.

Then, on another page, she found *I am sad, Dear Diary. B. will not . . .*

Risa squinted at the watery words. *B. will not . . . What will he not do?*

Risa thumbed through more crinkled pages.

Must marry J. came pages later. And by June, there were entries that had escaped the water. In June, Maddie had gone from happy to hateful. B. was her nemesis. B., she declared, was also her only love.

By August there were large blocks of print that declared *DESPERATE!* and *MUST LEAVE SOON!* with exclamation points that had gouged the paper. Maddie was either angry or sad. *CRYING,* she wrote on one page, *ALL THE TIME!*

Then July came and Maddie wrote of escaping to Sandown.

Finally, Risa turned a few pages with only the dates on them and then—

August 5, 1880

Dear Diary,

Risa sat straighter. Less ink had run on these latter pages. The writing was water-marked, but legible.

I am escaping! Tonight! I must pinch myself to believe it. My mistakes and my failures, I can at last put behind me. He has asked me to marry him, and I cannot refuse. His understanding is all I ever asked for, to turn my days to gold. Now I shall be happy.

I pray it will be so. Given the choice between bringing more shame to the title of countess of Rossborough, and doing what I must to save some shred of my self-respect, I know what I must do.

*I hope to God that he and I may depart Sandown unde-
tected and quickly. But after we are gone, I do wonder if we
will be able to live in peace or if*

Maddie's script trailed off as if she had been surprised at something or someone.

Maddie was about to run away to be happy and
someone stopped her.

Who?

She ran down the stairs and saw Ariel leaving the library. "Have you seen Blake?"

"Yes. He went riding. I wanted to go with him, but
he begged off. He looks awful, Risa. Are you having a
lovers' quarrel?"

"We're not fighting. We're debating."

"Isn't that the same thing?"

"I do hope not. Where did he go riding? Did he give
you any indication?"

"None."

Risa headed for the stable block. "Perhaps the
grooms have an idea."

But they didn't. Both stood shaking their heads at
her.

"Thank you then. I appreciate your kindness."

She decided to go to the studio and try to work. She
trudged up the lawn and into the house, then to her
room to change out of her gown.

Within minutes, she was crossing the grass, headed
for the shore and her work. The sky was the clearest
blue she'd ever seen. Ironic, that, when she had so
many clouds on her personal horizon.

Forcing back any despair, she vowed to put her
problems out of her mind and let it be filled with her
art. Her project must go on. The sooner she finished
it, the sooner she would be a married woman.

Or to be exact, if she let her instinct lead her to a solution to that dilemma, the sooner she might think of a way to show Blake he could not exist without her.

But the sun began to set before she could say she had any finite idea of what she must do.

Idly, she put her drawings and tools away and ran up the dunes to the lawn and the house. She changed for dinner, Mary assisting her with the folderol of corset, petticoats, and dinner gown. Having worn her comfortable linen for so many hours, Risa chafed in the starch and whale bones. Confined once more, Risa's mind turned to Maddie's death.

Dinner was dispirited. Elizabeth was mute. Ariel was tired. Blake was trying to do his duty as host, but he seemed to be preoccupied. When Risa tried to start a conversation, Blake joined her efforts. But Risa was affected by her aunt's recalcitrance and bad manners. Risa herself grew too tired to participate. When her aunt and Ariel made their excuses, Risa remained. She did not really want to talk with Blake, but she knew she must tell him about what she had read in Maddie's diary.

"Can I offer you a brandy?" Blake offered.

"Yes. Please."

"Why don't we go into my study?" he suggested when he had two snifters in hand.

Risa chose a big leather chair, while Blake stood by the fireplace.

They drank in silence for a minute when Blake said, "I went riding today. I heard you were looking for me."

"Yes, I have more news to tell you. Mary brought me Maddie's diary." She summarized the condition of the book, the variety of entries and their contents. "My conclusion is that Maddie was pregnant. I have a suspicion from the diary entries that the father was this B., but I cannot be positive."

"So that's why she wanted to marry so urgently."

"I think so, yes. If she could not have B., instead she would marry your brother John. But when you met her on the dock that night and told her you forbid John to marry her, she was bereft. After that she got into the sailboat and . . . never returned." She took a sip of her brandy and looked listlessly at the fire dance behind the grate.

"Risa." Blake went down on one knee before her, put her brandy on the table and then reached for her hands. "Darling, are you saying that now you think Maddie may have committed suicide?"

"I don't have enough evidence yet, Blake. I certainly don't want to believe it now. I could not before I learned she might have been pregnant, but . . . it is true, that if I loved a man who deserted me, I would be forlorn."

"You would not hurt yourself," he protested.

"Perhaps not. But if I were carrying his child and he would not marry me, the thought would cross my mind."

He searched her eyes. "You would never be in that circumstance with me."

She blinked. "Are we suddenly talking about you and I?"

"We are."

"But our circumstances are different from Maddie and her lover. He was not so careful as you. You promised me to take care not to give me a child before we wed, and except for our first time together, you have taken that precaution. Why would I think ill of you?"

He examined their intertwined hands. "I have given you cause to doubt me and I don't mean to. I said I would leave you here after this weekend because I wanted you to be certain that you could love me forever."

Suddenly his logic, wrong as it was, became clear to her. "You mean that you are concerned that *I* would leave *you?*"

"Eventually. Over the years. Perhaps you would grow tired of me. Want someone new who could stimulate your creativity more than I." He knit his brows. "I don't know how to explain it other than to say that if I married you and I could have you beside me every day, how could I ever let you go? If you became bored with me or—"

"Stop, please, there." She had to bite her lip not to shriek at him in laughter or outrage. How did men think? She was just beginning to learn. And she wondered if they had a brain in their heads when it came to understanding women. "Tell me, did you ever become bored with any of your mistresses?"

He blanched.

"*Did* you?"

"Yes. Every one."

"I see." She pursed her lips. "And do you doubt you will become bored with me?"

"Absolutely."

"Good. Very good." She tried desperately not to gloat. Instead, she rose and lead him toward the door.

"Where are we going?"

"Your room."

"Why?" He halted in the middle of the room.

"We are going to spend the night together. I am going to count how many times you can bore me. Now please, darling," she said after she opened the door, "tip-toe, will you?"

He was suppressing laughter.

He had continued trouble with that as he followed her up to his suite where he thrust open the door, scooped her into his arms, and shut the thing with a thud.

"You'll wake the house," she scolded.

"Just wait until you hear how."

"I am all ears."

He chuckled as he laid her on his mattress. "My love, your ears are very pretty. But I thank the good Lord you are not all ears. In fact, I like your legs better."

"Good. You are doing very well not to bore me. Anything else you like about me?"

He rolled her over to unhook her gown. "Let me see the rest of you and I will sing your praises as I go."

"That sounds fair. But do you carry a tune well?" she said into the mattress.

"Better than you, I wager."

She rolled around to face him. "What will you wager?"

"What do you want that I have?" he asked in a silken tone.

"All of you," she breathed, her fingers combing through his rich black hair.

"You have me."

She was heartened. "And that you will reconsider leaving here after the party."

"Yes, Cerise, I thought it through this afternoon. I promise to discuss it with you. Tomorrow."

"Excellent. Now what can I wager, let me think . . ."

He hovered over her, his lips a kiss away. "What would you like to give me?"

"Ohhh, I am sorry to say I did not anticipate this wagering business and I did not bring it with me."

"No?" he eyed her breasts so leisurely that she felt them swell with want of him. "I'd say you have everything I need."

She became innocent. "I could leave now and get it. Or can you wait until morning?"

His green eyes went to slits. "You will not leave this room until dawn."

"Get busy quickly then, will you? I am getting bored . . . talking."

18

⚜

When I sit down to make a sketch from nature, the first thing I try to do is forget that I have ever seen a picture.
John Constable

"That was a waste of time," Risa tugged at her gloves the next morning as she and Blake left Sir Giles Evelyn's house.

"He told us nothing we did not know, true," Blake said of the judge, as he helped her into his brougham.

"The same as Doctor Viner. Honestly, a less likely character to be a women's physician I have never met." Her distaste for the coroner whom they had seen just before the judge, matched Blake's.

"Gruff," Blake conceded.

"Rude. When did you say he moved here from London?"

"Almost a year ago."

"He would suit better in the city, although, even there, I doubt many women would seek him out. I would not."

"He has a small practice. People go because they must," Blake added, "or suffer."

"I am very disappointed that he was so uncooperative," Risa said. "I never thought he would be so protective of his doctor and patient relationship."

"I know, darling. But I thought I did see a spark come to his eyes when you asked if he examined Maddie's body for any signs of pregnancy."

"Yes. But obviously we did not know how to make him tell us anything he knew or suspected. He simply said no that he had not examined her body for that."

They sat a while in silence as the carriage rumbled over the country roads.

"Sir Evelyn was more congenial," Risa said at last.

"Even if we now know he still thinks Maddie died accidentally," Blake regretted.

They had shared with the judge the fact that Maddie had kept a deposit box with cash in it and they suspected she hid the cash because she had gained it illegally. To that, Evelyn had arched two white brows and asked "The connection to her death is what, exactly?" Risa nor Blake could prove there was one. They told him of her diary entries and then Risa dug it from her reticule to show him the last entry.

"Again, this gives me no cause to reopen the case," Evelyn had said.

They went on to recount their discussion with Arnie Crowley the previous day, and the judge proclaimed, that for lack of evidence there too, he could find no reason to order another inquest.

"It does not matter what Crowley thought when he first saw Lady Lindsay's body on the beach," the elegant gentleman told them with sarcasm that spoke of their audacity to question his ruling. "It does not signify that he thought her artless in her pose. It does not give me any cause to question the coroner's analysis. There seemed to be no signs of brutality to the body that the sea might not have inflicted. Bring me evidence that I should reconsider, and I will. Otherwise, I am delighted to see you in such good health, Lord Hargrove, and to meet your acquaintance, Lady Lindsay."

"Crusty old bugger," Blake muttered, as he settled beside her.

"Likes his power, doesn't he?"

"South of Cowes, he ranks just below me in station. He never lets me forget it, either."

"You bear your neighbors well," she vowed.

"Thank you, darling."

"Why not come over here? I'll help you bear other burdens."

His body, hungering for hers, responded immediately to her smile. "In my carriage?"

"Unless your coachman is used to being stopped along the road for rendezvous?"

He crossed his arms. Warned himself not to accept such an invitation to make love to her without benefit of condoms and so dangerously near home. But hell, he would marry her if she became pregnant before she finished her statue. He would take the chance that she would stay by him always. God knew, if she kept up this business about not boring him, he was going to be so greedy to have her in his bed he would marry her today if he could get a damn special license. But he couldn't. He had to get those on the mainland from a bishop. *Tough thing, to have to please her anyway, old man.* "Eager, aren't you?"

"Aren't you?"

He sat forward, scooped her up, and sat her in his lap. "Didn't have enough last night?"

"What is," she crooned as his fingers undid buttons of her gown and thrust inside to lift her breast from the damned corset, "your definition of enough?"

"With you? None," he murmured as he skimmed

his lips atop the swell of one smooth-as-cream nipple.

"I'm very good," she arched backward, "with numbers."

"And it was—" He yanked at the infernal hook on her corset. "—how many?"

"Four. Definitely four."

He had barely been able to walk straight this morning. He had exerted himself, careful of her novelty to the art, only too eager to love her again and then again. Even now, he could not tell her no. "I forbid you to wear these contraptions," he murmured as he lowered her corset more.

"Oh, do. I hate them. Pantalettes, too."

"Convenient." He pushed up her skirts and trailed his hand up her thigh to find to his surprise, no such garment. "Terribly convenient." He showed her just how much so—and had her clutching him in the fulfillment of her ardor and him groaning in his frustration as the coachman turned them into his drive.

Blake brushed down her skirts, righted his own clothes and thought of himself ruefully. For a man who had enjoyed many a woman, wherever, whenever he wanted, enjoying this one whom he loved was a treat as sweet as candy—and a torment bitter as gall.

He could not deny her or himself last night, nor today. Nor any day. So he would give them both what they wanted, and pray she married him and stayed married to him till he died.

He had wanted to wait to marry her until after she had enjoyed a long strong dose of independence. But if she did not agree, if she cut him out of her life, what good was his decision? He could be noble—and alone.

He wanted to be with her as her lover, her husband, perhaps the father to her children. But he recognized

in her the signs of her total dedication to her work.
Signs he himself had noted when he was in love with
his art . . . and nothing else quite equaled the ecstasy.

He raised her chin now, adored her star-bright eyes,
so filled with lust and love for him. "You need to work
today."

"Yes," she said. "Come model for me?"

"You want me there today?"

"Yes." She kissed him languidly. "Will you?"

"Of course."

While he waited for the guests to arrive, and this
weekend to be recreated, he would do as she wanted
and make love to her. Because when the event was finished, they would talk more about his decision to leave.
And barring the possibility that she might be pregnant
from these few times when he had rashly failed to use
protection, he feared that conversation would not solve
their conflict.

He would go away.

Vienna, perhaps. Or a quieter place like Napoli.

He could not stay here.

Would not. Because he could not bear to watch her
grow, as she surely would. And perhaps, grow beyond
him and his love.

But his delightful torture did not end.

She wanted him to model for her. So he went to his
rooms to change out of his morning attire and don a
shirt and trousers similar to what he'd worn when he
had posed for her in London.

The shirt, however, she quickly removed.

"Your trousers, too," she urged, a finger tapping her
lips.

He balked.

Her eyes delved into his. "What can be the problem?" she asked, innocent of her demand.

He grabbed her hand and pressed it to him. "This."

"Oh." A grin lit her face. "And I am so pleased."

He snorted. "Darling, your pleasure can be contained." When she wrinkled a brow, he explained, "Remember the coach?"

"Yes, of course," she replied, her cheeks going pink.

"A man's can't. Not for hours and hours. And if you strip me to my skin, my love, I will be in pain."

"Pain?"

He rolled his eyes toward the roof and prayed for strength of his own. "A man cannot walk around in a perpetual state of want, lest he find himself in pain. The . . . uh . . . body was not meant to want for too long, darling, without reward."

"Well, then—" She became an imp. "—I shall have to reward you, won't I?"

"You won't finish this marble."

"Ah, maestro. Observe!"

He did.

By day, he watched her in her absorption at her work.

And by night, he watched her in his bed. She learned to initiate their love play and to kiss him till he feared apoplexy. What amused him more than any fantasy she fulfilled was the way she stopped his heart with her inventiveness.

He hated the day to dawn when his guests began to arrive. But come they did, and their presence meant he must become more watchful of their secret hours, their playfulness on the beach, in her studio, in his suite. Careful now to wake her nearer four than five, he cut short their views of dawn together. And as soon as he had closed his door upon her to return to his lonely bed, he missed her.

* * *

Ben Woodward was the first to arrive on Wednesday.

"Curiosity is my excuse," Woody confided to Blake over a welcoming tea. "London buzzes with the potential match between you and Cerise. Good thing she brought her aunt and sister, buddy, or you would be the blackguard of the Season."

Blake was not particularly surprised that gossips had learned of Risa's early arrival here. But he was pleased that they did not brand her with a poor reputation. When Blake left here next Thursday or Friday morning to return to the city, many would wonder what relationship he did have with the lovely Lady Lindsay.

"Where is she, by the way?" Woody asked.

"My studio. Working."

"Sculpting? Good for her. Is she any good?"

Woody's tone struck a sour note. Was the American asking about other than Risa's ability in art? "Superb."

"May I have a peek?"

"You will have to ask her permission, Woody. She will join us at dinner."

"I look forward to renewing our acquaintance then."

Dinner began on a high note as Woody was his most charming, accepting Ariel at the table with an American's breeziness and being chatty with Risa about the debutante season she had abandoned. Elizabeth had begged off tonight with a headache, and Blake was glad. The woman was becoming more and more irascible as the days went on. However, by the soup course, the goodwill faded when Woody asked if he might come see Risa's work.

"I prefer that you not," she told him with a firmness to her decision Blake applauded. "I hope you don't mind. I am sensitive. It is crude, the figure barely emerging from the stone. The relief is not yet meaningful except to me."

Woody took her rejection with aplomb. "I defer to your wishes, of course. What is your subject?"

She gave him a thin smile. "I do not wish to say."

"Surely, you can tell me. I collect. I am no novice in these things. I am—"

"Forgive me, no. It is not the way I want to work on this piece."

Woody opened his mouth to argue.

Blake quieted him. "If Risa is protective, Woody, surely you can excuse her."

"I simply want to see it. Perhaps, if I like it, I will buy it."

"Blake owns the marble, Woody. I have not purchased it from him."

"Well, then." Woody was unperturbed. "I will buy it from you!"

"Woody, if Risa does not wish me to part with it, I won't."

"You don't even know what it is!"

Across the long table, Blake's eyes met hers. "I do." He knew the figure she urged from the marble was some representation of him, but he had no idea precisely what it was. Nor did he ask. The figure lived in her mind and, he thought, in her heart. It warmed him. Thrilled him. Made him want her all the more. Made his decision to leave her more difficult.

Woody sat a minute, examining both. "I see." Then he let the subject drop.

When Ariel retired, Risa rose.

"I think I shall retire, too. Then you two may have your brandy and cigars."

Woody accepted the brandy but not the cigar. His trip, he claimed, had tired him and he found his way to his suite soon afterward.

Blake watched him mount the stairs, waited until the

man's footsteps faded down the hall, then he himself took the steps two at a time.

He rapped on Risa's door, let himself in, undoing his cravat and draping it over a chair, discarding his tails and vest and shirt as he walked into her bedroom. He let out a chuckle at the sight of her.

She sat, red hair spilling over her full and pouting breasts, utterly nude, cross-legged like a girl, amid reams of her sketches, a crayon stuck between her teeth. The minute she saw him, she bounded from the fluff of her pillows and hugged him. "Come here, quickly," she urged him, flicking his flies open. "I need you badly." In a second, she had him naked as she. "Stand there, would you? Put your leg out. Like this." She put one foot before her, then sank to her knees in front of him and ran her fingertips up his inner thigh.

"Darling," he grimaced, "what is it you wish here?"

"This muscle—" She traced it. "—I need to see it flex."

Other muscles jumped at her touch. "Does it?"

"Mmmm," she licked her lips, and he imagined her before him using her mouth on him in another place. "Oh, yes. Beautifully." Her palm branded him. His heart slammed about like a cricket ball. "Now, come to bed and lie down. On your back." She giggled when he suckled her breasts. "No, later, later. I promise. I must see your leg."

"My love," he corrected as she wrapped her hand around him securely, "*that* is not my leg."

She was chortling, the witch. "But big enough to use for balance, don't you think?"

"Carve me that way," he growled as he rolled her onto her back, "and I shall lock you up and throw away the key."

"I'll gladly go if you come, too."
Would that I could—and you'd be happy.

And as the other guests arrived, her playfulness vanished. Her need to sculpt increased. Became a compulsion, a force, as vital to her as air or food.

"You must come to dinner, love," he insisted the Thursday afternoon that her cousin Georgie and Robert Dungarvon finally came with the Pierces and two other couples to complete the total of twenty-one guests. John, as expected, had not attended, nor even sent his regrets. "The stage is set now. Everything is as it was last August."

She faced him. In her linen tunic and trousers that she had donned after she had left his bed, she was covered in a fine powder from the marble. He had given her his old beret into which she had stuffed the wealth of her red hair. Now white, it matched her complexion and the film on her glasses. The whole effect made her look ghostly.

He was suddenly afraid, for the first time since he had discovered Bartholome's body.

"I will come. I am being petulant, I know." She swung round to view the marble.

From its mass, Blake saw the first definitions of what it would become.

Him. A man joining his lover in bed. It could be no other. From the cant of his head to the thrust of his thigh, this was a man utterly in love with the woman before him.

He had been so right to believe in her talent.

More right to love her.

Even now he would protect her.

He put his arms around her. Pressed a kiss to her head. "My love, we will come through this. We will learn what we can."

"And if we learn nothing new?" her old desperation resounded in her words.

He turned her in his embrace. "Then you must accept that, grieve for Maddie so that you can continue with your work."

"And then you will marry me."

He kissed her deeply. She took it as his agreement. He could not bear to say she should interpret it as *au revoir.*

19

~~~~~

I am risking my life for my work, and half my reason is gone.

<div align="right">

Vincent van Gogh to his brother, before his death

</div>

By Thursday, all twenty-one guests had arrived, been lavishly put up in their suites of last year, and the first dinner party of the four-day event began. The dinner conversation was lively, the guests eager to renew acquaintances and test the waters as to Blake's real intentions when he invited them down.

Blake, Risa noted with pride, was the consummate host. Making polite but bland replies to any inferences about his intent to have these visitors here again, he was charming, attentive—but more so to Risa. So much so that it spurred Lily Pierce to note afterward when the ladies had retired for coffee, how he deferred to Risa, "and seats you to his right."

Risa nodded, well aware her position at Blake's table would inspire a wealth of speculation that she was not merely his honored guest, but his hostess here.

Her seating, he assured her earlier, was the same as on the first evening of last year's event, when he had put Maddie to his right, attempting to keep his brother far from her sister. This year, however, John Hargrove's chair was empty.

"I did not expect him," Blake said later that night, one arm flung over his eyes as he lay upon Risa's bed. They had chosen her room to meet tonight because it was at the end of a hall nearer the back staircase. This way, he could come and go with less chance of others detecting his movements—and it afforded more privacy than his own suite, which was located at the other end of the house, past every guest's bedroom.

"We will do without him." Risa told herself that they must. "Everyone was very on their toes tonight, bent on proving to themselves this was not a re-creation but a true holiday. Even Aunt Elizabeth rises to the occasion."

"Don't you think Georgie gave her a swift kick to make her come round?"

Risa toyed with a smile. "I do." Then she removed her robe and lay down beside him. "Must I do the same to you to make you smile at me?"

His mouth curved up. "You know what you can do to get a smile from me."

She did.

But in the velvet hours before dawn after Blake left her, she felt the tension coil around her like a snake. This morning, there would be breakfast, and a shooting party, culminating in luncheon in tents near the edge of Blake's forest. The afternoon would begin with an hour of free time, permitting the ladies to rest or read. Some chose to ride. Last year, Blake told her, Maddie had chosen to nap.

With whom? John Hargrove? Or this other mystery man with the initial B.?

Risa rose from her bed and dressed for the dining room. A morning gown of blush sateen was what she picked. This was a dress Blake had never seen her in, but viewed with a wink of approval as she served herself eggs and ham patties from the sideboard.

A shooting party had never been her style. But she decided to go along, as Maddie had done.

The Pierces, Ben Woodward, Robert, Georgie, and Blake were in competition to pull as many pheasant from the air as possible. Blake had stocked his forest with them last September, as he did every autumn, so that they would be fat for the event. This year because it was spring, he apologized, they would not be quite as fat nor numerous.

If one liked such events, Risa told herself, attempting to rise above her need to desert these people in favor of her work. Her figure, or rather Blake's, came along nicely. Its squareness giving way to an elongated presence. The head, well shaped, tilted just so. The base, his spread legs, adequate to the task of balancing the form. Today, at nap time, she would begin the chisel work to outline more of the protruding portions and etch the relief higher.

"Don't you shoot?" Ben Woodward asked of her, when he had spent all his shot to bag one bird.

"I am not very good," she told him, trying to smile at this man whom she disliked. "My eyesight is better at distance, but even then, I am not quick enough. I prefer slow work."

"I really would like to come take a peek at your sculpture. It's invigorating to find a woman who sculpts."

"Yes, it is." She pretended to be interested in Georgie's aim.

"You will need all the help you can get if you wish to get commissions."

Was he inferring that he could help her? She shivered in dislike. "My best aid will be the excellence of my work."

He turned his head, narrowed his gaze. "Like your sister, aren't you?"

In very few ways. "Do you think so?" She wanted him to talk about Maddie, last year. That was why she was here. And him, too, for that matter.

"She could be independent, too."

"Circumstances made us that way. Popular wisdom has it American men like that in women." *Did you like Maddie?*

"The wisdom is right. I thought your sister was swell." Sorrow laced his tone.

Risa met his gaze. "Did she like you?"

"Not as much as I wanted her to." He screwed up his face, examined Robert pulling back for his set of shots. "She had a lover here at Sandown last August."

She gaped at him.

"You didn't know. I didn't think you would."

"Such things are not spoken of," she replied, lowering her voice lest others overhear.

"I had the feeling . . ." He scanned those in the party. ". . . that she wasn't proud of her relationship. Which means, he was a married man." He looked down, scuffing the dirt. "I hated that. That she wasted herself on him."

"Yes. I . . . Yes." She had misjudged this man entirely.

Blake caught her eye across the lawn. She could see he debated whether to join this conversation. So she smiled at Ben Woodward.

"I am so pleased you told me. I have had difficulty coming to terms with Maddie's loss. She was very dear to me and she helped me immeasurably by paying for my education when she did not have the means."

"I know."

"You do?" Nothing could have socked the wind from her more easily.

"She and I used to laugh that she was the first noblewoman of England, but she needed cash . . . and I was a scalawag's son with no pedigree and a bank full of greenbacks. How ironic life is."

Dinner began with a gathering in the conservatory. Georgie honored them with a turn at the piano and many joined in as they drank their aperitifs. A latecomer was Robert Dungarvon, however, and the reason for his delay was that he was utterly sloshed.

"Bobbie, darling"—Georgie rose from the piano— "you are not feeling well." She took his arm and tried to steer him past her mother, Blake, and Risa. "Excuse us, please."

As she walked him down the hall, Risa could hear Georgie scolding him and he returning insults.

Blake locked gazes with Risa who came forward, took his arm, and said, "Would you like me to tell the butler he may serve now?"

"A good idea, darling. Please."

Dinner was more strained than the previous evening. But Blake and Risa managed to get through it with a smile to their guests as they went out for a stroll on the beach, or up to their rooms to bed.

"Robert's drinking is becoming more frequent," Blake told her later in her room.

"Georgie becomes more of a harpy, too."

"Can't say as I blame her," Blake replied.

"No. But she shames him. She almost sounds as if she dislikes him."

"Hates him?"

"Yes," she said. "Interesting how suddenly you look at someone one day and he or she no longer looks like the person you knew."

"Perspective, they call it."

"Another person who is not what I thought is Ben

Woodward." She recounted her discussion with him that morning.

Blake expressed as much surprise as she over Woody's regrets about his relationship with Maddie. "And all this year," he said, "I wondered if he had a heart. Interesting, to find both of us had a different view of him."

Saturday's events consisted of croquet on the lawn in the morning, luncheon in the main dining room, rest and a nap. The evening was the re-creation of the supper party on shore and a moonlight sail for anyone who wished to take the offer of one of Blake's boats.

"I told you," Blake insisted early Saturday morning before he left her room, "you will not get into a boat."

"I will. There is no other way to ensure that we refresh people's memories."

"No one saw her cast off except me, and I forbid you to go."

"I am a decent sailor."

He took her shoulders. "I do not care if you are Christopher Columbus."

"Now who is being stubborn?"

He picked up his robe, looped the sash round his waist and cinched it. "You will *not* get into one of my boats."

"Why?"

"Bad luck."

"It is more than that. What?"

"A jinx." He strode toward her sitting room.

She caught his arm. "No." She stepped in front of the door. Traces of his old brooding etched his eyes. "Darling, no one is going to hurt me."

"I cannot be sure . . . so I will not let you go."

"If we recreate this evening exactly as it was last year, then you must come and watch me cast off."

He crossed his arms. "I see no new clues here. Nothing we didn't expect. Except Woody's revelation about how he cared for Maddie, and that isn't helping us in any way. And I worry."

She framed his face and felt a tremor from his tension. He had done a skillful job of hiding it from her.

What else had she not seen?

"What are you not telling me?"

"Arnie has called on the help of a few constables from Cowes and they are stationed at various points along my shore. One of the footmen is Arnie's recruit. When anyone goes out tonight, I am to give a list of those gone to the footman who will give it to Arnie."

"Whose suggestion was this? Arnie's?" She waited.

"I asked him to put on a few men for this evening."

"You are afraid for me?"

"You are getting close to discovering many secrets about Maddie. If your aunt is to blame or not, I do not know, but she certainly is a good choice for a suspect."

"Do you really believe that my aunt would hurt my sister?"

"Believe? No. Suspect? Yes, darling, I do. And I do not trust her. And if Maddie did die by someone else's hand, then I do not trust him or her to leave you alone for long. And that is the reason I asked Arnie for help."

Blake ended her questions about that, but she felt there might be something else he was not telling her.

What was it?

The question drove her, not to the croquet match, but to the studio. There, in her linen and beret, with her chisel in hand, she worked on a substance that would render up its secrets to her. She went about discovering them with a determination she had not known in over two years.

The sun was setting when she stepped away from the finer outline of the throat and shoulders when the sounds of footsteps had her turning toward the door.

At the knock, she called for them to come in, and felt the mallet grow heavy in her hand as she stared at her visitor. "Doctor Viner, please . . . please, come in."

He did so, gingerly.

She stepped down from her wooden riser, removed her beret and wiped her hands on a clean damp cloth. "Please, have that chair." She indicated the only one in the studio. "I have few visitors. Let me clean my glasses, won't you?"

He did as she told him, removing his top hat and twirling it like a boy come to call. So totally at odds with the self-assured man she had met days ago was this fellow, that Risa marveled he was the same one. But here, she thought with shock, was one more man she had not seen in full perspective. The doctor was nervous.

Why?

"I wish I could offer you tea, but I'm sorry to say, I have none. If you prefer we go up to the house, I—"

"No, thank you, Lady Lindsay. I prefer this. I asked for you at the door, and the butler told me you were here. I hope you forgive my intrusion."

"Of course, I do." *Tell me why I do.*

He concentrated on the figure of the man before him. "Impressive. You are talented."

"Thank you."

"Your sister spoke of you."

Risa's breath left her lungs. He knew Maddie when she was alive? "When?"

"Over a year ago. In London. She did not give me your name, but said her younger sister would one day be famous."

She wanted to fly at him, shake the rest out of him. But she stood, unmoving. Did he think her composed about such a revelation? "Please . . ."

He inhaled, looked about at everything and nothing in particular. "She came to see me at St. Margaret's when I was staff there. She was carrying a child—a child she did not want—and she had heard that I aided women with such a problem."

In Florence, Risa had known a model of Ambrusco's who conceived a baby, had an abortion, and died of a hemorrhage. "Did you help her?"

"No."

"But if you say you aided women who—"

"I did, Lady Lindsay. I did. By the time your sister came to me, I had decided against such actions. A few clergymen in London had heard of my endeavors. They had informed the directors of St. Margaret's. Needless to say, those men did not approve of my actions. I hated the idea that they might dismiss me, and instead I resigned my post. Sold my practice. Retired here. Where I do not perform such operations."

"Why come to me now?"

"I am tired, my lady, of lies and subterfuge. I thought I had left such acts behind me in London. I performed abortions there because I saw much misery resulting from unwanted children—and from abortions done by those who knew little of the surgery. I thought I did a good deed to help women, but I did not count the toll it took on me or my own wife. Your sister was one of the last women to come to me with such a request, and I turned her away there."

"Did she visit you here in Sandown?"

"No. When the constable came to me to ask me to perform an autopsy on a drowning victim last August, I agreed, name unknown to me. Then Crowley told me the dead woman was Lady Madelaine Lindsay. I still had no idea who the dead woman was until I saw her. You see, I had known your sister as Madelaine Rossborough."

The same name as the one on the safety deposit box.

"So you did the autopsy."

"And determined she had drowned. The signs were there. A collapsed lung. Water in the other. A broken leg. Bruising about the head and torso."

"Was she pregnant when she died?"

"Yes. About four months along, I'd say."

"You did not put that in your report."

"I truly thought it had no relevance to her death. I liked her; I felt sorry for her; I did not wish to shame her in her death. She was a woman with a terrible problem. A countess. A debutante. An innocent young woman, I think I can say she was, before . . . events overtook her."

"Why tell me now?"

"I saw your devotion to her the other day when you and Lord Hargrove came to me. I saw your desperation to come to closure about her death."

"Are you implying that she may have allowed herself to be drowned?"

"No. I did not think her capable then. I see now you do not think her capable, either. But I wanted you to know. My conscience demanded I tell you what I knew. For whatever it is worth to you." He struggled to his feet. Older, sadder, he moved more slowly to the door.

"Wait!" She strode toward him, hand out. "Thank you. I appreciate your honesty."

He took her hand warmly. "I appreciate your objectivity."

As darkness seeped into the corners of the studio, Risa sat, hands folded, her sight trained on memories of her older sister. The child who had wanted affection, approval, and gotten so little. The girl who tried to please her father and her aunt. The young woman who assumed the responsibilities for an ancient title and vast estate. The countess who had coddled her youngest sister and ordered her younger one to leave home and take the opportunity to become what she wished. The vulnerable woman who had loved unwisely and lived to regret it.

Tears of mourning ran down Risa's cheeks. Outrage ceased the flow.

Who among the men here had hurt her sister so? *Maddie. How do I find out?*

"I swear to you, ma'am," Mary told her when Risa insisted she recollect any detail at all about the man she'd glimpsed with Maddie in the maze. "I don't recall him. I wish I could, seein' how you want him so bad but—"

"All right, Mary. I hear you. Please unlace me a bit more, will you? I am unused to these whalebones." She wiggled in her sailing dress. Dinner was to be al fresco on the beach. Tonight the wind was steady off the Channel, a storm coming in from the Atlantic, Mary had said.

So similar to the night Maddie died.

"Thank you, Mary. That will be all."

The girl frowned. "You will be careful tonight, ma'am."

"Very." *With every man I meet here.* "Do not worry."

But she did not see relief in Mary's eyes. She shook off the need for restraint and took the hall down to her aunt's room and knocked.

"Come in!" It was Georgie's voice. "Hello, darling! Why, don't you look grand." She clapped her hands. "You look peaked though. What's wrong? You have Lord Sandown eating out of your hand and the model of him is divine. It will make you a fortune—and a career, just you see."

"You've seen my sculpture?" *When? Why?* Tired, outraged, Risa felt like a cat, restless, ready to pounce.

"Don't be testy, love. It's there for anyone on the beach to go see . . . and last night I took Bobbie for a stroll for air after his little illness, and we went inside. He wanted to see it."

Bobbie. Robert Dungarvon. Georgie had always called him Bobbie. Risa recoiled from the possibility that this might be the man her sister had written about in her diary.

"He says you will be absolutely the rage," Georgie rattled on. "No one has ever tried to portray erotic love . . . and this man of yours is—" she kissed her fingertips and made Risa's stomach twist.

"I like your sailing dress," her aunt told her, emerging from her own bedroom in a navy blue concoction.

Risa felt bile churn at her thoughts. "I would like to speak with you alone, Aunt Elizabeth."

"Georgie can stay."

"Pardon me, Georgie, but I must speak to your mother." Elizabeth stiffened. "I wish to talk about Maddie."

"I tire of the subject, Cerise."

Risa dare not speak for fear she'd curse.

"Very well." Her aunt took to examining her gloves. "What about her, now?"

Risa stared at Georgie. "Please, do me this favor."

Georgie's eyes had hardened to glass. "No." She folded her arms. "I stay."

Risa rubbed her temple. "I do detest your lack of co-operation."

Her aunt and cousin showed no signs of caring what Risa liked.

"It is time for us to have total truth between us about Maddie. I asked you a few weeks ago what happened to Maddie's diary and you said you did not know. But you knew where it was. In her desk drawer. Yes. And you came back to try to open the drawer and take it out.

Why? To read it? I venture to say you wanted to destroy it "

"You are insane. I never returned to her room."

"Lie. Again. Just as you did when I asked you if you
had ever heard of a man named Deville."

Elizabeth's lips firmed to white.

"How could you do that?"

Elizabeth moved not one muscle.

Risa would make her talk. "I have also learned that
Maddie was expecting a baby."

Elizabeth sucked in her breath.

"And you knew about that, too."

But Georgie unfolded her arms. "Who told you?"

"Does it matter?"

"Of course, darling. We don't want any scandal."

Risa gave her a withering look. "Who was the father
of her child?"

"John Hargrove," Elizabeth spat out.

"Impossible." *John met her about the time she became
pregnant.* Risa would bet her life that Maddie had slept
with him only here at Sandown to influence him to
marry her and run away with her.

"He slept with her here," Georgie sneered.

"My God," Risa breathed. "And you knew that, too.
Did you know that Maddie was desperate to have a
husband? That she didn't want the disgrace on herself,
her family name? She might have married John, too."

"*Your* precious lover made certain that did not happen," Elizabeth shot back, whipping her gloves against
a chair.

"Yes, and Maddie had her hopes torn from her again.
Blake was protecting his brother from a woman he
thought was another man's lover." She narrowed her
gaze on her aunt and her cousin. "Who was he?"

"What makes you think we'd know?" her aunt asked,
a quiver in her voice.

"Because, Aunt Elizabeth, you seem to know so much else. Bartholome, Deville, Maddie's pregnancy. What, pray tell, have I not covered?"

Georgie snorted, turned to walk away.

"Leaving your mother to bear the brunt, Georgie?"

Georgie whipped around, apology on her face for her mother, and hatred there for Risa. "You never had one, and mine became yours. You can't have anything more that is mine. Not you, or your little sister, or even your silly little Maddie."

Years of standing alone when her father criticized her dedication and her decisions had given Risa stamina she had not measured until now.

"What did Maddie have that was yours?" Risa asked, but knew the answer in her heart. It was Georgie's husband.

20

The sleep of reason produces terrible monsters.

Francisco de Goya

Why is she so late?

Blake shook his head at his butler, refusing his approval to serve the first course of dinner.

"Problems?" Woody asked, hand out for another refill of his champagne glass.

"Wondering what keeps Cerise." Blake glanced up toward the house. "She's usually very prompt."

"Primping," mumbled Robert Dungarvon. "Or is she over in the studio?" He stuck out his flute to a footman who refilled it for the fourth or fifth time. "Working on her man. S'wonderful pose, Blake. Make you both no-notorious." He hoisted his glass in a toast.

Woody frowned. "Don't get a snoot full, Bobbie. You said you wanted to sail. You won't be any good in a boat."

"I can't let you get in if you continue," Blake said.

"Been sailing since I was a pup." Robert swished the liquid in his mouth.

Blake would tie him down if Robert tried to sail away. No one would be hurt tonight, by God. He began to rap his knuckles on the arm of his chair. "I think I'll go see what keeps her." He rose when he saw Elizabeth Elgin march down the lawn. "Good evening," he approached her when she set foot into the tent pavilion and she had finished greeting the other guests. "You look wonderful." She didn't but he said it anyway. He wanted to be as good a host as he could— and asked if she'd seen Cerise.

"She sent me with her thanks, and her hope you will begin without her. She is indisposed."

Blake focused on the house. The event she longed to know so much about, and she was indisposed? "What's the matter with her?"

"Too much work. She is exhausted. Yes," she accepted a glass of champagne from his footman.

"Hello, Mother," Robert stood, grinned lopsided and sought his seat again.

"Is Georgie with her?" Blake persisted.

If looks could have killed, Elizabeth would have done in her son-in-law. "No. No, of course, not. Georgie is coming soon. She tried to help Cerise. Put her to bed. She is so overwrought," she said as an aside to Blake.

Robert chuckled. "Georgie as nurse. Odd pickchure."

Blake raised his hand toward his butler. "Dinner can begin and I'll go see—"

Elizabeth caught his arm. "No. Georgie said there was no need for you to look in on her." Elizabeth smiled at him, such an uncharacteristic expression that Blake felt the hair on his neck stand up. "She knew you would want to. She said Cerise must rest. Bobbie is right. She works too hard."

"The results—" Woody sank into his chair. "—are worth it. At least what I can see from the beach."

"I say"—Dungarvon leaned forward, one arm slung on the table—"Risa's going to be a smash. Ev'ry coll'-tor from here to New York will want a copy of that marble. Make you a fortune, 'specially from brothels."

Woody shook his head. "I'm sure that's not quite the audience Cerise has in mind. Or Blake, either."

"And it is not for sale," Blake affirmed.

"Why the hell not?" Dungarvon was astounded. "Oh, I see. You're in love with her. She duzzn't want the news to get out yet to the world. Look bad before the wedding to have seen your man without hiz clothes. And fine idea to fall in love with the maestro, eh?"

Others in the party were noting his behavior and the Pierces, who sat closest, consulted Blake with sympathetic eyes. Blake was torn between asking him to retire or punching him in the mouth.

"Have at her, I say. She'll marry you. My mother-in-law brought all four of them up to marry. Didn't you, Liz?"

Elizabeth could have felled him with her eyes. "Robert, do be civil."

"Aye, ma'am." He snapped up in his chair.

She beseeched Blake with a glance. "May he retire?"

"Retire?" Robert stood. "You insolent biddie. What the blazes d'you mean ordering me about. Just like your daughter. Do this. Do that. She wants this. She must have that. She cannot stand it that Maddie had this or that. Drives me to my creditors with my hat in my hand."

Blake took his arm. "All right, Robert. Time for a walk to the house."

Elizabeth walked to Robert's other side.

Dungarvon shot to his feet. "Do not put your hands on me." He straightened his coat. "I can do it myself." He bowed deeply to the assembly. "Do forgive my early departure. But as you can see, I am—" He flourished a hand, snickering. "—sent to my room without dinner."

Blake grasped his arm. "Come along, Robert."

Elizabeth was right beside Robert as they made for the house.

"Lady Elgin. I will see he gets to his suite."

"I will—"

Dungarvon growled. Then shook her off with such a wrench that even Blake staggered a few steps.

"Is she really so bad?" Blake could not help but ask as they made the front porch and Robert grew morose. Dungarvon was too far in his cups to give him an accurate answer, but Blake wished to understand this woman.

They were halfway up the lawn when Robert replied.

"Oh, yes. Poor Mother."

Blake took him across the foyer and they began to climb the central stairs.

"Wish I could sail," Robert said.

"I wish you could, too."

"Will you do this again next year?"

"I doubt it."

"Thank God. Why'd you put us through this torture?"

"I recreated the weekend only for Cerise, who needed to experience it to let Maddie go."

"Wish I could."

They'd gone another step before Blake was staring at him. "What?"

"Maddie. I miss her."

Blake did not know if this was a drunken man's ravings or truth. "I am so sorry she went the way she did."

"Me, too," Robert muttered. "Oh, me, too. If she hadn't helped me we never would have known . . ."

Blake focused on another step. "Known what?"

"We loved each other. That she should've been my wife, not *her*. Think, man. Could've been the consort of the countess of Rossborah."

"Georgie." Blake couldn't think of a damn pertinent thing to say to keep him talking. They took another step.

"Yeah. Never fall for the pretty ones, Blake. They can eat you alive."

"Did she do that to you?"

"Yes. And can't have children, either. Jes think, I would've been a father by now, living in America if she hadn't put a stop to it."

A father? "Georgie stopped you from—?" *Running off with Maddie?*

Robert got a smirk on his face. "Never marry a clever woman, my friend. Greedy cuss, too." He put a finger across his lips. "Had a good deal with Maurice, too."

Bartholome.

"Ya know, if you want to make copies of that nude of Risa's, we could make a forchun. We did it with Allure and—Hey! What are you doing?" Blake had hefted him under his arm securely and was double-timing his walk to his own suite. "Ya don't haf to . . . Gonna make me sick. Where we going?"

"My rooms. You can sleep. Georgie won't know."

"She yells, ya know."

"I am certain she does."

Inside his room, Blake dumped Dungarvon on his bed and yanked at his bellpull three times to get a footman up here fast. When the young man appeared, Blake praised heaven that the man was burly.

"Yes, sir! What can I—"

"See that Lord Dungarvon has every convenience, Smith." He crooked a finger at the servant and lowered

his voice. "Hear me well, Smith, when I say the gentleman must not, under any circumstances, leave this
room. Do you understand me?"

"Completely, my lord."

Blake was out to the hall, running for Risa's suite.
He didn't knock but threw open the door and took the
rooms in four strides. *Empty.* He pulled the bell for
Mary, but on second thought, had no reason to wait.

He took the hall at a dead run. Georgie's and Robert's
suite was at the other end. He skidded to a stop. Was she
in there? With Cerise? He put his shoulder to the door,
his hand to the knob, and burst through.

Christ! This room is empty too.

"She's gone, Blake."

He spun.

"Elizabeth."

Refractions of light glittered from her hand. She
held a gem-studded pistol.

He walked forward, fear for Cerise a monster un-
coiling in his guts. "Where have you taken her?"

"I will show you." She backed up a pace.

He flung out a hand, confident he would grab the
gun from her—and she shot him.

Risa felt the dragging weight of the water from the
floor of the boathouse in her skirts. She was cold, wet,
hungry. The cords Georgie had bound her hands with
cut her wrists. Wouldn't Blake wonder where she was?

"I won't be able to row with my hands tied."

"Darling, that's the idea," Georgie replied, snaking
the rope of one small boat from its moorings and heading it toward the sea. The cove at the back of Blake's
house was prepared for this evening's fun. "Eight boats,
each personally inspected by the great Lord Hargrove.
Tonight, he boasts he made a point to inspect them
twice. Fool."

Georgie continued to mutter to herself as she had since she had turned on Risa in her suite.

"It will be much too convenient that I die the same way Maddie did."

"Not quite the same, but at sea. Rather fitting." She picked up the lead rope to another sailboat and tied it to the mast pole. The other boat would be her means to return.

Would Arnie Crowley see my death as murder?

Blake would make Arnie investigate, Risa knew for certain. "Blake will find out."

"He'll be in gaol—hanged, dearest."

Her cousin hoped that Blake would be charged with her murder. *Ridiculous.* "He has no motive."

"When I cry and tell them that he seduced Maddie to marry her, get his hands on Allure, and you found out about his *amour* this year and became jealous? When I show them that you were so in love with the infamous Lord Hargrove that you sculpted him in that shameless pose? Dear heart, the police will tell me it was a crime of passion."

"Is that what yours was?"

"I had sound reason."

"Jealousy."

Georgie snorted. "After all, he is *my* husband."

"How long had Maddie and Bobbie been having an affair?" Risa had to know the awful details.

"Off and on again for over a year. She tried to find another man who charmed her as much, but the poor thing couldn't. The fool. I warned her."

"When?"

"When I learned about them seeing each other year before last."

Risa wished she had her glasses. They had fallen off when Georgie and her mother forced her toward the back stairs down to the cove. Squinting, she could only see so far into the gloomy night. A fog was rolling in, too.

"Get in."

"No."

"I said"—Georgie rushed over and hooked an arm under Risa's—"now." Bound, Risa was taller and had more muscle than her cousin, but Georgie hauled her nearer the boat. "Get in."

Georgie could not throw her in—that would make the boat pitch too much and sink. So she picked up an oar and raised it above her shoulder. "Get in or I knock you silly."

"Is that what you did to Maddie?"

"No."

"How then did you—"

"Mama did."

Risa forced down her outrage and her grief. "Why?"

"Maddie was going to bear their bastard. She tried to get Bobbie to marry her. But I told him he couldn't. That's why she accepted John Hargrove. The two of them were going to pretend Bobbie's baby was theirs. They were going to disgrace me."

"By pretending that the baby was—"

"No. I can't have children. Bobbie wants them, too. But, imagine. Me, who had so many offers. How could I bear to be outdone like that? I put a stop to that, I tell you." She nudged Risa so hard, Risa stumbled into the boat. It rocked madly.

Risa sat. *Think. Think fast.* She had come this far in her discovery and she faced death now because of it. For such a price, she'd learn the rest. "How did Maddie know Bartholome?"

Georgie's head came up, respect in her eyes. Without answering, she got into the boat, sat down and, instead of unfurling the sail, picked up two oars. Georgie had never been an accomplished sailor.

"How?"

Georgie pushed them from the shore.

Panic rose with disgust and bile in Risa's throat. *Georgie meant to throw her overboard?*

"Bobbie introduced her." Georgie's beautiful lips spread in a sardonic smile. "When she said she needed money for you and to buy a plough and seed for her precious tenants, Bobbie told her how she could earn money. Then he told her what we'd been doing for over three years."

"Copying the art in Park Lane." Risa choked. "Did you copy more than Allure?"

"Bravo, dearest." She looked over her shoulder, aiming for the Channel. "Yes, we did. A few Reynolds and a Fragonard. One Goya paid for our holidays to the south of France last year."

"Your mother helped too." *Hiring her own housekeeper to let the forgers inside the house.*

"Of course. She had to and we paid Alberts well to co-operate, too. My mother cannot refuse me anything."

"Obviously not."

"We had to get in. Had to have the keys to the kingdom, didn't we, to let the copyists have their look, hmmm?" Georgie was beginning to labor now with her effort, sailing or any exercise never her forte.

"Meanwhile, you were befriending Maddie. Being watchdog for when she came to London."

"Yes. Not easy. But we did it." Her triumph was dwindling with the exertion of rowing.

Risa could wait until Georgie tired. But Risa might not live that long.

She cast a lingering look at the shore. The tent pavilion with its torchères were but specks of light upon the void of sky and sea. She could easily swim to shore, now before she lost sight of it, if only she could undo her ropes. She twisted. And they held fast.

Broken sounds, vaguely reminiscent of human shouts, drifted to them across the waves. The repeating slice of Georgie's oars became the only constant in Risa's universe. The wind picked up. The mast caught her eye. The sail ruffled, unraveling from its ropes. If it unfurled more, rowing would be useless against the force.

"Maddie once loved you dearly." Risa whispered, marking time, praying that the sail would billow out of control.

"Enough to seduce my husband from me."

No one could do that if the husband truly loved his wife. Risa understood that clearly now. She thought of Blake and how she wished she would be able to tell him how she had learned this.

"Enough to help you forge masterpieces. How sad."

"I am not crying, Cerise."

"You took advantage of Maddie. All of you. Bobbie taught her illicit love. You taught her betrayal. And your mother . . ." Risa could barely put into words the horror she felt when she thought of how her aunt could have injured the little girl whom she had once hugged and kissed and consoled after her mother had died.

"My mother had to help me. I warned her if she didn't I would find a way to let the police know that she was the one who had authorized the forgeries."

"You are a fiend." She paused, then wondered aloud, "How did you get that way?" What did it matter? The bigger question was, "How could you kill your own cousin, Georgie?"

"No one is more important than I am."

Risa laughed.

Risa's change in attitude seized Georgie's attention. Risa could see only shadows of her face in the faint moonlight, but she saw Georgie's body stiffen, spring up when the sail unwrapped like a demon let from hell and whipped round with such a force it swept Georgie off her feet and into the water.

The boat rocked so wildly, that Risa threw herself to the floor, the only means for her to steady the craft after such a pitch.

Cries pierced the doom. Georgie pleaded for help. But hands bound, Risa had no means—and no pity— with which to help her.

Risa lay there, sobbing for Maddie as the boat skimmed across rough waves and she prayed that Blake would find her before her sailboat broke in the crucible of the sea and swept her body off toward France and death.

"Blake, for God's sake, let me do this!" Woody yelled at him the next afternoon as the American lassoed the broken mast and lashed the missing sailboat to their own. The two men had been part of the search party Blake and Arnie had ordered last night. Two men to each of the seven sailboats, it was heaven-sent that he and Woody had spotted the missing Sandown sailboat, bobbing near the shore like a toy. "You'll reopen that bullet wound of yours."

Blake shifted, pain in his shoulder restraining him from walking on the water to get to Risa. Her body lay limp, unmoving in the hull of the boat. Her hair was encrusted with salt, her white and navy gown, shades of gray, and sopping wet. Her eyes were closed. "She's unconscious." *She is not dead. Cannot be.* "Let's get her home."

He could not have Woody sail them fast enough.

"Lord Hargrove." Doctor Viner took his stetho-scope from his ears, unsmiling, hours later in Risa's suite. "Lady Lindsay has a high fever and she may be getting pneumonia from the exposure all night on the Channel. She also suffers from a sunburn, but happily that is only on her hands, neck, and face. So see that she has sponge baths to keep her cool, and warm her when she shivers. Also feed her lots of liquids. But she is healthy and should do well. She'll need rest and I am certain you will see she gets it. Then, too, you must rest. I know that will be difficult for you, since I suspect you will take up a position here by her bedside, but do be careful of yourself. You could reopen that wound. It was very close to an artery and we don't want to aggravate it."

"Thank you. I will do whatever I can to see her healthy again."

Blake forbade anyone to visit Cerise except himself and Mary. He sponged Cerise's bruised and burning body, he moistened cloths and held them to her chapped lips and scarlet cheeks. He would leave occasionally for minutes at a time to deal with the necessities.

The first one was to ask Robert Dungarvon what he wished done with Georgie's body. Robert sat in the morning room, stunned but talking to Arnie about his forgery of the Rossborough collection. "I should like to have her buried at my family's estate in Dorchester. The funeral should be there, too." He inquired of Arnie, "Do you suppose I will be able to go to the services?"

"I could probably send you with a policeman, yes. But only for the day."

Blake could not bear to hear anymore. He returned to Cerise, felt her forehead and bathed it, then sat down only to fall asleep. He had been up all night with Arnie's contingent of police, scouring the shore for any signs of Cerise and Georgie. It was against Doctor Viner's orders that he went out on two excursions into the Channel as dawn came. If anyone found Cerise, Blake wanted to be among the first ones to see her, comfort her. With the loss of blood he had suffered from Elizabeth's gunshot wound, Blake knew he drove himself beyond his capacity. Now that he had found her, he was helpless to give in to his fatigue.

"My lord." Mary was jostling his good shoulder.

"Yes." He sat up, noticed that Cerise still slept soundly. "What is it?"

"Constable Crowley would like a word, sir."

"Arnie," Blake met him in the hallway. "You need me?"

"I have detained Elizabeth Elgin in her suite, Blake. I put handcuffs on her because she is such a spitfire. She refuses to talk to me. I thought if you came in, she might spit at you a bit more. I hate to ask you but I must know more about why she attacked you."

"Let's see if I can rile her a bit for you," Blake said and led Arnie toward the lady's suite.

"Good evening, Lady Elgin. Comfortable, are you?" Blake eyed her, stiff as iron, arms before her, wrists in cuffs.

Blake took a chair to sit before her. He shifted his arm sling, pain stabbing him and making him wild to wrap his hands around this woman's throat for all the harm she had done to Cerise and Maddie. "What good will your money do you now that you will go to prison?"

She set her teeth.

"Not too ready to talk, are you? Well, I am. I know you had fun. Must have been a lark to pull the wool over so many people's eyes. Maddie and then Cerise." A thought struck him. "Or did you start your forgeries before your brother died?" He leaned forward. "I bet you had a wonderful time doing that. Making a fool of him as he lay in his bed, suffering."

Triumph flooded her features. "He was a monster. He deserved it. What I took from him, I deserved. It was a gross injustice that he inherited all of Rossborough. I was a better person."

What an appropriate word, *was*. "So you thought of the idea to earn money by copying works from the family collection."

"Yes. I thought of it. Why not? Bobbie kept complaining to Georgie about her spending habits. I told her to have what fun she could. I knew how to find a man like Deville. I told Bobbie to arrange it through Bartholome. Maurice had run a forgery ring for over a decade. Charles and I knew about it. Charles ignored Maurice, but I sought him out. Cultivated him, the bastard. Then he had the audacity to make up that silly story about Maddie buying a painting by Ritter."

"And though the tale was false, nonetheless it led Cerise down paths to find clues to the forgery." Blake saw her wince. "Did you kill him?"

She met his gaze. "He deserved to die. He was a stupid man."

Blake felt unclean just listening to this woman. "You have no remorse, do you?"

She scoffed. "Why should I? A woman deserves everything she can get from a man. Especially," she said the word with venom, "when she learns he is seeing another woman."

"So you forged art not only to spite your brother, but later also to spite Bobbie and Maddie?"

"Of course. It humbled them, made them beholden to me. Bobbie needed the money. So did Maddie to pay the taxes on Rossborough." She grinned, sardonic in her glee. "When Maddie complained about needing money for Cerise's education, too, Bobbie let slip there was a way to earn a bit. Maddie refused at first to agree, but in the end, she came around to our way of thinking. The money was too appealing to refuse."

"So appealing that you would kill your own niece to ensure you could continue forging art?" he asked.

"I did not kill her. I tried to get her into the boat. She wouldn't. I picked up an oar and hit her on the head with it. She fell. Georgie got her in the boat."

"And drowned her."

Elizabeth looked away.

Blake shot from his chair. "I think you have what you need to prosecute her, Arnie."

"Thank you for that, Blake."

Blake rubbed his elbow. "I need to talk to Robert. May I?"

"He's still downstairs. I have a constable from Cowes sitting with him. He is quite pitiful."

"I am glad you can think so. I have none for him." Blake thought of those who deserved more pity. Maddie. Cerise.

"Dungarvon says he will go with me to gaol, but he asks to speak to Cerise before he goes."

"Cerise will not be talking to anyone for awhile. And when she does recover, I do not think it wise to have her upset by the likes of Bobbie," he said the name with disgust. "But I would like to ask him a few questions."

"By all means." Arnie lifted his chin.

At the first sight of Robert, Blake was startled by the change since he had seen him more than an hour ago. The man had been crying. Recovering his senses after his bout with too much champagne, he looked more disheveled than last night. His hair was mussed. His clothes askew. His eyes bloodshot. "'lo, Blake. Did not think you'd care to lay eyes on me again."

I don't. "Do you have a list perhaps of the works you three had forged?"

He nodded. "Yes. At home." He glanced at Arnie. "I will turn it over to you."

Blake asked, "Did Maddie open the safety deposit box to put all of the payments in as M. Rossborough?"

"Yes. She handed most of the money over to me or Elizabeth or Georgie. She kept ten percent for herself and to send to Florence to pay for Cerise's study. Toward the end, she kept it all. For the copies of one Rembrandt and for Allure. She used it to pay all her bills because she wanted to start with a clean slate when she got married. When she told me she was pregnant last June, I wanted to divorce Georgie and marry her. But I knew the divorce would take over a year—and the baby would be a bastard and Maddie shamed by it. So I thought the only way to solve our dilemma was to run away, but Georgie found out and stopped me from leaving."

"How?"

"She threatened to expose me. Blame me for the forgeries. She would pretend to be the innocent wife."

"So you stayed with Georgie. What happened then?"

"Maddie told me she tried to have an abortion, but the doctor would not perform it for her. She knew she must marry soon and she began to try to charm someone into it. She met your brother and he liked her. And then . . ." Bobbie's face turned bitter.

"You became jealous," Blake concluded.

"That was my baby and she let him make love to her here. She was going to pretend my child was his."

"She was rather far along by August," Blake stated. "How was she going to explain the baby's early birth to John if he had not made love to her until then?"

Bobbie shrugged. "Maddie was too innocent for her own good. She believed that all things would come aright. And they don't."

Blake rose, unable to bear more of Bobbie's morose attitude. The man deserved everything he got. Prison. Humiliation. A loveless future.

Blake took the main stairs two at a time to return to Cerise. He turned the knob silently and let himself in.

Mary was sitting by her bedside, sponging her face. "She's quiet, my lord. She opens her eyes a bit and then falls back to sleep."

"Good, Mary. Thank you. I will sit with her now."

"Would you like some broth, my lord? Or tea?"

"Yes, please. Bring us both some."

"Anything else, sir?"

Bring me a way to make Cerise wake up quickly so that I can tell her I love her and won't ever leave her.

"No, Mary. I don't think so."

"You must rest, my lord. The doctor told me to insist. He wants you well for when Lady Lindsay awakens."

"Do not fear, Mary. I will recover." His good hand was flexing, needing activity, employment.

Mary noted it and inclined her head. "But, my lord, you will become bored sitting here, doing nothing."

Bored? He wanted to laugh or cry. "No, Mary. I will never be bored again. In fact . . ." He felt a burst of hope, whose cause was debatable given the current situation, but certainly undeniable. "Bring me some clay."

EPILOGUE

If I had not created heaven, I would have created it for you alone.
  Gianlorenzo Bernini's inscription on the Corona chapel

Sandown Manor, Wight
August, 1885

"*C*ome along, Maddie." Risa beckoned to her four-year-old daughter. The chubby brunette climbed down from her perch, the pure white plinth of *Devotion*.

"Papa says we can go now?" she asked, her green eyes at once attentive and curious.

"Yes, angel. He said he would be ready for us after I got home and you had finished your lunch."

"I am!" The little girl brushed cookie crumbs from her lap to the foyer tiles. Her dog, a frisky Scots terrier, lapped up the mess and sniffed at her pinafore to see if there were more he'd missed. Maddie giggled at him. "You can come, too, Pludo."

This dog was Maddie's birthday gift from Ariel last June. Returned for a holiday from Rome where she studied classical languages, Ariel had named the puppy Pluto for his black coat. Maddie mangled the name, though she did get obedience from the animal that no one else commanded.

"Thank you, Mary," Risa dismissed the young maid who had decided to stay on with Lord Hargrove and his new wife five years ago. Risa took Maddie's little fingers in her own and led them toward the garden doors. This path to the south wing was quicker than taking the long corridors through so many enfilade rooms. And she was eager to see Blake today, not only because she had exciting news for him, but especially because he had invited her.

For the first time in over nine years, Blake Hargrove had finished a sculpture. And today would be the first time that he invited his wife to see it—and the first time she had ever set foot into his studio.

Risa pushed open the doors and felt the golden sun warm her face. The sky was clear and blue today, a crystal moment filled with serenity. She wished she could scoop Maddie up to carry her to Blake's studio, but Doctor Viner had cautioned her this morning not to do any lifting.

"You remember we thought you might lose Maddie because you were constantly picking up your heavy tools to finish *Devotion*. Now, don't forget that. You are a strong woman, but when it comes to having a baby, you must be cautious. Let your husband pamper you." The doctor smiled wide and long at her. "He wants to, so accept it, will you, and for six more months pretend to be frail?"

She promised she would.

"You are not in the final stages of a project are you?"

"No." She had created a *modello* for a new statue, which she would call *Delight*. She liked the theme, and thought the composition worthy of marble. The woman stood, her hands in her lover's hair as he knelt before her and kissed her between her naked breasts. Her eyes focused on him, her mouth parting in the rapture that he brought her. He, too, was naked, one arm around her waist, one to her thigh. His eyes were closed, his ecstasy a reverence.

But now she would wait to carve this piece until after her next child was born. "I shall devote myself to this project, Doctor." She patted her stomach.

"Wonderful. Go home and tell your husband he will be a father again."

"Thank you," she had kissed his cheek. Over the years, the doctor and Blake and she had become friends. Risa liked him because he had volunteered much information about pregnancy and childbearing that Risa badly needed to learn. Without her mother or her aunt to inform her after the birth of her first child, Risa welcomed the knowledge about colic and nursing schedules and breast-feeding. Risa shared with him stories about renowned artists she had come to know personally.

Blake was responsible for that, as he was for so much else in her life. He had advised her on how to save money by being more frugal with her household spending in Northumbria and in Park Lane. She had paid off her bank loan one year earlier than it was due. Blake had also counseled her about estate management, giving her insight into agricultural issues that she had not had any experience with before. She was able to not only buy more seed for her tenants to plant, but also advised them on prices to ask for their grain.

Blake had been also invaluable in giving her insight into the professional art world. By introducing her to others artists whom he knew, such as Toulouse-Lautrec and Auguste Rodin, she gained a perspective on her work which she had not acquired from Signore Ambrusco. When guests came to the Hargroves' annual weekend parties at Sandown Manor, many remarked on the quality of *Devotion* which Blake and she had moved to the main foyer. A few had offered to buy the statue of the man who extended one hand to his lover, his urgent stance an eloquent declaration of his love for her.

"*Devotion* belongs here," Risa had told the potential buyers.

Word of her talent had spread. She received offers for commissions and accepted a well-chosen few. She continued to sculpt her own designs in her studio by the sea here during the summers. The autumns, she and Blake spent in London, alternately residing in his Grosvenor Square townhouse or hers in Park Lane. Winters were in his country home in Surrey and spring found them in Northumbria. In each home, Risa had established a large studio for herself, but her favorite one was here on Wight.

And here, she had awakened from the nightmare of her quest to solve the mystery of her sister's death.

Two days after her harrowing escape from Georgie, she opened her eyes in her room to see Blake sleeping in a chair. His left arm was in a sling, his legs stretched out, his feet propped on the bed. Lax in his fingers lay a lump of clay.

She thought she was dreaming.

She reached over to touch his hand and learned she wasn't. He awoke with a start. "What—?" His clay rolled off his lap and he caught it midair. "You're awake?"

She tried to smile but her cheeks felt as if she had stretched them thin already. "What are you doing in my room?" she asked when she looked around and realized she was in her suite in Sandown Manor.

He told her everything. Slowly, the horror of the evening came back to her conscious mind. And she asked about Georgie's fate, her aunt's, and Robert Dungarvon's.

Blake told her that, too. Afterward, in his arms, she

had cried for all of them. For Maddie, first, for whom she had been unable to shed any tears. For the rest of her family, whose sins she might never forgive. And finally, she wept for Blake who recounted how Elizabeth had shot him.

"How did you survive it?" she asked of him.

"Fortunately, your aunt is a very poor marksman and I wrested the pistol from her hands easily. I pointed it at her, and got to the bellpull to call for help. After that, Arnie and Woody and I concluded you had probably been forced to go with Georgie. When we found two sailboats missing, it was natural to think she had taken you out to sea."

"As she had Maddie," Risa whispered. "Why weren't any of Crowley's men able to stop Georgie before she got into the boat?"

"A man had just finished patrolling the boathouse before the two of you got there. When he returned minutes later and saw the boat gone, he yelled for help. We came to his side quickly, but the night was so dark on the water, we had a devil of a time searching. It was not until the next afternoon that Woody and I found you." He leaned forward to stroke her hair back from her face. "I was terrified that you had left me. I looked at you then and knew I would die, too, if you were gone."

"But I'm not going anywhere," she whispered back, her throat thick, wanting to discuss here and now his reasons for leaving soon for London.

"No. You're not. You're staying here to marry me. Next week."

"I am?"

He bit his lip, his need to stop his tears a torment. "I will have a special license to marry in approximately four days. I sent a cable to London to my secretary to petition for one without delay. He is usually very efficient."

"I hope so," she declared. "You don't need to talk about this?"

He gave her a hard, sweet look. "There is nothing to debate. I don't want to leave you and you don't want me to go."

"You have come far, my lord."

"Loving you has made it possible."

She took his good hand and urged him to open his fingers. "And why do you have clay?"

"To calm my nerves."

She cocked her head and reclined against her pillows, satisfied. "What are you creating?"

"Nothing. Mindless manipulation was all it was. Until I saw you smile at me again, I knew I was going to be mindless."

"This is a sea change."

"It might be only one small step."

She accepted that.

But over the years, she saw him reach for it whenever he felt sad. Such as those days his brother John refused yet another letter from him. Or the day they heard the news that her aunt Elizabeth was sentenced to life in gaol for murder, and Robert was convicted for ten years for the international crime of misrepresenting a work of art.

Blake reached for clay whenever he was happy. During the days of their wedding trip in Naples and Florence, after they would return to their hotel and make love in the hot Italian afternoons, he would hold it for minutes, fashion her face or her breast—and say it was not equal to the perfection of the woman in his arms.

Then the day that she told him she was expecting their child, he picked up a clump of it and tossed it around like a ball. And the days after that, he had it with him every day, all day long, tucked in a trouser pocket, dunking it in a glass of water to keep it moist.

Finally, just before Maddie was born, he told Risa he had decided to clean up his studio in the south wing. He was going to sculpt. And the day that Maddie came into the world, he picked up a hammer and chisel for the first time in years and whittled away at a tiny block of pink limestone.

He worked on small and inexpensive stones to learn his skills once more. And she had never asked to come into his domain, never expected him to change his need to work in solitude. That he could come to her studio at any time he wished was something they both accepted as simply her different work style. So his invitation today to her and Maddie was a momentous one.

She stood before the door, wondering if she should knock.

"Mama?"

"Yes, angel." She ran her fingers through Maddie's honey brown hair.

"Don't you want to see Papa?" Maddie was shuffling her feet.

"I do." *I need to see how well he has recovered his love of his art.* She rapped on his door and it fell open.

He grinned down at them. With a beret over his hair and wearing a set of linens he had adopted as his own work clothes, he was covered from head to toe in a fine white dust from his final sanding of his work. "Come in, my ladies." He picked a cloth from his back pocket to wipe his face. "Come in."

" 'lo, Papa!" Maddie cast out her arms to be taken up into his.

"Hello, angel." He leaned over to draw Risa against him. "How are you?" he asked her.

"Very well, thank you."

"Are you really? What did Doctor Viner say?" His eyes probed hers.

"Actually, he told me that you will have some troubles soon."

"In what way?" He grew alarmed.

"You'll need another arm to hold all three of us at once."

He threw back his head to laugh and then kissed her deeply, quickly. "I thought so. You looked the same way you did when you became pregnant with Maddie."

"Oh?"

"Ripe as a strawberry." He nuzzled her behind her ear. "Good enough to eat."

She was certain she blushed like a strawberry, too.

He chuckled and cleared his throat. "Well, ladies, I brought you here today to see something rare."

Maddie was looking over his shoulder. "It's me, Papa! You made *me*!"

He let her down to scamper away.

Risa's gaze followed her daughter—and her heart leaped in her chest.

The statue of elegant white Carrara was an ensemble. Not only a child, but a trio stood there in the center of his room. A man, a woman, and their daughter.

Blake examined Risa's expression as she did the statues'. "You like it," he breathed at last.

She raised her face, words inadequate.

"I need to hear what you think of it, Cerise."

She went to inspect it more closely.

The life-size statue before her was she. And he. With Maddie.

The man stood, his daughter in one arm, much as Blake had held Maddie a minute ago. His other arm circled his wife's waist as he bent to her, his half-lidded eyes focused on her mouth. Any moment, his lips would touch hers and the circle of love would close around the three of them.

Risa caressed the man's cool cheek, thrilling to the

stubble Blake had carved to illustrate his own. She felt the woman's arm, strong as hers. She traced a finger over the brows of the little girl and silk would never feel so soft.

Risa met Blake's gaze across the marble he had molded to represent their life together.

"It is," she vowed, "breathtaking."

His eyes twinkled. "It is," he murmured, "how we are, all of us."

"What do you call it?"

"Cherished."

Tears clogged her throat. She went to him, arms out, to pull him close and kiss him. The thousand words she wished to say, deserted her. Instead, she clung to him and whispered words he heard her repeat often. "I love you."

He took pins from her hair and ran his fingers through the tresses. "What do you think I should do with it?"

She matched his smile with her own. "I would say it would look best in the foyer of your London house."

"My thoughts exactly."

"Then when we have our little dinner parties there, people can see how talented Lord Hargrove is."

"Ah." He shook his head. "I have no delusions that my work compares to your artistry, my love. But I did want to try my hand at this again, if only to see if I could complete it."

"And how does it feel?"

He took her face between his hands. "What I have created in stone brings me a small joy, my darling, compared to the ecstasy of what we have created together in love."

AUTHOR'S NOTES

No statue of Allure exists. Gianlorenzo Bernini never created any work which depicted a woman's desire for a man. But therein lies the nub of my tale.

In fact, until Auguste Rodin began to create his sculptures of lovers, such as *I am Beautiful* in 1882 and his more well-known work *The Kiss* in 1886, no artist in the Western cultures had sculpted any piece which portrayed the ecstasy of human love between a man and woman. Yes, Bernini sculpted the famous Daphne and Apollo (which I transport from its abode in the Galleria Borghese in Rome, to place in Blake Hargrove's collection for my purposes here). But as you can read, this ensemble portrays fear and lust, not the rapture of reciprocal love.

Other conditions of the art world in 1880s I have kept factual.

Few women took up art. Mary Cassatt, noted here in the text, was one of the very few who ventured out and who prospered. Most women were discouraged from it. It did not pay then; it does not pay now. The life is erratic, the work consuming. Many women then had not the financial means, to say nothing of the encouragement, to defy social dictums which bade them stay home. Cassatt took copying lessons from a Philadelphia school of art beginning in 1861. It was one of the few schools which admitted women. She moved in 1874 to Paris, however, where she thought the atmosphere more welcoming to artists.

But not necessarily to female artists.

In Paris, women were not admitted to the prestigious art school, L'Ecole des Beaux-arts, until 1897.

Illustrative of this climate was the now-renowned sculptress Camille Claudel. Unfortunately, her life tells a tale of a woman too much in love with a man and driven to madness by her obsession with him, his rejection, and her art. Her lover? None other than Auguste Rodin.

At the other side of the coin, agents who sold art from artist to patron were becoming more prominent—and wealthy. Most of these men had been trained in art themselves, and like Blake, they experienced failure. They would then employ their knowledge of art and artists to make a living for themselves.

Some of these agents were also dealers. Some, like Maurice Bartholome, were failed artists. They could and did become a means by which many collectors could earn money, by permitting other artists to duplicate their works.

And for those of you who write to ask me for more of my little tidbits, here are a few:

- Toulouse-Lautrec, at age 16, did indeed sketch two Englishwomen as umbrellas.
- The famous bust of Louis the Fourteenth by Bernini was sculpted in a flurry of activity

within ninety days. Louis, ever guarding his grandeur, thought he looked too ordinary, hence, his question to his brother, "Is my nose really that crooked?"

- Many of the now famous Impressionist artists who came to prominence in this period lived in poverty. Degas took loans from art critics. Rodin never thought he earned enough to pay for his ever-moving, ever-enlarging studios. In 1869, Renior sold a painting of his for 100 francs, the equivalent today of ten American dollars!

I hope you enjoyed our trip into the art world! If you like Internet news, please visit me at

http://www.powerontheweb.com/Jo-AnnPower.htm

or e-mail me at

jpoweron@aol.com

If you wish to receive my regular newsletters, please send a legal-sized self-addressed stamped envelope to

Jo-Ann Power
4319 Medical Drive, #131-PMB298
San Antonio, TX 78229-3325